Ecofeminist Science Fiction

Ecofeminist Science Fiction: International Perspectives on Gender, Ecology, and Literature provides guidance in navigating some of the most pressing dangers we face today. Science fiction helps us face problems that threaten the very existence of humankind by giving us the emotional distance to see our current situation from afar, separated in our imaginations through time, space, or circumstance. Extrapolating from contemporary science, science fiction allows a critique of modern society, imagining more life-affirming alternatives.

In this collection, ecocritics from five continents scrutinize science fiction for insights into the fundamental changes we need to make to survive and thrive as a species. Contributors examine ecofeminist themes in films, such as *Avatar*, *Star Wars*, and *The Stepford Wives*, as well as television series including *Doctor Who* and *Westworld*. Other scholars explore an internationally diverse group of both canonical and lesser-known science fiction writers including Oreet Ashery, Iraj Fazel Bakhsheshi, Liu Cixin, Louise Erdrich, Hanns Heinz Ewers, Larissa Lai, Ursula K. Le Guin, Chen Qiufan, Mary Doria Russell, Larissa Sansour, Karen Traviss, and Jeanette Winterson.

Ecofeminist Science Fiction explores the origins of human-caused environmental change in the twin oppressions of women and of nature, driven by patriarchal power and ideologies. Female embodiment is examined through diverse natural and artificial forms, and queer ecologies challenge heteronormativity. The links between war and environmental destruction are analyzed, and the capitalist motivations and means for exploiting nature are critiqued through postcolonial perspectives.

Douglas A. Vakoch is President of METI, dedicated to Messaging Extraterrestrial Intelligence and sustaining civilization on multigenerational timescales. As Director of Green Psychotherapy, PC, he helps alleviate environmental distress through ecotherapy. Dr. Vakoch is editor-in-chief of the book series Space and Society (Springer), as well as general editor of Ecocritical Theory and Practice (Lexington Books). He has explored ecofeminism in six of his other books, including *Dystopias and Utopias on Earth and Beyond: Feminist Ecocriticism of Science Fiction*.

Routledge Studies in World Literatures and the Environment

Series Editors: Scott Slovic and Swarnalatha Rangarajan

For more information about this series, please visit: https://www.routledge.com/Routledge-Studies-in-World-Literatures-and-the-Environment/book-series/ASHER4038

"Unexpected kinships, cautionary tales, problematic intimacies, and visions of futures embedded in our present: for more than a century, speculative fiction has spoken the language of our ecological imagination. Enriched by political engagement and theoretical rigor, this is the same language that ecofeminism has been speaking since its inception. With an impressive ensemble of voices, perspectives, and experiences, *Ecofeminist Science Fiction* finally bridges in a systematic way sci-fi and ecological feminism, masterfully expanding the canon of environmental literary studies."

Serenella Iovino, Professor of Italian Studies and
Environmental Humanities, University of North Carolina
at Chapel Hill, USA, and author of *Ecocriticism and Italy*
as well as co-editor of *Environmental Humanities: Voices
from the Anthropocene*

"Writing into the lacuna where the intriguing cultural worlds of ecofeminism and science fiction meet, the international voices collected here delight and instruct as they grapple provocatively with intellectual challenges of our time, including female space and embodiment, queer ecology, ecoterrorism, and capitalism and colonization. This fine collection of ground-breaking essays convincingly depicts the continued need to engage the twin problem of violence to women and damaging the earth, while taking that engagement to new intellectual heights by reading the moving mirror of science fiction as a comment on our world."

Etienne Terblanche, Extraordinary Professor of
Literature, North-West University, South Africa, and
author of *T.S. Eliot, Poetry, and Earth* as well as *E.E.
Cummings: Poetry and Ecology*

"This is a wonderful book for all those interested in innovative ecocritical and ecofeminist analyses of science fiction, and indeed popular culture. The volume is impressive in its extensive international sweep, as well as employing multiple ecofeminist critical theories, including queer, animal studies, indigenous, material feminism, and anti-colonial emphases. Fresh and engaging, the authors examine a number of often-overlooked texts as well as those better known, including literature, films, TV shows, and a graphic novel. The historical range is astonishing, reaching back to sf precursors in the 19th century and stretching to contemporary works. The authors of the separate essays are in clear dialogue with one another, making this volume a great teaching tool."

Noël Sturgeon, Professor Emerita of
Environmental Studies, York University,
Canada, and author of *Ecofeminist Natures* as
well as *Environmentalism in Popular Culture:
Gender, Race, Sexuality and the Politics of the
Natural*

Ecofeminist Science Fiction

International Perspectives on Gender, Ecology, and Literature

Edited by Douglas A. Vakoch

Routledge
Taylor & Francis Group

NEW YORK AND LONDON

First published 2021
by Routledge
52 Vanderbilt Avenue, New York, NY 10017

and by Routledge
2 Park Square, Milton Park, Abingdon, Oxon, OX14 4RN

Routledge is an imprint of the Taylor & Francis Group, an informa business

Library of Congress Cataloging-in-Publication Data
A catalog record for this title has been requested

ISBN: 978-0-367-71641-7 (hbk)
ISBN: 978-0-367-72022-3 (pbk)
ISBN: 978-1-003-15304-7 (ebk)

Typeset in Sabon
by Deanta Global Publishing Services, Chennai, India

To Françoise d'Eaubonne,
for creating the word *écoféminisme*

Contents

Contributors

Başak Ağın, PhD, teaches English at Middle East Technical University (METU), School of Foreign Languages, Turkey. She has also taught several English literature courses in the Department of Foreign Language Education at METU. Her most recent publications include "Ecological Imperialism in the Age of the Posthuman: David Fedele's *E-Wasteland*" in Rayson K. Alex and Susan Deborah's *Ecodocumentaries: Critical Essays* (Palgrave Macmillan, 2016) and "The Ecological Posthuman in Lee's *Tarboy* and Tan and Ruhemann's *The Lost Thing*" (*CLCWeb: Comparative Literature and Culture*, Purdue, Vol. 18.3, 2016). She has also published several book chapters and journal articles and presented at various international conferences on ecocriticism and cultural studies. Ağın's research interests include posthumanism, material ecocriticism, and science fiction studies.

Teresa M. Bartoli, an independent scholar and activist, earned her MA in Speech Communications from California State University, Fullerton, USA. Her areas of research include ecofeminism, agnotology (culturally induced ignorance), and inequality. She specializes in youth issues and leadership inspired from her time as the director of a youth program that served urban youth in Los Angeles County. She was instrumental in designing and organizing youth leadership opportunities that addressed homelessness and other social issues. Bartoli is a public speaker, and while working for California State University, Fullerton, she taught public speaking and held a position at the Social Science Research Center. Bartoli is the co-author of *Pink Hats and Ballots: An Ecofeminist Perspective of Women's Political Activism in the Age of Trump, Coronavirus, and Black Lives Matter* (Lexington Books, 2021).

Sarah Bezan is Postdoctoral Research Associate in Perceptions of Biodiversity Change at the University of York's Leverhulme Centre for Anthropocene Biodiversity, UK. Prior to this she held a British Academy Newton International Fellowship at the University of Sheffield's Animal Studies Research Centre (ShARC), UK, where she remains an Honorary Research Fellow. She is the author of the book *Dead Darwin: Necro-Ecologies* *in Neo-Victorian Culture* (Manchester University Press, 2021) and co-editor of several volumes and special issues, including *Animal Remains* (Routledge, 2021) and *Seeing Animals After Derrida* (Lexington, 2018), along with a special issue on "Taxidermic Forms and Fictions" for *Configurations: A Journal of Literature, Science, and Technology*. Her next book monograph (in progress) examines cultural imaginaries of species loss and revival. To learn more, visit sarahbezan.com.

Benay Blend received her doctorate in American Studies from the University of New Mexico, USA. She has taught at the University of Georgia, Memphis State University, and the University of New Mexico. Currently, she is a retired professor of Native American, American, and New Mexico history. She has published widely in such fields as southwest women writers, Native American studies, and nature writing. Her published articles include "Challenging the Official Story: Alicia Kozameh, Alicia Partnoy, and Mother Activism During Argentina's Dirty Wars (1976–1983)," in *Mothers under Fire*, Arlene Sgoutas and Tatjana Takseva, Eds. (Demeter Press, 2015); "Intimate Kinships: Who Speaks for Nature and Who Listens When Nature Speaks for Herself?" in *Ecocriticism and the Global South*, Scott Slovic, Vidya Sarveswaran, Swarnalatha Rangarajan, Eds. (Lexington Books, 2015); "'I Learnt All the Words and Broke Them Up / To Make a Single Word: Homeland': An Eco-Postcolonial Perspective of Resistance in Palestinian Women's Literature," in *Ecofeminism in Dialogue*, Douglas Vakoch and Sam Mickey, Eds. (Lexington Books, 2017); and "'Neither Homeland Nor Exile Are Words': 'Situated Knowledge' in the Works of Palestinian and Native American Writers," in *Ecopoetics and the Global Landscape: Critical Essays*, Isabel Campos, Ed. (Lexington Books, 2018). Her current research focuses on place as a means of resistance in Native American and Palestinian writers.

Deirdre Byrne, PhD, is Head of the Institute for Gender Studies at the University of South Africa and editor of the academic journal *scrutiny2* as well as a member of the editorial collective of the journal *Gender Questions*. She has published research on Ursula K. Le Guin, science fiction, fantasy, and South African women's poetry.

Aslı Değirmenci Altın is Assistant Professor in the Department of English Language and Literature at Hacettepe University, Turkey. She earned her bachelor's degree in English Language and Literature at Bogazici University, Istanbul, and her master's degree in American Culture and Literature at Hacettepe University. She completed her PhD in English Literature at the University at Buffalo, USA, in 2013. Her dissertation focused on magical realist literature from the developing and postcolonial world. Her research interests are postcolonial theory and literature, the contemporary British and American novel, science fiction, climate fiction, and environmental humanities.

Melissa Etzler received her MA in German from California State University, Long Beach, USA, and her PhD in German with a Designated Emphasis in Film from the University of California, Berkeley, USA in 2014. Her dissertation, *Writing from the Periphery: W. G. Sebald and Outsider Art*, explores intersections of pathology, marginalization, creative production, and politics. She has since published two book chapters on Sebald. She is also interested in ecocritical thought and recently published "Pernicious Plants: Imitation and Uncanny Ecocritical Thought in Gustav Meyrink's 'Die Pflanzen des Dr. Cinderella'" in *German Quarterly*. She is the co-editor of *Outreach Strategies and Innovative Teaching Approaches for German Programs with Gabriele Maier* (Routledge, 2021). Etzler is a lecturer of German and First Year Seminar at Butler University in Indianapolis, USA.

Peter I-min Huang (黃逸民), PhD, is Professor Emeritus of English at Tamkang University, Taiwan. Huang's areas of interest are English and Chinese Literature, ecofeminism, ecopoetry, postcolonial ecocriticism, indigenous studies, science fiction, and climate fiction. He is a founding member of ASLE-Taiwan. He was chair of the English Department (two terms, 2007–2011), and he served as the conference organizing chairperson for *The Fourth Tamkang International Conference on Ecological Discourse* (23–24 May 2008) and *The Fifth Tamkang International Conference on Ecological Discourse* (17–18 December 2010). Huang's journal articles include publications in *Neohelicon*; *Journal of Poyang Lake*; *CLCWeb: Comparative Literature and Culture*; and *Foreign Literature Studies*. He has published book chapters in *Transecology: Transgender Perspectives on Environment and Nature* (Routledge, 2021); *Literature and Ecofeminism: Intersectional and International Voices* (Routledge, 2018); *Ecocriticism in Taiwan: Identity, Environment, and the Arts* (Lexington Books, 2016); and *East Asian Ecocriticisms: A Critical Reader* (Palgrave Macmillan, 2013). Huang also is the author of *Linda Hogan and Contemporary Taiwanese Writers: An Ecocritical Study of Indigeneities and Environment* (Lexington Books, 2015).

Zahra Jannessari Ladani, PhD, is Assistant Professor of English Literature at the University of Isfahan, Iran. She is the Persian translator of Kristina Nelson's *The Art of Reciting the Quran* and the English editor of *Quran Recitation Skills*. She has also translated a number of Stanley G. Weinbaum's science fiction stories into Persian for the first time. Her major contributions to science fiction consist of her lecture "The Rise of the Pulps, 1900s–1930s" given to Lars Schmeink's *The Virtual Introduction to Science Fiction*, and her chapter "John W. Campbell and his Writers" published in Leigh Grossman's *Sense of Wonder: A Century of Science Fiction* (Wildside Press, 2011). Her new book chapter, "Robert A. Heinlein in Historical and Cultural Context," has been published in

Rafeeq McGiveron's *Critical Insights: Robert A. Heinlein* (Salem Press, 2015). She has published articles in such diverse journals as *Research in Contemporary World Literature, Lesan Mobin,* and *Translation Studies.* Her most recent publication, coauthored with Sharareh Kashi, is "The Representation of Fukuyama's Pathways to a Posthuman Future in *Brave New World* and *Never Let Me Go*" in the *Journal of Literary Studies.*

Lesley Kordecki received her MA and PhD from the Centre for Medieval Studies at the University of Toronto, Canada, and is Professor Emerita of English at DePaul University, USA. A recipient of DePaul University's Excellence in Teaching Award, she is a former director of the MA in English at DePaul and served as chair of English at Barat College, USA, for over 20 years. She worked as a dramaturge for the Shakespeare on the Green productions in Lake Forest, Illinois, USA, for seven years and coauthored with Karla Koskinen *Re-Visioning Lear's Daughters: Testing Feminist Criticism and Theory* (Palgrave Macmillan, 2010) as a result of that collaboration. She is the author of *Ecofeminist Subjectivities: Chaucer's Talking Birds* (Palgrave, 2011).

Imelda Martín Junquera, PhD, is Associate Professor in the Department of Modern Languages, Universidad de León, Spain. Her fields of research and interest include Chicano and Native American literature and culture, as well as border studies, all under the framework of ecocriticism, ecofeminism, and environmental justice. She is a member of GIECO (Grupo de investigación en ecocrítica de España) from the Universidad de Alcalá- Franklin Institute and a former member of the Advisory Board of EASLCE (European Association for the Study of Literature, Culture and the Environment). From 2010 to 2016, she was the Executive coeditor of *Ecozon@ (European Journal of Literature, Culture and Environment).* Currently, she is the main editor of the journal *Estudios Humanísticos Filología* published by the Universidad de León. Recent publications include her edited volume *Landscapes of Writing in Chicano Literature* (Palgrave Macmillan, 2013), her book chapter "Healing Family History/ (Her) Story: Writing and Gardening in Pat Mora's *House of Houses*" in *International Perspectives on Chicana/o Studies: "This World is My Place"* (Routledge, 2014), and the journal articles "The Inscription of the American Southwest in Navajo Tribal Parks" in *Iperstoria. Testi letterature linguaggi* (2017), "The Wolf: Reenacting the Myth and Archetype in American Literature and Society" in *Revista Canaria de Estudios Ingleses* (2018), and "Dialogical Ecofeminist Perspectives in 'The Moths' by Helena María Viramontes and 'Women Hollering Creek' by Sandra Cisneros" in *Ex-Centric Narratives: Journal of Anglophone Literature, Culture and Media* (2019).

Meghna Mudaliar has been a teacher, writer, and editor since 2002. Her PhD research, conducted from 2008 to 2011 at Stella Maris College,

University of Madras, India, focused on the contrapuntal rhetoric in constructions of the "imaginary homeland" in the works of Sri Lankan-Canadian novelist and poet Michael Ondaatje and Kashmiri-American poet Agha Shahid Ali. Before joining Christ University in 2015, she taught at Stella Maris College and the Indian Institute of Technology Madras (IITM). Currently, the coordinator of the interdisciplinary MA in English with Cultural Studies programme at Christ University's School of Business Studies and Social Sciences, Bangalore, Mudaliar is also working on a postdoctoral Major Research Project on is narratives in gender studies, funded by Christ University. In addition to written papers and conference presentations, she has created syllabi for gender studies at the undergraduate and graduate levels. She also has a keen interest in the Romantic period, with particular reference to Samuel Taylor Coleridge and his brothers John and Frank, who died in India. Her most recent publication in the *Rupkatha Journal on Interdisciplinary Studies in Humanities* is titled "Rethinking Romanticism: Mary Shelley, *The X-Files*, and the Postmodern Prometheus."

Patrick D. Murphy is Professor Emeritus of English at the University of Central Florida, USA. He earned a BA in history from University California, Los Angeles, USA, in 1973, an MA in English from California State University, Northridge, USA, in 1983, and a PhD in English from the University of California, Davis, USA. in 1986. Recent publications include *Persuasive Aesthetic Ecocritical Praxis* (Lexington Books, 2015) and "Pessimism, Optimism, Human Inertia and Anthropogenic Climate Change," special climate change issue, *ISLE: Interdisciplinary Studies in Literature and Environment* (2014).

Katja Plemenitaš is Assistant Professor of English in the Department of English and American Studies of the Faculty of Arts at the University of Maribor, Slovenia. She earned her BA degree in English and French in the Faculty of Arts at the University of Ljubljana, Slovenia, and later completed her master and doctorate in Linguistics in the same faculty. As Assistant Professor of English, she gives lectures at the BA and MA levels. She currently teaches courses in morphology, discourse analysis, and language and gender. Her research interests include all aspects of discourse analysis and cognitive linguistics, and she also takes a keen interest in language and gender. She is a member of the Gender Studies Network (ESSE). Plemenitaš's work is predominantly based on the systemic-functional model of language in context. She has published several papers and book chapters based on her research. Her recent academic interests focus on linguistic appraisal in political rhetoric, the application of cognitive linguistics to discourse analysis, and the gendered forms of political discourse. She is currently working on a book about the analysis of logico-semantic relations in political texts.

Lydia Rose is Associate Professor in the Department of Sociology at Kent State University, USA. She earned a PhD in sociology from Purdue University, USA. Her research centers on environmental justice, ecofeminism, and inequality. Rose's teaching and scholarship emphasize the intersectionality and impact of race, class, gender, and other inequalities in our social institutions, including education, family, economy, food systems, and the environment. Her praxis emphasizes the connection of theory, research, and social action to alleviate the injustices created by social inequalities from both a micro and macro level. Rose is the coauthor of *Pink Hats and Ballots: An Ecofeminist Perspective of Women's Political Activism in the Age of Trump, Coronavirus, and Black Lives Matter* (Lexington Books, 2021).

Preface

Douglas A. Vakoch

Ecofeminist Science Fiction: International Perspectives on Gender, Ecology, and Literature provides guidance in navigating some of the most pressing dangers we face today. Science fiction helps us face problems that threaten the very existence of humankind by giving us the emotional distance to see our current situation from afar, separated in our imaginations through time, space, or circumstance. Extrapolating from contemporary science, science fiction allows a critique of modern society, imagining more life-affirming alternatives.

In this collection, ecocritics from five continents scrutinize science fiction for insights into the fundamental changes we need to make to survive and thrive as a species. Contributors examine ecofeminist themes in films such as *Avatar, Star Wars,* and *The Stepford Wives,* as well as television series including *Doctor Who* and *Westworld.* Other scholars explore an internationally diverse group of both canonical and lesser-known science fiction writers including Oreet Ashery, Iraj Fazel Bakhsheshi, Liu Cixin, Louise Erdrich, Hanns Heinz Ewers, Larissa Lai, Ursula K. Le Guin, Chen Qiufan, Mary Doria Russell, Larissa Sansour, Karen Traviss, and Jeanette Winterson.

Ecofeminist Science Fiction explores the origins of human-caused environmental change in the twin oppressions of women and of nature, driven by patriarchal power and ideologies. Female embodiment is examined through diverse natural and artificial forms, and queer ecologies challenge heteronormativity. The links between war and environmental destruction are analyzed, and the capitalist motivations and means for exploiting nature are critiqued through postcolonial perspectives. In the chapters that follow, contributors liberally cross-reference each other, as they engage in a dialogue on these topics that are critical to envisioning a better future.

Acknowledgments

For their innovative contributions that bring together ecofeminism and science fiction, I thank the authors of the chapters that follow: Başak Ağın, Teresa M. Bartoli, Sarah Bezan, Benay Blend, Deirdre Byrne, Aslı Değirmenci Altın, Melissa Etzler, Peter I-min Huang, Zahra Jannessari Ladani, Lesley Kordecki, Imelda Martín Junquera, Meghna Mudaliar, Patrick Murphy, Katja Plemenitaš, and Lydia Rose. I gratefully acknowledge the scholars who reviewed and commented on the full manuscript: Serenella Iovino, Noël Sturgeon, and Etienne Terblanche.

In my work as president of METI International, my colleagues have shared with me their insights about what it takes for civilizations to remain stable across the millennia—a prerequisite for the success of our organization's namesake Messaging Extraterrestrial Intelligence, given the immense timescales of interstellar communication. It is rare to find a community that sees a natural link between sustainability and the search for life in the universe, as reflected in METI's strategic plan that affirms the "ways that ecofeminism can provide insights into fostering environmental sustainability on multigenerational timescales." This book's focus on environmental critique and engagement is informed by conversations with current and past members of METI's Board of Directors: Jacques Arnould, Jerome Barkow, Kim Binsted, Steven Dick, David Dunér, Abhik Gupta, Adam Korbitz, Derek Malone-France, Anson Mount, Alan Penny, Florence Raulin Cerceau, Dalia Rawson, Ian Roberts, Jill Stuart, John Traphagan, Ariel Waldman, Laura Welcher, and Sheri Wells-Jensen.

For presenting early versions of their chapters in our panel on ecofeminist science fiction in the academic track of the international science fiction convention Worldcon 76, I thank Peter I-min Huang and Katja Plemenitaš, as well as those who joined them for the follow-up workshop at METI's headquarters in San Francisco: Abhik Gupta, Mike Matessa, Ted Peters, Iris Ralph, Dalia Rawson, Vandana Singh, Scott Slovic, and Laura Welcher.

For collaborating on ways to increase accountability for environmental threats and disasters, I am grateful to Otabek Suleimanov, founder of the Stihia Festival.

I warmly acknowledge the insights I have gained in integrating sustainable actions into our everyday lives through the clients I work with as director of Green Psychotherapy, PC, a clinical psychology and ecotherapy practice in the San Francisco Bay Area.

My thanks go to Scott Slovic and Swarnalatha Rangarajan for including this book in Routledge Studies in World Literatures and the Environment. To Michelle Salyga at Routledge, I am indebted for her help in shaping this book and for shepherding it through the editorial process. Bryony Reece has my gratitude for moving the book swiftly and efficiently into production. Finally, I thank Louise Peterken and Rachel Cook for conscientiously overseeing all aspects of the production process, as the final manuscript was transformed into the published volume you are now reading.

I am grateful to Ursula K. Le Guin for *The Left Hand of Darkness*, the novel I assigned for a course in the psychology of women that I taught as a graduate student a quarter-century ago, which opened the possibility for me to start reimagining gender and nature.

Most importantly, I thank my wife Julie Bayless for helping me understand what it means to be an ecofeminist.

Douglas A. Vakoch
San Francisco, California

Introduction

Patrick D. Murphy

As many claims about the origins of science fiction in western literature exist as definitions of this prose genre. These even include the argument that it is a "mode" of representation rather than a genre as such. Identifying western utopian literature is easier to date thanks to Plato. Given patriarchal institutional efforts throughout that history since Plato to limit women's literacy in general and authorship in particular, science fiction is usually defined as having a much shorter lifespan than utopian literature, based on the argument that its inception requires the development of modern science, from biology and medicine through astronomy and physics. The notion of what is "modern" in science, though, is quite irregular and uneven. It requires greater clarity about Islamic and Chinese science during the so-called Middle ages and any literary production in Arabic and Chinese based on those advances. Restricting themselves to western literature, critics often view science fiction as developing in the eighteenth century, although some put it as late as the twentieth. Again, it is likely that ongoing research in renaissance literature will push the origination point farther back in time depending on which sciences are analyzed as necessary preconditions for the "science" in science fiction.

Without fretting too much about that, one can easily argue that science fiction as a mode of imaginative prose fiction certainly arrived in full force with the publication of Mary Shelley's *Frankenstein* (1818), given its impact in its day, its influence on subsequent literature, and its enduring appeal. Gerry Canavan (2014, 271) describes *Frankenstein* in these terms: "widely acknowledged as the first SF novel, dramatizes man's overstepping of his natural bounds in a manner that would become paradigmatic for the genre." It is unfortunate that Canavan does not also mention its feminist dimension, although certainly that aspect could not be declared "paradigmatic." While not likely the earliest work of science fiction by a woman, *Frankenstein* is the most celebrated and influential launching of a tradition of women's participation in the writing of SF now spanning 200 years.

Women have clearly been participating in the writing of science fiction in English for at least 200 years. They have won numerous awards for their novels and short stories, becoming an increasing presence among the ranks of the best writers in the field. A quick scan of the Locus Awards, the Nebula Awards, and the Hugo Awards prove that. Their novels and stories repeatedly appear in lists of "must read" works. Likewise, many writers celebrated in the "mainstream" have also chosen to use this mode for some of their novels because it enables them to develop themes addressing crucial issues less amenable to the so-called "realism," to which some male critics wanted the Margaret Atwoods and Doris Lessings to limit themselves, such as alternative forms of pregnancy and childbirth, climate change, psychic capabilities, and post-capitalist economics.

From the earliest authors, such as Cavendish and Shelley, feminist and environmental issues have often been intertwined, such that ecofeminist, or, if you will, proto-ecofeminist works have been a staple feature of SF for several centuries. To their names, one can add the American author Mary Griffith, who wrote *Three Hundred Years Hence* (1836), as well as Mary E. Bradley Lane, author of *Mizora* (1890). Writers in the 1970s, such as Joanna Russ, Marge Piercy, and Ursula K. Le Guin, shifted the emphasis in science fiction from engineering and an extrapolation of the economic status quo to alternative economies, sexual relations, and alien encounters. No other science fiction author than Piercy has attempted to reshape the gendered pronouns of English, nor has any male writer suggested, as Russ (1977) did in *We Who Are About to...*, that not only should human beings not colonize every planet they land on but should choose death in order to protect the ecosystem of an off-limits one.

One might assume, then, that feminist and ecofeminist analyses of science fiction would have simply become part and parcel of any collection of essays on such literature. And, further, that any ecocritical anthology would also have to include a substantial body of ecofeminist critique. Unfortunately, such has not yet occurred. The critical anthology, from which I quoted Gerry Canavan earlier, *Green Planets: Ecology and Science Fiction*, co-edited by Canavan with Kim Stanley Robinson (2014), an author who has had female protagonists in numerous novels, gives short shrift to feminist and ecofeminist issues. Out of 260 pages, "feminism" is listed in the index as appearing on roughly ten pages, while "ecomaterialism" is lumped in with feminism for an additional four pages. "Ecofeminism" is listed under "feminism" and as appearing on one page and in one additional endnote, which happens to be a reference to some of my work on Le Guin. All of these references pertain to only two female authors: Ursula K. Le Guin and Maggie Gee. The representation of female science fiction authors and ecofeminism in their collection is utterly inadequate for a volume published as recently as 2014. Need I say more regarding a justification for this volume with its focus on ecofeminist science fiction?

The chapters in this present volume are organized into four sections, facilitating an appreciation of the intertextuality of the many contributions as well as highlighting the kinds of topics and issues pertinent to understanding ecofeminist science fiction. The authors of the chapters comprise a stellar international group of critics, both female and male.

Part 1. Female Bodies: Plants and Animals, Cyborgs and Robots

In the first chapter, Melissa Etzler discusses the early twentieth-century German novel, *Alraune*, by Hanns Heinz Ewers. In this Frankenstein-like tale, with Ewers drawing on folklore for his key conceit, scientists create a child by means of the mandrake root with the goal of enabling sex without love. The novel, according to Etzler, reflects the pessimism and decadence of the fin de siecle Berlin. But, despite the best-laid plans of mad male scientists, Alraune proves to be a rebellious offspring and reflects masculinist anxiety over the "new woman" of the twentieth century. The novel reveals the prevalent misogyny of its cultural and historical milieu. A reading of the novel against the grain as Etzler performs facilitates a greater appreciation of those works by women writers of the late nineteenth and early twentieth century that depicted ecological and feminist utopian possibilities for the future.

Apparent utopias are not always what they seem as the traveler in H. G. Wells's *The Time Machine* (1895) discovered. A similar misapprehension on the part of main characters occurs in Mary Doria Russell's *The Sparrow*, analyzed here by Lesley Kordecki. As she demonstrates, the male human space mission colonists rely on a series of false dichotomies: the pastoral versus the urban as separate spheres, the feminine as inferior to the masculine in the form of two distinct species, and people with a developed economy as more civilized than those with a primitive one. Through the lens of Critical Animal Studies, Kordecki dissects the novel in terms of these dichotomies and the revelations that dawn too late for the human colonists.

Imelda Martín Junquera analyzes a television series *Westworld* and the film *Sleep Dealer*. Film and series alike dramatize how uncontrolled technology leads to the exploitation of both androids and migrant workers and the need to break down artificial hierarchies of owners/exploiters and workers/exploited. In *Westworld* it is mainly two female androids who lead the rebellion in that environment, while in *Sleep Dealer* it is the racially oppressed. The film also critiques the use of military drone technology.

Continuing with attention to the film, Katja Plemenitäs analyzes the original version of *The Stepford Wives*, with its much grimmer conclusion than that of the remake. The film is a satiric dystopia of suburbia exposing masculinist anxiety about independent women. Along the way it expresses concern about the impact of technoscience on the environment, patriarchal shaping of living spaces in terms of various forms of enclosure, and the objectification of women as another resource to be exploited. The simulacra, Plemenitäs shows, are ones in which wild variability has been eliminated and as an embodied consumerist product they are manicured, contained, maintained, and restrained.

Part 2. Queer Ecologies

Aslı Değirmenci Altin analyzes one of the works of avant-garde novelist Jeanette Winterson, *The Stone Gods*. Using a narrative structure filled with radical temporal and cosmic shifts, Winterson produces a cautionary tale that Değirmenci argues demonstrates that an anthropocentric continuity will destroy any opportunity to reverse course and provide humanity with a second chance to develop a sustainable inhabitation of Earth. The novel includes a parallelism between cosmetic surgery for women and the artificiality of a totally domesticated biosphere. Drawing on the theories of Plumwood, Dolozel, and others, Değirmenci demonstrates how two of the central characters who fall in love—both of them female, but one of them a human and the other an android—function as posthuman subjects voicing and experiencing the destructiveness of the current trajectory of ecocide.

Sarah Bezan provides a reading of Canadian author Larissa Lai's *Salt fish Girl* and its treatment of embodiment. Mixing myth with a narrative of cloning for reproduction, Lai's novel counters the heteronormative depictions found elsewhere in science fiction outside of feminist texts. As with other texts that challenge the idea of the body as a discrete object, Lai, according to Bezan, emphasizes aqueous nature rather than the solidity of terra firma. A disruptive ecofeminist politics challenges masculinist bio-techno-capitalism.

Meghna Mudaliar switches our attention to two long-running television series, *Doctor Who* and *Supernatural*, both of which she argues loosely fit into a broad definition of SF. She focuses on the representation of a major lesbian character introduced late into each of the series, analyzing them by means of Greta Gaard's arguments about ecofeminism developing beyond any "charges of gender essentialism" and combines that with insights from animal studies. Mudaliar notes that the ecological dimensions of characters are associated mainly with other worldly characters with whom the two lesbians, Bill Potts and Charlie Bradbury, interact. These associations facilitate an initial critique of the series' representations in terms of patriarchal dichotomies. Yet, in each series, after Bill and Charlie are killed off, they are eventually brought back in "alt" forms that tend to be far more progressive than their original versions, demonstrating a more nuanced representation of the two both in terms of their sexualities and in terms of their environmental relationships.

Part 3. War and Ecoterrorism

In my chapter that opens this section, I focus on the six-volume *The Wess'har Wars* series written by Karen Traviss, who is mainly known in SF circles for writing *Gears of War* and *Star Wars* novels with military emphases. But in this series, she delves deeply into a variety of ethical questions that have been foregrounded by ecofeminist philosophy. First noting that the narrative structure is dialogical and internally persuasive rather than mono-logical and authoritative, I consider its development in relation to feminist-developed invitational rhetoric and the responsibility it places on readers to work out appropriate answers to complex problems. Then, the chapter distinguishes the tending instinct displayed by certain species in the series from any form of essentialist reductionism and considers the concept of relationality as a fundamental aspect of human entanglement with the rest of nature. I also look at how Traviss addresses the economic limitations of commodification in relation to patterns of consumption and the distinction between wants and needs. Finally, the complexities of trying to rebalance environmentally damaged ecosystems require a nuanced approach with no easy answers, reflective of ongoing debates over conservation, preservation, and restoration.

Başak Ağun turns attention to the *Star Wars* franchise of films, particu-larly the most recent ones arguing that they have increased their representa-tions of diversity in response to audience expectations and provide positive portrayals of female characters. She analyzes these films by means of the posthumanist materialist turn in feminist and ecofeminist theory advanced by such thinkers as Jane Bennett and Félix Guattari. From that perspective, the "force" can be viewed as agentic and a type of vibrant matter compa-rable to "dirt" as a performative actant in the world. The "force," then, represents the ways in which the inorganic can demonstrate agency.

Peter I-min Huang provides a contrastive analysis of two works of Chinese science fiction. One of these texts, he argues, caters to masculinist fears of environmentalist agendas as terroristic plots. The other sympathetically rep-resents the themes that the first novel castigates. The first novel promotes faith in science and technology with no concern for environmental conser-vation. In it, the Cultural Revolution provides a backdrop for the pathetic and ineffective actions of a Rachel Carson-like character who wants to save old-growth forests and invites aliens to help stop the despoliation of the planet. While the invitation is reminiscent of the conclusion of *The Wess'har Wars* series, the results are disastrous rather than beneficial. While this first novel promotes an androcentric fantasy of the technological sublime, the second one depicts a techno-dystopia based on the actual e-waste capital of mainland China. The "woman warrior" of this novel leads a migrant work-ers' revolt against their plight and the environmental destruction in which they are coerced into facilitating.

Part 4. Capitalism and Colonization

Lydia Rose and Teresa M. Bartoli turn attention from fiction to film with a critique of the blockbuster *Avatar*. They consider the ways in which the film demonstrates connections between patriarchal attitudes of domination toward women, nature, and indigenous peoples. Deploying the key con-cept of Antonio Gramsci's political theory, they look at the paradigm of hegemonic masculinity. At the same time, they consider how indigenous cultures are presented as the antithesis of capitalist expansionism.

Zahra Jannessari Ladani introduces readers to two novels by an Iranian author, Iraj Fazel Baksheshi. In these works, idealistic women undermine the techno-domination plans of male scientists thereby producing feminist counternarratives to hyper urbanization and totalitarianism, including the increasingly pertinent problem of ubiquitous surveillance. In *The Sun's Sons*, Baksheshi portrays human beings colonizing another planet as parasitic rather than symbiotic in their goals of domination. According to Jahnessari-Ladani, Baksheshi's "heroines are the initiations of a new version of heroism, one that collates social responsibilities with ethical mandates and an egalitarian outlook."

Benay Blend combines Indigenous Studies with ecofeminism in her analysis of two novels, one by the award-winning Native American author, Louise Erdrich, and the other by a pair of authors, one Israeli and the other Palestinian. These anti-colonial works upend the recurring trope of colonization disguised as exploration. Erdrich, Blend argues, critiques genetic engineering and reproductive technologies as exploitative of nature through a cautionary tale about "womb volunteers." The Palestinian/Israeli duo have written their comic-book style novel as a collaboration that is itself a form of resistance to domination and exploitation. Blend views their work as demonstrating that "Ecofeminists hold cooperation, too, as a core value." Both novels, she argues, analyze the problems of frontiers and the need for a statelessness that abolishes arbitrary and illusory boundaries.

In the final chapter, Deirdre Byrne considers Ursula K. Le Guin's representations of environmental threats in two of her early novels, *Rocannon's World* and *The Word for World Is Forest*, published in 1966 and 1972, respectively. She argues that Le Guin seeks to represent a "vision of equipoise and collaboration" rather than the models of domination and conquest of natural worlds and other sentient species that littered the science fiction scene prior to the 1960s. In particular, femininity is presented as a species-wide ethical capacity for care and not solely an attribute of females. Byrne invokes Deleuze and Guattari's concept of "becoming-ecology" in the course of analyzing the surrender to a forested way of thinking in the second of these two novels.

All in all, these chapters provide a wide-ranging ecofeminist analysis of an international array of novels, films, and stories produced in the past two centuries. Some of the works considered have already become science fiction classics, while others are just beginning to receive adequate critical attention. In addition to readers developing a strong primary reading list out of these discussions, they also benefit from the different ecofeminist methods and theoretical orientations adopted by the chapters' authors. Both the critical approaches and the literary works and films analyzed, then, provide a rich reading experience.

Bibliography

Canavan, Gerry. 2014. "Of Further Interest." In *Green Planets: Ecology and Science Fiction*, edited by Gerry Canavan and Kim Stanley Robinson, 261–279. Middletown, CT: Wesleyan University Press.

Canavan, Gerry, and Kim Stanley Robinson, eds. 2014. *Green Planets: Ecology and Science Fiction*. Middletown, CT: Wesleyan University Press.

Cavendish, Margaret. [1666] 2016. *The Description of a New World, Called the Blazing World*. Peterborough, ON: Broadview.

Griffith, Mary. [1836] 1975. *Three Hundred Years Hence*. Boston, MA: Gregg Press.

Lane, Mary Bradley. [1890] 1999. *Mizora: A Prophecy: A Mss. Found Among the Private Papers of Princess Vera Zarovitch: Being a True and Faithful Account of her Journey to the Interior of the Earth, with a Careful Description of the Country and its Inhabitants, their Customs, Manners, and Government*. Lincoln, NE: University of Nebraska Press.

Russ, Joanna. [1977] 2005. *We Who Are About to…*. Middleton, CT: Wesleyan University Press.

Shelley, Mary. [1818] 1994. *Frankenstein, or, The Modern Prometheus*. Mineola, NY: Dover.

Spender, Dale. 1986. *Mothers of the Novel*. London: Pandora Press.

Wells, H. G. [1895] 2017. *The Time Machine*. Oxford: Oxford University Press.

Part 1

Female Bodies

Plants and Animals, Cyborgs and Robots

1 "Mothered by the Arid Sand"

Hanns Heinz Ewers' *Alraune* with an Ecofeminist Twist

Melissa Etzler

In Germanic folklore, few plants are as notorious as the hallucinogenic *Mandragora officinalis*, or mandrake root. Its primary attribute outlined by Aristotle's pupil Theophrastus of Eresus on Lesbos (c.370–c.287 BCE), which is later adopted by Germanic culture, is the association of the aphrodisiac plant with fertility. Theophrastus explains that Greek custom required one to "dance around the plant [during the harvest of mandrake apples], uttering as much as one can remember about lust, sex and the full mysteries of erotic passion" (Scarborough 2006, 13–14). During the Renaissance, the mandrake root appeared in an artistic form that was a peculiar conjoining of science and fiction. In reference to medical illustrations that anthropomorphized the root, Melodie Slabbert writes that "art in general was a mixture of realism [science] and idealism [fiction] and this applied to medical illustrations" (2010, 134). Such illustrations made the mandrake root an easy target for appropriation in twentieth- and twenty-first-century pop culture, for example in texts and films ranging from J. K. Rowling's *Harry Potter and the Chamber of Secrets* (1999) to Andreas Marschall's short film *Alraune* (the German term for mandrake root), which was one of three films featured in the horror trilogy *German Angst* (2015). What has remained consistent over time is that the mandrake has always existed within a liminal space between science and fiction and which points to configurations of gender and sexuality.

In addition to, or perhaps because of, the plant's natural humanoid physical attributes, it was sought out for medicinal purposes despite the rumored risks associated with the collection of the plant. According to legend, if one removes a mandrake root from the ground, the plant emits so harsh a scream that the sound will be fatal to anyone in the vicinity. Nonetheless, it is said that people would fill their ears with wax, tie a rope between a dog's tail and the mandrake and then force the dog to run. The dog never survived, but the human gained possession of the precious plant. By 1390, there were plenty of German illustrations representing this legend and, in nearly every instance, the mandrake is feminized and uprooted from the ground by a man (Gassen and Minol 2006, 304). Along with the gender-based illustrations, the mandrake legend claims that the root only comes into existence when the earth is fertilized by the semen of a hanged man. Because of its rumored fatal capabilities and, somewhat contradictory, medicinal benefits (a fertility aid) and pitfalls (to oversexualize an individual), by the late Middle Ages, belief in the precarious nature of the plant was widespread and associated with witchcraft. The mandrake was considered evil and only if it were properly treated could it be employed for its utilitarian function, aside from as an aphrodisiac that is, to sublimate sexual desire.

It is this legend that German writer Hanns Heinz Ewers (1871–1943) translates into the realm of science fiction in *Alraune* (1911). In this novel, a scientist artificially inseminates a prostitute with the mandrake root, thereby creating a female child, named Alraune. She/it is a creature "neither man nor beast" who is oblivious to love but understands sexual desire all too well (15). While in 1911 this premise was the stuff of which dreams are made, scientific developments beginning in the 1950s would make births vaguely similar to Alraune's reality. On July 25, 1978, Louise Brown, the world's first "test-tube" baby, was born via *in-vitro* fertilization, a procedure for which Robert Edwards won the Nobel Prize in 2010 (Northwestern University 2010). Sixty-seven years before *in-vitro* fertilization, Ewers' tale depicts the Promethean birth of a creature that prompts the reader to ponder human subjectivity and its formation. Alraune embodies the in-between state outlined by theorists of the posthuman such as Rosi Braidotti. She/it is emblematic of an erasure of the nature-culture divide (Braidotti 2013, 3). Alraune is indicative of cultural production through her genesis via technology and she is also intimately linked with the organic, feminized realm of plants. She/it is a figure that exists between multiple borders and I argue that this text can be read through an ecofeminist, science fiction lens. As Christie Tidwell and Bridgitte Barclay observe, "many texts are ripe for ecocritical and gender readings in sf [...] because science fiction texts often ask questions such as *where is nature, what is natural, and who is equated with nature*" (Tidwell and Barclay 2019, ix). Wavering between such borders, Alraune reveals how Ewers' novel is in dialogue with the shifting social roles and gender norms that many believed were leading women into an "unnatural" way of life.

Something about the taboo tale appealed to the public and withstood the test of time. *Alraune* launched Ewers to world fame, he sold over a million copies and the novel was translated into over 25 different languages. Perhaps its longevity is even due to the ubiquitous ecofeminist, *avant la lettre*, undertones. It was quickly adapted to film, appearing over five times between 1918 and 1930, the most famous version being the 1928 horror film directed by Henrik Galeen and starring Brigitte Helm. Outlining the various appearances of *Alraune* but focusing on the Ewers novel, I show how this figure, despite diverse sociological contexts, manages to persist as a quintessential proto–femme fatale and even proto-ecofeminist of pop culture.

Fin de Siècle Berlin: Industry, Technology, and the Birth of the New Woman

Hanns Heinz Ewers was born in Düsseldorf in 1871 and moved to Berlin in 1901 where he quickly ensconced himself in Berlin's cultural life and both the pessimism and decadence of *fin de siècle* Berlin informed *Alraune*. Despite the fact that the novel takes place in Cologne, *Alraune*'s creation occurs in Berlin. Much like Ewers' contemporary, Gustav Meyrink, whose works I read through an ecocriticist lens due to his theorizing of the potential negative environmental ramifications of scientific experimentation within the city (Prague) space, I view Ewers' organic creature Alraune as the rebellious offspring of an increasingly mechanized Berlin (Etzler 2017). As a novel written during a period of extreme cultural, economic, sociological, and political upheaval, this novel fits the description offered by Roger Luckhurst regarding a commonality between Gothic and science fiction works. He claims that "both genres lever open imaginative possibilities at the boundaries of advancing knowledge, exploiting underground phrases of 'extraordinary' science where norms are unraveling and have not quite established a new norm" (Luckhurst 2018, 36). In order to read *Alraune* from an ecofeminist perspective, it is important to understand the shifting role of women in Berlin, a city frequently depicted and often cited as the apocalyptic, biblical "Whore of Babylon" (Smith 2013, 3–4).

At the turn of the century in Berlin, one female figure gained a public presence like never before—the prostitute. The dichotomy of the prostitute, always either viewed as victim or monster, is recreated in Ewers' *Alraune*. Much like the dual nature of the prostitute, the legend states the mandrake root can, on the one hand, bring fame, fortune, and love to its possessor. On the other hand, it can bring death. In Ewers' novel, the young bachelor and hedonistic playboy Frank Baum knows that in order to help his uncle, the lucrative Privy Councilor ten Brinken (who uses animals for his artificial insemination experiments), to create the perfect *alraune*-creature, he must first locate a prostitute to use as a surrogate. It is clear that to Frank Baum, a person in the know, Berlin ranks second on the scale of debauchery, just under Paris. Baum considers his impending task in Berlin: "Too bad, because Paris would have been the right place. There they would have an easier time of it and they would find something better ... Let it be Berlin" (Ewers 2013, 70). The fact that Baum refers to the woman as a "something" reveals the project as dehumanizing. Though Berlin is not Baum's first choice, the city offered, especially for women, the contrary lifestyles of licentiousness and depravity or financial and social mobility and freedom.

Between 1871 and 1905, Berlin's population grew from 826,000 to over two million and, with this influx of people, the seeds of women's suffrage began to grow. This is an increase of 247% in 34 years, compared to the 54.2% population increase from 1905 to 2020. Many single women were lured into Berlin by the possibility of financial and social autonomy that enabled them to have access to disposable income. Suddenly, women were participating in the workforce, in mass entertainment, and in metropolitan consumer culture (Smith 2013, 4–5). The growing presence of women in the workforce made inequality painfully obvious, and women "banded together and rallied support for increased educational and occupational opportunities, making Berlin the seat of the German women's movement" (Smith 2013, 5). However, women in the bourgeois workforce were not the only ones fighting for their rights—prostitutes also came together and fought "to publish their own newspapers and file legal petitions with state and local governments" to pass laws to regulate prostitution and prevent the spread of venereal diseases (Smith 2008, 449). Society was shocked by prostitutes demanding rights. As such, the prostitute punished in *Alraune*, who dies just after birthing the *alraune*-creature, can be viewed as a fantasy of restoring the hierarchical, gender-based order in which women, particularly prostitutes, regress to being silent objects and obediently fulfilling men's desires whatever the cost.

The changing roles of women in the socioeconomic sphere were as extreme as the alteration in women's style and appearance. By 1900, female fashion journalists were encouraging women to embrace a new look: "the dresses became shorter and more comfortable to wear, and the pants, suit, and tie were adopted as part of the female wardrobe" (Ganeva 2008, 24). The new, androgynous look of women with their bobbed hair and male suits implied a threatening overturn of hegemonic power. The in-betweenness of the New Woman is mirrored in Ewers' Alraune figure, as she too is between boy and girl and shifts between oppressor and oppressed as well as inorganic and organic. As Katja Plemenitaš mentions in her chapter on *The Stepford Wives*, the satirical science fiction novel captures the anxieties and vulnerabilities that both men and women faced with new social developments (this volume). *Alraune* too is a reflection of the historical unconscious of rapidly developing German cities which culminated in the roaring 1920s. Urbanity encouraged social change in the form of reactionary individuals who defied traditional gender roles, causing further anxiety over the loss of normative structures.

Alraune embodies the many women who were harshly critiqued for abandoning the countryside. These women became emblematic of the loss of warmth associated with the natural, female organic space, in exchange for a realm that was unnatural in its cold, mechanical state. The changing look of women, their physical presence on the streets of cities, and their mobility (both literally and socially) resulted in the assumption that with such freedom must come moral lapse. The *femme fatale* was born, a woman perceived to be as cold and indifferent as the city space itself. These women were dangerous to men and "created a public sphere in which they were no longer simply objects of male voyeurism but also active subjects who shaped their urban environments" (Petrescu 2010, 276). While Ewers' text is quite early to be considered in discussions of Germany's New Woman because the novel was adapted to film in 1928 and again in 1930, one sees how the *alraune*-creature spoke to the New Woman during her heyday.

Alraune, as a character, fits in perfectly with the *femme fatale* and science fiction figures of Germany's roaring 1920s. Alraune is like one of the most iconic female figures from German science fiction, Maria, or the *Maschinenmensch* (Machine Man), from Fritz Lang's film *Metropolis* (1927). Maria/*Maschinenmensch* is both the emotional, Virgin Mary figure and a monster since her double is literally a robotic machine, exactly in her image, created by a mad scientist. Both versions (virtuous and villainous Maria) are played by Brigitte Helm, who also plays Alraune in Henrik Galeen's 1928 cinematic version of Ewers' novel. Because the New Woman is in part a critique of women abandoning the countryside (organic realm) and adapting to life in the big city (which requires a relinquishing of the organic), one can see how a New Woman figure such as Alraune would fit into an ecofeminist discussion. As Greta Gaard explains: "Ecofeminists have described a number of connections between the oppressions of women and of nature that are significant to understanding why the environment is a feminist issue, and, conversely, why feminist issues can be addressed in terms of environmental concerns" (Gaard 1993, 8). The obliteration of nature occurring in rapidly developing turn-of-the-century Berlin became a mirror for the shifting roles of women who seemed to be moving beyond their "natural" states on the countryside: mother, homemaker, caretaker.

Alraune as Science Fiction *avant la Lettre*

Broadly, the science fiction genre analyzes the dehumanization of science. In *Alraune*, genetic engineering produces a plant-human hybrid femme-fatale who can bring temporary good fortune and wealth but who ultimately wreaks havoc on anyone who crosses her path. Metaphorically, she reflects the concerns of conservative, bourgeois individuals in early twentieth-century Berlin regarding increasing the emancipation for women. This fear resulted in the artistic construct of female figures that were dangerously monstrous. Science fiction is particularly suited to reflect cultural upheavals and scientific-technological developments. Having experienced the Second Industrial Revolution or Technological Revolution first-hand by moving to Berlin at the turn of the century, Ewers was qualified to capture one major rupture that ripped through the fabric of Berlin society, namely the aforementioned women's movements which resulted in the birth of the "New Woman" in the 1920s. Alraune is much like the Stepford wife discussed by Katja Plemenitaš: she is a highly paradoxical figure. "Stepford wife" as a term had its origins in a parable about the sexist backlash to female liberation seen in the American middle class of the 1970s, and yet today the term is used mainly for the negative evaluation of women (Plemenitaš, this volume). Likewise, Alraune is both a dangerous femme fatale and a savior, born during a time of women's liberation. Part of what makes Alraune an Other is not just her connection to the new archetype of the monstrous *femme fatale*, but rather her intimate connection to the male-dominated realm of science.

Adam Roberts writes about the science fiction genre's genesis by naming a few tales that could potentially be considered part of the genre pre-1920, which is the date in which the *Oxford English Dictionary* claims it originated: "[These tales] were specific and sometimes one-off examples of imaginative fiction. It was not until the 1920s that these sorts of writing became identified as belonging to a family of literature, Science Fiction" (2000, 3). In order for enough works to share similarities that would serve as the impetus for introducing a new genre, there must have been something already in art before this time. Ewers was not alone in creating such works, for nearly contemporary examples of proto–science fiction from Australian women writers who explore the capabilities of women beyond historically bound gender limitations, see Nicole Anae (2021). Thus, assuming the 1920 date is rather arbitrary and also considering the fact that *Alraune* was adapted to film several times during the 1920s under the category science fiction, I will outline the elements of *Alraune* that classifies it as science fiction based on the definitions provided by Roberts.

Many Germans were writing "imaginative fiction" which, rather than focusing on accuracy, "invents things not found in our world" (Roberts 2000, 2). While *Alraune* is an imaginative text, it is also grounded in the material world and the "events are made plausible within the structure of the text" (Roberts 2000, 5). This stipulation that a form of explanation in the "style of scientific discourse" of the otherwise implausible process is required within the context of the narration enables *Alraune* to fall under the science fiction category (Roberts 2000, 8). The clarification of Alraune's birth via *in vitro* fertilization is, to use Roberts' example of Kim Stanley Robinson's *Red Mars* (1992), the equivalent of introducing a gene re-splicing bath which extends the human lifespan, which is "*not* within the discourse of current science, ... but the plot development is integrated into the pseudo-scientific idiom of the book" (2000, 5). Thus, in order for a work to be qualified as science fiction, there must be a clarification, presumably in scientific discourse, of the otherwise impossible event.

In *Alraune*, the central "novum"—a term coined by Darko Suvin from the Latin for "new thing" or "point of difference"—between the real world and the world invented by Ewers that is "material rather than conceptual or imaginative" and can be systematically worked out within the text is the process of *in vitro* fertilization (Roberts 2000, 6–7). Ewers initially establishes the character of Privy Councilor ten Brinken as a well-respected scientist. When he is visited by Duchess Wolkonski, he is eager to tell her "about his experiments in the transfer of the germ-cell and in artificial impregnation" (Ewers 2013, 47). He explains that this was his first attempt and he has since successfully conducted the experiment on rats, guinea pigs, and monkeys. At first hesitant about the idea of creating a live *alraune-*creature when approached by Frank Baum, he is sold by the chance to translate an old superstition, "mystical nonsense," into fact (Ewers 2013, 58). While details of the actual operation do not occur in the novel, scientific discourse continues in a vain that prompts the reader to ponder to what extent the subordination of nature is mirrored in the violent acts against women. Alraune is born of an invasive experiment resembling technologically mediated rape; the intrusion within the female body is not unlike the way many individuals at this time viewed industrialized society's encroachment on and exploitation of feminized nature, a word that is a female noun in German (*die Natur*) among many other languages.

It is apparent that the men of Ewers' novel see a direct correlation between women and the earth, which they disdain, thereby revealing their misogynistic and anthropocentric tendencies. When Frank Baum is convincing ten Brinken to create the *alraune*-creature, he explains why the mandrake root, which will ultimately become the *alraune*-child, needs to be implanted into a prostitute:

> But the earth is also the eternal prostitute. Does not she give herself to all, freely? She is the eternal mother, she is the wench ever ready to sell herself to untold millions. She never denies herself, whoever desires her may take her wanton body.
>
> (Ewers 2013, 59)

If Mother Earth could speak for herself, she would likely attack Baum for this defamation of character. In Baum's rhetoric, he makes her a "prostitute" (which she actually cannot be as there is no legitimate transaction at stake, her resources are taken and she is physically altered by mankind with no compensation—"victim" would therefore be a more appropriate term), a "wench" (female servant or prostitute), and "wanton" (lustful, sensual). Baum thereby establishes the earth as desirous (wanton) of its own exploitation (wench). Because for Baum and his uncle, women equals earth, and the earth equals a lustful body *desiring* its own subjugation. They betray a mindset that enables them to act violently toward women without the slightest qualms.

As a societal commentary, Baum and ten Brinken provide a stab at the feared aforementioned prostitutes of Berlin who were suddenly appearing in the metropolitan male realm of courthouses demanding rights. In the above quote, Baum equates prostitutes with the earth and expresses his opinion that both deserve to be subjugated. The mindset of Baum and his uncle is a fictional embodiment of the following quote by ecofeminist author Greta Gaard:

the way in which women and nature have been conceptualized historically in the Western intellectual tradition has resulted in devaluing whatever is associated with women [and] nature, while simultaneously elevating in value those things associated with men, reason, humans, culture, and the mind.

(1993, 5)

Because the comments by Baum are hyperbolic, I believe Ewers is poking fun at those who feared the strides not only of prostitutes but of all women who were thriving in the metropolitan areas of the Western world at this time.

Women and Mother Earth—Alignments with the Age of Romanticism

When Frank Baum sees Alma Raune for the first time, he knows she is the prostitute he needs for his uncle's experiment since she is, in his view, the consummate embodiment of a Mother Earth desirous of subjugation. Baum describes Alma:

her hips and her breasts all cried out with a single, wild wish: Take me – take me! She was no longer a whore; she was the final mighty archetype of all womankind. From head to foot she was sex and sex only. 'Oh, she's the right one!' Frank Baum whispered. 'She is Mother Earth – Mother Earth – '

(Ewers 2013, 99)

Alma Raune's exploitation by Baum and ten Brinken, particularly because of her presumed affinity with an uncanny nature that seems to long for its subjugation, is not unique to Ewers' tale. It is usurped from the Germanic Romantic genre to which many authors of the early twentieth century returned due to a melancholy arising from nature's loss and a contradictory drive to technologically control and alter it for mankind's benefit. One tale which reveals this particularly well is Ludwig Tieck's (1802) novella "The Rune Mountain" ("Der Runenberg").

In Tieck's tale, protagonist Christian leaves his childhood home because he is afraid of turning into his father, a gardener with the ability to communicate with plants; however, his attempts to find his own path in life are thwarted by his interaction with a mandrake. While journeying away from the lowlands, he travels up a mountain and absentmindedly pulls a mandrake root out of the earth: "He had heard of the mysterious *mandragora*, which was said to utter such a heartrending cry when it was pulled up that it drove people out of their minds" (Tieck 1802). The root instantly morphs into a man who urges Christian onward up the mountain. At the mountaintop, Christian observes a beautiful, naked woman of "otherworldly beauty" who is "large and powerful" (Tieck 1802). She is alone, singing a song and gazing at a tablet laden with gemstones—this woman is the shape-shifting mandrake root in its more sensual and irresistible form. Because of the woman's peculiar behavior, the reader interprets this sequence to be Christian's waking dream or a sexual fantasy: he lusts equally after the woman and the wealth she represents by way of the gemstones.

This is a tale of domination of women (the mandrake post-metamorphosis) and the earth (the gemstones). Nonetheless, a feminist reading of this scenario is possible and relies on the mandrake root/woman's self-awareness of fulfilling Christian's sexual and monetary desire. As punishment, she turns up the sexual appeal and forces him to become a mad miner, making him believe the stones he collects are precious gemstones. Similarly, Ewers' Alraune uses her sexual appeal to provide fortune for those in her favor and punishment for those who are not. Her creator, ten Brinken, is punished when Alraune learns how he created her in his laboratory. She seduces him, convinces him to engage in mining ventures, to make her the sole heir of his fortune, and to kill himself. Incidentally, the hanged murderer whose semen is used to impregnate Alma Raune in ten Brinken's experiment was also "a miner for the Phoenix Mining Company in the Ruhr" (Ewers 2013, 113). In "The Rune Mountain" and *Alraune*, the men who originally took from the earth are forced to continue on this path which results in their rapid deterioration and destruction, meanwhile, the plant/human *femme fatales* reap the benefits.

In Galeen's film *Alraune* (1928) there is also a quote of Tieck's "The Rune Mountain" in the scene in which Alraune performs a dance routine knowing her creator is observing her as a means of coercion. The particular movements stem from "the body culture movement [that] was conceived in part as therapy for the dehumanizing effects of technology, [but Alraune dances] in an effort to empower her explicitly unnatural body" (Whitney 2010, 252). Like the mandrake-woman's dance on the mountaintop for Christian from "The Rune Mountain," Ewers' and Galeen's Alraune uses her bodily movements to coerce men into bad business ventures and even deadly situations. Alraune's subversive nature makes her like Frankenstein's monster or modern cyborgs who have developed their own agency and use their bodies and minds to turn against or destroy their creators (see Plemenitaš in this volume where cyborgs are contrasted to Stepford wives with perfect bodies but artificial minds).

Exploitation and Vivisection of Parallel Bodies Women and Earth

Expectations of male hegemony and the subservience of women are apparent in all levels of society in *Alraune*. Ten Brinken and Frank Baum first devise the plan to create the *alraune*-creature when a mandrake root, which is displayed in a cabinet of curiosities, falls from the wall. From the beginning, the mandrake is objectified, indicative of the treatment of women in the novel: "The *thing* had been hanging way up above all the other curios, and the long tear it had made in the tapestry as it dragged its nail out from the crumbling mortar, was plainly visible" (Ewers 2013, 50, italics in original). The *thingness* of the mandrake root is associated with the women who could serve as surrogates. When "His Excellency" ten Brinken searches for a surrogate, he finds it difficult to convince anyone from the "working-class" to participate in his experiment since "these creatures" have "some very queer notions regarding artificial insemination" (Ewers 2013, 77). Ten Brinken is relieved when he must travel to Berlin to attend the International Congress of Gynecologists since "there was little doubt that a metropolitan city would offer them a wider choice of material" (Ewers 2013, 78). Ten Brinken assumes the women of Berlin won't have the "narrow-minded attitude of their provincial sisters," which means that, to ten Brinken, the women of Cologne have "less common sense than the guinea pigs and monkeys" that did not protest his experiments (Ewers 2013, 78). Ten Brinken's words are a prime example of the "ways in which feminizing nature and naturalizing or animalizing women has served as justification for the domination of women, animals, and the earth" (Gaard 1993, 5). The conflation of feminine and animal qualities as justification for dominance continues throughout the science fiction genre, see for example Lesley Kordecki's chapter in this volume. As mentioned, because the comments by characters such as ten Brinken are hyperbolic, I read this as a proto-ecofeminist text: the equation of women, animals, and the earth and the argument for their subservience is so extreme, it comes across as absurd.

Ten Brinken's rhetoric rarely diverges from the realm of science and objectivity, even when talking about invasive experiments on women. He is surprised that "at the mere whisper of the word vivisection the public runs amuck" (Ewers 2013, 77). Ewers, however, is careful to align ten Brinken's violent acts against women with those of the murderer whose semen he uses in his experiment. The murderer, Peter Noerrissen, is condemned to death after he rapes and murders Anna Trautwein: "The victim had been cut into pieces in a most horrible fashion and to a large extent with almost professional skill" (Ewers 2013, 114). Similarly, Alma Raune, who survives the birth of Alraune for only a few seconds, is "assigned for dissection" and while her "body contributed vastly to the education" of an anatomy professor's pupils, her head was set aside for the senior medical student, who forgot it when he went on vacation and, finding it "too far gone" when he returned, "threw it out" after reserving only the skull pan to be "fashioned into a pretty dicebox" (Ewers 2013, 125). The abuse of and disrespect for the female body in *Alraune* is emblematic of the mindset critiqued by ecofeminists which enables the objectification of women and nature so that they may be exploited for commercial gain, consumerist pleasure, or, in this case, scientific knowledge and technological advancement.

As ten Brinken's created *alraune*-creature grows up, she brings both wealth and death to each member of ten Brinken's family. In most cases, Alraune's actions seem as arbitrary as those of nature itself: she simply convinces people to act in a certain way, sometimes beneficial, sometimes destructive, but she is always indifferent to the outcome. When Alraune develops a relationship with her co-creator Frank Baum, she discovers feelings for the first time, as does Baum, which was to a certain extent inevitable given Baum means "tree" in German. Baum, aware of the destruction she causes to everyone she knows, secretly wishes her dead, yet desires her at the same time, despite the fact that the relationship becomes increasingly vampiric—at the end of the novel, Alraune even cuts him and drinks his blood. Because Alraune is constructed as a male fantasy of desire and wish fulfillment, yet one which is ultimately destructive, she cannot exist. While sleepwalking on the roof after an evening with Baum, she is awoken by another member of the household calling her name to warn her, yet at this moment she slips and falls, enabling Baum an Oedipal return to the safety of his mother's home where he'll presumably spend his life as a bachelor.

Conclusion

In the end, the figure that the reader tends to sympathize with is Alraune. During her relationship with Baum, she ponders those questions which make us quintessentially human. As Barry B. Luokkala claims, what makes us human is exactly what Alraune tends to do: "We ponder the nature of our own existence, by asking questions, such as 'Who am I?' and 'What does it mean to be human?' We are able to analyze the human condition" (2014, 196). Additionally, the hyperbolic descriptions of her "nothingness" instigate the reader's allegiance toward her and their anger at descriptions such as "mothered by arid sand … no one can describe this creature, for he is as indescribable as nothingness itself" (Ewers 2013, 127). The "arid sand" implies the womb that ten Brinken artificially inseminates and, again, simultaneously aligns women with nature. Additionally, Ewers employs several metaphors to describe Alraune, thus the gender varies as in the above reference to "he." Because Alraune is an organic, yet also a technologically created figure striving, much like the New Woman in Germany at the time, for independence and acceptance in a male-dominated society, I read this text in alliance with ecofeminist works that are "politically engaged discourses that analyze conceptual connections between the manipulation of women and the nonhuman" (Buell, Heise, and Thornber 2011, 425). The task that Ewers seems to take up in *Alraune* is in line with "the projects of feminism and environmentalism [that] notice the similarities between androcentric logic and the cultural logic that constructs a culture/nature opposition, places a higher value on culture, and as a result authorizes human domination over nonhuman nature" (Otto 2012, 13). Alraune is a *femme fatale* who overcomes dichotomies that create a delineation between organic and inorganic, male and female, natural and technological, and thus serves as a quintessential example of a proto-ecofeminist.

References

Alraune. 1928. Directed by Henrik Galeen, performances by Brigitte Helm and Paul Wegener.

Anae, Nicole. 2021. "Ecofeminist Utopian Speculations in Henrietta Augusta Dugdale's *A Few Hours in a Far-Off Age* (1883), Catherine Helen Spence's *A Week in the Future* (1888), Mary Anne Moore-Bentley's *A Woman of Mars; Or, Australia's Enfranchised Woman* (1901), and Joyce Vincent's *The Celestial Hand: A Sensational Story.*" In *Dystopias and Utopias on Earth and Beyond: Feminist Ecocriticism of Science Fiction*, edited by Douglas A. Vakoch, 98–113. Abingdon, Oxon, UK and New York, NY: Routledge.

Braidotti, Rosi. 2013. *The Posthuman*. Malden, MA: Polity Press.

Buell, Lawrence, Ursula K. Heise, and Karen Thornber. 2011. "Literature and Environment." *Annual Review of Environment and Resources* 36: 417–440.

Etzler, Melissa. 2017. "Pernicious Plants: Imitation and Uncanny Ecocritical Thought in Gustav Meyrink's 'Die Pflanzen des Dr. Cinderella'." *German Quarterly* 90, no. 4: 459–474.

Ewers, Hanns Heinz. 2013. *Alraune*. Translated by S. Guy Endore. Birchgrove Press.

Gaard, Greta, ed. 1993. *Ecofeminism: Women, Animals, Nature*. Philadelphia, PA: Temple University Press.

Ganeva, Mila. 2008. *Women in Weimar Fashion: Discourses and Displays in German Culture, 1918–1933*. New York, NY: Boydell & Brewer, Camden House.

Gassen, Hans Günter, and Sabine Minol. 2006. "Science & Fiction: Die Alraune oder die Sage von Galgenmännlein." *Biologie in unserer Zeit* 5, no. 36: 302–307.

German Angst. 2015. Directed by Jörg Buttgereit, Michal Kosakowski, and Andreas Marschall. Artsploitation.

Luckhurst, Roger. 2018. "Interrelations: Science Fiction and the Gothic." In *The Cambridge History of Science Fiction*, edited by Gerry Canavan and Eric Carl Link, 35–49. Cambridge, UK: Cambridge University Press.

Luokkala, Barry B. 2014. *Exploring Science through Science Fiction*. New York, NY: Springer.

Metropolis. 1927. Directed by Fritz Lang. Kino Video.

Northwestern University. 2010. "Inventor of *In Vitro* Fertilization Wins Nobel Prize." October 4, 2010. Accessed October 12, 2020. http://oncofertility.nort hwestern.edu/blog/2010/10/inventor-vitro-fertilization-wins-nobel-prize.

Otto, Eric C. 2012. "Ecofeminist Theories of Liberation in the Science Fiction of Sally Miller Gearhart, Ursula K. Le Guin, and Joan Slonczewski." In *Feminist Ecocriticism: Environment, Women, and Literature*, edited by Douglas A. Vakoch, 13–39. Lanham, MD: Lexington Books.

Petrescu, Mihaela. 2010. "Domesticating the Vamp: Jazz and the Dance Melodrama in Weimar Cinema." *Seminar* 46, no. 3: 276–292.

Roberts, Adam. 2000. *Science Fiction*. London: Routledge.

Robinson, Kim Stanley. 1993. *Red Mars*. New York, NY: Bantam Books.

Rowling, J. K. 1999. *Harry Potter and the Chamber of Secrets*. New York, NY: Arthur A. Levine.

Scarborough, John. 2006. "Drugs and Drug Lore in the Time of Theophrastus: Folklore, Magic, Botany, Philosophy and the Rootcutters." *Acta Classica* 49: 1–29.

Slabbert, Melodie. 2010. "'A Curious Incident Involving a Dog': The Legal-Historical Significance of Dog Images in Medieval and Renaissance Medical Illustrations." *Fundamina* 16, no. 2: 121–146.

Smith, Jill Suzanne. 2013. *Berlin Coquette: Prostitution and the New German Woman, 1890–1933*. New York, NY: Signale, Cornell University.

———. 2008. "Working Girls: White-Collar Workers and Prostitutes in Late Weimar Fiction." *German Quarterly* 81, no. 4: 449–470.

Tidwell, Christy, and Bridgitte Barclay. 2019. *Gender and Environment in Science Fiction*. Lanham, MD: Lexington Books.

Tieck, Ludwig. 1802. "Der Runenberg." Accessed October 12, 2020. https://en.wiki source.org/wiki/The_Runenberg.

Whitney, Allison. 2010. "Etched with the Emulsion: Weimar Dance and Body Culture in German Expressionist Cinema." *Seminar* 46, no. 3: 240–254.

2 The Runa and Female Otherness in Mary Doria Russell's *The Sparrow*

Lesley Kordecki

An unlikely narrative to carry an ecofeminist undercurrent is *The Sparrow*, a 1996 speculative fiction novel by Mary Doria Russell. The story seems far more concerned with a Jesuit space mission and its religious, not scientific or ecological, goal to find and presumably convert other cognizant beings of the universe. As such, we are introduced to mostly male characters that interact with the inhabitants of the planet Rakhat, seemingly an Eden. But, as I will argue, the abstract female becomes embodied, literally and prophetically, in the animal/human species of the Runa. Here instead of plants and robots, like in the other chapters in this section of the present book, stereotypes of human females are imposed on the animalistic beings of the new planet's environment. These people are shockingly consumed by the planet's second cognizant species, the predatory, masculinist Jana'ata, in this horrifying story of tragic errors that link environment and gender. In many ways, the ecology of the planet reinforces the stereotypes of human gender. The lovely countryside where the humans live for years with the feminized Runa is in stark contrast to the masculinized trade city of Gayjur, the home of the Jana'ata, a deceptively similar species that, like the Runa, cuts across the boundary between humans and other animals. In this humbling tale of human error, the foreign Earthlings completely misinterpret the relationship between these two economically interdependent groups, the novel's sly emblems of human gender typing.

A unique aspect of the space mission, set in the future (2024), is that the majority of individuals on the project are actually clerical missionaries, albeit of a more enlightened ideology than many in history. The financing of the trip is controlled by Jesuits who, although opportunistic and even a bit corrupt at times, remain strangely earnest in their missionary zeal to find new children of God. Others have written on the book's spiritual quest for God and its colonialist quest for material acquisition or at least knowledge (Lembert 2004; Khader 2005). My focus is on how tellingly Russell breathes life into the characters of the book, both those of Earth and those of the planet Rakhat, for the animal-like Runa are indeed people, all fully possessed with the ability to speak, which distinguishes them profoundly from nonhuman animals that we may individually know and love. The disposability of the Runa as food reveals something ineffable to readers, even those who try hard to imagine the souls within the animals around us, often the animals we ourselves eat.

The planet calls to the Earthlings with songs radioed across space, and this lyricism leads to the ensuing action. Their mission is to find the singers of this intergalactic song. The tunes that bring the small group of humans to Rakhat turn out to be pornographic lyrics that represent the kind of atrocities later inflicted upon Emilio Sandoz, the Jesuit the book follows most closely. He ends his time there as a raped concubine of an unscrupulous aristocrat, Hlavin Kitheri. The book revolves around a series of fatal ironies; this mistaken glorification of the Rakhati songs, those that serve as the initial recognition of extraterrestrial life, is but one. The account of the trip is interspersed between the story of Emilio after he returns from space, a broken man whose mangled body and soul make this eloquent and charismatic priest nearly inarticulate. As fellow priests learn his story, so do the novel's readers, a plotting that builds suspense about how everything goes so drastically awry.

The music and song that draw the human foreigners are heavily immersed in the novel's symbolism. Music is akin to poetry, to literature, and the death of the musical scholar earlier on the mission begins the downward spiral of the Earthlings. The Runa, the first people the group encounters, fear music, which they associate with their predators, the Jana'ata, one of many clues lost on Emilio (311). Such gender representation of groups is instructive: in the present collection, we see Karl Zuelke argue a depiction of feminized and masculinized cultures of future humans (Zuelke 2021).

Music is also related to bird song, an association that conjures up the sparrow in the title, a creature linked with Emilio, who becomes the bird whose song (both his love song to God and his clerical conviction) is torn from him as he bitterly loses his faith in a God who allows the sparrow to fall. Near the end of the book, the Father General of the Jesuits who are investigating the failure of the mission strives to explain God's tolerance of the brutalities committed against Emilio by quoting Matthew 10:29, "Not one sparrow can fall to the ground without your) Father knowing it." Another more cynical priest retorts, "But the sparrow still falls" (479).

The sparrow reference has a long and revered tradition. Bede (1990, 129–130) in his *Historia ecclesiastica gentis Anglorum* (CE 731) famously equates the sparrow with the human soul. In Shakespeare's play, Hamlet prophetically utters before his own fatal duel, "There is special providence in the fall of a sparrow" (Shakespeare 2014, 5.2.197–198). Bird imagery, moreover, has vital aftermaths in today's critical animal studies: Gilles Deleuze and Felix Guattari (1987, 278–279) present a complex philosophical notion of "becoming-woman" and "becoming-animal" that interrogates the existence of these "others" in a patriarchy, forming a matrix for ecofeminism.

Indeed, animal studies can help us interpret the animalistic presentation of nonhumans in the novel, as we will see. Steve Baker, in attempting to see how Deleuze and Guattari's "becoming animal" can reveal new insights into what we call animal and what we call human, tells us that "The real radicalism of the concept lies not in its reframing of the question of living subjects and their identities, but rather in its charting the possibilities for experiencing an uncompromising sweeping-away of identities, whether human or animal" (Baker 2002, 67–68). Compare also Sarah Bezan's analysis of queered fish-like humans (this volume).

The first encounter of Earthlings with the attractive Runa demonstrates why we care about one more science fiction depiction of alternate cognizant species. The scene is suffused with enlightened beauty, goodwill, and spiritual rapture. The humans see the Runa returning to their village, carrying baskets of flowers with "exquisite scent." Emilio and the travelers stand quiet. "There was no panic in either group. The villagers ... were unclothed, but around their limbs and necks many wore bright ribbons, which fluttered and floated sinuously in the wind." The humans take note of the crowd and the people themselves. "The two species were not grotesque to one another. They shared a general body plan: bipedal, with forelimbs specialized for grasping and manipulation." The physician and anthropologist among the travelers, Anne Edwards, "found them beautiful" with

> Large mobile ears, erect and carried high on the sides of the head. Gorgeous eyes, large and densely lashed, calm as camels'... There were many differences, of course ... humans were tailless ... and another human oddity stood out, here as at home: relative hairlessness. The villagers were covered with smooth dense coats of hair, lying flat to muscular bodies. They were as sleek as Siamese cats.
>
> (269–270)

Further observation makes Anne say "They are so beautiful" and she worries that they would find the humans "repulsive ... We are outlandish, she thought, in the truest sense of the word" (270). In this meeting, humans are the less appealing animals.

This description from the point of view of humans is markedly open, humble, and accepting. Still, the many comparisons to Earth animals, likening the Runa, for example, to camels and cats, establish these people as other, not quite people. Russell herself notes in an Afterword written for the twentieth anniversary of the publication of the book:

> Bipedalism has developed in several lineages on Earth: hominids; dinosaurs and birds; wallabies and kangaroos. I had worked in Australia in the 1980s and liked the idea of kangaroos as the physical model for the VaRakhati [both species on the planet]. Take it from me: if you come

face-to-face with an adult male red kangaroo in the Outback, you will feel a very definite respect.

(490)

And yet a few sentences later, Russell notes that kangaroos are "dumber than a five-pound bag of sand."

We are also faced with the "identity-suspension" (Baker 2002, 68) of the "becoming-animal" in this occurrence of beings clearly not easily slotted into the binary of animal or human. That binary comes under constant interrogation throughout the text. The animalization of beings has an adverse effect on human valuation. Some biologists today are challenging the human speciesism that serves to denigrate nonhuman differences, but the denigration is still inherent in our language (Haraway 1991; Calarco 2015).

In this scene, the physical differences seem to be taken in stride by the explorers, but the attempts at communication bring an almost sacred aspect to the meeting. Emilio is the humans' interpreter, and in the struggle to communicate, the Runa put forward a child, Askama, who apparently is their own interpreter. In exchanging greetings and introducing themselves, she endearingly calls Emilio "Meelo." On his part, "He had come somehow to the conclusion that she was a little girl and he was already deeply in love, his whole soul open to her" (272), a powerful point in the narrative in which we follow the tender attempts at connecting. Performing some charming sleight-of-hand tricks involving plucking a flower from behind the child's ear, Emilio enchants them all with magic:

> Soon other children came forward, and their parents moved closer as well, until the two groups, alien and native, merged, enthralled, surrounding Emilio and Askama as he made pebbles and leaves and flowers multiply and vanish and reappear, gathering possible numbers and nouns and, more important, watching Askama's face as he worked, glancing at the adults and other children to check responses, already absorbing the body language and mirroring it in a dance of discovery.
>
> (272–273)

In this wondrous moment, "Smiling and in love with God and all His works, Emilio at last held out his arms and Askama settled happily into his lap." The magic is both figurative and literal, involving the natural flowers and scents of the Edenic Runa people.

But this brief summary does not do justice to the transcendent event. Part of the strength of the writing derives from Russell's careful introduction of the humans involved. We learn to love the intelligent, appealing, talented, witty, and well-meaning humans who are almost all good friends on the mission. They subtly reinforce the gender interrogation of the story, and we are invested in their success and deeply shocked by their slaughter. The personalities of the humans are well developed in the first half of the book, so much so that when we read through their confrontations with the two alien species, we work through the tensions for their sake. The gentle Runa do the rest.

The Humans

First, Emilio, the doomed sparrow, is paradoxically a macho Hispanic male, with "Indian ancestry plain" (9) and a feminized divine. He is described by others in contradictory terms, with comments like "Sandoz's damnable machismo" (282) and "Today I may have looked upon the face of a saint" (284, 400). His physical stature is similarly variable. His small physique makes both the Runa and Jana'ata take him to be a child, like all the others from Earth, except Jimmy Quinn, whose height is more comparable to the people of Rakhat (276, 374), and yet Emilio has the muscle of a street fighter (370). When the Rakhati discover that Emilio is an adult, they think he must be a feeble man because of his stature. He indeed becomes defenseless as the book goes on. The female Runa must shield him, encircle him, as they do their children and their own men. Another irony is that female Runa, but not Jana'ata, are more martial than the males of the species, who are smaller, even though the species as a whole is feminized when juxtaposed with the Jana'ata.

Emilio's role as interpreter gives him his most predominant trait. Language plays a key role in the paradox and bitterness of the novel. The foreigners' misunderstanding of the gender of the Runa foreshadows the fatal miscalculation of the villagers' prey position in relation to the Jana'ata (308, 400). The travelers think that the Runa who care for the children of the village are female, but they are not; the women are the larger, the more mercantile and mobile sex. Emilio is the human responsible for communication, but despite his prowess with words, he misses the most significant point: the Runa's total vulnerability to the Jana'ata.

The other men on the trip include three Jesuit priests and two brilliant and kind scientists, one of whom is married to shrewd, humorous, and emotive (395) Anne Edwards, a woman whose point of view becomes second only to Emilio's in the novel. Like Sofia, the other female on the mission, Anne is powerfully drawn to Emilio. The women serve as representatives of heart and head, with Anne, the emotional pivot, mothering the crew as well as Emilio, who upon finding her butchered and half-consumed body late in the story, calls her "the mother of my heart" (443). Sofia, younger and lovely, is almost machinelike in her precise scientific affect, so much so that one of the Jesuits found her "almost unfeminine" (348). She, the smallest of the humans, fatefully teaches the Runa resistance at the end of the mission (45). These women are indispensable to the story, with a pregnant Sofia even contributing to the novel's procreative subtheme, nature's exuberant replication. And yet we learn early on that the Jesuit Father General judges that "the mission went wrong at its inception, with the decision to involve the women. A breakdown in discipline from the beginning" (13). The monastic influence becomes apparent in significant ways. Celibacy and the right of childbearing underlie the destructive motivations of the Jana'ata and their control of the Runa. With the humans, the androcentric character of the mostly celibate group helps form not only misinterpretation but also flawed judgment. After all, what's a paradise without fertility?

The Runa

The Runa, the species with whom the humans live for almost three years, continue to be animalized and feminized in both positive and negative ways. The social structure of the Runa is branded by the male scientists as "closer to a herd" (279). Like animals, the Runa and Jana'ata use their ears expressively (290–291) and are intensely scent driven. The aroma of coffee beans brought from Earth becomes the commercial draw of the foreigners on this planet of animals/humans. Even from the Runa's point of view, the text tells us that they had assumed, because Emilio and Sofia looked alike, that they were "littermates" (295). The humans thought the Runa as "harmless as deer" (369), a comment directly before the first Jana'ata appears. Embittered and pushed by uncomprehending priests later on Earth, Emilio, former "lover" of the Runa child Askama, fallen away "lover" of God, spits out, "The Runa are not unintelligent and some are marvelously talented, but they are essentially domesticated animals. The Jana'ata breed them, as we breed dogs" (394). But he also notes before the catastrophes to come that

> there is a sort of simplicity to Runa thinking, but we barely speak their language and we hardly know them...What seems like simplemindedness may be our ignorance of their subtlety. And it's very difficult, sometimes, to tell ignorance from lack of intelligence. We may seem a little dim to the Runa.
>
> (313)

Indeed, humans are more than "a little dim" about the planet. An analysis like this can be found in biologists today studying Earth's animals, those who question the standard notion of their supposed diminished capacities compared to that of humans. The assessment of the Runa by humans is reciprocated. Earlier we hear that, from a Runa perspective, the foreigners are "like children" (292). Russell perpetuates the misconceptions with these parallel and fuzzy appraisals.

So too, the Runa species is not only animalized but concurrently feminized, oftentimes in ways that echo enforced female behavior in heavily patriarchal societies on Earth. In their language, the Runa refer to themselves as "someone" not "I," and this linguistic display conveys humility and self-abnegation in all their passive dealings. When humans and even Supaari, the

Jana'ata who trades with them, speak in this tongue, Ruanja, it suggests an automatic subservience. For example, after Supaari, as typical of a Jana'ata, succumbs to his "overpowering urge to attack" Emilio, he finds that the latter pins him down like he would a street thug. The priest then tells him "in the soft lilt of the Ruanja, 'Someone regrets your discomfort. Even so, harm is not permitted. If someone lets you up, will your heart be quiet?'" (370–371). A mixture of mildness and care is present in the language of the Runa, and also we might add, it is accompanied by a female decorum even when in a position of strength.

Further, the Runa are "intensely social" (279) and the village is a contributor to the "fragrance industry" (310) of the planet, traits often associated with human females. Emilio thinks the Runa "unselfconsciously physical and affectionate. Like Anne ... only more so." The other male humans, as primates, covertly think less of the Runa and find them somewhat boring. Once they meet Supaari, their first Jana'ata, they think they understand: "The stateliness and deliberation and placidity of Runa life made the humans feel almost drugged; the constant eating, the constant talk, the constant touching dragged on their energy" (397). These attributes of the species, many of which as we discover later, occur because the rural Runa are insufficiently fed and constantly vulnerable, are also reminiscent of dominated women. We learn that Runa "do all the productive work" on the planet (391). And we are shown a clever Runa female living in the city, educated and bred, like many, to be tutors and artists to make the point that what the rural Runa have become is culturally dictated. This division between the Rakhati species mirrors that of the stereotypes of human gender, especially in the underdeveloped countries of Earth. Lydia Rose and Teresa M. Bartoli, as well as Aslı Değirmenci Altın, also explore the question of the exploitation of nonhuman females in their analysis of other texts (this volume). Perhaps most indicative of the gendering of species, Jana'ata males even take Runa females as concubines. No such reciprocity occurs.

The Jana'ata

The Jana'ata, so like the Runa physically (but with claws and carnivorous teeth), are nourished solely by the flesh of harvested Runa. This fact becomes the haunting subtext throughout the story. Our notion of the male is ruthlessly prioritized over the female in that nearly all the Jana'ata in the story are indeed male. It is implied that their genitalia is so exaggerated that they must be clothed, unlike the Runa (389). In this novel, female Jana'ata are concubines only, leading to the further feminization of Emilio, who likewise becomes imprisoned in a harem.

Hands, both of the two species and the alien humans, become symbolic of the gendered power plays of the planet. Thus, the procedure to disable Emilio's hands, cutting the nerves so that the fingers spread like willow branches (352), becomes revelatory of his increasing powerlessness, another irony, since the claws of the Jana'ata are symbolic of their dominance. Through a language error, Emilio agrees to the ritual which cripples him inexorably, much like the binding of feet for Earth women, a rite couched in gendered power plays.

Similar to Supaari, the dissolute Jana'ata, Hlavin Kitheri, is "Third born" in a noble family and not allowed to procreate, once again underlining the cultural inexorability of fertility and sterility. He therefore indulges in art and sexual dissipation and thus becomes the source of the songs that draw the humans to the planet. So the music, the language of the spheres, is representative of corruption, not communication, of oppression and decadence, not joy and community between species, as the explorers thought. In *The Sparrow*, the basics of Jana'ata differences are explored and presented as perverted masculinity.

Yet the most significant difference between the Rakhati species is that the Runa are vegetarian and the Jana'ata are exclusively carnivorous; they eat only Runa, not non-cognizant animals (which are available) or plants. The eating of flesh is a subject too large to be covered here, but the basic consumption of one cognizant species by another, a variation on cannibalism, does figuratively parallel the absorption of one gender by another. Karl Steel (2016, 179) probes how the "horror" of anthropophagy "uncritically perpetuate[s] the distinction of humans from nonhuman animals." Further, Carol J. Adams (1990, 189) argues that "Through symbolism based on killing animals, we encounter politically laden images of absorption, control, domain, and the necessity of violence. This message of male dominance is conveyed through meat eating." *The Sparrow* projects a cannibalistic horror, even to the extent of having the saintly Emilio devour innocent Runa babies in order to survive (453). The butchering and ingestion of Runa, whom we see as fellow people, constitute the ethical watershed of the novel and its most provocative element. Both the grisly and metaphoric impact is exacerbated when humans become prey as well. So when Jana'ata "take meat" (437) by slaughtering Anne and the leader of the Jesuits, Sofia thinks, "what a meager meal they must have made" (443).

Once again, critical animal studies, especially ecofeminist ones, can be used to interrogate this aspect of the novel. In a later book by Adams, *Neither Man nor Beast: Feminism and the Defense of Animals* (1994), she adds that

> objects referred to by mass terms have no individuality, no uniqueness, and that when we turn an animal into "meat," someone who has a very particular, situated life, a unique being, is converted into something that has no distinctiveness, no uniqueness, no individuality. The existence of *meat* as a mass term naturalizes the eating of animals, so that consumers do not think "I am now interacting with an animal" but instead consider themselves making choices about food.
>
> (115)

How much greater the impact if you have previously conversed with your dinner. In Russell's novel, the Runa devoured are individual characters, like the humans who try to defend them. The fictional realm, with imaginary beings that cross the line between animal and human, provides a medium to see into the morality of dealing with nonhuman members of the environment, here animal-like people who capture our sympathies and whose slaughter challenges the kind of human exceptionalism fatal to others around us.

The parallel between Rakhati species and human gender stereotypes is not without exceptions, of course. The broad outlines are enough to call attention to the species and gender issues at stake, and Russell's ability to create believable characters makes the analogy instructive, discomfiting, and at times profound.

The Land

Finally, more conventional notions of ecology and environment in the novel reinforce these refrains of gender and species. The first sighting of Rakhat is revelatory: "It wasn't Earth but it was beautiful, and it had a powerful pull on their emotions" (216). Even the landing is in terms of birth since procreation serves as a constant undercurrent: "Each of them felt some of the same dizzying exultation as they emerged from the lander, spilling from their technological womb and blinking, and felt themselves reborn in a new world" (226). We once again return to birth, breeding, and reproduction. Overpopulation is Rakhat's chief ecological problem upon which the plot-line dramatically and ruthlessly hinges. The special process of birth control enacted by the Jana'ata for themselves and more horrifically, for their breeding stock, the Runa, becomes more appalling in light of the Catholic mores reflected by the Jesuit travelers. Other science fiction tales are worked in this volume by Patrick Murphy and Imelda Martín Junquera, as well as by Nicole Anae (2021) in another collection, to note fundamental connections between the environment and issues of containment, balance, and utilitarianism.

The story carefully builds up to these outcomes, made more striking because we are led to believe in intergalactic hope. For example, references to Eden are interspersed with youthful glee when the space travelers land: "There followed days of rapture and hilarity. Children on a field trip to Eden, they named everything they saw." And true to the wit of these people, the names of the insects and small animals are cleverly descriptive, sophisticated, and farcical, such as "Richard Nixons," "Dominicans," "Fast Eddies," and the often present "coronaries," styled as such because the creatures give them a dramatic start (226, 265). The allusion to naming harkens back to Judeo-Christian mythology of the first parents in Eden. The biology around them is frequently noted: "Even dozing, they were suffused with their surroundings" (228). And after the death of one of their number, a first serious setback, they leave "the Eden" they lived in for weeks (257).

But the tale's terrestrial resonances do not stop there. The biblical garden morphs into an experimental one that the humans plant to sustain themselves, and then to nourish their hosts, the Runa villagers (314). The plants become the forbidden tree, the knowledge of creation, that is, the secret to enhanced fertility, not the knowledge of good and evil. Without overt recognition, the humans are the serpents tempting the Runa, and the supposed Eden is profoundly violated. Sofia worried more scientifically that the "sharing of seeds and transplants from Earth might trigger some sort of ecological disaster," but they assumed that the plants would die off and not interfere with the ecosystem (413). However, they did fatally interfere with the Jana'ata cultural system of regulating Runa births through limited food supplies since the females became more fertile with additional nutrition. Emilio later says that "they breed to their feed" (448). Consequently, the dominant species needed to "cull" the new babies in a gruesome massacre in which they encountered the beginnings of an opposition that the humans instigated. Because of well-intentioned, miscalculated interference, both humans and Runa are murdered in a poignant tragedy that relentlessly unfolds throughout the novel. In his subsequent questioning, Emilio reveals "It was the gardens … The mistake. What you've been waiting for. The fatal error." (447).

The final sentence of the book buries the message in the ecosystem. The Jesuit Father General, on Earth years later, is pictured "looking for how long he had no idea, across a grassy open courtyard to a complex panorama of medieval masonry and jumbled rock, formal garden and gnarled trees: a scene of great and beautiful antiquity" (483). We return to the natural and built environment on Earth, the lessons probably unlearned despite Emilio's example.

How can we get this oddly moving novel, complete with its encounter with people who uncannily resemble animals, to help us think about nonhumans, both fictional and real? Will we continue to reflect on the animalization (a word with harmful biases) of humans? To what will these often alienating and oppressive distinctions of human and nonhuman animals lead? It seems we are struggling to remain in Eden, naming and dominating creatures as in the Judeo-Christian myth. Many today tell us that animals, as the element of our environment most similar to us and yet so prejudged, can open up our thinking about them as well as ourselves. Russell's book takes us off-world, but our own critical animal studies tell us that these questions are all around us. The Runa are not our Earth's animals, or are they? The book checks our smug assurance in human exceptionalism and pushes us to consider our responses to cannibalism when the Jana'ata speak and cognitively interact with their future food.

These animal/human beings trouble our hierarchy of environment, but in this tale, they also serve to combat the gendering double standards we live under, with the steady undertones of the two species paralleling the feminine and the masculine. *The Sparrow* demands that the reader consider in a wholly transformative way the nature of the human versus that of the animal and the intertwining of gender in those definitions. Russell does the unthinkable in having us emotionally participate in the consumption of fellow mammals, those whom we have learned to think of as people. The book is at its heart a profoundly moving exploration of the essence of the human animal as well as, more subtly, the force and limitations of our often flawed notions of gender.

References

Adams, Carol J. 1994. *Neither Man nor Beast: Feminism and the Defense of Animals*. New York, NY: Continuum.

———. 1990. *The Sexual Politics of Meat: A Feminist-Vegetarian Critical Theory*. New York, NY: Continuum.

Anae, Nicole. 2021. "Ecofeminist Utopian Speculations in Henrietta Augusta Dugdale's *A Few Hours in a Far-Off Age* (1883), Catherine Helen Spence's *A Week in the Future* (1888), Mary Anne Moore-Bentley's *A Woman of Mars; Or, Australia's Enfranchised Woman* (1901), and Joyce Vincent's *The Celestial Hand: A Sensational Story*." In *Dystopias and Utopias on Earth and Beyond: Feminist Ecocriticism of Science Fiction*, edited by Douglas A. Vakoch, 98–113. Abingdon, Oxon, UK and New York, NY: Routledge.

Baker, Steve. 2002. "What Does Becoming-Animal Look Like?" In *Representing Animals*, edited by Nigel Rothfels, 67–98. Bloomington, IN: Indiana University Press.

Bede. 1990. *Ecclesiastical History of the English People*. Translated by Leo Sherley-Price. Revised by R. E. Latham. London: Penguin.

Calarco, Matthew. 2015. *Thinking Through Animals: Identity, Difference, Indistinction*. Stanford, CA: Stanford University Press.

Haraway, Donna J. 1991. *Simians, Cyborgs, and Women: The Reinvention of Nature*. New York, NY: Routledge.

Khader, Jamil. 2005. "Race Matters: People of Color, Ideology, and the Politics of Erasure and Reversal in Ursula Le Guin's *The Left Hand of Darkness* and Mary Doria Russell's *The Sparrow*." *Journal of the Fantastic in the Arts* 166: 110–127.

Lembert, Alexandra. 2004. "Die Suche nach 'dem Anderen': Die Science-Fiction-Romane Mary Doria Russells." *Inklings: Jahrbuch für Literatur und Ästhetik* 22: 116–129.

Russell, Mary Doria. [1996] 2016. *The Sparrow*. New York, NY: Ballantine.

Shakespeare, William. 2014. *Hamlet: The Arden Shakespeare*. Edited by Ann Thompson and Neil Taylor. London: Bloomsbury.

Steel, Karl. 2016. "How Delicious We Must Be/Folcuin's Horse and the Dog's Gowther, Beyond Care." In *Fragments for a History of a Vanishing Humanism*, edited by Mrya Seaman and Eileen A. Joy, 175–192. Columbus, OH: Ohio State University Press.

Zuelke, Karl. 2021. "Keeping Grows; Giving Flows: Reciprocal Relations and the Gift of *Always Coming Home*." In *Dystopias and Utopias on Earth and Beyond: Feminist Ecocriticism of Science Fiction*, edited by Douglas A. Vakoch, 138–149. Abingdon, Oxon, UK and New York, NY: Routledge.

3 Reproduction, Utilitarianism, and Speciesism in *Sleep Dealer* and *Westworld*

Imelda Martín Junquera

The West, a traditionally masculine space inhabited by the lone ranger and the cowboy as the emblematic figures in search of a quest, is recreated in a theme park called Westworld where visitors can liberate their instincts by engaging in violent activities such as killing and rape without being punished, because the hosts are androids, not real human beings, created specifically for the purpose of enjoyment. The origins of this HBO series dates from the film released in 1973, based on a novel by Michael Crichton, in which Yul Brynner plays the android who starts killing humans as a result of a malfunction in his circuits. The whole central system suffers a failure and androids and humans exterminate each other except for the only human visitor who has not submitted to the pleasures of the park and who escapes successfully. The moral of the story warns against the dangers of relying too much on artificial intelligence at the time they were developing and alerts the viewers to the multiple possibilities the future brings about.

The classical Western motive of the domination of nature in terms of taming the wilderness seems out of the question in this computer laboratory designed space. Everything has been created from artificial matter: androids, animals, and even landscapes. Inspired by Mary Shelley's (1818) novel about Dr. Frankenstein's attempt to create life from dead matter, *Westworld* eliminates the danger of death because the humanoids are designed to be unable to inflict any pain on humans. Humans hold complete control over the landscape and the androids that inhabit it, but this ambitious project will finally turn back against its creators. Ynestra King (1990) blames this uncontrolled development of technology and the irresponsibility of human beings toward nature on how "capitalism is dependent on expanding markets and therefore ever greater areas of life must be mediated by sold products. From a capitalist standpoint, the more things that can be bought and sold, the better." Anthropocentrism also justifies the assertion that "human beings are entitled towards the dominion of nonhuman nature" (108). At the same time, it affirms that human beings dominate nonhuman nature to obtain true freedom, regardless of the fact that this domination in the case of *Westworld* and *The Sleep Dealer* makes the audience develop a sympathy for the android and the cyberbraceros instead of the human beings, contrary to what the viewer could experience watching the 1973 version.

In *Westworld*, androids' motor functions have been designed to be deactivated at the request of those in power so that they do not represent a danger in case of malfunctioning. When failure to respond at the command occurs, human technicians discover that the androids have started to take control of their lives. William S. Haney (2006, 4 affirms that "one difference between machines and organism noted by the physicist Jean Burns, however, is that human beings have volition or free will, which is associated with consciousness, while machines do not." The awareness of this lack of volition and its later acquisition, a key question in both visual materials analyzed here, mark the development of the characters in order to gain agency and independence from the orders of their superiors in rank and to run away from the spaces of oppression where they have been confined.

It is mainly two android women: Dolores and Maeve, who supposedly rebel against their creators, Arnold and Robert Ford. It must be noticed that the name of the latter makes clear reference to Henry Ford and the innovation he introduced in the car industry with the chain production and the popularization of the automobile as well as the control exerted on his factories. Parallelism between the car industry and the production of these androids for leisure can clearly be stated, as well as the reference to assembly lines and low cost effected on mass production of goods, as compared with the job of cyberbraceros at the "maquilas" in Tijuana. Whether their rebellious behavior belongs to one of the narratives associated with the park, so it has been planned by their creators, or it is a true acquisition of agency and independence on their part remains a mystery through the entire first season of *Westworld*. In fact, the sentence "These violent delights have violent ends," repeated and passed along as if the androids were victims of a contagious disease, as Christopher Orr (2016) points out in "Sympathy for the Robot," becomes a mantra in their consciousness that triggers this insubordination against their oppressors. As the sentence belongs to Act 2, Scene 6 of Shakespeare's tragedy *Romeo and Juliet*, the feeling of revenge can be appreciated from the beginning.

Apart from the distance created between humans and androids, the difference between men and women is also openly established from the first episode: women have been created to satisfy clients and, thus, we find Maeve taking care of customers at the brothel and Dolores showing her charm to visitors while Teddy has only been programmed to love her and dies once and again unable to protect her from the visitors that kill her family and rape her. The consideration of these androids as bodies deprived of conscience, of feelings, and of will reinforces the idea of the necessity to break this oppression and to introduce the ecofeminist tenet of breaking hierarchies between the human and nonhuman world as it is made explicit from the first episode when the characters are introduced. At the same time, there is no trace of ecological minds in any of the two species: nature and natural resources belong to the ones holding power, to the owners and designers of the park who manipulate and dominate them at their will. There is even a central control overviewing everything that happens in all the scenarios so nature, androids, and technicians are oppressed in the same terms. Kordecki (this volume) analyzes thecontrol of human beings and the Runa exerted by the Jana'ata, and told by Russell in *The Sparrow*, whose behaviour reminds of the treatment inflicted on Maeve and Dolores by technicians and visitors, to which they respond first, with a feeling of surprise, and, later on, with rebellion and revenge against the oppression they have been submitted to.

These two heroines, however, do not belong to the same social class, and this establishment of a hierarchy even among the androids is made explicit from the beginning of the series. It is necessary then, to introduce at this point a critique to the social hierarchy established that contradicts ecofeminist goals. In a sense, they are presented as opposites; while Dolores, which in English means pain, is a blonde and one of the first androids created by Arnold, Maeve, a mulatto prostitute, has been designed and programmed to satisfy men's sexual desires and, thus, she runs a brothel. With a special configuration that allows her to predict what her clients would require, Maeve provides the most satisfying pleasures to her customers as it is expected from a prostitute. As Plemenitaš (this volume) states when discussing *The Stepford Wives*, they become perfect market products themselves: Maeve and the female robots from Stepford reproduce a behavior prepared for immediate male satisfaction of his desire to dominate women.

Because of her condition and most likely her race, Maeve's naked body is constantly exposed during repairs while Dolores' body always appears covered in suggestive ways to avoid showing her most sexualized parts. Etzler (this volume) argues that this situation also takes place in *Alraune*, where women's bodies are the object of abuse and disrespect and used for commercial purposes until they die and their corpses end dissected for medical studies. Another clear difference between one woman and the other is the class of people with whom Dolores interacts, such as Bernard Lowe or Robert Ford—the men in charge. Besides, she has been in Arnold's house and she is often required for conversation with the head of the organization: William, son-in-law of the first owner, Mr. Delos, who becomes obsessed with her and the park. Maeve only talks to repairers, stating that class separation is important to establish a distance between them. She rebels in episode 8 after a repeated series of repairs provoked by her to understand why she had memories from a previous destination and decides to take control of her life. Apparently, she has the opportunity to be free but it seems that she has been programmed differently and her choices have also been established for her in advance, so she returns to the park in search of her daughter whom Felix, a technician, has located in another section of the park. She starts experiencing strong feelings of attachment toward this girl that acted as her daughter in a former narrative. The question of reproduction as it is addressed by Kordecki (this volume) also resembles the treatment that procreation receives in *Westworld* and *The Sleep Dealer*; she wonders what is a paradise without reproduction when this is exactly the idea: to create a space of immortality eliminating the need to bear new human creatures, who, grow up, age and finally die.

Feelings and emotions have traditionally functioned as the justification to oppress women, positing them at the side of dualisms where they stand for the body, inferior and irrational confronted to the superior mind, to reason. In the words of Greta Gaard (1993, 5)

> for example, the way in which women and nature have been concep-
> tualized historically in the Western tradition has resulted in devaluing
> whatever is associated with women, emotion, animals, nature, and the
> body, while simultaneously elevating in value those things associated
> with men, reason, humans, culture and the mind.

In the case of *Westworld* and *The Sleep Dealer*, this dualism that serves to retain Maeve in the park and Luz in Tijuana breaks apart after their rebellion and points out that social and ecological revolutions can happen parallel as Ynestra King (1990) points out in "Healing the Wounds: Feminism, Ecology and the Nature/Culture Dualism."

The Sleep Dealer tells the story of Memo, a Mexican young man whose father is killed by a drone suspected of terrorist actions against the USA because Memo himself has installed a radio station that intercepts private governmental frequencies. Running away from Santa Ana del Rio, Memo meets Luz and arrives at Tijuana where he starts working as a cyberbracero in a maquila, known as sleep dealer. Rivera (2012, n.p.) explains that

> the word 'cybraceros' alone signals the future of borderlands labor as
> a type of 'cyborg labor' (dehumanized and invisible), as well as the
> history of migrant labor along the border, specifically the midcentury
> practices, that initiated the rapid industrialization of the borderlands.

There, workers are connected through nodes previously attached to their bodies to electronic devices that transport their manual work to construction machines in the USA. Humans and androids in *Westworld* and Memo and Luz in *The Sleep Dealer* establish relationships in which the most technologically advanced being uses and abuses the one who is left behind and ignores how to profit from this technology. Rebeca Lemov (2015, 46) argues that the situation portrayed in these two visual documents responds to the fact that social relationships have been accepted to take place through machines:

> A growing body of research explores the question of how users interact
> with their gadgets and media outlets, and how in turn these interactions

transform social relationships. The defining feature of this heavily mediated reality is our presence "elsewhere," a removal of at least part of our conscious awareness from wherever our bodies happen to be.

In the case of *Westworld*, relationships not only take place through social networks but with machines themselves. Thus, transforming humans into cyborgs enhances the distance between them and the rest of the human beings which allows inflicting inhumane treatment on them, since they technically become less human and more machinelike. Bernard Lowe serves as an example of the transformation of humans into machines. He has been designed by Ford after Arnold, to work as his replacement, programmed with the same memories that tormented him, like the loss of his son that made him miserable. Before his human death, he tried to deliver androids a conscience but the discovery of his failure took him to desperation and to put an end to his tormented life with the help of Dolores. Later, in the third season, it is revealed that he hides the key to the destruction or salvation of the human world after the android's riot breaks out. Lemov (2015, 49) complains about the lack of research and preoccupation on "The status of the body that holds these devices, the body as platform—the body that is vacated—is curiously invisible," probably ignoring the extensive work done in ecofeminism by Karen Warren or Val Plumwood, especially in *Environmental Culture* who from their understanding of conceptual structures of domination have attacked value hierarchical thinking and reacted against the patriarchal models of domination based on the superiority of a race, gender, class, sex, or species: "A conceptual framework is a socially constructed set of basic beliefs, values, attitudes and assumptions that shape and reflect how one views oneself and others. It is oppressive when it explains, justifies, and maintains relationships of domination and subordination" (Warren 1996, xiv). Through this new ecofeminist criticism, the bodies of cyborgs or androids acquire visibility as they are rendered the importance they deserve without lessening the value of their labor. The progressive aging of humans versus the eternal youth of androids reveals as another weapon against the former. All of a sudden, the bodies of androids acquire the dimension of vessels for immortality without the need for perpetuation through descendants. Plemenitaš in her study about *The Stepford Wives* (this volume) explains how the substitution of human women for female robots transformed them into perfect bodies which do not age and as they are deprived of a human brain, of a will, therefore, they have lost the capacity of autonomous thinking.

More recently, Braidotti's thesis exposed in the third part of her work *The Posthuman* (2013) also focuses on how anthropocentrism has shaped the relationships between androids and humans which is a concept that perfectly describes the situation of cyberbraceros in *The Sleep Dealer*. The abuse of the worker is represented as an objectification, as inhuman treatment inflicted on what can be considered as just disposable bodies:

As a critical analysis of this historical moment, Marxism and its social-ist Humanism taught us that objectification is indeed a humiliating and demeaning experience for humans in that it denies their full humanity and can thus be truly called inhuman at a basic social level. The com-modification process itself reduces humans to the status of manufac-tured and hence profit-driven technologically mediated objects. This insight constitutes the core of the humanist heart of Marxism, which I analysed in chapter 1. Subsuming human relations into the nexus 'money-power' is for Marxists a form of inhumanity and the key social injustice of capitalist modes of production.

(106)

The Sleep Dealer shows how Mexican cyberbraceros have to be constantly substituted because of sudden high voltage or malfunction in their nodes. They die electrocuted and no one comes to help; the other cyberbraceros are only requested to disconnect the deceased one so that another one can be put in his place. A replacement worker is always found easily as the demand surpasses the offer both in the film and in real maquiladoras. Braidotti in *Posthuman Knowledge* (2019) regrets the position that humans have adopted toward technological developments, how we experience excessive joy, "euphoria" as she calls it, or suffer from "anxiety" in alternative peri-ods of time "in view of the exceedingly high prize that we—both humans and non-humans—are paying for these transformations" (13).

The model of Italian Renaissance and emblem of Humanism is the Vitruvian Man; created as the perfect measurement of its time, it acquires instead of a liberating character, one of bondage in contemporary times. Rosi Braidotti addresses its complexity in *The Posthuman* and its model is reproduced both in *The Sleep Dealer* and *Westworld*. The position that cyberbraceros adopt when they are connected through their nodes to the wires that send their virtual work simulates that of the Vitruvian man within the circle: oppressed by the nodes and in constant danger of being electro-cuted. As to *Westworld*, it is clear from the beginning that the androids are designed from the model of the Vitruvian man: the 3D printers that create their bones, muscles, and tendons are connected inside the circle that turns around. It is as if they were spinning from there:

> It is the image of Man as a rational animal endowed with lan-guage. Anti-humanists over the last thirty years questioned both the self-representation and the image of thought implied in the Humanist definition of the Human, especially the ideas of transcendental reason and the notion that the subject coincides with rational consciousness. This flattering self-image of 'Man' is as problematic as it is partial in that it promotes a self-centred attitude.
>
> (Braidotti 2013, 23)

Dolores, who paradoxically has been programmed by Arnold to destroy the park, appears in the first episodes of the series as an innocent being, carrying the pain and frustrations, the corruption of her creators in their abusive behavior toward other humans and nonhuman beings whom they consider their inferiors. She is always taken advantage of until she rebels killing Arnold and Ford. Eztler (this volume) discusses how Alraune, the creature born from a prostitute and the semen of a hanged murderer, also rebels against her creator, ten Brinken, upon discovering how she was made. The novel *Alraune* and the later adaptations made for the cinema reflect the same idea of male oppression over bodies of other human beings or more than human ones that appear both in *Westworld* and *The Sleep Dealer*. In the latter, Luz, Memo, and Rudy Ramirez feel trapped in a network of abusive situations and people who take advantage of their innocence since they acknowledge their absolute ignorance of the manipulation they are suffering. The external networks that connect the three of them use their nodes to exert firm control on their bodies and minds. Thus, Luz makes money out of telling stories about Memo; she betrays the poor man who has deposited in her his most intimate secrets. She connects through her nodes and shares, in an internet-based virtual space called Truenode, aspects about Memo's experience escaping from his home village to Tijuana which Rudy Ramirez buys, unknowingly of their connection. Luz is forced by the nodes to tell the truth and to talk about her relationship with Memo, so intimacy gets broken and private lives become full of interferences. Braidotti (2013, 109) refers to these exchanges as:

> The relationship between the human and the technological other, as well as the affects involved in it, including desire, cruelty and pain, change radically with the contemporary technologies of advanced capitalism. For one thing, the technological construct now mingles with the flesh in unprecedented degrees of intrusiveness, as we saw in the previous chapter. Moreover, the nature of the human–technological interaction has shifted towards a blurring of the boundaries between the genders, the races and the species, following a trend that Lyotard assesses as a distinctive feature of the contemporary inhuman condition. The technological other today – a mere assemblage of circuitry and feedback loops – functions in the realm of an egalitarian blurring of differences, if not downright indeterminacy.

As to Maeve and Dolores, they take control over the men who accompany them in episode 6, in the first season. It is very interesting how both become aware of their condition as part human, part machine, and how they learn to use their physical and intellectual attributes at the same time. This is how Maeve and Dolores, initially secondary characters, androids created for the satisfaction of human beings, take the reins of the narratives in the park, transforming them into an attack against whoever threatens them. Dolores's awakening starts when she shoots Robert Ford; it is a kind of trigger to a series of events that will culminate with her as the leader of a group of bandits who try to destroy William at first and the human race at large as it is announced in the third season.

Maeve is obsessed with recuperating her daughter even though she knows that, as an android, she lacks reproductive abilities and the girl has been created in a laboratory exactly the same as her. Thus, her role as a mother imposed by her gender codification prevails over her desire to obtain freedom from her creators and the rest of the humans that have used and abused her. In ecofeminist terms, following essentialist theorists, this response could be conditioned by her nature as a woman who makes her a caring, loving, and nurturing figure and supports the thesis that biology is destiny. On the other hand, Dolores and Maeve react against this essentialism as they attempt to eliminate all the masculine human power, the concept itself of a park created for masculine enjoyment in which, among many other advantages presented to male visitors, the danger of pregnancies has been eliminated. Following this patriarchal configuration, sexual relationships rarely take place under mutual consent: rape and abuse represent a constant, a repeated humiliation exerted on the bodies of female androids. Dolores is repeatedly and brutally forced to engage in sexual relationships but she has a consensual relationship with William and another with Teddy. Therese and Bernard apparently enjoy a healthy sexual relationship that takes place under mutual consent but Therese ignores he is an android so the consent is questioned as in the case of Dolores. From the first episode, the difference between men and women is clearly set: customers' satisfaction is the key. Women must be at the disposal of male visitors for sexual relationships while men cannot protect their women from the humans' advances toward them. Abuse and oppression are repeatedly exerted on them and their lives only make sense through this exploitation they are subjected to. Luckily, they apparently forget their suffering every day at dusk since their memory gets erased on a regular basis by technicians in the hub.

Gaining consciousness through awakening to memories implies misery and rejection toward the mistreatment inflicted by technicians and visitors. Humans in the park feel they can use the androids at their convenience and they find their punishment: human technicians are killed by androids as revenge for having abused them or having enjoyed them. In episode 6, human workers are shamed by Maeve about the fact that they enjoy sex with androids while they are being repaired. She makes them regret the fact that they use the bodies for their own sexual pleasure. During episode 10, one of the technicians is surprised masturbating in front of Héctor, the bandit that accompanies Maeve, so he gets killed by him. Their stories unite, making ecofeminist practice evident in the vindication of their rights to be respected as living entities with the same value as human beings.

The destruction of their creator acquires the symbolism of eliminating the oppression, the patriarchal linkage they attempt to escape from, both physically and intellectually. The pattern of oppression seems to find a repetition in both visual materials: those human/cyborg/androids perceived as inferior can be used and abused for the profit and enjoyment of those who hold the power in capitalist terms, in terms of money.

In a tour de force, in episode 3 of the second season, Dolores identifies herself in front of android confederate soldiers as Wyatt; she assumes the identity of the bandit whose narrative had just been inaugurated before she killed Ford. *Westworld* plays with gender roles and with the assumptions of the characters and the audience who does not expect a woman to lead a revolution like the one she initiates. Dolores transcends the roles imposed on her as a woman created to satisfy men and reveals her as the hero, the leader of the revolution of androids but also the center of the new narrative created by Robert Ford for the delight of the new visitors. Just as Ynestra King (1989,23) predicted: "There is no reason to believe that women placed in positions of patriarchal power will act any different from men." Dolores submits and oppresses animals and Teddy for her own benefit because she considers them weaker than she is. As she is an android, the codes she has been imprinted with can be changed from a sweet, pleasing woman ready to become a wife to those of a warrior defeating human beings and other opponents.

Dolores becomes the center of the labyrinth; she has been created after Arnold's son who died as a child and she has been given special qualities. However, she has been trapped in a loop of events that get repeated again and again. She is named pain because she holds all of Arnold's suffering and she carries the key to the suffering of the rest of the male protagonists of the series, both human and android: William, Ford, Theodore, and Bernard. Dolores reverts the suffering of the androids by rebelling and taking the reins of the revolution. She is the sweet Dolores and the bandit Wyatt who will take revenge for all the androids of the park in season two and the machine whose existence must be ended in order to save humanity during the whole third season. This ambiguity she exhibits manipulating androids and humans at her convenience will transform her into a non-reliable character for the other heroine, Maeve, as they fight each other in the decisive battle of saving or destroying the human race.

William, Dolores' nemesis, reveals himself as a controller, as the embodiment of the patriarchal relationships of domination that happen in the series. All his relationships have been planned in advance, even his marriage with Mr. Delos' daughter is a business contract to acquire the company from his father in law, to be the main heir displacing and disabling his brother in law. William and Dolores confront each other in season two after he falls in love with her: he realizes she is not a human being and regrets having had feelings for her. He desires to use her to show other people the way to find themselves, their own reflection. In this same second episode in season two, Dolores has taken command and refuses to be used and abused anymore. Reversing this situation of inferiority also implies the change of male androids so that manipulation of them can be useful to obtain their aims. Dolores convinces Teddy to march with her and then, transforms him to serve her effectively. At the same time, Maeve uses Héctor as well to help her fulfill her purposes. Both men have been reprogrammed to love these women and obey their orders, so they blindly follow the revolt started by their lovers who now command the actions in the park. From passive to active, from submissive to rebellious these two android women succeed in transgressing traditional gender roles and social stereotypes to become leaders of their own revolts.

Rosi Braidotti (2013, 103) defines how relationships between humans and nonhumans should take place: what kind of bonds can be established within the nature-culture continuum of technologically mediated organisms and how they can be sustained. Both kinship and ethical accountability need to be redefined in such a way as to rethink links of affectivity and responsibility not only for non-anthropomorphic organic others but also for those technologically mediated, newly patented creatures we are sharing our planet with.

In *The Sleep Dealer*, Rudy Ramirez realizes he is part of the oppressed when he buys Memo's story from the network Truenode and travels to Tijuana trying to amend his error. At the same time, Memo discovers his condition of inferiority when he learns that Luz has sold the history of his family on the internet. When Rudy shows Memo his nodes, the three of them realize their condition of puppets directed from above through a control system configured and programmed to make them obey without questioning. A reflection from Braidotti sustains the idea that a new reconsideration of the concept of what entails to be human seems necessary: "'We,' the dwellers of this planet at this point in time, are interconnected but also internally fractured. Class, race, gender and sexual orientations, age and able-bodiedness continue to function as significant markers in framing and policing access to 'normal' humanity" (2019, 114). In this sense, Memo is deprived of any decision capacity from the beginning of the story in Santa Ana del Rio. Rudy Ramirez drives a drone from the USA pointing at Mexico where, as Braidotti (2013, 123) points out, the enemy must be killed in cold blood. With drones or robots,

> *The Economist* points out other advantages of posthuman warfare and argues that autonomous robot-soldiers could do more good than harm: they would not rape women, burn down civilian dwellings in anger or become erratic decision makers under the emotional stress of combat.

He has been told what to aim at without questioning orders. At the same time, he experiences that the distance provided by drones between him and his target works as a protection from involvement with the victim; to prevent the development of any kind of empathy although he learns too late that he has made a mistake:

> Questioned on this issue by *The Guardian* (Carroll 2012), RPA or drone pilots argue that their jobs involve different types of courage from conventional warfare, not only because they have to take the consequences of possible mistakes, but also because a different degree of rigour and accuracy is needed to kill by remote control.
>
> (Braidotti 2013, 126)

Braidotti (2013, 126), however, sustains how Jimmy Carter used to defend that robots must be always controlled by humans. Alex Rivera projects his agreement with this sentence at the end of *The Sleep Dealer* and reveals his desire to establish poetic justice: the three protagonists, Memo, Luz, and Rudy use the technology that oppressed them to liberate Mexican people: breaking the dam which controls the water stolen from Mexican lands becomes symbolic of the break of the USA hegemony. Returning the resources to their lawful owners belongs fully to the aims of ecofeminist criticism, crossing the borders of imposition and oppression to envision a new sustainable future for the wretched people that live across the border from the USA, a future now more in danger than ever because of the current pandemic that we are suffering in the year 2020. The crashing of the train that takes the visitors inside the park in *Westworld* at the end of the second season also holds the symbolism of acquiring free will and consciousness for the androids; it represents taking the reins of their own present and future while breaking the last connection with the structures of power and domination imposed on androids in the park as it announces a new organization possibly based on more equal principles different from the ones exerted from the external control of the human race. As the third season shows, the androids led by Dolores threaten to exterminate the human race as if to end the cycle of destruction that Arnold and Ford started with the creation of the park itself but what ends being exposed and debated once more is how "such a hasty recomposition of an endangered Humanity reinstates anthropocentrism and fails to do justice to the violence humans are visiting upon other species, the planet included" (Braidotti 2019, 157).

References

Braidotti, Rosi. 2013. *The Posthuman*. Cambridge, UK: Polity Press.
———. 2019. *Posthuman Knowledge*. Cambridge, UK: Polity Press.
Gaard, Greta. 1993. *Ecofeminism: Women, Animals, Nature*. Philadelphia, PA: Temple University Press.
Haney, William S. 2006. *Cyberculture, Cyborgs and Science Fiction*. Amsterdam: Rodopi.

King, Ynestra. 1990. "Healing the Wounds: Feminism, Ecology, and the Nature/ Culture Dualism." In *Reweaving the World: The Emergence of Ecofeminism*, edited by Irene Diamond and Gloria Feman Orestein, 106–121. San Francisco, CA: Sierra Club Books.

—————— 1989. "The Ecology of Feminism and the Feminism of Ecology" in *Healing the Wounds: The Promise of Ecofeminism*, edited by Judith Plant. 18–29. New Society Publishers.

Lemov, Rebeca. 2015. "On Not Being There: The Data-Driven Body at Work and at Play." *The Hedgehog Review* 17, no. 2: 44–56.

Orr, Christopher. 2016. "Sympathy for the Robot." *Atlantic*, October, 38–40.

Plumwood, Val. 2002. *Environmental Culture: The Ecological Crisis of Reason*. New York, NY: Routledge.

Rivera, Lysa. 2012. "Future Histories and Cyborg Labor: Reading Borderlands Science Fiction after NAFTA." *Science Fiction Studies* 39, no. 3: 415–436.

Shakespeare, William. 1595. *The Tragedy of Romeo and Juliet*. Accessed October 12, 2020. https://www.gutenberg.org/cache/epub/1777/pg1777-images.html.

Shelley, Mary. 1818. *Frankenstein; or, the Modern Prometheus*. London: Lackington, Hughes, Harding, Mavor, & Jones. Accessed September 30, 2020. https://www .gutenberg.org/files/41445/41445-h/41445-h.htm.

Warren, Karen J. 1996. *Ecological Feminist Philosophies*. Bloomington, IN: Indiana University Press.

4 The Living Spaces of Robots

An Ecofeminist Reading of *The Stepford Wives*

Katja Plemenitaš

The Stepford Wives belongs to those rare works of popular fiction that have captured the imagination of the public to become part of the wider cultural knowledge. The phrase "Stepford wives" can be found in dictionaries and is now considered part of the general cultural lexicon beyond the English-speaking countries. The term is generally used as a synonym for mindless, submissive, and perfectly groomed housewives, and is commonly used as a slur. According to the dictionary definition, a Stepford wife is a derogatory informal expression for "a married woman who submits to her husband's will and is preoccupied by domestic concerns and her own personal appearance" (Collins Free Online Dictionary 2020). Paradoxically, the term, which had its origins in a parable about the sexist backlash to female liberation, is nowadays used mainly for the negative evaluation of women. The term originates from the titular wives of the satirical science-fiction novel *The Stepford Wives,* published in 1972, which was written by Ira Levin. Levin describes gender relations in the American middle class of the 1970s through a dystopia in which American suburban housewives in idyllic Stepford are conspired against by their husbands. One by one the women of Stepford are killed and replaced by robots. *The Stepford Wives* was published at a time when second-wave Anglo-American feminism was in full swing, capturing the anxieties and vulnerabilities of both women and men faced with new social developments. Its influence on popular culture was further established through several adaptations: two feature film adaptations (the 1975 version and the 2004 remake), and three made-for-television sequels (Maio 2004). Its trajectory through pop culture is somewhat similar to another cult film of the 1970s—the film *Westworld* based on Michael Crichton's screenplay of 1973, which is now experiencing a resurgence and renewed cultural relevance as an HBO series (Martín Junquera, this volume). Krugovoy Silver (2002, 60) notes that despite critical neglect and a relatively short theater run, the first film about Stepford has had a wide-reaching popular appeal and cultural influence lasting into the twenty-first century. The scholarly and critical interest in the story has eventually caught up with its popular appeal, at least since the publication of the DVD version of the film in 2001. Many studies have focused on the feminist readings of the story, but some have also examined other elements, such as the depiction of the characters within Jewish writing tradition (Pummill 2015) or the Freudian interpretation of the gaze (Helford 2006). The themes of the story also continue to resonate for a new generation of writers and filmmakers. One such recent example is the horror sci-fi satire *Get out*, a take on contemporary American racial relations that claims the author of *The Stepford Wives* as its "spiritual godfather" (Robey 2017).

This continued theoretical and popular interest proves that *The Stepford Wives*, whether as a book, feature film, or TV show, is a modern-day horror science fiction that provides "political/ sociological/ philosophical insights as well as genre entertainment" (Boruzkowski 1987). According to Maio (2004, 115), the book and the film are foremost "of the time," "a snapshot of the social landscape of an earlier time." At the same time, Maio notes that the story is also an ahead-of-the-curve study of the "male" backlash mentality, even before the media had put a name to the phenomenon" (Maio 2004, 115). Krugovoy Silver (2002, 60) even credits the film for "the diffusion of feminist theory from smaller, loosely connected consciousness-raising and activist groups to mainstream American culture as a whole." Therefore, it is no coincidence that the book and the first film adaptation appeared in the same period as the first edition of the work *Language and Woman's Place* by Robin Lakoff, which was published in 1975 (Lakoff 2004) and the early explicit mentions of ecofeminism (d'Eaubonne 1974). The Stepford fembots with their meek high-pitched politeness, restricted repetitive speech, and shiny surfaces, their insides and outsides devoid of organic matter, are a perfect embodiment of the linguistic concerns of Lakoff's deficit theory of empty exaggerated lady speech and the society's rising concerns about the effects of technoscience on the environment and humanity (Johnston and Sears 2011). Krugovoy Silver (2002, 60) notes that the story of the Stepford Wives can be read as "an important cultural document of second wave feminism that addresses three main issues drawn from the women's movement: a woman's domestic labor, a woman's role in the nuclear family and a woman's control over her body." My focus in this study is to examine the way in which the story of the Stepford Wives of the 1975 film approaches all these issues and integrates them by giving them an ecofeminist frame. My main argument is that the reading of the story of the Stepford Wives through an ecofeminism prism reveals the ways in which the patriarchal power structures of Stepford shape the living spaces of its women. Such a reading reveals the story's warning about the damaging effects of patriarchal values in building a perfectly functioning consumer society. The men of Stepford control the living spaces of the women of Stepford by gradually perfecting their living space into meticulously groomed and highly controlled "enclosures." In my analysis, I focus on the visual and verbal cues of the story which encode this message at different levels of explicitness and which provide a common ecofeminist framework for the central topics of second-wave feminism, such as the submission of women through domestic labor, their role as mothers and wives and the lack of control over their bodies. From an ecofeminist perspective, these topics are integrated into a pessimistic cautionary tale about the men's destructive domination of nature in general, and female nature in particular, whereby both types of nature are considered as two integral parts of the same conceptual whole.

There are two broad assumptions about the connection between women and nature: one orientation assumes an innate connection, i.e. the tendency of women to be more attuned to nature than men. The other orientation is critical of the focus on the innate nature of this connection and argues for explanations of the associations between women and nature which reveal the "social and historical factors that have led to women's oppression" (Vakoch 2012, 4). Čeh Steger (2015) argues that the essentialist equation of women with nature diverts attention away from the connection between environmental degradation and the discrimination of women. Catriona Sandilands (1999), who is also critical of essentialist positions, argues that social constructivism can be equally essentialist. What all the different essentialist positions have in common is their fixed, immutable, and uniform categorization of both women and nature. Sandilands (1999, 70) further argues that essentialist positions are part of identity politics, which "draws attention away from the fact that ecological degradation is a complex social problem." According to Sandilands (1999, 70) we have to open a way for new realizations of humans as "always already simultaneously natural and cultural beings, and to work in the world aware of our limitations." In my discussion, I attempt to show that the story of the Stepford Wives demonstrates a very postmodern sensibility in rejecting the essentialist position about women, a sensibility which is also reflected in the connections between the women, their living spaces, and nature. The categorical unification of women is imposed on the women through the destructive force of the main villains, the men of Stepford. In her discussion of climate fiction (cli-fi) by Bobis, Ralph (2021) observes that the transformation of the earth rests on privileged masculinist fears and desires. Similarly, in *The Stepford Wives*, the transformation of the women is driven by male desire and anxiety. Like indigenous science-fiction literary works analyzed by Blend (this volume), the story uses science-fictional elements to question the concept of Western progress, but unlike those works, it offers a defeatist rather than celebratory vision of the future.

The story of Stepford thus falls into a long tradition of feminist science-fiction literature which highlights parallels between the domination of women and the domination of the environment and in which, as Anae (2021) observes, female writers from the period of the nineteenth and early twentieth century played an important precursor role. Justine Larbalestier notes in her Introduction to *Daughters of Earth: Feminist Science Fiction in the Twentieth Century* (2006, xviii) that "women have written science fiction for as long as the genre has been around and (...) science fiction is always about the here and now, about this place where humans live."

Although written and directed by men, the story of Stepford belongs to feminist science fiction as it perfectly captures the sensibilities and fears stemming from the development of technology and gender divisions of its time.

The 1975 film was directed by Bryan Forbes and features Katharine Ross in the role of the protagonist Joanna Eberhart, Paula Prentiss in the role of Joanna's best friend Bobbie Markowe, and Peter Masterson in the role of Joanna's husband Walter Eberhart. Through a combination of science-fictional and horror elements, the film creates the atmosphere of a dystopian feminist nightmare with minimal effects. The science-fictional elements do not depend on special effects as the film does not focus on the internal complexity of the robots or show any details of the workings of the technology itself. The real women can only be distinguished from the robots through their behavior: the way they speak, move, and dress. The technological mechanism behind their existence is only indirectly suggested through visual allusions to electronics factories dotting the landscape around Stepford and through the mention that the character named Diz, the head of the men's association, used to work for Disney.

The story of *The Stepford Wives* follows the young urban housewife and aspiring photographer Joanna Eberhart, who moves from bustling and noisy Manhattan to the suburban quiet of Stepford, Connecticut, with her husband Walter and their two young daughters. She reluctantly follows the decision of her husband to live in the calm suburban town of Stepford, seemingly unperturbed by social divisions or unrest, where all the women are perfect housewives content with their lives and all the men belong to a men's association. She becomes friends with Bobbie Markowe and Charmaine Wimperis, and when these two also suddenly change into perfectly groomed submissive housewives, Joanna gradually realizes the town's dark secret: all the women are being murdered and replaced by robots and the men who are members of the men's association are responsible for this. Joanna tries to escape with her children to a safer place but is killed by her robot replica and her body and soul are replaced by an outer shell in the form of her robot body.

At the very beginning of the story, the reluctant heroine Joanna is at the start of a new chapter in her life, a journey into the unknown to escape the messiness of urban existence. From the first scene, it is obvious that she is hesitant to move and that she has been convinced by her husband that leaving New York is best for their family. The director Bryan Forbes takes his time during the title credits, showing long scenes of the family driving through the countryside to their new home. The scenes are set to soothing music, creating an atmosphere of calm and domesticity, but the visuals reveal a different story: the main protagonist's descent into a misogynistic nightmare runs through a landscape punctuated with electronics factories, laboratories, and shopping centers. Joanna has to sacrifice her noisy, diverse life in New York for a clean, quiet life in idyllic suburbia, far from the madding crowd, so to speak. What we see on the way to her new home is a foreshadowing of the events to come. The journey to Stepford is interspersed with glimpses of an industrial landscape sprawling through the fields of the countryside. While the female protagonist of *The Waste Tide* discussed by Huang (this volume) is constrained to recycling electronic waste in a toxic environment, in *The Stepford Wives*, the females are themselves transformed into toxic electronic waste. The ominous-looking electronic factories are among the first foreboding visual cues of constriction and uncanniness—the very first being the nude mannequin carried by a man through the streets of Manhattan. These visual cues signal that genre-wise, the story is not a family or relationship drama, but a horror story with the family and relationship dynamics providing the locus for the ensuing horror. We can see the apprehensive look on Joanna's face as they drive past these factories, since her husband Walter convinced her to move by claiming that their new life would be an antidote to the pollution, neuroticism, and noise of New York, a persuasive pitch which is later unmasked as a means of "friendly" persuasion used by all the Stepford husbands to motivate their wives to agree to move to Stepford. This "pitch" about the clean environment in Stepford is used several times by different men throughout the film, but it only really disturbs Joanna when it is repeated by her best friend Bobbie after she has been turned into a robot: "Leave Stepford? Good schools, low taxes, clean air." The promise of safety for the children, good schools, and clean air is the most effective manipulation the men are able to contrive, knowing with near certainty that the potential reluctance of their wives would be overcome by what is considered best for the children. The human women of Stepford can be manipulated based on their sensitivity and affection toward their families, and their fierce protectiveness toward their children. The pre-robotic women and the men of Stepford are presented along the typical gender lines of the difference approach to psychological gender differences (e.g., Tannen 1991), whereby men as a group are more status-oriented, while women as a group are oriented toward connection. However, it does not necessarily follow that such a portrayal of the Stepford men and their original wives embraces an essentialist view of women. In fact, the human women of Stepford are presented as a very diverse group. They cannot be reduced to their nurturing tendencies since they display a very wide range of different interests. The glamorous Charmaine likes to play tennis and has little interest in professional pursuits, the dynamic Bobbie is very extroverted, sarcastic, and sexually overt, while Joanna is the "everywoman" in the bunch—she is sensitive and restrained, but also curious and artistic, the one who suffers the most from the lack of a meaningful life—Friedan's (1963) problem that has no name. The husbands, on the other hand, conceptualize the women through an essentialist prism by ignoring their diverse interests. What is more, they use the women's genuine interest in the well-being of their families for their own nefarious purposes. Joanna accepts the argument about a safer and cleaner living environment in Stepford, but she also admits in her welcoming interview for the local newspaper that she misses the noise of New York, the exact opposite of what is expected of her.

This awareness about the pollution of the living environment and the role the development of technology plays in it is a recurrent motif throughout the film. The women worrying about the dangers of pollution affecting the life of their families and the role of technology in their eventual demise represent the most visually and thematically accessible ecofeminist reading of the story. In her discussion of the critical reception of the first film, Boruzkowski (1987, 16–19) observes that the film combines a genre formula with social commentary through addressing the changing role of women in contemporary society and apprehensions about technology. The development of technology means progress, but in Stepford, progress is positively framed only for the male villains, whereas the female victims experience technological progress as regression, ultimately as a tool of their total annihilation. The steadily progressing industrial sprawl of electronics factories and laboratories surrounding and encroaching upon the suburban towns presents a visual metaphor about the use of technology and science in the control of the physical and mental living space of the women. Women in Gearhart's feminist separatist utopia *The Wanderground* discussed by Tidwell (2021) reject science as masculine and dangerous, but the human female protagonists of Stepford still trust science, even looking for help in a chemical laboratory to uncover the cause of the sudden transformations. But the feminist fears are confirmed when rather than helping the women, science turns out to be their worst enemy. The development of technology and science in Stepford is a primarily male endeavor, and the real danger for the women comes from the people intimately closest to them. The men of Stepford such as Dale Coba, a.k.a Diz, a former engineer at Disney, Claude, the stuttering linguist, and the illustrator Ike Mazzard all use their ingenuity and creative potential to destroy the women they feign to befriend. The fear that men create and use technology for the purpose of dominating women and nature is a deeply ecofeminist concern. Johnston and Sears (2011, 76) focus on the gendered character of technology and science in the film by noting that it is "technoscience that informs and colludes with the film's misogynistic practices." The ubiquitous presence of the high-tech industries and "science parks" with names such as "CompuTech," "Data Systems Inc.," "COBA Biochemical Associate and General Electronics: A Division of Atlantic Eastern Homedale Plant" in the backdrop of the idyllic sequestered domesticity suggests a power struggle that is enacted over "gendered bodies" (Johnston and Sears 2011, 77). The men always remind the women about the main reason they moved to Stepford—to enjoy an easy life, clean air, and provide a safe environment for their children. They exploit the women's general anxiety about the environment which reflects the rising ecological awareness of 1970s middle-class America. This anxiety tragically became reality a few years after the release of the film in the notorious incident of chemical waste poisoning in Love Canal. The topic of pollution anxiety is the most explicit at three crucial points in the film. The first point is at the beginning, when the Eberhart family moves to Stepford, seemingly to provide for a better, cleaner environment for the whole family. The novel makes this general concern for the unpolluted environment even more explicit by mentioning the non-polluting detergent which is part of the welcome package for the new arrivals. The second point is after Joanna and Bobbie see the transformed Charmaine, which prompts Bobbie to blame the local factories for dumping toxic chemicals in the Stepford river and consequently influencing the change in the Stepford female population. Due to their distrust in government organizations, the women seek help from Joanna's former boyfriend, who is a chemist in charge of a laboratory. His analysis of drinking water shows no additional chemical pollutants, although he is no different than other men in his patronizing demeanor toward the women. The third point comes after Joanna discovers a transformed Bobbie and realizes that there are intentional sinister forces at work. Joanna visits a female psychiatrist, who is sympathetic and advises her to get her children and flee from Stepford. At this point, the film shows a close-up of a dead rat floating in water, a visual reminder of the general destruction of the wild nature offering no escape routes anymore, and a metaphor for the destruction of the female nature. As a matter of fact, Joanna's fate is already sealed at that point. The Joanna with an organic body and an organic mind has nowhere to return to—the spaces that await are made for her inorganic body and consist of the pretty but highly controlled and meticulously maintained artificial enclosures of the house, the manicured garden, and the shopping mall. The film shows the pre-robotic Joanna and Bobby enjoying themselves in the freedom of the wildflower meadows, almost covered from view by the tall grass. In contrast, the natural space of their robot copies consists of the tamed nature of manicured lawns, pruned fruit trees, pot plants, and flowers grown in the greenhouse. The nature outside the regulated spaces represents a free arena for spontaneity, and the controlled existence of robots represents a sharp contrast to the joy of creativity and unpredictability offered by wilderness.

In their article about the connection between wilderness recreation and women's everyday lives, Pohl, Borrie, and Patterson (2000) note that wilderness recreation provides different kinds of freedoms, such as freedom of body, freedom of mind, freedom of movement, and freedom from societal constraints. According to Pohl, Borrie, and Patterson (2000, 430), wilderness recreation thus offers women a new perspective, which entails "critiquing norms about materialism, body image, and acceptable social conduct." In addition, wilderness also offers women "solitude, absorption, and freedom from the distraction of everyday life," and thus contributes to their mental health and freedom of thought (Pohl, Borrie, and Patterson 2000, 430). Robot women represent the very antithesis of all these freedoms: the freedom of body, freedom of mind, and freedom of movement. Contented with their life in a confined environment, they represent the ideal woman in the eyes of the Stepford men. As Stepford begins to diversify racially, the story hints at an equally bleak future for the wife of the first black couple—her husband behaves exactly like the other Stepford husbands and she is destined to become a Stepford wife, too.

The story of Stepford women shows how limiting people's environment and preventing their access to natural spaces has damaging consequences for the experience of the freedom of body and mind. Here we can also draw parallels to the modern African American experience of the great outdoors, which has been harmed by historical racism. The consequences of historical racism continue to harm the cohesiveness of modern American society and are also reflected in racialized attitudes to living spaces. In her book *Black Faces, White Spaces*, Carolyn Finney (2014) examines how the legacies of slavery, Jim Crow, and racial violence have influenced the cultural understanding of the wilderness and controlled who should and can have access to natural spaces.

Similarly, Shelton Johnson (2012), a Black park ranger, observes that historically there were many laws that kept African Americans "in their place," and one of the places they were not supposed to be was outside, in the wild, and the legacy of these laws still has a powerful effect. Likewise, Donathan Brown, a Black college professor, relates his own personal experience while hiking in the Adirondacks mountains by noting there has always been this questioning by locals whether Blacks belong there (Figura 2020). This prompted the American Hiking Society to issue a statement in which they reinforced the mission to enable the outdoors to be a place of enjoyment for all and to fight against systemic racism that prevents Black, Indigenous, and People of Color from having equitable access to quality natural spaces and enjoying the great outdoors as a place of healing and encouragement (American Hiking Society 2020).

It is these questions of belonging, freedom, and identity that connect the fictional world of Stepford to the world of modern reality, a world facing several problems on a global scale: violence, environmental pollution, global warming, and pandemic disease. These crises have given rise to a critical new awareness of limited access and contribution of people with marginalized identities to the relationship with nature and conservation.

In the dystopia of Stepford, the question of individuals not belonging is resolved by the women simply being replaced by robots. What follows is the ultimate reduction of the living space of the "new" women to the regulated artificial environment controlled by the men, which ultimately leaves no space for the women's natural bodies and minds. The oppression of the natural world through the patriarchal power structure parallels the oppression of the women, whereby both oppressions finally intersect and culminate in the total annihilation of the women's perishable organic bodies and minds and their replacement by improved models—man-made products with limited and controlled artificial intelligence. The real horror is revealed gradually through the story—the man-created technology does not liberate the women from the drudgery of their housework to enable the diversification of their interests and their living spaces, but, on the contrary, actively attempts to reduce their environment both in size and diversity in order to eschew their imperfect organic bodies and distracting agency. Ynestra King (2003, 458–459) notes that a healthy eco-system is a diverse eco-system, while biological simplification goes hand in hand with the homogenization of taste and culture, and in such circumstances, "social and natural life are literally simplified to the inorganic for the convenience of market society." The new robotic housewives are a perfect metaphor for this kind of society. The ultimate achievement of the men's use of technoscience to transform their wives is a perfectly functioning market society.

In his foreword to the 2011 edition of Ira Levin's novel, Chuck Palahniuk notes that the unsettling fantasy of Stepford has in some way become real for women in the twenty-first century. The book covers and TV shows are populated by well-groomed women in search of a husband. The feminists of the 1970s with their celebration of imperfect, ungroomed physical bodies and their unbridled carnal selves have given way to pretty dolls and domestic goddesses with their surgically enhanced bodies and faces in perfected photographic images. The shiny flawless Stepford fembots are a warning and foreshadowing of this trend toward homogenization of diversity in both nature and culture. A manifestation of this trend is visible in the media obsession with robotic silicone sex dolls. These are often marketed as a replacement for a real partner and have even prompted discussions about the rights of sex dolls (Žižek 2018). According to de Fren (2009), the fetishization of artificial female bodies poses the question about the objectivization of women and about the feminization of objects, whereby the line between the two is not entirely clear. The sexual objectivization of the Stepford dolls, however, has more to do with domestication than fetishization. Whereas the natural women of Stepford are sexually inquisitive and overt, freely talk about sexual desire and roam around in short skirts and revealing tops, the robots are covered up in frilly blouses and long skirts, and utter platitudes during sex. Colleen Stevenson (2007, 87) observes that science fiction often employs an optimistic vision of cybernetic transcendence of the human as an escape from the limitations of the flesh. In her "Cyborg Manifesto" (1991) Donna Haraway offers an optimistic vision of the gendered cyborg as a hybrid of machine and organism, opposed to traditional dichotomies of man/woman, human/machine. However, as I-min Huang (2018, 130) notes, women "share in common with the environment and the cyborg the stigma of impurity, hybridity." The Stepford cyborgs are even less than hybrids—they are simply inorganic, plastic objects for the satisfaction of their husbands' needs. Telotte (1983, 45) argues that the real terror is implicit "in their similarity to what is held up as a cultural ideal and in the fact that this duplication is obviously desirable to those closest to the women, their own husbands." When there is no escape left, Joanna asks what the men's motivation is for replacing the women, and Diz calmly replies: "Because we can." This shows, somewhat surprisingly, that the men themselves do not really believe in the inherent inferiority of the women, they just use their power to abuse the women's trust for the purpose of domination. Nor do the men particularly care about the women's natural reproductive abilities, since the robots seem to lack internal organs. But they effectively manipulate the women's maternal affection for their scheme, for example, in luring Joanna to the mansion with the recording of her children's distressed voices calling for mommy.

The story offers a very radical and pessimistic vision of male domination. The Stepford men are aware of the close integration of the female body and mind, which leads them to dispose of both. Instead of trying to "only" sedate the women, they resort to an irreversible fascist solution of completely annihilating their imperfect organic bodies in order to get rid of their organic minds. What they gain in the process is their wives' ageless perfect bodies, but even more importantly, the artificial minds that fit into those bodies. Compared to the animal/human species of the Runa in Doria Russell's novel *The Sparrow*, which embodies the abstract female (Kordecki, this volume), the robot species of Stepford embodies a distorted abstraction of the female. Kang (2005) observes the often subversive nature of cyborgs, who develop their own agency and become a threat to their creators. But the Stepford models show no autonomy—they may malfunction occasionally but they never develop any agency that would threaten their creators. They only represent an active threat to their human originals, not just as their more submissive and physically enhanced replacements, but also as the very instrument used in their murder in the film version. The film shows this in one of the final scenes in which Joanna is confronted with her own replica. In this scene, which is accompanied by ominously mellow music, the smiling robot with hollow eyes takes a nylon stocking as a strangling device and slowly approaches Joanna. We do not see what happens afterward, as the scene ends in a fadeout, but it is clearly implied that Joanna is killed by her robot replica. This can be interpreted as a metaphor highlighting the fact that in a modern market society, the women themselves are willing accomplices in their own subjugation as they actively participate in the underlying consumerism of the narrow definitions of womanhood and beauty. The women of Stepford are transformed into perfect products by the technological and creative know-how available to their husbands and tweaked to perfection in accordance with the precise wishes of their commissioners. Although one of their primary functions is sexual, they appear to be void of any sexual agency. Unlike Hanns Heinz Ewers's character of Alraune, a sexual creature with an unnatural yet organic origin discussed by Etzler (this volume), the Stepford creations are devoid of human desire and are akin in their nature to a sex toy that can cook and shop. Pre-transformation Joanna and Bobbie are good-looking women, sexual creatures attuned to their carnal desires, but in their inorganic versions, they are shiny and faultless, a strangely sexless yet gendered embodiment of consumerism—they are recreated as market products themselves. Their posthuman bodies, even though seemingly alive, perfect and timeless, do not present the positive force of posthuman embodiment from the materialist feminist approach discussed by Ağın (this volume), because they lack the very force that gives matter meaning.

Unsuitable for the vast spaces of nature, these strange animated objects end up circling in the same enclosures—the kitchen, the house yard, and the shopping mall. The women's domestic labor, their handling of their own artificial bodies, and even their roles as mothers and wives are now reduced to their one true purpose—making daily consumer decisions. When we see Joanna and Bobbie meeting for the first time, they interact energetically in the tall grass of the community meadow, but in their last scene, they glide silently through the shopping aisle briefly exchanging platitudes. In the last scene, there is also a brief glimpse of the new arrivals, the first Black couple in Stepford, fighting in a shopping aisle. We hear the husband repeating the well-known "pitch" about the advantages of Stepford. We know there is no hope for the new woman in Stepford, as it is obvious that the husband has already joined the ranks of Stepford men. In Stepford, gender lines prevail over all the other divisions and all the women, regardless of race or status, will eventually end up circling through the same spaces. The end result is a cautionary tale about capitalism using patriarchal values to its own advantage. The manipulation of women runs parallel to the domination of their living spaces and the reduction of their environment is an instrument in annihilating the diversity of their human nature. The diversity of the environment and of human nature is replaced by an illusion and a semblance of diversity in the form of endless shelves brimming with products.

References

American Hiking Society. 2020. "Racism in the Outdoors Resources." Accessed September 2, 2020. https://americanhiking.org/hiking-resources/racism-in-the-outdoors/.

Anae, Nicole. 2021. "Ecofeminist Utopian Speculations in Henrietta Augusta Dugdale's *A Few Hours in a Far-off Age* (1883), Catherine Helen Spence's *A Week in the Future* (1888), Mary Anne Moore-Bentley's *A Woman of Mars; Or, Australia's Enfranchised Woman* (1901), and Joyce Vincent's *The Celestial Hand: A Sensational Story*." In *Dystopias and Utopias on Earth and Beyond: Feminist Ecocriticism of Science Fiction*, edited by Douglas A. Vakoch, 98–113. Abingdon, Oxon, UK and New York, NY: Routledge.

Boruzkowski, Lilly Ann. 1987. "The Stepford Wives. The Re-created Woman." *Jump Cut: A Review of Contemporary Media* 32: 16–19.

Čeh Steger, Jožica. 2015. *Ekokritika in literarne upodobitve narave (Ecocriticism and Literary Depictions of Nature)*. Maribor: Litera.

Collins Free Online Dictionary. 2020. "Definition of 'Stepford Wife'." Accessed April 30, 2020. https://www.collinsdictionary.com/dictionary/english/stepford-wife.

d'Eaubonne, Françoise. 1974. *Le Féminisme ou la Mort*. Paris: Pierre Horay.

de Fren, Allison. 2009. "Technofetishism and the Uncanny Desires of A.S.F.R. (alt .sex.fetish.robots)." *Science-Fiction Studies* 36: 404–440.

Figura, David. 2020. "Race in the Adirondacks: What's behind NY's Effort to Make the Region Welcoming to All." *Syracuse.com*, September 3, 2020, updated September 9, 2020. Accessed October 12, 2020. https://www.syracuse.com/outdoors/2020/09/race-in-the-adirondacks-whats-behind-nys-effort-to-make-the-region-welcoming-to-all.html.

Finney, Carolyn. 2014. *Black Faces, White Spaces*. Chapel Hill, NC: University of North Carolina Press.

Friedan, Betty. 1963. *The Feminine Mystique*. New York, NY: W. W. Norton.

Haraway, Donna J. 1991. "A Cyborg Manifesto: Science, Technology, and Socialist–Feminism in the Late Twentieth Century." In *Simians, Cyborgs and Women: The Reinvention of Nature*, edited by Donna J. Haraway, 149–181. New York, NY: Routledge.

Helford, Elyce Rae. 2006. "The Stepford Wives and the Gaze: Envisioning Feminism in 1975." *Feminist Media Studies* 6, no. 2: 145–156.

Huang, Peter I-min. 2018. "Cyborg Goddesses, Linda Hogan's Indios, and Jade Chen's Mazu's Body-guards." In *Literature and Ecofeminism: Intersectional and International Voices*, edited by Douglas A. Vakoch and Sam Mickey, 128–140. London and New York, NY: Routledge.

Johnson, Shelton. 2012. "Reclaiming the Wilderness." *Earth Island Journal*. Accessed August 28, 2020. https://www.earthisland.org/journal/index.php/magazine/entry/reclaiming_the_wilderness/.

Johnston, Jessica, and Cornelia Sears. 2011. "The Stepford Wives and the Technoscientific Imagery." *Extrapolation* 52, no. 1: 75–93.

Kang, Minsoo. 2005. "Building the Sex Machine: The Subversive Potential of the Female Robot." *Intertexts* 9, no. 1: 5–22.

King, Ynestra. 2003. "The Ecology of Feminism and the Feminism of Ecology." In *Worldviews, Religion and the Environment: A Global Anthology*, edited by Richard C. Foltz, 457–464. Belmont, CA: Wadsworth Publishing.

Lakoff, Robin. 2004. *Language and Woman's Place*. Edited by Mary Bucholtz. Oxford: Oxford University Press.

Larbalestier, Justine. 2006. "Introduction." In *Daughters of Earth*: *Feminist Science Fiction in the Twentieth Century*, edited by Justine Larbalestier, xv–xix. Middletown, CT: Wesleyan University Press.

Levin, Ira. 1972. *The Stepford Wives*. New York, NY: Random House.

Maio, Kathi. 2004. "The Town Hollywood Couldn't Forget." *Fantasy & Science Fiction*, 115–120.

Palahniuk, Chuck. 2011. "Revisionist Herstory: Everywhere is Stepford." Introduction to *The Stepford Wives*, by Ira Levin. London: Corsair.

Pohl, Sarah L., William T. Borrie, and Michael E. Patterson. 2000. "Women, Wilderness, and Everyday Life: A Documentation of the Connection between Wilderness, Recreation and Women's Everyday Lives." *Journal of Leisure Research* 32, no. 4: 415–434.

Pummill, Tricia. 2015. "The Stepford Wives: a Jewish American Novel." *Western Tributaries* 2. Accessed October 12, 2020. https://www.reed.edu/gls/Tricia.Pummill.pdf.

Ralph, Iris. 2021. "Ecofeminist Climate Fiction: Merlinda Bobis's *Locust Girl*." In *Dystopias and Utopias on Earth and Beyond: Feminist Ecocriticism of Science Fiction*, edited by Douglas A. Vakoch, 67–79. Abingdon, Oxon, UK and New York, NY: Routledge.

Robey, Tim. 2017. "Get Out's Paranoid Godfather: Why *Stepford Wives*' Author Ira Levin Still Gives Us Nightmares." *The Telegraph*, March 18. Accessed October 12, 2020. https://www.telegraph.co.uk/films/0/get-outs-paranoid-godfather-stepford-wives-author-ira-levin/.

Sandilands, Catriona. 1999. *The Good-Natured Feminist: Ecofeminism and the Quest for Democracy*. Minneapolis, MN: University of Minnesota Press.

Silver, Anna Krugovoy. 2002. "The Cyborg Mystique: *The Stepford Wives* and Second Wave Feminism." *Women's Studies Quarterl* 30, no.1/2: 60–76.

Stevenson, Melissa Colleen. 2007. "Trying to Plug In: Posthuman Cyborgs and the Search for Connection." *Science Fiction Studies* 34, no. 1: 87–105.

Tannen, Deborah. 1991. *You Just Don't Understand: Men and Women in Conversation*. London: Virago Press.

Telotte, J. P. 1983. "Human Artifice and the Science Fiction Film." *Film Quarterly* 36, no. 3: 44–51.

Tidwell, Christy. 2021. "'The Revolt of the Mother': Romanticizing Nature and Rejecting Science in Sally Miller Gearhart's The Wanderground and Other Feminist Utopias." In *Dystopias and Utopias on Earth and Beyond: Feminist Ecocriticism of Science Fiction*, edited by Douglas A. Vakoch, 150–162. Abingdon, Oxon, UK and New York, NY: Routledge.

Vakoch, Douglas A. 2012. "Introduction: A Different Story." In *Feminist Ecocriticism. Environment, Women, and Literature*, edited by Douglas A. Vakoch, 11–13. Lanham, MD: Lexington Books.

Žižek, Slavoj. 2018. "Do Sexbots Have Rights?" *RT*, April 20. Accessed April 22, 2020. https://www.rt.com/op-ed/424709-sexbots-sex-dolls-rights/.

Part 2
Queer Ecologies

5 Anthropocentric and Androcentric Ideologies in Jeanette Winterson's *The Stone Gods*

An Ecofeminist Reading

Aslı Değirmenci Altın

Ecofeminist theory emerges from the premise of parallels between the oppression of nature and women, and as such borrows from both feminist and ecocritical studies in its undertaking of exposing any form of subjugation, alienation, or otherization of both humans and non-humans on the planet. As Greta Gaard explains, this is because "the ideology which authorizes oppressions such as those based on race, class, gender, sexuality, physical abilities, and species is the same ideology which sanctions the oppression of nature" (1993, 1). The awareness of the nature/culture dualism of Western civilization also proves influential in understanding and implementing an ecofeminist worldview. Drawing from other critical works, Val Plumwood succinctly explains that "women in Western culture have been historically associated with the 'lower' order of nature and materiality, and men with the contrasting 'higher' order of mind, reason, and culture" (1998, 214). This ingrained patriarchal view, then, serves to justify the control and oppression of both women and nature. A significant component of ecofeminist criticism is to lay bare these connections, especially in literature and culture. As Irene Sanz Alonso suggests literary fiction in general, and science fiction in particular, provide fertile ground to offer a critique of social systems we are surrounded with as it gives the reader the chance to experience the dystopic futures that will most likely be true if everything stays the same as well as the alternative ways that could be employed (Sanz Alonso 2021). Similarly, Deininger and Scammell (2021) reiterate the importance of science fiction as a form of environmental literature in its ability to make room for women writers not only to imagine new worlds but also to instigate change.

Jeanette Winterson's *The Stone Gods* (2007) presents us with a dystopian future in which the dominant ideology that is intent on subjugating—and in the process destroying—both nature and women seems to succeed at it. In four parts of the novel, three first-person narrators, all playfully named Billie/Billy Crusoe, and all occupying different temporal and spatial positions, tell their respective stories of "a repeating world—same old story" (2007, 49). In the first and longest part of the novel, titled "Planet Blue," the narrator is Billie Crusoe, a lesbian scientist and dissident, who has to work for the government of Central Power on Orbus, a dying planet in which the highly advanced technology does not help the inevitable end. Her job, as the novel opens, is to advertise the new planet the Central Power found, Planet Blue, which strikingly resembles our own planet Earth. In this sense, Winterson actually depicts a distant past of humankind on a different planet surrounded with futuristic technology, a history of people who did the same mistakes we are doing now, and could not save their planet from total ruin. Winterson also explores the potential for a posthuman future in this part by imagining an interspecies love story between Billie and a conscious, evolving robot (a "robo sapiens") named Spike. The second chapter of the novel takes us to the eighteenth century, to Easter Island where an English sailor named Billie Crusoe watches fighting rival tribes on the island cut off the last standing tree to be in their gods' grace. In that sense, this short chapter serves as an interlude that shows the destructive potential of humankind at a micro-level. In the last two chapters, titled "Post-3 War" and "Wreck City," Winterson depicts a near-future London after a nuclear war, which renders all the government systems obsolete, enabling a global capitalistic company named MORE to fill in as government. In this space-time, Billie is a scientist working on the prototype of the first robo sapiens Spike, who at that point consists of just a head. When she takes Spike for a walk outside the limits of the city to what is called Wreck City, she encounters all kinds of outcasts refusing to live in the new world order, and furthermore witnesses the hidden remnants of the nuclear war: a dead radioactive forest, people with cancerous diseases and bodily deformations, sick children that are left behind. All these chapters give testament to humankind's apparently irremediable insistence on destroying our planet. That's why Ursula K. Le Guin (2007) suggests that *The Stone Gods* is "a vivid, cautionary tale—or, more precisely, a keen lament for our irremediably incautious species."

In the technologically advanced world of Orbus, there are no wild lands left anymore; traditional farming and agriculture are non-existent; the meat is produced in labs; and even the pets are robots. In the same way, the human body is modified in many ways by using biotechnology: people are genetically fixed at a certain age so they do not get old; excessive cosmetic surgery is the norm; children are now born "womb-free." Just like the unnatural and highly technological environment, the human body is also presented as extremely artificial, and the pressure is felt even more on the female body. The parallels between the women and nature in the novel become most apparent in the sense that the dominant patriarchal ideology that has already abused and completely destroyed nature is about to give up on women as well. Yet, women are not the only ones suffering from this totalitarian hierarchy hiding under the disguise of technology and a thin veil of democracy. Winterson depicts other groups that are also oppressed:

racial others in the form of abused children from the Eastern Caliphate, and non-human/machine others in the form of Spike, the robo sapiens who was a part of the discovery mission to Planet Blue. With Spike as an evolving intelligent robot in female form, Winterson also questions the concept of humanness and the possibility of a world without humans, thus providing a truly posthuman critique as well. This chapter argues that *The Stone Gods* emphasizes the importance of ecological and feminist undertakings by showing how depressing the future can be for nature, women, and other minorities oppressed under the dominant ideology. The analysis of the novel is limited mostly to the first and longest chapter of the novel, to the dystopian future of Orbus, and provide an examination of the anthropocentric, androcentric, and ethnocentric ideologies dominant in the society while positing two protagonists Billie and Spike as the posthuman, queer, and anti-anthropocentric subjects that challenge the dominant and normative ideologies.

Winterson's critique of how citizens of Orbus were able to completely destroy their planet is inseparable from the dominant anthropocentric ideology presented through many characters and the portrayals of media in the novel. Anthropocentrism can be simply described as the thought that "nothing has greater value than human beings, and that everything else can legitimately be bent to the service, use or interest of humanity" and it also places "humankind at the pinnacle of value in the world, and to privilege human existence over other kinds" (Grayling 2010, 27). The robo sapiens Spike, who predicts that Orbus has about 50 years left, tragically but quite rightfully suggests that "There are many kinds of life...Humans always assumed that theirs was the only kind that mattered. That's how you destroyed your planet" (Winterson 2007, 65–66). However, not everyone is of the same idea. In fact, the denial of humankind's culpability for the planet's death accompanies the anthropocentric ideology in the novel. When Billie's boss Manfred, the ultimate mouthpiece of the Central Power, states in a politically correct way that "Orbus is evolving in a way that is hostile to human life," Billie is quick to retaliate: "OK, so it's the planet's fault. We didn't do anything, did we? Just fucked it to death and kicked it when it wouldn't get up" (2007, 7). Winterson positions Billie as the counter-argument to the dominant androcentric and anthropocentric ideologies of Central Power.

Since it is too late to bring back Orbus from total destruction, the real question becomes whether human beings will repeat the same mistakes on Planet Blue. The first few pages of the novel carry a celebratory feeling as the new planet is introduced to the public. Billie, looking at the images of this new planet is hopeful at first: "This is a great day for science. The last hundred years have been hell. The doomsters and the environmentalists kept telling us we were as good as dead and, hey presto, not only do we find a new planet, but it is perfect for new life. This time, we'll be more careful. This time we will learn from our mistakes" (2007, 6). However, Winterson is quick to remind us that this is not quite the case, and the same bleak results will most probably await them on the new planet. Apart from its viability for human life, one of the first things revealed about the new planet is that it has very large dinosaur-like animals. The President of Central Power assures his citizens that "monsters will be *humanely* destroyed with the possible exception of scientific capture of one or two types for the Zooeum" (2007, 5, emphasis added). Thus, even before they relocate to the new planet, the citizens of Central Power feel entitled enough to change the whole ecosystem of a planet. At the end of this first part of the novel, a space privateer named Captain Handsome who is sanctioned by the Central Power makes an asteroid hit Planet Blue to create a dust storm to kill dinosaurs, but he miscalculates and instead starts a mini ice age, making immediate relocation to Planet Blue impossible. Thus, the incredible chance given to the people of Orbus to make a new start is crushed by the ingrained anthropocentric idea that human beings can colonize and use nature as they see fit. In this particular example, the anthropocentric view is carried even further, into deep space, altering the course of asteroids, creating human-made collisions of planets, reshaping cosmic bodies so that humankind can go on living.

This reshaping, remodeling of nature (and even cosmos), as a direct result of anthropocentric worldview, is also observed in the gendered practice of genetic fixing and major cosmetic surgeries, which reveals the androcentric ideology on Orbus. In a world where age is considered as "information failure," the norm is to get fixed at a certain age so everyone does it (2007, 9). However, Billie, who is later revealed to be not genetically fixed for political reasons, is uncertain about some implications of this high technology: "Science can't fix everything, though – women feel they have to look youthful, men less so, and the lifestyle programmes are full of the appeal of the older man" (2007, 9). We learn that most men prefer getting fixed before their forties whereas "there are no women who Fix past thirty" (2007, 9). Even in this seemingly innocuous use of technology, the inequalities emerge in a way that puts more pressure on the female body. This idealized youthfulness and obsession with beauty also create unprecedented problems:

> we're all perverts now. By that I mean that making everyone young and beautiful also made us all bored to death with sex. All men are hung like whales. All women are tight as clams below and inflated like lifebuoys above. Jaws are square, skin is tanned, muscles are toned, and no one gets turned on. It's a global crisis...
>
> So, sexy sex is now about freaks and children. If you want to work in the sex industry, you get yourself cosmetically altered in shape and size. Giantesses are back in business. Grotesques earn good money. Kids under ten are known as veal in the trade.
>
> (2007, 19)

In these normalized uses of biotechnology to alter bodies, the dominant mainstream ideology at first leads people toward the same standard of beauty developed by the male gaze, then creates differentialized bodies that are sexually objectified. Reading these biotechnologically altered bodies as "posthuman," Yazgünoğlu (2016, 144) suggests that Winterson presents us with the "dehumanization of the human in the process of posthumanization."

Mrs. Mary McMurphy, or "Pink," whom Billie has to visit for her job, exemplifies the extent of this internalized male gaze in women. A 58-year-old woman genetically fixed at 24, Pink wants to undergo a new, illegal, and possibly very dangerous operation called "genetic reversal" to return to childhood so she can continue to attract her now-pedophile husband. Dolezal reads Pink as "a parody of normalized femininity" as she is completely conforming to the patriarchal wishes of her society and her husband (2015, 99). She tells Billie that she wants to be like Little Senorita, "twelve-year-old pop star who has Fixed her-self rather than lose her fame" (Winterson 2007, 16). Apparently, Pink's husband is "mad about Little Senorita" and rejects having sex with Pink on the basis that she is too old (16). "I love my husband and I want his attention. I'll never get it aged twenty-four," Pink says (2007, 58). The heterosexual male gaze is so internalized in Pink that she is willing to risk her life for a chance to continue being the object of that gaze. As Dolezal suggests the purpose of these biotechnological surgeries is "to fulfill the sexual fantasies of mainstream male heterosexual desire," and in the process, make women more suppressed: "Biotechnologies do in fact often reproduce and reinforce negative heterosexual patriarchal dynamics, where women are figured as passive, receptive, and dominated, while men are active, self-determining, and productive" (Dolezal 2015, 99–100).

Mainstream male heterosexual desire inscribes its wishes and dominance not only on female humans but also on machine subjects as seen in the example of Spike. Billie is surprised when Spike explains the reason why she was made in an "absurdly beautiful" female form: "they thought I would be good for the boys on the mission" (Winterson 2007, 28). Although interspecies sex is illegal and punishable by death in Orbus, it is not in space, and Spike is used for the sexual gratification of male astronauts on the mission; she explains she used up "three silicon-lined vaginas" during the mission (2007, 28). Billie is extremely surprised and incredulous as she reminds Spike that she was "the most advanced of the crew" to which Spike answers "I'm still a woman" (2007, 28). Winterson's critique of androcentric and anthropocentric ideologies converges in this instance of subjugating Spike as both the female and the non-human Other to the male and human-centered "master."

Winterson's critique of anthropocentric ideology present on Orbus is mainly focused on the Central Power, a government body quite similar to the Western or Euro-American world in terms of their technological advancement and capitalistic system. Apart from their anthropocentrism, the ethnocentric and colonizing tendencies of the Central Power are likewise criticized though there are not many references to the rest of the world which mainly consists of two other governmental bodies: The Eastern Caliphate and The Sino-Mosco Pact. Billie states that these countries will not have a place on the new planet:

> The way the thinking is going in private, we'll leave this run-down rotting planet to the Caliphate and the SinoMosco Pact, and they can bomb each other to paste while the peace-loving folks of the Central Power ship civilization to the new world.
>
> (2007, 7)

Thus, the accepted hierarchy between nature and human, privileging human life over the survival of the others on the planet, emerges also in the form of privileging some human beings over others based on their race, ethnicity, or nationality. This becomes even more manifest when it is revealed that children used in sex industry in Central Power are from the Eastern Caliphate. When Billie is in a perverts' bar, she sees a man "heading for the Jacuzzi with a ten-year-old boy on his shoulders and a ten-year-old girl in his arms," and further informs us that "Both of them are Caliphate kids. We buy them. We wouldn't do it to kids born in the Central Power because (a) it's illegal and (b) we're civilized" (2007, 19). Though Billie's sarcasm in this sentence is palpable, it is also obvious that what she says is the common and accepted discourse of her society. Brandão and Cavalcanti (2021), in their discussion of Margaret Atwood's *Oryx and Crake*, brings up the similar issue of pedophilia and child prostitution in the example of Oryx, who is of Asian origin, sold by her mother at an early age, starts making porno movies at the age of eight, and grows up to be a prostitute. Brandão and Cavalcanti read Oryx's body as an ecodystopic body, and as such an expressive text that shows the extent of sexual exploitation of women and children in patriarchal environments. The fact that future dystopias imagined by other women writers also depict children as sexual objects and pedophilia as normalized should come as a warning for the high probability of this kind of horrid practices. On her way out of the bar, the bouncer reveals to Billie that he is "getting [a wife] from the Eastern Caliphate—it'll be legal, believe me, but she's nine years old and I'm gonna Fix her" (Winterson 2007, 21). For the civilized man, the master, it is quite customary to objectify children this way as sex slaves and also justify this slavery on the basis of their ethnicity.

One implication of all these sexual politics on Orbus is also the fact that women can be rendered obsolete. Billie is particularly pessimistic about the future:

> The future of women is uncertain. We don't breed in the womb any more, and if we aren't wanted for sex ... But there will always be men. Women haven't gone for little boys. Women have a different approach. Surrounded by hunks, they look for 'the ugly man inside'. Thugs and gangsters, rapists and wife-beaters are making a comeback.
>
> (2007, 22)

Billie cannot complete her sentence when she considers this possibility of what might happen to women if the patriarchal society does not need them anymore. This fear of Billie is not uncalled for. Val Plumwood (1997, 337) explains that within the "centric structure" of androcentrism, the masculine is seen as the center and the feminine as the other. She further suggests that the female other's agency is included in the male partner traditionally, and thus she is regarded as passive. This results in the fact that "she is valued as a means to ends rather than accorded value in her own right, deriving her social worth instrumentally from service to others, as the producer of sons, etc." (1997, 338). Plumwood categorizes certain features between anthropocentrism and androcentrism, and in the category "instrumentalism" she explores how each of these centric structures uses nature and women respectively. Winterson, in a similar way, draws strong parallels between what anthropocentric ideology did to nature on Orbus and what androcentric ideology is doing and might do to women in the same manner.

Through this association between women and their potential to "serve" to the patriarchal society emerges a questioning of technology since even the most utopian-sounding technologies, as seen, are used to subjugate women. Plemenitaš (this volume), for instance, in her discussion of *The Stepford Wives*, shows how dangerous technology can be both for women and nature at the hands of dominant patriarchal ideology that can go as far as killing and replacing suburban wives with their artificial robotic replicas. Hope Jennings (2010) analyzes Winterson's position on technology by drawing from Carol Stabile's article "Feminism and The Technological Fix" in which Stabile (1997, 509) suggests that

> Given the fact that technology has more often than not been utilized to oppress those who do not possess it, or cannot engage with it, these feminists have tended to be more generally critical of technoscience, while at the same time aware of its liberatory potential.

Jennings (2010, 138) reflects that this is exactly what Winterson does:

> *The Stone Gods* employs these tactics in order to resist oversimplifying the dangers and promises of science, using technology at the level of parody in order to demonstrate how our fantasized utopias concerning the benefits of science often lead to dystopian futures or worlds.

Yet, it can be noted that, although Winterson criticizes the way some technologies are used in Orbus as a cautionary tale, she does not implement a technophobia in the novel, which becomes most obvious in her imagination of Spike as a robo sapiens.

With Spike, Winterson creates a different posthuman machine than those typically conceived in science fiction cyborg stories which "dramatize our fears as we become targets in the world of cyborg weapons, while anticipating the demise of the flesh-and-blood body and the gradual extinction of humanity" (Dinello 2005, 12). In Winterson's narrative, "the gradual extinction of humanity" is imagined as a possible reality yet it is clear the reason will not be any attack from cyborgs. In fact, Winterson also draws attention to the lack of this common science fiction element in this novel. When Spike criticizes humanity for their destructive ways on the planet, Pink and Billie start questioning the difference of Spike from humans, and the following conversation ensues:

> 'I never heard of an activist robot,' said Pink.
> 'It's just one more thing we're going to have to be on your behalf,' said Spike.
> 'What are you going to do?' I said. 'Overthrow us?'
> Spike laughed. 'Revenge of the Robots? No, but you see, Robo sapiens is evolving—Homo sapiens is an endangered species. It doesn't feel like it to you now but you have destroyed your planet, and it is not clear to me that you will be viable on Planet Blue.'
>
> (2007, 65)

Spike cleverly suggests that there is no need for a violent "overthrow" when the human species takes care of exterminating themselves. Spike is not homogenized into a group of machines that look the same and just take orders. With her ability to evolve as a robo sapiens, and despite the subjugation she suffers, Spike becomes a subject in the novel rather than an object. Oppermann (2013, 32) suggests that with Spike, Winterson is able to challenge the boundaries of human/machine and nature/culture, and thus creates "a posthuman subject as an 'embodied' consciousness."

At the end of the first part of the novel that focuses on Orbus, Billie and Spike fall in love with each other, which opens up the possibility of a posthuman and queer future. Both Billie and Spike transgress their assumed identities, which enables us to view them both as posthuman and queer. In all three spatial and temporal locations Winterson depicts in the novel, she narrates the stories of three queer pairs: in Orbus, Billie falls in love with Spike; in the eighteenth century in Easter Island, Captain Cook's left-behind sailor Billy falls in love with Spikkers, a native of the island whose father was a Dutch sailor; and again, in the very last part of the novel, in post-nuclear war London, a different Billie is forming a relationship with another Spike, the first robo sapiens she is responsible for programming. However, it is not solely the sexuality of these lesbian and gay characters that render these relationships queer. As a matter of fact, in the dystopian future Winterson imagines in Orbus, the same-sex relationships are quite normalized, which is most clearly seen in the homonormativity of Billie's boss Manfred, who is gay, quite conformist, and the representative of the capitalist, anthropocentric, racist and sexist system of the Central Power. So, these three couples, but most importantly Billie and Spike in the first part of the novel, are queer in the sense that Halberstam (2005, 6) defines the term as "nonnormative logics and organizations of community, sexual identity, embodiment, and activity in space and time." In Central Power where almost any sexual act and any way to attain sexual gratification is normalized, interspecies sex between a human and a robot or cyborg remains the only prohibited sexual act. So even by making love to each other, Billie and Spike defy the accepted notions of normalized sexuality, break the law, and enter the realm of "non-normative," and thus become queer.

Apart from the liberating implications of this interspecies relationship, it is significant that these two characters posit a counter-argument to the anthropocentric ideology of Orbus. Spike, as a cyborg that is able to evolve, feels emotions for the first time when she is recounted a love poem. The fact that she is able to react to a poem while literature is rendered obsolete in Orbus posits her as a subject that defies the limitations put on her by the androcentric and anthropocentric ideology. Spike wants to feel, fall in love, and thus she actively chooses Billie, and starts their relationship. Billie, on the other hand, as the narrator and female protagonist of the novel, questions all forms of oppression she encounters. As she confesses to her boss Manfred before she escapes from Orbus, she doesn't "believe in the system" as it is "repressive, corrosive and anti-democratic" (Winterson 2007, 45). Although at the beginning of the novel she seems to conform to this lifestyle albeit criticizing it, as the novel proceeds we learn that Billie lives on a now-obsolete farm that is leased to Living Museum; she actually has a real dog and not a robotic pet as many do; she is not genetically fixed for "political" reasons, and most importantly she helped other dissident activists place a bomb at the headquarters MORE-Futures, the capitalistic corporation closely connected to the government. The fact that Winterson depicts Billie as an active agent against capitalist and patriarchal institutions is particularly important in order not to overemphasize her evident connection to nature and non-human animals, and thus inadvertently suggest that there is an innate affinity in women toward nature. Billie is aware of humankind's interdependency with the planet and critical of the dominant ideology that brings forth most of the problems on the planet. Thus, Billie's dissidence carries her queerness beyond the sexual act and helps define her.

Yet, despite all these critical views and non-conforming life choices, remnants of speciesism also surface in Billie in her prejudiced treatment of Spike as she questions her humanity. When Spike attempts at kissing Billie for the first time, she surprisingly blurts out "You're a robot" which she realizes sounds more like Pink McMurphy than herself (2007, 63). Billie, at first, is reluctant to give in to her physical attraction toward Spike, and questions Spike's motives:

'Do you want to kiss a woman so that you can add it to your database?'
'Gender is a human concept,' said Spike, 'and not interesting. I want to kiss you.' She kissed me again.

'In any case,' she said, very close, very warm, and I am responding, and I don't want to, and I can't help it, 'is human life biology or consciousness? If I were to lop off your arms, your legs, your ears, your nose, put out your eyes, roll up your tongue, would you still be you? You locate yourself in consciousness, and I, too, am a conscious being.'

(2007, 63)

In this conversation and in others that questions "the essential quality of humanness," Spike deconstructs the idea of the superiority of humans (2007, 63). It is also important that Billie, too, overcomes her ingrained human/machine dualism and falls in love with Spike. In outlining her theory of "posthuman feminism," Rosi Braidotti (2017, 21) suggests firstly that "feminism is not a humanism." Defining the ideal "Man" of humanism, she states that "the dominant subject is implicitly assumed to be masculine, white, urbanized, speaking a standard language, heterosexually inscribed in a reproductive unit, and a full citizen of a recognized polity" (Braidotti 2017, 23). What Winterson imagines with Spike as a non-human/machine other and Billie as a non-conformist, anti-anthropocentric, and queer subject defies all these qualities of the "male dominant subject," and as such, both Spike and Billie emerge as truly posthuman subjects.

Although Billie is at first attracted to Spike because of her physical beauty in a female form, it is Spike's difference and her consciousness that makes Billie fall in love with her. Billie describes Spike as "unknown, uncharted, different in every way from me, another life-form, another planet, another chance" (Winterson 2007, 88). Billie not only challenges the norms of her society by being able to see beyond the physical appearance that every normative person fixates on in Central Power, but also by describing Spike "as another planet, another chance," she draws a parallel between Spike and Planet Blue. This similarity is also evident in the choice of gendered pronoun to refer to Spike and Planet Blue; although both entities are genderless, the pronoun used for them is "she." This equation of the planet and the non-human machine other as females resonates with the ecofeminist theories that suggest women and nature are subjugated by the same forces. Similarly, Martín-Junquera (this volume) draws our attention to the fact that the androids, working-class technicians, and nature are all oppressed in the same manner by the patriarchal dominant power in the television series *Westworld* while emphasizing the necessity of ecofeminist ideologies to break the hierarchy between humans and non-human androids. In the case of Spike and Planet Blue, they are both represented as chances not to repeat the anthropocentric and androcentric ideologies that have misused both nature and the female subjects in Orbus. Just as Billie accepts an anti-anthropocentric outlook and embraces her love for Spike, humans will have to let go of their speciesism and anthropocentrism if they want to continue their existence on this new planet.

When things go wrong on Planet Blue, Billie chooses to stay with Spike instead of traveling with the rest of the group to the relatively safer colony.

This part of the novel ends with the triggered ice-age making it too cold for Spike and Billie to continue walking on Planet Blue, so they shelter in a cave, where they spend their remaining time together. Spike, dying due to lack of sunshine, slowly takes out body parts to conserve energy until she is reduced to a head, thus to consciousness, to mind. In that last moment, Winterson posits love as the possible remedy we need. "Love is an intervention" Billie muses to herself, and Spike describes love as "the chance to be human" (Winterson 2007, 68, 90). And perhaps, their kind of love, without being limited to and by any centrism is the way forward. The fact that Winterson ends this first part of the novel with Billie's acceptance of Spike as a lover, a partner, someone to die with, regardless of Spike's gender or existence as a non-human other, indicates and advocates a posthuman and queer future for our planet. Sarah Bezan (this volume), in her discussion of Larissa Lai's *Salt Fish Girl*, also takes up the issue of interspecies human-cyborg sex which she calls "speculative sex" and posits it as a challenge to the futuristic advanced capitalism and its use of biotechnology to oppress racial, sexual, and nonhuman others to create sameness. Similarly, Debra Wain suggests that the implication of posthuman hybrids gaining acceptance at the end of Margaret Atwood's *MaddAddam Trilogy* offers a possible posthuman future for our planet (Wain 2021).

In *The Stone Gods*, Winterson creates a futuristic dystopian world that frighteningly resembles our world in its dominant ideologies of anthropocentricism and androcentricism and their practices. If we are to accept Ursula K. Le Guin's (1979, 156) statement that "science fiction is not predictive" but rather "descriptive," the warnings in the novel becomes even more pressing. Stacy Alaimo (2017, 90) suggests that "Feminist theory, especially material feminisms and posthumanist feminisms, offer cautionary tales, counterpoints, and alternative figurations for thinking the Anthropocene subject in immersive onto-epistemologies." That is what Winterson does with a critique of anthropocentric, androcentric, and ethnocentric ideologies present in Orbus as well as our world, and also rendering two main characters, Billie and Spike, as posthuman, queer, and anti-anthropocentric subjects that go beyond real and imagined boundaries of oppressive ideologies.

References

Alaimo, Stacy. 2017. "Your Shell on Acid: Material Immersion, Anthropocene Dissolves." In *Anthropocene Feminism*, edited by Richard Grusin, 89–120. Minneapolis, MN: University of Minnesota Press.

Braidotti, Rosi. 2017. "Four Theses on Posthuman Feminism." In *Anthropocene Feminism*, edited by Richard Grusin, 21–48. Minneapolis, MN: University of Minnesota Press.

Brandão, Izabel F. O., and Ildney Cavalcanti. 2021. "Margaret Atwood's Ecodystopic SF: Approaching Ethics, Gender, and Ecology." In *Dystopias and Utopias on Earth and Beyond: Feminist Ecocriticism of Science Fiction*, edited by Douglas A. Vakoch, 37–49. Abingdon, Oxon, UK and New York, NY: Routledge.

Deininger, Michelle, and Gemma Scammell. 2021. "'Extinction is Forever': Ecofeminism and Apocalypse in Louise Lawrence's Young Adult Short Fiction." In *Dystopias and Utopias on Earth and Beyond: Feminist Ecocriticism of Science Fiction*, edited by Douglas A. Vakoch, 83–97. Abingdon, Oxon, UK and New York, NY: Routledge.

Dinello, Daniel. 2005. *Technophobia: Science Fiction Visions of Posthuman Technology*. Austin, TX: University of Texas Press.

Dolezal, Luna. 2015. "The Body, Gender, and Biotechnology in Jeanette Winterson's *The Stone Gods*." *Literature and Medicine* 33: 91–112.

Gaard, Greta. 1993. "Living Interconnections with Animals and Nature." In *Ecofeminism: Women, Animals, Nature*, edited by Greta Gaard, 1–12. Philadelphia, PA: Temple University Press.

Grayling, A. C. 2010. *Ideas That Matter: The Concepts That Shape the 21st Century*. New York, NY: Basic.

Halberstam, Judith. 2005. *In a Queer Time & Place: Transgender Bodies, Subcultural Lives*. New York, NY: New York University Press.

Jennings, Hope. 2010. "'A Repeating World': Redeeming the Past and Future in the Utopian Dystopia of Jeanette Winterson's The Stone Gods." *Interdisciplinary Humanities* 27, no. 2: 132–146.

Le Guin, Ursula K. 1979. *The Language of the Night: Essays on Fantasy and Science Fiction*. New York, NY: G. P. Putnam's Sons.

———. 2007. "Head Cases." *The Guardian*, September 22. Accessed August 15, 2020. https://www.theguardian.com/books/2007/sep/22/sciencefictionfantasyand horror.fiction.

Oppermann, Serpil. 2013. "Feminist Ecocriticism: A Posthumanist Direction in Ecocritical Trajectory." In *International Perspectives in Feminist Ecocriticism*, edited by Greta Gaard, Simon Estok, and Serpil Oppermann, 19–36. New York, NY: Routledge.

Plumwood, Val. 1997. "Androcentrism and Anthropocentrism: Parallels and Politics." In *Ecofeminism: Women, Culture, Nature*, edited by Karen J. Warren, 327–355. Bloomington, IN: Indiana University Press.

———. 1998. "The Environment." In *A Companion to Feminist Philosophy*, edited by Alison Jaggar and Iris Marion Young, 213–222. Oxford: Blackwell.

Sanz Alonso, Irene. 2021. "Alien Ecofeminist Societies: Sharers in Joan Slonczewski's *A Door into Ocean*." In *Dystopias and Utopias on Earth and Beyond: Feminist Ecocriticism of Science Fiction*, edited by Douglas A. Vakoch, 114–125. Abingdon, Oxon, UK and New York, NY: Routledge.

Stabile, Carol. 1997. "Feminism and the Technological Fix." In *Feminisms*, edited by Sandra Kemp and Judith Squires, 508–512. Oxford: Oxford University Press.

Wain, Debra. 2021. "An Ecofeminist Treatment of Nourishment and Feeding in Margaret Atwood's MaddAddam Trilogy." In *Dystopias and Utopias on Earth and Beyond: Feminist Ecocriticism of Science Fiction*, edited by Douglas A. Vakoch, 25–36. Abingdon, Oxon, UK and New York, NY: Routledge.

Winterson, Jeanette. 2007. *The Stone Gods*. Orlando, FL: Harcourt, Inc.

Yazgünoğlu, Kerim. 2016. "Posthuman 'Meta(l)morphoses' in Jeanette Winterson's *The Stone Gods*." *Ecozona* 7, no. 1: 144–160.

6   Speculative Sex

Queering Aqueous Natures and Biotechnological Futures in Larissa Lai's *Salt Fish Girl*

Sarah Bezan

New materialist and feminist approaches to embodiment in recent years have foregrounded the fluidity of past, present, and future ecological relationships. Astrida Neimanis's *Bodies of Water: Posthuman Feminist Phenomenology* (2017, 4) suggests, for instance, that "to figure ourselves as bodies of water not only rejects a human separation from Nature 'out there'; it also torques many of our accepted cartographies of space, time, and species, and implicates a specifically watery movement of difference and repetition." Drawing from French philosophy (Maurice Merleau-Ponty and Gilles Deleuze) and French feminist theory (Hélène Cixous and Luce Irigaray), Neimanis's work articulates how a posthumanist and feminist approach to aqueous natures might enable us to rethink spatial, temporal, and corporeal boundaries.

The speculative fiction of Larissa Lai's *Salt Fish Girl* (2002) is representative of such an approach to aqueous natures. As writing that Lai describes as "situated in time" and yet constructed "in the loosest and most fluid way possible," *Salt Fish Girl* reflects Lai's commitment to "break away from a unitary Western liberal subject" (Lai 2004, 22) and to address the Western logic of the nature/culture divide that guides our thinking about ecological destruction (Lai 2016, 30). Lai's novel engages with aqueous natures by queering origin myths and futures that figuratively connect the shared prehistoric origin and habitus of all organic life (that is, *water*) with "past and future bodies [that] swim through our own" (Neimanis 2017, 4). Utilizing a bifurcated narrative that conjoins the reincarnated Chinese creation goddess Nu Wa with a young woman named Miranda Ching, the novel, according to Serenity Joo, "intentionally challenges the concept of origins by interweaving myths of creation and reincarnation with stories of cloning and genetic modification as the means of reproducing humans" (2014, 47). Along with a shift from heteronormative biological reproduction to queer (pro)creativity, this strange interweaving of past and future narratives guides the process of Asian-Canadian and Asian-American subject formation, which is foundational, as scholar Paul Lai contends (2008, 184), to the novel's politics of "queer kinship."[1]

Elaborating further on existing scholarship of the novel's political significance, and focusing specifically on Lai's depiction of water and birthing as queer conventions of ecofeminist science fiction,[2] I contend that Lai's novel engages with ecological crises through representations of *speculative sex*—a term I use to interpret the wet and unwieldy practice of human-cyborg sex that inspires strange conceptions and oceanic (re)births. In its portrayal of past, present, and future aqueous natures, *Salt Fish Girl* emblematizes the fluidity and slipperiness of queer women's writing and also responds to the protracted future of environmental violence imagined in the novel's concluding pages. As such, this chapter considers how the biotechnocapitalist machine depicted in Lai's fiction (in which all-female human-hybrid clones are bioengineered and exploited for their labor) reflects an Anthropocenic future that contemporary feminist scholars have critiqued for its rigidly masculinist logics. Alternatively, I propose that the wet sexual politics of the novel counters this rigidity with a flexible and fluid ecofeminist political paradigm.

My critique of speculative sex in the novel takes Neimanis's theoretical examination of bodies of water as a focal point, elucidating how a shift from terrestriality to aqueous natures allows for an affirmative ecofeminist politics. For a volume such as this (which gathers approaches to ecofeminist science fiction), my contribution also showcases how the mythopoetic and futuristic conventions of the genre can be explored through the otherworldliness of water. Similar in approach to Iris Ralph's (2021) analysis of Merlinda Bobis's *Locust Girl* and Peter I-min Huang's critique of 4th-wave manifestations in science fiction (SF, this volume), my reading of Lai's novel critiques the logic of climate change that undergirds Euro-Western heterosexualities and also highlights the importance of hybridized identity categories as a strategy of political resistance to settler colonialism in the twenty-first century. I organize this analysis into two sections. The first section, "Speculative Sex and the Hydro-Logics of Space," focuses on the spatial coordinates of Dr. Rudy Flowers's laboratory, the Unregulated Zone, and the Zodiak Aquarium, illuminating how Miranda and her lover Evie's intersecting bloodlines, sexual encounters, and conceptions inside and outside of these spaces (and especially in water) enable us to trace movements of ecofeminist resistance. The second section, "Amniotic Corporealities: Lai's Posthuman Gestationality," examines evolutionary and biotechnological mythologies by close reading the birth of Miranda and Evie's baby through the conceptual lens of "posthuman gestationality" (Neimanis 2017). In this section, I examine how the novel's fishy labors reveal the creative potential of queer women's writing to respond to an uncertain future of biotechnological innovation and intervention. In keeping with Neimanis's assertion that bodies of water jumble our accepted cartographies of space, time, and species, this chapter demonstrates how the novel's queering of aqueous natures and biotechnological futures can be creatively configured in and through the slipperiness of sex.

Submersive Ecofeminism

Ecofeminist approaches, as outlined in Catriona Sandilands's genealogical overview of the field in *The Good-Natured Feminist* (1999), are to some degree oriented toward a consideration of aqueous natures. From Mary Daly's conception of *Gyn/ecology* (1978), which is attuned to the watery "labyrinthine inner ear" (188), to Donna Haraway's critique of biological essentialism, which advances a reading of the partiality and hybridity of subject positions under the rubric of the cyborg (1991), early ecofeminists strove to articulate the "nonsolidity of nature itself" (Sandilands 1999, 99). In their rejoinder to the rigidity of phallogocentrism, French feminist writers like Cixous and Irigaray made this fluidity even more explicit, advocating for a literary play on "ocean" [*mer*] and "mother" [*mère*] (Cixous 1994, 102). These approaches echo the work of the visionary conservationist Rachel Carson, who proclaims in the introduction to *The Sea Around Us* (1950, 3) that "beginnings are apt to be shadowy, and so it is with the beginnings of that great mother of life, the sea."

More contemporary engagements with this maternal trope are located in Anthropocenic discourse, but are often related in a less fluid mode, and in more pejorative terms. Utilizing the metaphor of childbirth, Jeremy Davies's *The Birth of the Anthropocene* (2016, 2) describes the "present environmental crisis" as evidence of "the birth pangs of a new epoch." While the ravaged mother-earth trope is familiar, this figurative construction reinforces a heteronormative logic that construes nature as a body subject to violation. The framing of this problem has been set: it has been well-established that the initial constitution of the scientific board responsible for coining the term "Anthropocene" was largely composed of male scientists (Schneiderman 2017, 170), and that several centuries of history in the West, from the industrial revolution to the present, carry a record of androcentric (and colonial) conquests that treated nature as the source for innumerable extractable resources. With this history in mind, we might instead read the maternal trope in this context as a concept in the service of a fixed cartographical and geological discourse that announces the advent of *geontopower*—described by Elizabeth Povinelli as a "malignant force on the meteorological, geological, and biological dimension of the earth" (2016, 21). Affirming Povinelli's view, Richard Grusin writes in the introduction to his edited collection, *Anthropocene Feminism* (2017),[3] that "scientists and engineers continue to rely on many of the same masculinist and human-centered solutions that have created the problems in the first place" (ix), and that ecofeminism (following the legacy of Vandana Shiva, Val Plumwood, and Greta Gaard) ought to advance an "ethos of disruption" (xi). Donna Haraway's *Staying With the Trouble: Making Kin in the Chthulucene*

(2016) is one such example of this ethos, offering a creative critique of the Chthulucene (contra Anthropocene) as a mode of engagement with multi-species feminisms and SF forms. Similarly, Stacy Alaimo's latest work in the emerging field of blue ecologies has taken aim at the "stark terrestrial figurations of man and rock in which other life-forms and biological processes are strangely absent" and in which the "acidifying seas, the liquid index of the Anthropocene, are disregarded" (2017, 89).

As a rebuttal to the rigid discourse of the Anthropocene, water in *Salt Fish Girl* can be seen as an originary element that erodes the "monolithically heterosexual" (Mortimer-Sandilands and Erickson 2010, 176) and predominantly geological conception of environmental futures, replacing it instead with a malleability of form that allows for a submersive (and subversive) ecofeminism. Unlike Anthropocene discourses that might conventionally define the present era as concrete, catastrophic, and geologically distinct, this kind of submersive ecofeminism is, in the mode of the French feminist *écriture féminine*, multi-labial, fluid, cross-pollinatory, mutant, variant, unstable, intersectional/interspecies, and (pro)creatively (re)productive. As I argue in the following section, Lai avails herself of this rhetorical fluidity in the novel's prescient response to the negative impacts of Anthropogenic change.

Speculative Sex and the Hydro-Logics of Space

If Lai's preceding novel, *When Fox is a Thousand* (1995), is written as a "literary geography" (Lai 2004, 23), then *Salt Fish Girl* is composed as a *literary hydrology* that meditates on space, reproductive cycles, and time(scales) beyond the human. Merging together the ecofeminist symbol of the mother-sea with the SF trope of otherworldliness, the novel presents water as a queer substance that links bloodlines and suffuses the flow of historical trauma, while also containing the (re)productive possibilities for future species. The novel's *hydro-logics of space* can therefore be defined as the watery spaces of (pro)creative sex that link bodies together across past, present, and future temporalities.

The hydro-logics of space extend from the novel's odorous scene of creation at the bank of the Yellow River to the cool and misty mountain pools of the Pacific Northwest. In the novel's opening pages, water is defined as the substance of creation: the narrator Nu Wa relates that "in the beginning there was me, the river and the rotten-egg smell. I don't know where the smell came from, dank and sulphurous, but there it was, the stink of beginnings and endings" (2). This aqueous beginning, and its attending stench, follow through multiple generations of bawling, black-haired baby girls (48, 269), including the Salt Fish Girl, born in South China in the late 1800s, and Miranda Ching, conceived sometime before 2044 in Serendipity when her post-menopausal mother miraculously comes into contact with the pepper-pissy juices of a durian fruit procured from the Unregulated Zone.[4]

Water, and the stench it carries, fill every nook and cranny of the book. Miranda's "unpleasant cat pee odour oozed...and flowed into every room. It swirled around the coffee table, glided smoothly over the couch and poured over the rug," swirling, coiling, gushing, leaching, infusing, and flooding every room with its permeating smell (15–16). This watery stench also becomes the primary marker for the "dreaming disease" that is believed to infect people. Bearing the ineluctable weight of the trauma of collective memories, sufferers are enticed to begin "their compulsive march into the rivers and oceans, unable to resist the water's pull" (71). In addition to this smell that moves like water, Miranda and her lover Evie Xin (a human-carp clone) bear the mark of a fistula—a "small hole that itches periodically and releases a thin stream of briny-smelling fluid when rubbed" (107) and which "serve[s] the function of memory, recalling a time when we were more closely related to fish, a time when the body glistened with scales and turned into the dark, muscled easily through water" (108). The final scene of the book, which is set in a mountain pool that smells "faintly of salt" (268), similarly treats the stench of bodies of water as a vehicle that transports characters into other temporal and spatial realms.

In *Salt Fish Girl*, the commingling of bloodlines overrides and re-encodes the trauma of colonial geographies, while the subsequent act of sex produces new shape-shifting forms for traversing the bounds of time and space. Colonial geographies can be read beneath the surface as the Island of Mist and Forgetfulness and the urban sprawl of Serendipity, often implicitly, and sometimes explicitly, reminding readers of past traumas: the Gold Rush in British Columbia (1858–1863), the treacherous expansion of the Canadian Pacific Railway (1881–1885), the racist and exclusionary Chinese Immigration Act of 1885, and the Japanese Canadian Internment of 1945, which left thousands of Japanese-Canadian immigrants dead or displaced (Chan 2017, n.p.). The allegorization of these colonial geographies and Asian diasporas reflects, according to Paul Lai, "a common trope of science fiction in the presentation of the island as an uncanny other world" (2008, 172), but also demonstrates how the world of science fiction functions as a referential corollary of our own (Landon 2002, xii). Employing these tools of science fiction, Lai gestures to Canada's hematic history through repeated references to blood in the chapters "The Island of Mist and Forgetfulness" and "A Song for Clara Cruise." These chapters, which connect Nu Wa's narrative with Miranda Ching's, treat blood as water: the ancestral substance of belonging that connects bodies across time and space.

Symbolizing a longing for a motherland and a mother tongue, the seeping wounds that Miranda and Evie endure—and inflict—transport them through time and space by overlapping their stories with the narrative of Nu Wa and the Salt Fish Girl. These chapters are significant because Miranda and Evie learn the origins of one another's bloodlines and begin to reclaim the bodily autonomy that had been breached by biotechnological processes of cloning and experimentation. In the chapter, "The Island of Mist and Forgetfulness," the reincarnated Nu Wa has betrayed the Salt Fish Girl by running away with Edwina, who she later kills with a fish-gutting knife, spilling blood "like water" (146). Just as the trope of reincarnation leads to the repetition of bloodlines, this scene with Nu Wa in the 1800s similarly spills over into subsequent pages with Miranda in 2062. Here we discover that Miranda is interrupted in the process of taking blood from Evie at the private clinic of Dr. Rudy Flowers (who is the mastermind of the cloning scheme and the physician treating patients who suffer from the "dreaming disease"). While later reunited with Evie, Miranda is for a time held at Dr. Flowers's laboratory to undergo invasive experimentation, where she is frequently described as bleeding or bloody: her fistula is "crusted with dried blood" (147), and her nose spurts with blood following her escape from Dr. Flowers in response to a mist of tear gas (148–150). When Evie and Miranda come together again (both away from Dr. Flowers's clinic), Evie retrieves the thin vial of blood that Miranda had partially extracted, explaining that she is "point three percent *Cyprinus carpio* freshwater carp" (158), which has been supposedly sourced from the bloodline of "a woman named Ai, a Chinese woman who married a Japanese man and was interred during the Second World War" (160). In this critical scene, "blood as water" informs the novel's hydro-logics of space: through its bisected narrative, the blood from Nu Wa and the Salt Fish Girl is drawn together with the blood of Miranda and Evie in a circular loop. Like the tide, their bloodlines jointly refer back to Canada's colonial legacy of bloodshed and to the trauma of Flowers's biotechnological regime.

The fluidity of bloodlines in these overlapping chapters reveal Lai's repeated return to aqueous natures, but the novel's (pro)creative potential for political action becomes fully realized through Miranda and Evie's sexual encounters, which take place outside of the sterile spaces of the laboratory and enclosed partitions of the Zodiak Aquarium (the site of Evie's "birth"). It is no surprise that Miranda and Evie escape from spaces that seem to ominously capture the ravaged mother-earth trope. Housed in an abandoned hotel in the Unregulated Zone after a catastrophic flood in 2017, Flowers's laboratory is surrounded by ocean water with a wall of sturdy Plexiglass that keeps the ocean

> pressed, full and furious at being shut out of this territory, which clearly belonged, by natural rights, to it and not to us...It slammed things against it—seaweed, old bottles, frayed rope, scrap metal, swaying schools of fish—whatever it could conjure up from its polluted floor.
>
> (112)

It is in this space of confinement that Dr. Flowers administers his biotechnological program, known as the Diverse Genome Project, which is responsible for bioengineering an all-female labor force out of racial minorities, Indigenous peoples, and groups facing extinction. Flowers's attempt to control nature and ferry it into contained spaces and discrete ontological categories is echoed in the logical structure of the Aquarium as well, which contains brightly colored fish in the tanks: an octopus with undulating tentacles, a lungfish the length of a human body. The parallels between Evie's own body and the shimmering lungfish are presented alongside the sterile tables of the laboratory, upon which sit vials of fertilized and unfertilized eggs. Yet the fecundity of the scene strikes Miranda as unsettling: "all these tidy attempts to control the mud and muck of origins upset me" (268).

While the laboratory and aquarium are voyeuristic spaces of bodily confinement and invasion (complete with their own "logics" of scientific knowledge), the queer hydro-logics of the Unregulated Zone return Miranda and Evie to their aqueous origins. These sexual encounters are infused with watery metaphors: their coupling at the subdivision of a group of escaped Sonia cat-clones, for instance, is described as a heavenly stew, in which "steam rose" from their bodies "like water splashed on a hot pan of garlic greens" (225). In the mountains, their sexual encounter is construed through a "stream" of consciousness narration:

> The fishiness of her drew me, but I tried not to think about the strangeness of her conception. Her fingers moved over my skin, cool and tingly as ice water. I wanted to turn into water myself, fall into her the way rain falls into the ocean. I moved through the cool dark with her, my body a single silver muscle slipping against hers, flailing for oxygen in a fast underwater current, shivering slippery cool wet and tumbling through dark towards a blue point of light in the distance, teeth, lip, nipple, the steel taste of blood, gills gaping open and closed, open and closed, mouth, breath, cool water running suddenly piss hot against velvet inner thighs and the quick shudder silver flash of fish turning above the ice-blue surface of the lake.
>
> (161)

Through a play on the fish's own occasionally indeterminate gender (termed by biologists as biological hermaphroditism) and its non-normative sexual and reproductive practices, Lai reconstructs the movements of a body breathing underwater, muscling through a stream, melding together flesh. Juxtaposed with the linear and prescriptive logic of Flowers's cloning regime, this stream of consciousness account of inter-species copulation utilizes the unstable figure of the cyborg to challenge the dark forces of biotechnology, illustrating Haraway's insistence that "cyborg politics is the struggle for language and the struggle against perfect communication, against the one code that translates all meaning perfectly, the central dogma of phallogocentrism" (1991, 176). As a result of these fishy-human couplings, Evie and Miranda create mutant multiplicities and fluid variations of resistance to the colonial traumas and the dark powers of biotechnology.

In so doing, these "monstrous reproductions" rework the genre of science fiction by considering how it remains "entwined with the racist medico-scientific discourses that upheld notions of white Western superiority" (Sharp 2019, 223). These discourses are perhaps no more deeply entrenched than in Asian cultural stereotypes. Figured as "machines, insects, robots, cyborgs" and "generally nonhuman" beings, as Lai writes in a recent essay, Asians are often depicted as an unindividuated and "collective horde" (Lai 2020, 2). Yet through these fishy-human couplings that intersect bloodlines and bodies across time and space, *Salt Fish Girl* explores the primordial pleasures of sex along with its historically situated relationships with colonial and biotechnological origin stories. Indeed, Mónica Calvo-Pascual argues that this maternal mode of alternative reproduction counters the narrative of "hetero-patriarchal utilitarian techno-scientific control" and the "Judeo-Christian prescription of procreation as the main purpose of sex" (Calvo-Pascual 2018, 407). As such, Lai's novel breaks through the generic conventions of science (which are yet further rooted in white Western narratives like Mary Shelley's 1818 text *Frankenstein*) by submerging the genre's colonial and racist origin stories in queer ecofeminist imaginaries of bloodlines and posthuman pro-creativities.

Amniotic Corporealities: Lai's Posthuman Gestationality

While speculative sexual encounters inhabit queer spaces that move the protagonists beyond these traumas and dark powers, they also conceive of what Neimanis explains is a "more-than-human hydrocommons" (4). The conception and birth of the baby girl at the novel's end employs the watery amniotics of gestation and labor to represent a breakdown of human exceptionalism. Lai's ecofeminist figuration of water brings the outside in—and the inside out—by reflecting the fluid and multiplicitous variations between bodies and beings. In creating multiple sites of embodiment that cross species lines and temporal boundaries, these figurations encapsulate *posthuman gestationality*: the exploration of "evolutionary science and related stories of embodied indebtedness, where past and future bodies swim through our own" (Neimanis 2017, 4).

This posthuman gestationality is also relayed within the wider arc of the novel, which connects Miranda's seemingly immaculate conception with her mother's contact with a durian fruit. In the final chapter, it is revealed that durian trees were developed as a "fertility therapy for women who could not conceive" (258). The natural mutations engendered by the fruit of these trees create unexpected results. Just as the fishiness of Evie and the other clones is a decidedly "unstable factor" in their being (159), Miranda determines that

> we are the new children of the earth, of the earth's revenge. Once we
> stepped out of mud, now we step out of moist earth, out of DNA both

new and old, an imprint of what has gone before, but also a variation. By our difference we mark how ancient the alphabet of our bodies. By our strangeness we write our bodies into the future.

(259)

Having apprehended her own origins, and the origins of the baby growing in her womb, Miranda sees her body as an alphabet figure; a genetic code creatively recomposing itself out of its primordial, aqueous substance, and into an unfurling future.

Miranda and Evie's labor establishes a politics of queer kinship that sprawls millennia. The birth of their queerly conceived progeny is similar to the mirrored surface of the lake itself, which reflects back upon the previously reincarnated figures of Nu Wa and the Salt Fish Girl, and which becomes a medium for mixing Miranda's amniotic fluid with blood in the saltwater pool:

> Yes, I thought, an ancient ocean bubbling up through the rocks, salty and full of minerals. I scrambled desperately towards it, shed my clothes and slipped in. No shame as the coils unravelled. And to my surprise, Evie too slipped out of her clothes and slid into the water. Her legs fused together, and as her skin met water, a thin layer of tiny silver scales began to form and glisten in the moonlight. She stretched her tail though mine and our coils interlocked and slid through one another and then all of a sudden I found myself breathing these great heaving breaths. My belly heaved and contracted. Blood streamed into the water, staining it. I howled with the pain of womb spasming deeply, and then a dark head emerged six inches below my navel, from an opening in my scaly new flesh. The head had a wrinkled human face. Evie reached under water, guided the thing out, black-haired and bawling, a little baby girl. Everything will be alright, I thought, until next time.

(269)

Unlike the vials and tubes of manipulated biomaterial in Dr. Flowers's laboratory, which convey a sense of a singular and authoritative administration of evolutionary development, the creation of a child in the novel's concluding pages illuminate the multiplicity and multi-labial meanings of life that rail against a prescribed biotechnological future.

These scenes reflect more broadly and self-reflexively upon the nature of queer women's writing and upon the liquid imaginaries of ecofeminist science fiction. In emulating the spirit of *écriture féminine*, Lai's conception of the queer body as an alphabet figure provides evidence for Julian Murphet's claim that "writing is breeding, and breeding is writing" (2016, 209). However, it also addresses the negative logic of reproductive futurism, which holds that the fantasy of the future and the figure of the Child are co-extensive (Edelman 2004, 3–4). This is because writing in a biotechnological future also activates the anxiety that accompanies the asexual mode of biotechnological reproduction, as Luciana Parisi suggests. Biotechnology, Parisi argues, is "caught in the middle of a positive paradox: the more it guarantees control of the reproduction of life, the more it challenges its biological forms and functions" (2008, 283). Biotechnocapitalism is a system fuelled by the use of life forms deemed stable and therefore vulnerable to exploitation. It holds, as its founding vision, the promise that through the means of asexual reproduction, the human can "control not only its destiny but also its origins" (Stephens 2001, quoted in Essed and Schwab 2012). The reproductive future conceived by biotechnocapitalism sees a profit in the normative replication of sameness, yet it remains embedded in the cultural imaginary of difference that undergirds the nuclear family, the racially freighted fantasy of whiteness and nationhood, and the teleological narrative of human exceptionalism. But it is this normative replication of sameness—conceptualized in gendered, racial, ethnic, national, and sexual terms—that Larissa Lai reconfigures in her treatment of speculative sex. Lai's posthumanist representation of the queerness of the female body marks *Salt Fish Girl* as a watershed work of speculative fiction that presents an affirmative politics of resistance in an increasingly perilous future. From immaculate human-vegetal conceptions to fishy labors and births in water, Lai's novel opposes the geological and stratigraphical epistemologies of the Anthropocene, conveying it fluidly into an unstable and affirmatively pro-creative future.

Notes

1 Lai describes this queer kinship in her own words as a "politics of contingency" (2004, 22). I prefer to use the term "queer kinship" because it conveys a wider and more inclusive set of relationships (race, ethnicity, sex, and gender), and because it is more frequently used by scholars in the field. As a proponent of the term, Helen Merrick (2008, 229) writes that "'queered kin' seems a highly appropriate aid for re-reading and potentially destabilizing the heteronormative surface of ecofeminist stories."

2 Non-heteronormative sexual reproduction (i.e., parthenogenesis, cloning, and other biotechnological forms of reproduction) is a key trope of ecofeminist science fiction. Primary examples include early speculative fiction, such as Charlotte Perkins Gilman's utopian novel *Herland* (1915), and New Wave era fiction, such as Joanna Russ's *The Female Man* (1975). In the subfield of Canadian queer ecofeminist science fiction, Lai's focus on queer reproduction could be described as similar to the work of the Japanese-Canadian writer Hiromi Goto, whose novel, *The Kappa Child* (2001), explores queer conceptions. For a definitive overview of queer sexualities in SF, consult Wendy Gay Pearson's (2008) "Towards a Queer Genealogy of SF" in *Queer Universes*.

3 The first chapter from Elizabeth Povinelli's book, *Geontologies*, also appears in Grusin's edited volume.

4 While a reading of the olfactory sense lies beyond the parameters of my analysis, there are two excellent treatments of smell that readers might find useful, including Stephanie Oliver's (2011) "Diffuse Connections: Smell and Diasporic Subjectivity in Larissa Lai's *Salt Fish Girl*," and Paul Lai's (2008) "Stinky Bodies: Mythological Futures and the Olfactory Sense in Larissa Lai's *Salt Fish Girl*."

References

Alaimo, Stacy. 2017. "Your Shell on Acid: Material Immersion, Anthropocene Dissolves." In *Anthropocene Feminism*, edited by Richard Grusin, 89–120. Minneapolis, MN: University of Minnesota Press.

Calvo-Pascual, Mónica. 2018. "'The New Children of the Earth': Posthuman Dystopia or a Lesbian's Dream in Larissa Lai's *Salt Fish Girl*." *Orbis Litterarum* 73: 405–417.

Carson, Rachel L. 1950. *The Sea Around Us*, Special Edition. Oxford: Oxford University Press.

Chan, Arlene. 2017. "Chinese Immigration Act." *The Canadian Encylcopedia*, March 27. Accessed October 12, 2020. http://www.thecanadianencyclopedia.ca/en/article/chinese-immigration-act/.

Cixous, Hélène. 1994. *The Hélène Cixous Reader*. Edited by Susan Sellers. London: Routledge.

Daly, Mary. 1978. *Gyn/Ecology*. Boston, MA: Beacon Press.

Davies, Jeremy. 2016. *The Birth of the Anthropocene*. Oakland, CA: University of California Press.

Edelman, Lee. 2004. *No Future: Queer Theory and the Death Drive*. Durham, NC: Duke University Press.

Essed, Philomena, and Gabriele Schwab. 2012. "Introduction: Cloning and Cultures of Replication." In *Clones, Fakes, and Posthumans: Cultures of Replication*, edited by Philomela Essed and Gabriele Schwab, 9–22. Amsterdam: Rodopi.

Gilman, Charlotte Perkins. 1915. *Herland*, edited by Barbara H. Solomon. New York, NY: Signet Classics.

Goto, Hiromi. 2001. *The Kappa Child*. Red Deer, AB: Red Deer Press.

Grusin, Richard. "Introduction." In *Anthropocene Feminism*, edited by Richard Grusin, vii–xix. Minneapolis, MN: University of Minnesota Press.

Haraway, Donna. 1991. "A Cyborg Manifesto: Science, Technology, and Socialist-Feminism in the Late 20th Century." In *Simians, Cyborgs and Women: The Reinvention of Nature*, 149–181. New York, NY: Routledge.

———. 2016. *Staying with the Trouble: Making Kin in the Chthulucene*. Durham, NC: Duke University Press.

Joo, Hee-Jung Serenity. 2014. "Reproduction, Reincarnation, and Human Cloning: Literary Form and Radical Forms in Larissa Lai's *Salt Fish Girl*." *Critique – Studies in Contemporary Fiction* 55, no. 1: 46–59.

Lai, Larissa. 2002. *Salt Fish Girl*. Toronto: Thomas Allen Publishers.

———. 2004. "Sites of Articulation–An Interview with Larissa Lai: Robyn Morris in Conversation with Larissa Lai," *West Coast Line* 38, no. 2: 21–30.

———. 2016. "Life/Fiction: Speculative Fiction and Environmental Emergence." *The Goose* 14, no. 2: 30–33. Accessed October 12, 2020. http://scholars.wlu.ca/cgi/viewcontent.cgi?article=1193&context=thegoose.

———. 2020. "Familiarizing Grist Village: Why I Write Speculative Fiction." *Canadian Literature* 240: 20–39, 178. Accessed October 12, 2020. doi:10.14288/cl.vi240.192487.

Lai, Paul. 2008. "Stinky Bodies: Mythological Futures and the Olfactory Sense in Larissa Lai's *Salt Fish Girl*." *MELUS* 33, no. 4: 167–187.

Landon, Brooks. 2002. *Science Fiction after 1900: From the Steam Man to the Stars*. London: Routledge.

Merrick, Helen. 2008. "Queering Nature: Close Encounters with the Alien in Feminist Science Fiction." In *Queer Universes: Sexualities in Science Fiction*, edited by Wendy Gay Pearson, Veronica Hollinger, and Joan Gordon, 216–232. Liverpool, UK: Liverpool University Press.

Mortimer-Sandilands, Catriona, and Bruce Erickson. 2010. *Queer Ecologies: Sex, Nature, Politics, Desire*. Bloomington, IN: University of Indiana Press.

Murphet, Julian. 2016. "Poetry in the Medium of Life: Text, Code, Organism." In *Writing, Medium, Machine: Modern Technographies*, edited by Sean Pryor and David Trotter, 208–223. Ann Arbor, MI: Open Humanities Press.

Neimanis, Astrida. 2017. *Bodies of Water: Posthuman Feminist Phenomenology*. London: Bloomsbury.

Oliver, Stephanie. 2011. "Diffuse Connections: Smell and Diasporic Subjectivity in Larissa Lai's *Salt Fish Girl*." *Canadian Literature* 208: 85–108.

Parisi, Luciana. 2008. "The Nanoengineering of Desire." In *Queering the Non/Human*, edited by Myra Hird and Noreen Giffney, 283–311. London: Ashgate.

Pearson, Wendy Gay. 2008. "Towards a Queer Genealogy of SF." In *Queer Universes: Sexualities in Science Fiction*, edited by Wendy Gay Pearson, Veronica Hollinger, and Joan Gordon, 72–100. Liverpool, UK: Liverpool University Press.

Povinelli, Elizabeth. 2016. *Geontologies: A Requiem to Late Liberalism*. Durham, NC: Duke University Press.

Ralph, Iris. 2021. "Ecofeminist Climate Fiction: Merlinda Bobis's *Locust Girl*." In *Dystopias and Utopias on Earth and Beyond: Feminist Ecocriticism of Science Fiction*, edited by Douglas A. Vakoch, 67–79. Abingdon, Oxon, UK and New York, NY: Routledge.

Russ, Joanna. 1975. *The Female Man*. London: Orion Publishing.

Sandilands, Catriona. 1999. *The Good-Natured Feminist: Ecofeminism and the Quest for Democracy*. Minneapolis, MN: University of Minnesota Press.

Schneideman, Jill. 2017. "The Anthropocene Controversy." In *Anthropocene Feminism*, edited by Richard Grusin, 169–195. Minneapolis, MN: University of Minnesota Press.

Sharp, Sabine Ruth. 2019. "Salt Fish Girl and 'Hopeful Monsters': Using Monstrous Reproduction to Disrupt Science Fiction's Colonial Fantasies." *Contemporary Women's Writing* 13, no. 2: 222–241.

7 Queering *Doctor Who* and *Supernatural*

An Ecofeminist Response to Bill Potts and Charlie Bradbury

Meghna Mudaliar

Introduction

As scholars have observed, feminist criticism is a difficult term to define; does it refer to works written by all who identify as female, or to works read through the perspectives of feminist discourse, regardless of the author's gender identity, or something else entirely? Vakoch (2012) observes that the term is "inclusive enough" to refer to works by writers of any gender, "as long as the analysis is informed by feminism" (1). Consequently, it may be beneficial to think of ecofeminism also from a similar perspective, given that the "authors" of visual texts such as television series are often identified in the plural: is the "author" the show-runner who conceptualized and brought the show into existence; the episode writer who writes the script after discussion with the show-runner and other advisory members; or the actor, who is arguably the most important point of contact between the audience and the character? Debating these questions seems to detract from the spirit of ecofeminist inquiry, which, after all, is deeply concerned with understanding the relationship between gender roles and ecological discourse, regardless of the authorial origins of fictional narratives. Suffice it to say that the narrative, plot, and character in visual texts are driven by several heterogeneous forces, and that our ecofeminist concerns lie with the ways in which we read and interpret the text rather than the nature of the origins of the text and the forces that shape it (although, of course, we may reserve the right to bring into our area of inquiry any pertinent detail regarding the origin of the show that we may believe is necessary to understand the "nature" of the text).

Ecocritical discourse has come a long way since it emerged as a discipline in the late twentieth century, and one of the many ways in which literary studies has moved into interdisciplinary realms of discourse is through its engagement with, and interrogation of, visual and media-based texts such as television shows. Sarah Bezan and Aslı Değirmenci Altın, in their chapters on queer ecofeminism, have both illustrated elsewhere in this volume the ways in which theoretical frameworks such as speciesism and the posthuman relate to contemporary ways of examining literary texts that engage with science. Science fiction as a genre, it may be argued, has almost always been related to ecocritical ways of thinking, long before academia identified theoretical frameworks based around issues relating to the environment; also, iconic science fiction texts such as Arthur C. Clarke's *2001: A Space Odyssey* were simultaneously conceptualized as both book and film, emphasizing the interdisciplinary nature of interpretations of the narrative's textuality. Additionally, in observing that "the many systems of oppression are mutually reinforcing," Gaard (1997, 114) emphasizes the fact that women (and, by extension, all marginalized genders) cannot be liberated unless nature is, and vice versa. In this, the interdisciplinary nature of the texts under analysis reinforces the need to examine systems of oppression as interrelated, also implying that the removal of these structures of oppression necessitates the perception of identities and their contexts as essentially connected.

Both genres show that straddle the line between science fiction and related genres such as horror and fantasy, *Doctor Who* and *Supernatural* have each presented multiple viable options for engaging with ecocritical discourse, particularly in terms of the posthuman contexts of ideological discourse in the twenty-first century. As Laura Wright's (2015) book *The Vegan Studies Project* demonstrates, the post-9/11 era has brought back into focus our relationship with animals and their capitalist exploitation in the form of turning them into "products" such as meat and leather, specifically in terms of how human potency (and impotency) in the face of violence are expressed in the American context after the attacks on New York City and the subsequent "war on terror." Such fears, perhaps part of a hegemonic collective unconscious, often reveal themselves in texts from popular culture in which non-human characters are presented as alien or violent. For instance, a species of tree people figures prominently in the 2005 episode of *Doctor Who* in which the Ninth Doctor and Rose Tyler travel forward in time to the end of the universe, and *Supernatural* often features pagan gods ("Scarecrow," "A Very Supernatural Christmas") as violent forces that punish human beings for their failure to adhere to ancient rituals that revere the forces of nature.

Bill Potts and Charlie Bradbury have several characteristics in common, the most prominent of which is their status as iconic lesbian characters in television shows that have a cult following. While both *Doctor Who* and *Supernatural* have repeatedly succeeded in pushing the boundaries of the genre, neither show is known for its prominent LGBTQ+ representation (unlike, e.g., shows such as *Orphan Black*, another iconic science-fiction drama that features a recurring gay character, Felix, who is intrinsic to the main plot). It is perhaps the very rareness of queer female characters in the broader narratives of both shows that brings Bill and Charlie into prominence in the context of queer ecofeminist studies of the shows since both characters provide near-unique perspectives on the male protagonists of the shows while simultaneously providing the opportunity to engage in explorations of "women-identified women" and their experiences in the context of narratives that are almost always coded as masculine (as science fiction narratives often tend to be).

Character Introductions

Introduced in the first episode of Series 10 of "New Who," the colloquial term referring to the new series of *Doctor Who* that premiered in 2005 with Christopher Eccleston as the Ninth incarnation of the Doctor, Bill Potts is the third lesbian character to be featured on the show after Jenny Flint, a nineteenth-century human woman, and Madame Vastra, a "lizard woman from the dawn of time" (as she describes herself), who are married to each other. However, unlike her predecessors, who feature rather rarely and only in supporting roles, Bill is the first lesbian character to have a starring role on the show, featuring as the Doctor's companion throughout series 10. There have also been other queer female characters on the show and its spinoffs such as *Torchwood*, in which Toshiko Sato, who first appeared in an episode of *Doctor Who*, is shown in one episode in a relationship with Mary, an alien entity in human form. River Song, Alex Kingston's recurring character on *Doctor Who*, is also hinted at as being queer. The newest incarnation of the Doctor, played by Jodie Whittaker, now officially indicates that the show's currently female protagonist is married to River, although the latter has yet to appear alongside the Thirteenth Doctor.

Bill's introduction is interestingly complex, informed by sensitivity as well as a problematic perception of the girl she has a crush on and whom she claims to have "fatted" up by feeding her too many chips:

> BILL: Okay, so my first day here, in the canteen, I was on chips. There was this girl. Student. Beautiful. Like a model, only with talking and thinking. She looked at you and you perved. Every time, automatic, like physics. Eye contact, perversion. So I gave her extra chips. Every time, extra chips. Like a reward for all the perversion. Every day, got myself on chips, rewarded her. Then finally, finally, she looked at me, like she'd noticed, actually noticed, all the extra chips. Do you know what I realised? She was fat. I'd fatted her. But that's life, innit? Beauty or chips. I like chips.

The first objectionable statement made by Bill is that the girl is beautiful like a model, "only with talking and thinking," a statement that clearly indicates that models are not known for either of these activities. While such stereotyping of women in the modeling career is unacceptable in any context, it is exceptionally alarming when such typecasting is done by so-called "women-identified women," or women who, being lesbians and/or feminists, should presumably know better. Bill also uses the word "perved" to signify her crush on the girl, a word normally used in heteronormative contexts to signify the ways in which heterosexual men look at women who are considered attractive in certain terms. In one sense, much of queer studies—the word "queer" itself, in fact—is about reclaiming language and reappropriating it to empower oneself, suggesting that to "perv" is not an activity that needs to be restricted only to one kind of gender or sexual orientation. On the other hand, is it somehow better for a woman to be "perved" on by another woman rather than a man? Surely the act of being a "pervert" is equally problematic no matter who is performing it.

The final point of contention in Bill's monologue is, of course, the fact that she eventually realizes that by plying her crush with chips, she has turned a woman who was "beautiful, like a model" into someone who was "fat." She seems to make the problem worse by commenting that it has to be "beauty or chips": even from the point of view of a lesbian of color, there can be no middle ground between beauty and chips. One is either "beautiful" (from a certain point of view) and presumably eats nothing, or one is inclined toward chips and, presumably, not beautiful.

While this instance of body-shaming and fat-shaming does not bode well for Bill's tenure on the show, the introduction of Heather is truly when Bill's narrative takes on elements of ecofeminist interest. As Gaard (1997, 119) has observed, queer identity has often been devalued by the perception that same-sex relations are "against nature," and therefore, reclaiming female queerness and sexuality from the label of "deviant" also indicates that our very idea of "nature" needs to be revisited and redefined: "the 'crime against nature' argument stands out as having the greatest immediate interest for ecofeminists." In this, Heather's identification with an otherworldly but definitely "natural" alien race suggests that a romantic relationship between her and Bill is finally possible only toward the end of Bill's tenure on the show, when she has presumably had experiences that have helped her evolve from the body-shaming person of her first episode into someone who, having gone through horrific body modification herself, has progressed into being someone who can fully appreciate the change that Heather has gone through. The medium of water that helps them reconnect strongly indicates a definition of "natural" that blends ecological concerns with a reimagining of aspects of the natural world that see it not as fixed and stagnant but rather as transitory and progressive. Such a redefinition of the natural suggests new ways of perceiving the environment not only in terms of something essential for our survival, such as water, but also in terms of giving the ecosystem an identity and life of its own, distinct from the role it plays in sustaining human life.

Charlie's introduction in *Supernatural*'s Season 7 episode "The Girl with the Dungeons and Dragons Tattoo"—with the title being a clear reference to the popularity of Stieg Larsson's *The Girl with the Dragon Tattoo* in popular culture—is as the quintessential lesbian geek who fangirls after Hermione Granger and Arwen Undomiel and has to be walked through a flirtation scene with a male security guard because she is clueless about how to flirt with men. In "LARP and the Real Girl," Charlie is much more in her element, roleplaying as the Queen of Moondor, complete with loyal subjects. Her reunion with Sam and Dean Winchester is less than enthusiastic on her part, having been injured before on a dangerous mission the Winchesters set her on:

SAM: Charlie.
CHARLIE: Charlie Bradbury is dead. She died a year ago. You killed her. My name is Carrie Heinlein. Oh, and guess what. Now you killed her, too.

Both of Charlie's pseudonyms are references to seminal writers in the genre of science fiction, Ray Bradbury and Robert Heinlein. In many ways, Charlie brings into the series a sense of rootedness about its origins and the genres it engages with, reminding us of the classics as well as bringing in a much-needed female perspective on events. While the show had briefly attempted a feminist outlook with the character of Jo Harvelle, the primary narrative of the series, focused on two "codependent" brothers, did not leave much room for exploration of the identities and motivations of female hunters of the supernatural. (Dean dismisses Jo's argument about women being able to do the job just as well as men with a terse "This ain't gender studies," and the subject is pushed aside.)

Charlie, on the other hand, not only becomes "the little sister I never wanted," for Dean, but is also the first lesbian character on the series since Lily Baker from Season 2, who is murdered by Sam and Dean's early nemesis, Azazel, after having been cursed with a psychic power that makes her kill everything she touches, including her own girlfriend. An unfortunate exploration of Lily's doomed character also appears in the *Supernatural* anime series, in which her girlfriend is reduced to the status of Lily's roommate, and no mention of Lily's sexual orientation is made.

While Charlie does not have a significant other in her first episode, she is constantly represented as connected to narratives such as that of Arwen from *The Lord of the Rings*, whose status as Elrond's daughter and identity as elf connect her, in turn, to an ancient, pre-industrial society of non-humans that gains much of its magic from its communion with the natural world. The establishing of Moondor, the LARPing arena that is represented as pre-industrial (no cellular phones or electronic devices are allowed in Moondor, although there is a "tech" tent for digital emergencies), is also coded as Middle Earth in many ways; the villains of the game are an army of "Shadow Orcs." Also, LARPing connects the show's fictional narrative and setting to the many real-world contexts in which fans of science fiction interact with each other through mediums such as online message boards, cosplaying, and science-fiction conventions. The environmentally friendly world of Moondor particularly suggests a space in which technology is marginalized and natural alternatives centralized, reversing the dichotomy of technology/nature in a way that prioritizes and empowers the idea of "naturalness." This technique has the effect of "naturalizing" Charlie's sexuality and thereby reclaiming lesbianism from the traditional criticism of being "unnatural." Moreover, Charlie's attraction to the faerie Gilda, which is enthusiastically reciprocated, suggests her compatibility with a being from a "magical" world. Like Middle Earth, therefore, Moondor becomes a space in which harmony with elements of the natural world and of the ecological domain become representative of identities that are not hidden or "artificialized" by societal conventions but rather expressed openly and proudly as an embracing of sexuality as a natural expression of selfhood and self-determined identity, as is evidenced when Charlie and Gilda are interrupted mid-kiss; Charlie's reaction betrays only frustration at being interrupted rather than embarrassment or regret at having been found in a passionate embrace with another woman.

Bill/Heather, Charlie/Gilda, and Charlie/Dorothy

Bill and Charlie's relationships with Heather and Gilda respectively also forge strong connections between the science fiction contexts of the series and the ecological dimensions of the stories of two otherworldly characters. The "alien" identities of Heather and Gilda may be read in ways that connect the ecofeminist inquiry into dichotomies such as "natural/unnatural," particularly in terms of how women are consistently told that maternal instincts are "natural," as is compulsory heterosexuality, leading to essentialist discourses that code female sexuality as dependent on, and necessarily related to, the idea of masculinity. As Gaard (1997, 119) points out, the essentialist discourse against both women's identities and the construction of the natural world contains an inherent paradox:

> Here again is one of the many contradictions characterizing the dominant ideology. On the one hand, from a queer perspective, we learn that the dominant culture charges queers with transgressing the natural order, which in turn implies that nature is valued and must be obeyed. On the other hand, from an ecofeminist perspective, we learn that Western culture has constructed nature as a force that must be dominated if culture is to prevail.

Gaard's observations bring to the forefront the central paradox of the dominant, essentialist ideology: that while queer identity and female sexuality that exists beyond the purpose of procreation are both criticized as "unnatural," suggesting a reverence toward nature, the existence of the "nature versus culture" argument also strongly suggests a fear of the so-called "natural," which must constantly be repressed and overcome in order to reinforce and promote one's ideologies.

Bill and Heather's first meeting is in a crowded bar in which they make eye contact but are unable to converse, and Bill subsequently comes across Heather sitting on a bench:

BILL: You okay?
HEATHER: Yeah, I'm fine.
BILL: Sorry, can I ask? What's that in your eye?
HEATHER: It's just a defect in the iris.
BILL: Looks like a star.
HEATHER: Well, it's a defect.
BILL: At least it's a defect that looks like a star.
HEATHER: I'm getting it fixed.
BILL: Okay. Sorry, none of my business, but are you freaking out about something?
HEATHER: Please. You can say no. Would you come with me? Can I show you something?
BILL: God, yes!

Interestingly, both Heather's name and the defect in her eye are expressive of ecological emblems: her name refers to the plant that is often found growing in the wild, suggesting an unchecked and natural energy, and the "unnatural" defect in her eye, shaped like a star, is what seals her destiny at the hands of the alien race that is responsible for her death, or at least of the cessation of her life as a human entity. In this, Heather's character clearly moves into a realm beyond the "natural"; however, this transition may also be seen not as a move into an "unnatural" realm but rather as a shift in the ways in which the "natural" is defined.

Also, Bill's encounter with Heather takes place in the context of her initial meetings with the Doctor, before she is aware that he is not human; interestingly, this continual "reboot" of the Doctor's identity also involves revisiting our notions of what constitutes science fiction:

BILL: I don't know. Look, I know you know lots of stuff about, well, basically everything, but do you know any sci-fi?
DOCTOR: Go on.
BILL: Well, what if she's possessed. Something like that.
DOCTOR: Possessed by what?
BILL: I don't know. I saw this thing on Netflix. Lizards in people's brains.
DOCTOR: Right. So, you meet a girl with a discoloured iris and your first thought is she might have a lizard in her brain? I can see I'm going to have to up my game.

It seems significant that Bill, a newcomer to the universe of *Doctor Who*, chooses to identify "sci-fi" as not necessarily science-based but rather something that deals with supernatural elements such as possession, suggesting a link with *Supernatural* and other contemporary series that constantly interrogate and trouble existing definitions of the genre. Also, Heather herself becomes an otherworldly being, subsuming into her identity aspects of both the characteristic sci-fi alien and the ethereal ghost that is ubiquitous in contemporary sci-fi:

DOCTOR: Bill, listen to me. Whatever she's showing you, whatever she's letting you see. It's a lure, it's a trap. She's making you part of her, and you can never come back.

BILL: I see what you see. It's beautiful.

DOCTOR: Bill, let go! You have to let go! She is not human any more.

Interestingly, the Twelfth Doctor, for all his established broadmindedness, becomes here the epitome of the essentialist argument that rejects Heather's identity as "not human"; also intriguing is Bill's statement that although she sees what the Doctor does, she perceives it as "beautiful." The essentialist discourse is, therefore, summarily rejected by Bill as she finds beauty in the "not human": the so-called "unnatural" is perceived by her as beautiful, suggesting a readiness to accept her "natural" sexuality as well as foreshadowing her own transition toward the end of the series, when she can finally be with Heather. Bill says: "I saw it all for a moment. Everything out there. She was going to let me fly with her. She was inviting me. I was too scared." The Doctor replies: "Scared is good. Scared is rational. She wasn't human any more." Gaard's idea of subverting the correlation of "rational" with "masculine" and "heterosexual" may clearly be identified here, since Bill's "instinctive," "female," and "homosexual" perception of Heather is expressed in terms of "seeing it all," of broadening the mind and the perception of identity as heterogeneous and full of unexplored possibilities. (This idea of seeing "it all" for a moment also occurs in classic science fiction tales such as *2001* and its sequels, in which Dave Bowman ceases to be human but continues to exist as a being that has evolved to a place that other humans have not, even to the extent that he can take along with him the consciousness of HAL-9000, a machine.)

Similar to Bill's relationship with Heather, who evolves into a different species, Charlie's first relationship that we see on *Supernatural* is with the faerie Gilda, who has been summoned to Moondor, the Live Action Role Playing (LARPing) arena by a magician and is being forced to murder for the sorcerer. Toward the end of the episode, the two women share a passionate kiss, and Charlie gets the opportunity to save Gilda from the (male) sorcerer who is controlling Gilda. Although Gilda is never seen again, having gone back to her faerie realm, Charlie's next encounter with a woman is in the episode "Slumber Party," in which she meets Dorothy Baum, daughter of

L Frank Baum, on whom the character of Dorothy from the Oz books is revealed to have been based. Dorothy, a real-life hunter of the supernatural, who has been frozen in time with the Wicked Witch, is an effective foil to Charlie's character: she is a woman from the early twentieth century who wears trousers, rides a motorcycle, and is keenly adept at hunting monsters. The end of the episode, in which Charlie accompanies Dorothy to Oz to help her with the war waging there, is coded in vivid yellows and greens, as the women walk through a magical door to enter Oz, the naturalistic colors and setting adding to the emphasis on Oz as a pre-industrial and pre-technological society. As with the Oz books, the Wizard himself is implicitly coded as a figure of patriarchal authority who will presumably be outwitted by two women.

Alt!Bill and Alt!Charlie

While both Bill and Charlie are killed in the course of the series, each of them returns in some form, suggesting that a "death" of their former selves is essential for them to evolve into more progressive versions of themselves. Other than their sexuality, they also share a similar history of growing up without parents, and their mothers play significant roles in their lives: the Doctor goes back in time to take photographs of Bill's mother since Bill has none. Significantly, Bill observes: "My mum always said, 'With some people you can smell the wind in their clothes.'" If the wind can be seen as emblematic of the natural world, a "natural" force that figuratively represents following one's instincts rather than the constraining norms of societies, then Bill's memory of her mother also serves to reclaim the idea of femaleness and connect it to instinctual drives in a positive rather than regressive way (regressive in the sense that problematic correlations are often made between definitions of femaleness and the ability to give birth). Similarly, a significant phase in Charlie's history comes to a close when she finally allows her comatose mother to be taken off life support in the episode "Pacman Fever," reading to her mother during her final moments from *The Hobbit*, as her mother used to do for her when Charlie was a child. As has already been discussed, Tolkien's envisioning of Middle Earth as a pre-industrial space in which nature is reclaimed from notions of primitiveness and savagery may be seen here as indicative of a shared relationship between Charlie and her mother that is free from confining and normative notions of femaleness and motherhood.

Bill, who is fatally shot before suffering an even worse fate by being subjected to cyber-conversion, is saved from her fate by Heather, who makes her second and final appearance at the end of series 10, and the women leave to explore the universe together. The context is that of a dystopian, post-apocalyptic wasteland, a common trope in science-fiction narratives that promote cautionary tales of the disastrous possibilities for the human race if environmental concerns continue to be ignored. Significantly, Heather rises out of a pool of water as rain begins to fall, and when Bill asks if she is dead, Heather kisses her and says, "Does that feel dead to you? You're like me now. It's just a different kind of living... I can make you human again. It's all just atoms. You can rearrange them any way you like." She then opens the TARDIS door to reveal a bright star shining in space, and invites Bill to "Let me show you around."

This notion of "a different kind of living" may be correlated with the argument proposed by Cuomo (1998, 3) against the Cartesian dictum that sees non-human animals as machines rather than living beings. One of the primary ways in which ecofeminism presents its prerogatives is to deconstruct Cartesian notions of the primacy of rationality and the subjugation of instinct and intuition—almost always coded as feminine—as "primitive" and base. Heather's declaration that "it's all just atoms" signals a transition for her, and an introduction to Bill, of ecofeminist mediums of perception that "rearrange" preexisting notions of femaleness and sexuality into new, progressive, and revolutionary ways of seeing the universe, as indicated by the shining star visible through the TARDIS doors. Moreover, the Doctor's regeneration from a male character to a female one begins as Bill and Heather head out into the universe, signaling that a new era of the series has begun. With Jodie Whittaker currently playing the first female regeneration of the Doctor, the world's longest-running science fiction series finally has a female character at the helm, suggesting exciting possibilities for ecofeminist discourse in the context of science fiction in television.

Charlie's return to the series, unlike Bill's, takes a much longer trajectory. The original Charlie meets her death in the Season 10 episode "Dark Dynasty," killed by the Styne family, who are descendants of Victor Frankenstein. The connection with Mary Shelley's classic, which is often regarded as the book that established the genre of science fiction, reinforces *Supernatural*'s status as a genre show that has its roots in the science-fiction tradition while also having evolved to include the conventions of contemporary science fiction, which borrows from conventional narratives while simultaneously crossing the thresholds of different genres to create a forum for discussion and representation of multiple identities and various tropes in popular culture. The evolution of the genre may also be seen as a parallel to what Warren (1987) suggests in a seminal work that helped establish the discipline of ecological feminism: that rather than using more conventional forms of feminism as a base, ecofeminism must be transformative in its frameworks since traditional categories of feminist discourse are often problematic in terms of the ways in which ecofeminism is conceptualized. Similarly, contemporary science fiction moves beyond conventional definitions of the genre in multiple ways, providing new and transformative frameworks of interrogation.

Charlie returns to *Supernatural* in Season 13 in the form of an alternative Charlie from a different universe that is opened through an inter-dimensional portal. Like the dystopian world in which Peter Capaldi's Twelfth Doctor begins his regeneration into Jamie Whittaker's Thirteenth Doctor, Charlie's world, often referred to on the show as "apocalypse world," is a place in which Sam and Dean never existed and consequently never stopped the Biblical apocalypse. Alt!Charlie, unlike the original Charlie, is a hunter right from the start, leading a force of resistance fighters against the archangel Michael and his followers, who control the post-apocalypse world. While she does not appear in the finale of Season 13, alt!Charlie is now in "our" universe, road-tripping with Rowena the ancient witch, suggesting exciting possibilities for the future of both characters. Rowena, who in Season 10 likens herself to Charlie by stating that they're both "sexually progressive," is also a strong character in terms of ecofeminist discourse; being a witch, she channels ancient pagan powers that present a powerful alternative to the guns and machines with which hunters such as Sam and Dean battle the forces of supernatural evil.

In the contemporary post-human discourse, Pearson et al. (2008, 14) have pointed out how lesbian identity is often seen as "anti-human" in promotions of essentialist ideologies that see queer identity as being "against" the natural order of things; subsequently, characters such as Bill and Charlie serve to remind us of humanistic discourses that continue to engage with and include representations of queer identity in the context of understanding what it means to be human. In its explorations of technology that are often coded in terms of worlds and universes that are pre-industrial or otherwise informed by non-human characterizations that serve to remind us of our continually evolving definitions of what it means to be human, ecofeminist science fiction remains a powerful contender in literary and cultural contexts that both engage with and interrogate our developing notions of hybrid and heterogeneous forms of identity.

References

Cuomo, Christine. 1998. *Feminism and Ecological Communities: An Ethic of Flourishing*. London and New York, NY: Routledge.

Gaard, Greta. 1997. "Toward a Queer Ecofeminism." *Hypatia* 12, no. 1: 114–137.

Pearson, Wendy Gay, Veronica Hollinger, and Joan Gordon, eds. 2008. *Queer Universes: Sexualities in Science Fiction*. Liverpool: Liverpool University Press.

Vakoch, Douglas A., ed. 2012. *Feminist Ecocriticism: Women, Environment and Literature*. Lanham, MD: Lexington Books.

Warren, Karen J. 1987. "Feminism and Ecology: Making Connections." *Environmental Ethics* 9, no. Spring: 3–20.
Wright, Laura. 2015. *The Vegan Studies Project: Food, Animals, and Gender in the Age of Terror*. Athens, GA: University of Georgia Press.

Part 3
War and Ecoterrorism

8 No Easy Answers in Karen Traviss's *The Wess'har Wars* Series

Patrick D. Murphy

Dialogical Narrative

The Wess'har Wars consists of six novels, *City of Pearl* (Traviss 2004a), *Crossing the Line* (Traviss 2004b), *The World Before* (Traviss 2005), *Matriarch* (Traviss 2006), *Ally* (Traviss 2007a), and *Judge* (Traviss 2008), published from 2004 through 2008. They tell the story of Shan Frankland, Environmental Hazards Officer, and her mission in outer space initially to retrieve a flora and fauna seed bank. Over the course of the novels' 2,300 odd pages, the story addresses numerous issues of concern to environmentalists, feminists, and ecofeminists. The author, Karen Traviss, though, is quite explicit about distancing herself from any of the ideological positions of her characters (Morgan 2006; Traviss 2007b). That is actually well and good because it results in an internally persuasive narrative without an authoritative center that would allow readers to receive passively a singular message. Thus, John Heckman (2007) in "Implacable Justice" is misguided in his analysis when he attributes thematic positions to the author, failing to recognize this dialogical narrative structure. Rather, readers are treated to dialogical plot development and a narration that always presents perceptions through the viewpoint of the different characters, human and alien, rather than a monological, authoritative implied author (see Murphy 1995). Like the characters debating within and among themselves, readers are thrust into the position of evaluating and re-evaluating ethical stances, arguments, and significant actions to make decisions about appropriate ecofeminist ethics.

Throughout the six books, no easy answers are proposed about environmental crises, interspecies ethics, or gender dynamics. Rather, they reflect Erika Cudworth's argument in *Developing Ecofeminist Theory* that "Systems are not teleological—we cannot predict the paths adopted, and we are likely to be surprised by patterns of change in social systems, captured in the blink of a human lifetime" (2005, 176). The title of the second volume, *Crossing the Line*, describes the difficulty depicted repeatedly in making ethical judgments that lead to a particular course of action. First, despite the clear-cut ethical reasoning behind the decision to take a specific course of action, one that often has a "must" attached to it, the laws of unforeseen circumstances and unintended consequences invariably alter or undermine the anticipated results. Although the philosopher Targassat, whose beliefs guide the Wess'har aliens of Wess'ej that Frankland first meets, states that those who have a choice must act, she also states that "There is no single point of perfect balance" (Traviss 2006, 94 [her beliefs often comprise the epigraphs for various chapters]). Second, in response to the inability to maintain hard and fast ethical absolutes, several different characters, human and alien, recognize the need to keep drawing such lines to practice restraint, seek limits, and achieve dynamic balance.

The viewpoint adopted, then, is one in which the conflict between differing moral values is actually displayed as a positive condition of cooperation and compromise. As Cudworth notes, "The complexity of systems, natural and social, indicates that diversity is a strength. So too, is it likely to be in an attempt to unpick the matrix of social domination" (2005, 177). The antiteleological narrative, then, reflects a fundamental ecofeminist recognition of the diversity and complexity of reality, of which social formations and species differences are but aspects. Such questions as when is intervention necessary for ecological rebalancing and how extreme should be the measures taken, when is nonintervention an appropriate form of action even when a species is being self-destructive, and what is the difference between violence that reduces one population for the benefit of another and unintentional environmental degradation that leads to extinction, all require ethical approaches and moral behaviors that will unavoidably result in the imposition of one set of values on a group holding a different set of values.

Invitational Rhetoric

Much like the feminist concept of an invitational rhetoric, Traviss's Wess'har Wars encourages readers to consider reflexively actions, motives, intentions, potentials, and possibilities. Even in the case of intention, which the Wess'har initially dismiss as unimportant, it eventually begins to become a shared concern between Wess'har and human. Feminist scholars continue to be the main promoters of invitational rhetoric. Foss and Griffin (1995) provide a definition that emphasizes the intention of such rhetoric to go beyond attempts at persuasion and the imposition of power over another that the effort to persuade invariably entails, particularly in the patriarchal tradition of Western rhetoric. They state that

> Invitation rhetoric is an invitation to understanding as a means to create a relationship rooted in equality, immanent value, and self-determination. ... In presenting a particular perspective, the invitation rhetor does not judge or denigrate others' perspectives but is open to and tries to appreciate and validate those perspectives. (5)

In many respects, Eddie, the embedded human journalist on Frankland's interstellar voyage, is the best example of an attempt to implement invitational rhetoric because of his initial commitment to ethical journalism and presenting all sides of a story. Yet, he epitomizes the difficulty of implementing nonjudgmental news stories as the future of human survival on Earth nears its testing point when the most technologically advanced and interventionist alien group, The Wess'har of Eqbas Vorhi, prepares to visit Earth for punishing individuals responsible for a disastrous military action on the planet Bezer'ej where the seed bank is located and for the environmental rebalancing of species on Earth.

Unlike Eddie, Shan Frankland, having functioned as a law enforcement officer, begins from the opposite end of the spectrum, initially always evaluating information in order to pass judgment and take action. Gradually, though, she moves increasingly toward the invitational rhetoric position of trying to see reality from an alien, in every sense of that term, perspective. As with numerous ethical positions in the complete narrative, the attempt to practice invitational rhetoric is more significant than the inability to maintain a stance of openness. At the end of the day, numerous characters, despite whatever understanding they have achieved through an invitational openness, like Eddie, must, as the title of the sixth book states, "judge." Readers may see, and vicariously participate in, the benefits of invitational rhetoric that occur as different characters function as both rhetors and listeners who are "willing to engage each other's beliefs and be willing to let go of some of their own desire to move toward mutual understanding" (Ryan and Natalie 2001, 71). The part of invitational rhetoric as defined by Foss and Griffin (1995) that is rendered most problematic in the narrative is that of "self determination" because of the ethical limits of the impact of such determinations on other species. As Kathleen Ryan and Elizabeth Natalie note, "The conditions of freedom, in particular, that bound the rhetorical situation may operate quite differently across contexts" (83).

With the Isenj, another alien species with whom the Wess'har of Wess'ej engage in conflict, there is the question of intervening or not intervening on their home planet Umeh when environmental overreach there pushes the Isenj into space colonization. On Bezer'ej there is the dilemma of a species saved from extinction by the Wess'har only later to demonstrate a "fascist" mentality, as the Earthlings see it, of hunting practices that drive other species to extinction. How long should a dialogue be carried on with those who champion a self-destructive industrialism and resource consumption that will exhaust their own, our own, planet? In *Judge*, that question is answered by the arrival of the Eqbas Vorhi Wess'har on Earth, but the strategy for rebalancing to be employed will depend largely on the willingness of the wrangling regional powers to enter into not only a transformative dialogue but also a demonstration of environmentally responsible practice. Interestingly enough in terms of the issue of rhetoric, the Wess'har always only intervenes on the basis of being invited by at least one species, not necessarily the dominant one, or one segment of the dominant species. On Earth, the Australasians invite intervention because they know the Wess'har are coming anyway to punish people responsible for attempted species extinction on Bezer'ej. For the Isenj, it is one foreign minister who invites their intervention. But, the invitation element stops there insofar as the Eqbas Vorhi Wess'har may not be uninvited. Their general lack of interest in the reservations of the dominant species about the extremity of their strategy for ecological rebalancing is only ameliorated by their willingness to offer tactical options. As a result, their behavior provides an opportunity for readers to consider the limitations and problems of an invitational rhetoric after the point at which a group has gained an understanding of the others' viewpoints but finds that their positions on environmental degradation are morally unacceptable.

Gender Dynamics and Tending

At its most basic level, Wess'har Wars is a story of alien contact, primarily between Frankland and the "female" leaders of the Wess'har of Wess'ej and the "male" Wess'har Aras, with whom she eventually has a cohabitational relationship. These Wess'har, and their Eqbas Vorhi counterparts, have their society organized along matriarchal lines. That matriarchy does not arise from some essentialist argument that having women in charge automatically produces different political outcomes but from the specific evolutionary history of the Wess'har species. Nor does it arise from the notion of a reductionist maternal instinct. Instead, Traviss portrays an alien society in which both male and female versions of the Wess'har, as their sexual dimorphism is seen through the eyes of the Earthlings, demonstrate what Shelley Taylor (2002) has labeled the "tending instinct" and display variations of maternal attitudes. An evolutionary argument that explains certain differences in a fundamentally dimorphic sexual reproductive species is not automatically an essentialist one and the narrative in nearly every book is at pains to complicate such a binary perspective. As with many species on Earth, the Wess'har "females" are larger than their "male" counterparts. And like some other species here the "males" are the ones that carry a child to term and nurse it.

The Wess'har also engage in a dimorphic form of physical interaction, similar to sexual intercourse, called *oursan*, through which DNA is transferred horizontally between the participants, which is necessary for maintaining the health of the males (see Crisp et al. [2015] on horizontally acquired genes on Earth). So, while the males give birth and play a major role in child-rearing, the females play a crucial role in maintaining bondmate health, that is, nurturing the males. As a result of the necessity of such genetic transmission for the benefit of the species, there is no "single" Wess'har. Nor is it accurate to consider them either "male" or "female" in terms of human gender expectations and social norms. Everyone is bonded to someone else (Traviss 2004a, 314). Traviss thereby joins a group of feminist science fiction authors who have played with and subverted traditional dimorphism and gender binaries, such as Marge Piercy and Ursula K. Le Guin.

This issue of "tending" to others is played out on numerous levels. Of the five sentient species with whom the Earthlings engage in verbal dialogue, four of them are clearly portrayed as highly community-oriented. For the Ussissi, community and family are so important that when one of their number becomes infected with a microorganism that renders him an outcast, he commits suicide rather than continue life as an *isolato*. Being an isolated individual is portrayed explicitly as a curse and it is only among the human beings from Earth that we find such individuals in the novels, including initially Frankland. Although not explicitly stated, it seems strongly implied that this sense of community leads the Wess'har to extend their sense of community beyond their own species, to the point of engaging in radical environmental rebalancing when a sentient species asks for help in addressing either their decimation by other species' pollution or self-inflicted decimation through ecocide. Daniel Smail (2008), who references Taylor's (2002) book, *The Tending Instinct*, also cites primatologist Blaffer Hrdy, who claims that "brain receptors for oxytocin, one of the 'peace and bonding' hormones, are typically more numerous in species where males bond with their mates and participate in rearing offspring" (2008, 115). Smail then goes on to wonder:

> But if such receptors are not hardwired in humans, if they have to be formed through development and experience, if cultural norms militate against them, then fathers will not necessarily have the neural equipment to process injected prolactin and oxytocin. . . . the bodies of deadbeat dads cannot easily generate or use the hormones that undergird the bonding process.

(2008, 115–116)

From this perspective, then, many contemporary people are undergoing significant malformation, from the lack of adequate parent bonding and attention to their children and from the lack of adequate direct social and personal intimacy as their interactions are increasingly mediated by various technological filters. When a "family" is seen seated in a restaurant and each person is on a different electronic device, while some of them are wearing earbuds, and when not looking down at his phone the father is checking the sports event on the big screen, there is a fundamental disconnect underway in which psychotropic stimulation, as Smail would call it, is being sought and received from every direction except relational personal conversation and engagement.

Relationality

Mary Judith Ress in her study, *Ecofeminism in Latin America*, turns to the scholar and activist, Ivone Gebara, for her argument for a fundamental reorientation of human societies to end oppression and exploitation. She quotes Gebara regarding the need to reperceive "relationality." It, she states,

> Is constitutive of all beings. It is more elementary than awareness of differences or than autonomy, individuality, or freedom. It is the foundational reality of all that is or can exist. It is the underlying fabric that is continually brought forth within the vital process in which we are immersed. (Ress 2006, 126)

Such a reperception, similar to the one that many environmental activists draw from Buddhism, *pratityasamutpada*, mutual co-arising, reflects a repeated refrain running through ecofeminism from its earliest proponents, such as Kaza (1993) in her "Buddhism, Feminism, and the Environmental Crisis." It takes on added meaning in the Wess'har Wars story because of the symbiotic role that a particular microorganism, *c'naatat*, plays in the lives of major characters, but also in terms of how Traviss portrays co-evolution of species, particularly that of the Ussissi and the Wess'har. While feminist new materialists use such terms as "entanglement," "relationality" has the benefit of foregrounding a volitional as well as nonvolitional aspect. While being related to someone else is not a choice, relating to that person is one.

It is important to note that Traviss's most developed depictions of alien societies do not rely on a nuclear family construct but on an extended one, not only through living arrangements and Wess'har polyandry, but also through the sharing and transfer of genetic memories. Here she shows another aspect of dialogics in the recognition that our thoughts to the degree that they are put into words are never completely our own because the language we use is replete with the voices, intonations, and connotations of others who have used the words before us. Likewise, our memories of places and events are shaped, altered, and sometimes substituted by the images made and impressions expressed by others.

Part of the storyline in this six-volume narrative involves the main Wess'har character, Aras, a warrior infected with the "parasite"—at other times it is labeled a "symbiont"—*c'naatat*. *C'naatat* is a microorganism that infects him and has the ability to bioengineer his body to maintain its health and longevity as the host site of its existence. His body is literally a "planet" for this organism that apparently makes choices about the ways it mutates any host body. Without direct communication, its sentience can never be adequately ascertained, but throughout the various books, it displays a tendency to experiment with the bodies it inhabits beyond simply maintaining life support. Many years ago, Allen (1990) made the remark that our bodies are planets, and scientific research has borne this out as not some New Age or spiritual ecofeminist claim but as fact. Over the past decade, researchers have been mapping the human microbial genomes and discovered that for every human gene of DNA there are 360 microbial ones and that nearly 90% of the cells in our body do not actually belong to us, but are "alien" organisms: microbes, viruses, and bacteria. Many of these are becoming understood as necessary, such as gut bacteria, for maintaining human health as well as influencing the development of our immune system and contributing to human evolution (Yong 2013; Brumfield 2015; Crisp et al. 2015).

For the purposes of the plot, Aras cannot remain the sole carrier of *c'naatat* and so to save Frankland's life after she is wounded in a firefight with the Isenj, he infects her with the symbiont. Later, she accidentally infects one of the Marines, Ade, a member of the initial expedition that she heads. Symbiosis represents the most basic form of the relationality that Gebara defines and reflects the kind of material entanglement that contradicts illusions of autonomy, the ideology of individualism, and static concepts of the self, all of which are promoted by patriarchies as aspects of multivalent domination (see Murphy 2009). As Frankland recognizes in her thoughts, "*I am a world, too*" and "*a world has responsibilities*" (Traviss 2004a, 390–391; italics in original).

Commodification and Consumption

There is a significant critique of commodification and colonization that echoes—either purposely or inadvertently—ecofeminist arguments about the deleterious effects of patenting seeds, both in terms of bioprospecting as a form of colonization and as a form of the destruction of local control of food production. The latter part of this critique connects with the ecofeminist subsistence perspective developed by Bennholdt-Thomsen and Mies (1999) in *The Subsistence Perspective,* and Shiva (2005) in *Globalization's New Wars,* and other works authored and co-authored by these three.

On Earth, in 2299 all seeds are owned by corporations and global ecosystems are in sharp and rapid decline. Yet in deep space, there is the seed bank shipped off to preserve unpatented seeds for future generations. Frankland believes she is being sent to retrieve that seed bank, even though it would take 150 years round trip. Unfortunately, the team of scientists that accompany her is also interested in colonization and at least one of them is a government agent whose mission is to find out if *c'naatat* really exists and if so to retrieve it for use as a bioweapon creating nearly immortal soldiers.

Readers quickly learn, though, that the religious colony who traveled with the seedbank would have died out without Aras's assistance because they mistakenly believe they could either grow Earth plants on a planet with a similar atmosphere or else eat native flora, but the latter is laced with cyanide. With Ara's help, they establish a strictly vegan diet of Earth-based plants because he sets up a biobarrier on one island to prevent contamination of the native flora. There is then no monocultural farming, but a strict subsistence orientation (Traviss 2004a, 59). And the colony's daily life is basically structured as a gift economy, which is the same basis on which the Wess'har in that solar system exchange goods and services. Commodification is critiqued in terms of the environmental problems it creates. Although the colony Christians believe that they are on a religious mission to preserve and then restore the Earth's biota, they would have failed due to a lack of understanding xeno-ecology. The problem of the facile and disruptive introduction of alien species into a local environment has significant implications for Earth's global agro-economics because of the ongoing problem here with export-oriented plantation crops.

The first book, *City of Pearl*, emphasizes the importance of unpatented seeds for survival—they are necessities of life that should not be owned by corporations (Traviss 2004a, 255). This same argument extends to the current problem of the privatization of freshwater supplies and global land grabs by multinational corporations and sovereign wealth funds (see Murphy 2015; Pearce 2006; Parr 2013; and Pearce 2012). The value and importance of the seed bank alongside the rejection of commodification and exchange value, rather than use-value, as the determinant of what gets created or produced, are reiterated throughout all six books. Along with that appear a variety of remarks by different characters, especially the Wess'har followers of the Targassat philosophy, about the distinction between wants and needs (Traviss 2004b, 46). For instance on Wess'ej, Aras's home planet, and where Frankland lives for much of the series, there are communal stores with an eco-sufficiency economy based on sharing surplus food, handicrafts, and tool making. There is no hoarding or possessing and no currency.

Veganism

Relationality is then linked with economics through the rejection of commodification because other species are viewed by the Wess'har as people and not resources to exploit. They are strictly vegan, although here again there is the recognition of no easy answers in that some species have evolved to be carnivores or omnivores. Positions on vegetarianism and veganism have been a staple of ecofeminist thought from its earliest articulations. And while critics of ecofeminism have invariably tried to make the vegan positions within it appear authoritarian and dogmatic, they can only do so by ignoring the nuanced features of the discussion. Moral vegetarianism has been a staple thread in ecofeminist thought and activism, although not universally adopted or supported, from its earliest days and continues to develop and evolve in complexity and sophistication. The work of Adams, for instance, is exemplary from her early *The Sexual Politics of Meat* (1990), through essays included in her edited collection, *Ecofeminism and the Sacred* (1993), to her more recent book co-edited with Gruen, *Ecofeminism: Feminist Intersections with Other Animals and the Earth* (2014). Gaard in

"Ecofeminism Revisited" points to Curtin's (1991) "Toward an Ecological Ethic of Care" as an early example of an ecofeminist "carefully nuanced approach to consumption that eschewed universalizing" (Gaard 2011, 38). Most recently, the journal *ISLE*, in the Autumn 2017 issue devoted a "cluster" of five essays under the title "Vegan Studies and Ecocriticism."

The problem, for instance, with the recovering Bezeri aquatic species, who are reviving as a result of being intentionally infected with *c'naatat* by one of the humans, is not that they are hunters and omnivores, but rather that they willfully and knowingly hunt other species to extinction, justifying their action on the basis of intellectual superiority. This position creates a dilemma for Aras, who has been their protector for centuries. He played a major role in wiping out the colonization of their planet by the Isenj because that species' pollution would have led to the extinction of the Bezeri. But he also cannot allow the Bezeri to flourish at the expense of the other species they would extinguish. Through this dilemma, Traviss demonstrates that moral arguments to determine a correct how and what of any significant action are always flawed or limited because priority is given to one aspect of moral considerability over another and the good of the whole outweighing the harm to the individual— although that may only be short-term harm with long-term benefits.

So, a focus on species rather than individual members of the species and a focus on multispecies flourishing rather than a dominant species' power and health always remain complicated issues. We see this complication repeated in the environmental realm today in the differences between proponents of ecological restoration and ecological conservation. At the same time, it is suggested in *Ally* that the individual and society are really not distinguishable as discrete entities since they are mutually co-constructive and hence there is always a responsibility for others of various kinds (Traviss 2007a, 4). That takes us beyond the new materialist notion of entanglement since that term always implies that there is the potential for un-entangling, while the depiction of symbiosis in the Wess'har Wars more accurately reflects the reality of any species existence. In *Matriarch* this complexity is remarked upon through the representation that a minimum impact lifestyle of a tool-making species means being agriculturally intensive while keeping high tech mechanics in reserve as much as possible to reduce energy production and consumption (Traviss 2006, 150).

Wants, Needs, and Rebalancing

The recognition of the distinction between wants and needs both reinforces this minimalist practice as well as raising the specter of the need for population self-regulation. An economy based on the creation of "wants" rather than the fulfillment of "needs" will tend to generate population pressures based on rates of consumption (Traviss 2006, 151), while commodification and justifications based on intellectual superiority will allow the ignoring of the needs of other species, including their needs to reproduce and maintain a sufficient population for generational continuity. In *Judge,* an epigraph from Targassat helps to demonstrate the complexity of finding the right balance among no easy answers in that causing no harm is a utopian dream not a practical reality, and so then as with the concept of *ahimsa* in Buddhism, the achievable goal is the causing of the least harm. Because no simple yardstick can apply in every situation, then a sentient community has a responsibility toward its own balance in relation to others, but that community should not try to assume too much responsibility that then denies responsibility to others (Traviss 2008, 231).

This last point leads to a consideration of the galactic rebalancing strategy of the Wess'har of Eqbas Vorhi, the home planet from which the Wess'har followers of Targassat split. While I agree with much of Heather Sullivan's (2010) analysis in her "Unbalanced Nature" essay, I disagree with her bifurcation of technology and "biological forms" and her claim that Traviss provides no critique of the Eqbas Vorhi rebalancing project. The Wess'har rely on nanotechnology and biodegradability extensively and the humans understand too little about their technology to ascertain how much of it is organic or biological and how much inorganic. Second, technology refers to the application of scientific knowledge for practical purposes and not just to machinery. Once Esganikan, the leader of the Eqbas mission to Umeh, initiates her rebalancing project there it becomes clear she relies on a mixture of bioweapons and mechanical ones. From the beginning of their invitation of these Eqbas relations, the Wess'har of Wess'ej discuss with Frankland concerns about their aggressive interventionism. And, just like the human interest in *c'naatat* as a bioweapon, so too Esganikan wants her scientist, Shapakti, to learn how to control and eventually to infect her with it when she heads for Earth. That this action represents a disastrous techno-logical decision and not that "technology in Traviss' series appears neutral and helpful" (Sullivan 2010, 282), is seen when Esganikan is fragged for her action by a Skavu soldier under her command. In addition, Shapakti realizing that there will always be an Eqbas temptation to use *c'naatat* as a weapon, flees his home planet and takes refuge on Wess'ej, where he and the Wess'har leaders there opt to destroy all of his research on *c'naatat* extrac-tion. Repeatedly, the arguments against the excesses of unlimited technol-ogy are expressed by the Wess'har followers of Targassat and by Frankland, who attempted suicide to keep *c'naatat* out of human hands, while the rationalizations of the Eqbas Wess'har are held up to critique by them.

While the Wess'har Wars provides no easy answers to any of the major issues that appear in this multi-volume narrative, Traviss has her characters express many ideas about ethically appropriate courses of action, the fre-quency with which the best intentions produce results that have unintended consequences, and the necessity both of seeking balance and being unable to achieve some sort of stasis. Many of the best ideas expressed can be found in ecofeminist thought while ecofeminist criticism elucidates the complexities that the narrative develops.

References

Adams, Carol J. 1990. *The Sexual Politics of Meat: A Feminist-Vegetarian Critical Theory*. New York, NY: Continuum.

———, ed. 1993. *Ecofeminism and the Sacred*. New York, NY: Continuum.

———, and Lori Gruen, eds. 2014. *Ecofeminism: Feminist Intersections with Other Animals and the Earth*. New York, NY: Bloomsbury.

Allen, Paula Gunn. 1990. "The Woman I Love Is a Planet: The Planet I Love Is a Tree." In *Reweaving the World: The Emergence of Ecofeminism*, edited by Irene Diamond and Gloria Feman Orenstein, 52–57. San Francisco, CA: Sierra Club Books.

Bennholdt-Thomsen, Veronika, and Maria Mies. 1999. *The Subsistence Perspective: Beyond the Globalised Economy*. Translated by Patrick Camiller, Maria Mies, and Gerd Weih. London: Zed Books. Originally published in German in 1997.

Brumfield, Ben. 2015. "You May Be Your Germs: Microbe Genes Slipped into Human DNA, Study Says." *CNN*, March 13. Accessed October 12, 2020. http://www.cnn.com/2015/03/13/health/microbe-genes-human-dna-evolution/.

Crisp, Alastair, Chiara Boschetti, Malcolm Perry, Alan Tunnacliffe, and Gos Micklem. 2015. "Expression of Multiple Horizontally Acquired Genes is a Hallmark of Both Vertebrate and Invertebrate Genomes." *Genome Biology* 16: Article No. 50. Accessed October 12, 2020. doi:10.1186/s13059-015-0607-3.

Cudworth, Erika. 2005. *Developing Ecofeminist Theory: The Complexity of Difference*. New York, NY: Palgrave Macmillan.

Curtin, Deane. 1991. "Toward an Ecological Ethic of Care." *Hypatia: A Journal of Feminist Philosophy* 6, no. 1: 60–74.

Foss, Sonja K., and Cindy L. Griffin. 1995. "Beyond Persuasion: A Proposal for an Invitational Rhetoric." *Communication Monographs* 62 (March): 2–18.

Gaard, Greta. 2011. "Ecofeminism Revisited: Rejecting Essentialism and Re-Placing Species in a Material Feminist Environmentalism." *Feminist Formations* 23, no. 2: 26–53.

Heckman, John. 2007. "Implacable Justice: Arguing Politics and Theories of Law via the Encounter with Powerful Alien Species." *Extrapolation* 48, no. 2: 302–313.

Kaza, Stephanie. 1993. "Buddhism, Feminism, and the Environmental Crisis." In *Ecofeminism and the Sacred*, edited by Carol J. Adams, 50–69. New York, NY: Continuum.

Morgan, Cheryl. 2006. "Interview: Karen Traviss." *Strange Horizons*, March 27. Accessed October 12, 2020. http://strangehorizons.com/non-fiction/articles/interview-karen-traviss/.

Murphy, Patrick D. 1995. *Literature, Nature, and Other: Ecofeminist Critiques*. Albany, NY: SUNY Press.

———. 2015. *Persuasive Aesthetic Ecocritical Praxis: Climate Change, Subsistence, and Questionable Futures*. Lanham, MD: Lexington Books.

———. 2009. "Subjects, Identities, Bodies, and Selves: Siblings, Symbiotes, and the Ecological Stakes of Self Perception." *Topia – Canadian Journal of Cultural Studies* 21: 121–135. Accessed October 12, 2020. doi:10.3138/topia.21.121.

Parr, Adrian. 2013. *The Wrath of Capital: Neoliberalism and Climate Change Politics*. New York, NY: Columbia University Press.

Pearce, Fred. 2012. *The Land Grabbers: The New Fight Over Who Owns the Earth*. Boston, MA: Beacon.

———. 2006. *When the Rivers Run Dry: Water – The Defining Crisis of the Twenty-First Century*. Boston, MA: Beacon.

Ress, Mary Judith. 2006. *Ecofeminism in Latin America*. Maryknoll, NY: Orbis Books.

Ryan, Kathleen J., and Elizabeth J. Natalie. 2001. "Fusing Horizons: Standpoint Hermeneutics and Invitational Rhetoric." *RSQ: Rhetoric Society Quarterly* 31, no. 2: 69–90.

Shiva, Vandana. 2005. *Globalization's New Wars: Seed, Water & Life Forms*. New Delhi: Women Unlimited.

Smail, Daniel Lord. 2008. *On Deep History and the Brain*. Berkeley, CA: University of California Press.

Sullivan, Heather. 2010. "Unbalanced Nature, Unbounded Bodies, and Unlimited Technology: Ecocriticism and Karen Traviss' Wess'har Series." *Bulletin of Science, Technology & Society* 30, no. 4: 274–284.

Taylor, Shelley E. 2002. *The Tending Instinct: How Nurturing is Essential for Who We are and How We Live*. New York, NY: Henry Holt.

Traviss, Karen. 2004a. *City of Pearl*. New York, NY: Eos.

———. 2004b. *Crossing the Line*. New York, NY: Eos.

———. 2005. *The World Before*. New York, NY: Eos.

———. 2006. *Matriarch*. New York, NY: Eos.

———. 2007a. *Ally*. New York, NY: Eos.

———. 2007b. "Karen Traviss Responds to John Heckman." *Extrapolation* 48, no. 3: 620.

———. 2008. *Judge*. New York, NY: Eos.

Yong, Ed. 2013. "Bacterial DNA in Human Genomes." *Scientist*, June 20. Accessed October 12, 2020. https://www.the-scientist.com/news-opinion/bacterial-dna-in-human-genomes-39147.

9 "The Force Is Strong with This One"

A Material Feminist Approach to *Star Wars*[1]

Başak Ağın

Traditionally dominated by the white male, science fiction as both a literary and a cinematic genre has habitually had phobic relations[2] with femininity and diversity. "A genre concerned first and foremost with masculine concerns," science fiction has almost standardized "the general sidelining of women," reducing their "role and space" mostly to "active sidekicks," which means women in science fiction can only exist as "the exception, not the norm" (Kac-Vergne 2016). This "virtual exclusion of women," as Jenny Wolmark (1988, 48) aptly points out, has inflicted so many constraints on women's production of science fiction that one can consider feminist science-fiction "a contradiction in terms."

A relatively recent example of this was experienced during the 2015 Hugo Awards. The proponents of a more conventional and mainstream science fiction complained about the publication of "left-wing diversity lectures" under the science-fiction label, and about "soft science majors (lit and humanities degrees) using SF/F as a tool to critically examine and vivisect 21st-century Western society" (Lovell 2016). Ironically, the complainers seemed not to be aware that science fiction has primarily been a genre of literature and that the first science-fiction novel, *Frankenstein* (1818), was penned by a female author, Mary Shelley. Unsurprisingly though, what they decried as "left-wing diversity lectures" and "critical examination of Western society by literature and humanities majors" had mostly been written by female and/or nonwhite authors. Leaving the archaic discussion of whether science fiction must involve "rocket science only" aside, I believe, there is a more crucial problem here. The problem of inclusion in science fiction seems to persist, despite the genre's openness and suitability to diversity. Science fiction, as Irene Sanz Alonso (2021) points out, could offer alternative modes to help prevent the replication of oppressive patterns, highlighting such values as respect, understanding, and interconnectedness. So, the resistance toward inclusion looks like a missed opportunity for science fiction.

Having been an area of contest for the role of the female and/or nonhuman characters since its debut with what came later to be known as Episode IV: *A New Hope* (1977), *Star Wars* has been no exception to this debate. Due to its under- or misrepresentation of the female, the racial, the ethnic, and/or nonhuman "Other," the saga formerly received plenty of criticism from both fans and academic circles. Some of these critiques include the notorious reduction of nonhuman figures like Jabba the Hutt and Jar Jar Binks to stereotypes of particular ethnic diversities, such as "the Italian gangster," "the Zulu leader," or "the Jamaican Rastafarian," and female heroes like Leia and Padmé to a mere function of the plot as the damsel-in-distress, an object of romanticism for the protagonist, or a heterosexual male fantasy. Including very few nonwhite actors in the whole saga was another point of criticism.[3] Following a similar thread, Jeffrey A. Brown (2018, 339) pinpoints the debate over the positioning of Leia and Padmé, concerning whether they are principally sturdy "heroines" or undeveloped types portrayed simply as "damsels." He argues that, in both the old trilogy and the prequels, these two figures were characterized in reduced strength, which confined them to supporting roles only. Philip L. Simpson (2006, 116) also states his discontent over the gradual decrease in autonomy in those initially significant and robust female characters.

Yet, these critiques appear to have worked, as Episodes VII, VIII, and IX play a different tune, allowing more space for the female and nonhuman characters. These *Star Wars* films, although there is still so much to achieve in this direction, transformed the saga from derogatory representations into a more inclusive and less reductionist universe. To quote Gwendoline Christie (2016, 65), who played the part of Captain Phasma,[4] "it just seems logical to me that people want to see a more diverse representation of our society," and if this is the case, then why not discuss diversity and ecofeminism in light of *Star Wars*? In what follows, I explore the evolutionary pathways that have led *Star Wars* to inclusion and discuss the concept of the "force" in relation to the idea of agential matter. Before further elaborating on the feminist links between the Force and agential matter, however, the extent of women's inclusion in the first two trilogies needs a visit. This can be discussed via three strong female figures in order of appearance: Leia, Shmi, and Padmé.

Leia is introduced in the 1977 movie as a fearless Alderaanian politician. Until her real identity is revealed, she is known only by her princess title, which she in fact gained from her adoptive parents, Queen Breha and Senator Bail Organa. Not to the audience's knowledge until very later in the saga, Princess Leia is force-sensitive and trained in the ways of the Force after the Battle of Endor, which reached the extent that she constructed her own lightsaber, although she admits to not completing this training later in the series.[5] Thus, even though the first three movies do not give much credit to her force-sensitivity, Leia has challenged the passivity attributed to the female characters. Supporting this claim, Berger (2012, 16) points out how

Leia "grabs a blaster, zaps stormtroopers, and shows herself to be a strong person." Diana Dominguez (2007, 116) also notes that Leia displays a hero

> without losing her gendered status; she does not have to play the cute, helpless sex kitten or become sexless and androgynous to get what she wants. She can be strong, sassy, outspoken, bossy, and bitchy, and still be respected and seen as feminine.

In the trilogy of Episodes VII, VIII, and IX, the respect that Leia receives reaches a higher level, with her force-sensitivity becoming more visible and her title, "General Organa," implying less a princess and more an army leader. This means that she does not only hold a title she inherited, but she has earned one through years of training as a pilot and fighter. Her capabilities as a military commander and a decision-maker help transform Leia from being questioned as a damsel-in-distress or a sex-slave[6] to attaining the status she deserves. Her wit, her piloting skills, and her competence with weaponry make Leia what she is. The character also became "a striking icon for a proudly feminist demonstration" in January 2017, which featured banners and posters displaying her as a princess and a general, stating "a woman's place is in the resistance" (Gibson 2017). She has become a clear symbol of women's empowerment so much so that Leia has clearly set the norm in her final years in *Star Wars*.

The feminine powers are also visible throughout the second trilogy, partly in Leia's grandmother, Shmi Skywalker, and partly in her mother, Padmé Amidala. In Episode I: *The Phantom Menace* (1999), Shmi is portrayed as a single parent who tries to raise her son Anakin as well as possible despite the poor living conditions brought about by slavery. When approached by Qui-Gon Jinn, who wishes to take Anakin away for his Jedi training, she is brave enough to say, "But you cannot stop the change, no more than you can stop the suns from setting." Despite knowing that she will never be able to see her son again, she agrees to send him with Qui-Gon to provide Anakin with the better life she believes he deserves. This scene presents a generous and influential female figure capable of making logical decisions without falling into emotional traps. In this sense, Shmi subverts the role attributed to a stereotypical female character, often associated with the natural, irrational, weak, passive side of the infamous, socially constructed dualism, employed to oppress women, as Imelda Martín Junquera (this volume) argues. Shmi can make a rational decision, putting her feelings and emotions at stake. We observe here a reversal of the traditional positions ascribed to male and female humans in the form of rationality and emotionality. Shmi, as a powerful single mother, skillfully controls her emotions and can thus be associated with rationality.[7]

In the following episodes, II and III, only when he sides with his emotions does Anakin fail in his decisions as a Jedi/Sith. In other words, Shmi represents Anakin's rational side, while his Jedi masters, Qui-Gon and Obi-Wan, implicitly symbolize his emotional attachments. One can think, for instance, about the moment when Qui-Gon insists that the Jedi Council take Anakin as a padawan. That insistence is mostly, if not solely, based on Qui-Gon's unavoidable feelings of sympathy, or perhaps pity and attachment, for young Ani. Along similar lines, the famous "You were like my brother, Anakin. I loved you!" quote from Obi-Wan in Episode III: *Revenge of the Sith* (2005) reveals an outburst of disappointment that flows from strong emotional bonding. This means that, despite the Jedis' claims of no attachment, they "sometimes" lack control over their feelings. In contrast to the Jedis' alleged preference for rationality over emotions, the one who is capable of battling with her emotions is Shmi, a non-Jedi female figure. Therefore, the conventionally hierarchical relationship between the so-called rational male with a higher rank (*bios*) and the allegedly emotional female with no status (*zoë*) is debunked. Zoë seems to have co-opted its centuries-old suppressor through the character of Shmi Skywalker, who is the only known ancestor to all the heroes that formulate the core of the *Star Wars* saga.

A similar debate over "emotions versus no emotions" is also observed in Anakin's attraction to Padmé, which primarily brings his downfall. Following his poignant side, Anakin lets the dark side grow inside him and breaks his oath for no attachment. Thus, Padmé is observed as strong a female influence on Anakin as Shmi. These two women form the basis of Anakin's Oedipal complex and trigger his struggle to release a loved one from the hands of death. Indeed, from a Freudian perspective, both Shmi and Padmé can be considered the underlying bricks that paved the way for the making of Darth Vader, on whose story the entire saga is built. In this sense, one can even claim that the narrative forces that compose *Star Wars* mainly rely on feminine powers. It was mostly because he failed to rescue his mother that Anakin strongly aches to save Padmé, and it was his love of and attachment to his mother and his wife that led to his turning to the dark side, hence becoming Vader. Padmé's various depictions as the Queen of Naboo and the ultimate voice of diplomacy in the Galactic Republic, especially after her becoming an invaluable member of the Galactic Senate during the Clone Wars, also indicate the powers attached to female heroes in the second trilogy.[8] The saga seems to have continued learning from past criticisms, which might explain the presence and influence assigned to Shmi and Padmé in the prequels (and to an assortment of nonwhite and/or nonhuman figures in the following movies and other media). Padmé's diplomatic position accompanied by her being the mother of two pivotal characters, the Jedi Master Luke Skywalker and the Princess/General Leia Skywalker Organa, makes her as crucial as Shmi. From a conventional ecofeminist reading, therefore, the (re)productive power of these two significant female figures may indicate the feminine energy of changing the course of events—by literally and metaphorically giving birth to the main characters of the old trilogy.

From the late 2000s and early 2010s onward, the snowballing figures of female and/or nonhuman characters in the *Star Wars* saga have signaled a change in favor of all "the Others" in science fiction. The *Star Wars* canon continues to thrive with new movies, fan-fictions, video games, and side-stories, to invent many new female and/or nonhuman heroes, who are not only increasing in number but also becoming more diversified in terms of race and species. Take Ahsoka Tano, for example, a Togruta female from Shili assigned as a young and restless padawan to Anakin in the animated film and series *Star Wars: The Clone Wars* (2008–2020). Ahsoka fought together with Anakin as a commander in the Grand Army of the Republic, leading frontline campaigns against the Confederacy of Independent Systems. Or take Mon Mothma, a Chandrilan human female who served as a powerful anti-war politician in both the Galactic and Imperial Senates, working closely with Organa for the establishment of a rebellion against the empire. The variety involves both humans and nonhumans who have appeared in the Expanded Universe, such as Sith Ladies Mara Jade (Human) and Asajj Ventress (Dathomirian), Jedi General Aayla Secura (Twi'lek), the leader/pilot of the Rebels, Hera Syndulla (Twi'lek), force-sensitive "pirate queen" Maz Kanata (Humanoid from Takadana), human female heroes Rose Tico, Jyn Erso, Vice Admiral Holdo, and finally, Rey, the young Jedi, who is so powerful to use her grandfather Palpatine's signature strike of force lightning in *The Rise of Skywalker*.

One can then suggest that the diversity issue is becoming more welcome in *Star Wars*, as exemplified by the opening lines of season 7, episode 1 of the animated series *Star Wars: The Clone Wars* (2008–2020): "Embrace others for their differences, for that makes you whole." Beginning with minor steps in the prequels (1997–2003) and the animated series, then continuing with the later films like Episode VII: *The Force Awakens* (2015), Episode VIII: *The Last Jedi* (2017), Episode IX: *The Rise of Skywalker* (2019) as well as with *Rogue One* (2016), *Star Wars* seems to have evolved into a more diverse universe. So, *Star Wars* is currently offering a more inclusive and an almost equally shared environment, which, symbolically speaking, aligns with the material turn, chiefly conjectured by feminist scholars. Incorporating into its body more females and more characters of other colors as well as of various species, *Star Wars* is in a state of *becoming*, assuming a more encompassing perspective. Even more notably, taking a more explanatory approach to what it means by the "Force" and how the Force surrounds the universe that hosts all life forms along with the non-living things, it is embracing diversity in a posthumanist and material feminist sense. As Episode VIII: *The Last Jedi* focuses more on how the Force is embedded within all beings and things, I argue that the concept of the Force in *Star Wars* is a reshaped and visually enhanced model of the "living matter" initiative.

The posthumanist ventures like material feminisms, the new materialisms, and material ecocriticism helped ecofeminism bypass a condemned view of women, synonymous with the Mother Earth, which was, in Rebekah Sheldon's apt depiction, "figured as the exploitable source of nurturance" (2015, 199). In synch with Sarah Bezan's arguments (this volume), for example, the aid of the new materialisms to feminism has brought about a new sense of fluidity in the ecological relationships of the past, the present, and the future. Such fluidity is increasingly epitomized in *Star Wars*, which has started, to borrow Stacy Alaimo and Susan Hekman's words (2008, 4), "to take the materiality of the more-than-human world seriously." One can then claim that the saga relieves itself from its past mistakes of under-representation or misrepresentation and draws attention to the indivisibly linked nature-culture continuum that works *"around, through,* and *in* us" (Sullivan 2014, 80; emphases in the original). In a sense, it returns to the core idea on which it is constructed; re-works on it, cultivates and conva-lesces it, and helps the audience more deeply comprehend what the Force is. Regardless of whether the producers are in a conscious attempt to make amends for the exclusionary practices or aim to increase the saga's popu-larity, what *Star Wars* has evolved into echoes a new materialist sense of matter in its lively, agentic, and all-binding formulation. Therefore, I argue, if matter is the interconnecting element for all animate and inanimate bod-ies in our universe, then the Force in the *Star Wars* universe is the science-fiction equivalent of matter on the metaphorical level.[9]

As a result, *Star Wars* in this chapter is considered and interpreted as a set of meaning-making practices, which, by the guidance of its plot, expli-cates a posthumanist form of ecofeminism. Just like ecofeminism, it is seen as part of a bigger context, not merely the saga that George Lucas started, or the fan-fiction of the Expanded Universe, or a Disney by-product that has hit the box-offices all around the world. Perhaps, the famous words of Karen Barad, the feminist author of *Meeting the Universe Halfway* (2007, 26), would elucidate this better: "*We are a part of that nature that we seek to understand*" (emphases in the original). And I suggest, metaphorically, that universe we meet halfway might as well be the *Star Wars* universe. Therefore, I wish to adapt this quote and claim: "We are part of that force we seek to understand." From this perspective, particularly considering the fresher viewpoints on the relationship between matter and meaning-mak-ing practices, *Star Wars* turns out to be an ideal site for drawing parallels between science fiction and ecofeminism in its twenty-first-century shape, which also corresponds with the motives behind this book. Therefore, the phobic relations of science fiction with femininity and diversity require a discussion in light of the links between the Force and lively, agentic, and vibrant matter. Though seemingly at odds at first glance, these two points, as what follows will clarify, are very closely linked indeed.

Returning to the debate in the Hugo Awards, I believe that when over-looking the concept of diversity, the advocates of a popular mainstream sci-ence fiction are following an erratic line of argument for several reasons. To begin, if what they think of science fiction involves yet another story imagin-ing some victorious humans in the face of an alien attack, then this is no dif-ferent than a male-dictated historical account of us/them binary, recapping how "we defeated the invaders" that are not from *our* "religion," "race," or "ethnicity." Too reductionist and too elementary an approach to science fiction in such a world of complex networks. Secondly, if their understanding of science fiction involves fantasies of attaining superhuman powers to dominate other planets (because in ours, we have depleted all resources!), then this is no more than a transhumanist justification of human exploitation of nature or any other "commodity," which is an innately problematic, anthropocentric discourse, dating back to ancient Greeks' distinction between *bios* and *zoë*. Why this distinction is problematic and how it relates to the phobic relations of science fiction with femininity and diversity comprise the basis of a posthumanist argument, which supports my ecofeminist discussions of the Force as matter.

The ancient Greek conceptualization of life consisted of two planes: *bios* (a privileged life) and *zoë* (a simple life). The former, as van den Hengel (2012, 2) reminds us, referred to "the life of the elite male citizens that make up the *polis*," which was exclusive to "rational" powerholders. In contrast, the latter represented "all the 'others' of Man" (Braidotti 2006, 37; capitalization in the original). It signified the absence of rationality, powerlessness, and confinement to home (*oikos*).[10] The division had three implications: It signified a separation of the public and the private; it implied gender-discriminative consequences; it demonstrated the segregation of the animate and the inanimate. These roots of liberal humanism tell us that "the Others" were discriminated against on the alleged grounds that they were not "humans." This means that humanism, as a "species-specific" discourse, can be employed to "oppress both human and nonhuman others" (Wolfe 1998, 42). Any discourse of exclusion, then, implies anthropocentrism and androcentrism, used at the expense of the others that fall into the category of *zoë*. Consequently, when asserting that "a more traditional and a non-diverse approach to science-fiction is necessary,' the supporters of more conventional science fiction are unknowingly or deliberately dedicating themselves to an almost purely male-privileged human domain, which is only preserving and spreading an anthropocentric discourse. Arguing against "left-wing diversity" and "soft science" in science-fiction is nothing more than "a kind of techno-masculinism of a self-caricaturing kind," to borrow the words Haraway (2006, 146) used in critiquing Hans Moravec's *Mind Children: The Future of the Robot and Human Intelligence* (1988), in which Moravec fantasized about the possibility of downloading human mind into a computer, thereby extending humans' social and technological competences. Such dreams of becoming superhumans by controlling nature and technology implicitly or explicitly complement a desire to maintain male exceptionalism which restricts women's, children's, and all the Others' access to and production of life in general, of which science-fiction is only a tiny portion. It is a reiteration of *bios/zoë* distinction. But there is a problem here. If I put the maxim "we are part of that force we seek to understand" on my Twitter page, that would probably receive quite a number of "likes" from *Star Wars* fans from all around the world, male and female alike, perhaps without understanding what it exactly means. And yet, there is no gender, age, color, class, or rank attributed to the first-person plural pronoun in this thought-experimental tweet. "We" refers to everyone.

That reference to everyone, as all living beings and inanimate things, brings us to the relations between the concept of the Force and the agential capabilities of matter as outlined by the new materialist approach feeding ecofeminism. Here, it is possible to draw upon JV Chamary's article on the Force, in which the author relies on Arthur Tansley's (1935) conceptualization of ecosystems, mentioning the interchange between the organic and the inorganic. Chamary (2018) convincingly argues that the Force adheres to the working principles of the ecosystem, where there is a constant interaction between the lively, organic bodies and the inanimate. He notes that this seamless exchange "fuels the ecological cycle." This is reminiscent of two Latin idioms; *Omnia mutantur, nihil interit* ("everything changes, nothing perishes"), which Ovid used in his *Metamorphoses* (circa 8th century AD), and *Omnia mutantur nos et mutamur in illis* ("all things change, and we change with them"), often attributed to the Roman Emperor Lothar I. When combined, these two renowned sayings could be interpreted as the exploration of the law of conservation of mass, to which Chamary also refers. He underlines that matter never disappears, but continuously flows as energy within the biomass, establishing the idea of interconnectedness of all life forms and non-living things.

Chamary's arguments on how the Force is consistent with the ecosystem resonate a lot with the way matter is conceived, first in material feminisms, then in the new materialisms, and finally, in material ecocriticism, all of which can be considered various perspectives of posthumanist-ecofeminism. According to this set of approaches, our assumptions on the "normative sense of the human and its beliefs about human agency" and our "material practices, such as the ways we labor on, exploit, and interact with nature" have been challenged (Coole and Frost 2010, 4). Every being and thing is considered alive in this paradigm. The concept of vitality, re-defined in this new understanding of ontology, rejects the image of the nonhuman as inert, passive, and inanimate, and brings forward the effect-inducing, agential power of matter. Agency here signifies a sense of flux and becoming that occurs "without will or intention or delineation" (Alaimo 2008, 247). The human is in a constant making "with the flows of substances and the agencies of environments" (Alaimo 2014, 187). What Tansley refers to as an ensemble within an ecosystem is called a state of enmeshment, an assemblage, an intra-action, or a mesh by several scholars who have shaped this new paradigm (see Alaimo and Hekman 2008; Barad 2007; Bennett 2010; Coole and Frost 2010; De Landa 2002; Kirby 2011).

Therefore, in correspondence with Chamary's ideas, I argue that this view of matter, as an agentic body, vibrates along with the concept of the Force in *Star Wars*. In Episode IV: *A New Hope*, Obi-Wan Kenobi enlightens Luke

Skywalker by explaining what the Force is: "The Force is what gives a Jedi his[/her/their][11] power," he says. "It's an energy field created by all living things. It surrounds us and penetrates us; it binds the galaxy together." From this definition, one can claim that the way the Force enacts itself and triggers change in a performative manner reverberates Ladelle McWhorter's example of dirt. McWhorter (1999, 166) writes, "dirt isn't a particular, identifiable thing. And yet it acts." Just as the Force leads to enactments and capabilities to trigger change, dirt also performs, "aggregates," and "perpetuates itself." And, so does the Force. If the agential realistic account of the world portrays one inhabited "not by active subjects and passive objects" (Bennett 2015, 224), but by dynamic matter that is in constant communication with the rest of the planetary inhabitants, then that dynamism is an unswerving route to the Force in the *Star Wars* universe.

Perceived this way, the Force bears a strong resemblance not only to the concept of matter in material feminism, but also to Qi as the life force in Eastern philosophy. Just like Qi and vibrant matter, the Force in the *Star Wars* saga refers to the source where all life comes from and returns to. Both Qi and the living matter are alternatives to our current social and cultural practices that neglect the existential power of all life forms, inanimate objects, and impersonal agents like rocks or electricity. Both of them, therefore, indicate an understanding of a cumulative, aggregate ontology based on assemblages, which problematizes the segregating dualisms that seek a linear causality and temporal difference between being and knowing, which arise from *bios/zoë* distinction. This is compellingly illustrated in Heesoon Bai and Avraham Cohen's exploration of Qi (2008, 36): "A dualistic consciousness that categorically separates the self from the world and mind from matter is probably the deepest source of humans' environmental degradation and exploitation of each other." This quotation, which can be treated as an elucidation of the Force metaphor in *Star Wars*, openly supports the idea of matter as vibrant, living, and interconnected *to* and *within* all entities.

To further support the link between the Force and matter as agentic bodies, one can also build another analogy between the Force and Jane Bennett's account of the vitality of matter. In season 6, episode 11 of the animated series *The Clone Wars*, Qui-Gon tells Yoda how he found a way to return by becoming one with the Force after he died in Episode I: *The Phantom Menace*. "I am a manifestation of the Force," he says. He explains how the Force is engendered by the living, and how this force creates a feedback loop to bring together all the things that have ever lived, to bind everything. Qui-Gon's words can indicate an understanding of matter as alive and vibrant, as pointed out by Bennett. As Bennett (2010, xvii) contends, the vitality of matter is not necessarily organic or biotic. The agency here denotes matter's predisposition to accumulate or construct "heterogeneous groupings," which can include both human and nonhuman elements that collaboratively hold the power to generate effect. It underlines the active and dynamic nature of matter. Social and natural phenomena, such as political decisions or natural disasters, are enacted via these coalescent bodies. Matter, therefore, is addressed as the coalescent agency of all entities bound together. It "draws together what appears separate and makes the totality subject to mutation and emergence" (Sheldon 2015, 196), hence the necessity to critically question or "vivisect" the problems of our current era. Such vivisection requires a rethinking of our role as humans, and perhaps leaving the comfort zone of *bios*, acknowledging that the divide between *bios* and *zoë* has never actually existed.

A final connection between the Force and agentic matter can be found in Episode VIII: *The Last Jedi* (2017) when Luke Skywalker tells Rey that the Force is "the energy between all things, a tension, a balance that binds the universe together." As Rey has already experienced how the Force enacts in Episode VII: *The Force Awakens* (2015), she has a sense of what it is like, but cannot fully articulate what it exactly is, which justifies her mistaken explanation, corrected by Luke. However, as I have already argued above, rather than a comprehensive definition, how the Force shows itself in various forms is more important, just as matter does in the new ontology offered by the material turn, as the igniting power behind the twenty-first-century ecofeminism. In fact, as the examples above also demonstrate, in this century, agency is re-defined and shared. It is no longer confined to the meaning of human intentionality, decision-making capabilities, or cognizance. It is carried beyond the capacities of the human domain to the various forms of biological entities and to nonhuman, inorganic bodies. This horizontally aligned ontology distributes agency equally among the human and the nonhuman, which reaches beyond segregations between, say, colors, ethnicities, beliefs, classes, and genders. After all, if the boundary between the human and the nonhuman, mind and matter, and the self and the world is eroded, the other binary oppositions that create discriminatory "-isms" remain moot. What comes instead is an amalgamation of compound agencies, both human and nonhuman, which necessitates a rethinking and reviewing of our ways of life, ways of understanding, and ways of meaning-making to balance our relations with the other inhabitants of our planet. And inevitably, this change asks us to revisit and reconsider what makes us human. If the concept of the human is rethought in this posthumanist way, then the age of resistance becomes the age of *zoë*. Under this light, if the Force is a unifying, living vibration that circulates within human and nonhuman feedback loops, then the core of the *Star Wars* saga has always already relied on a feminist, pro-diversity, new materialist philosophy. So, when someone says, "May the Force Be with You," they might not necessarily mean "you" as a gendered, biological body with reasoning skills, cognizance, and emotions, but may perhaps refer to an impersonal agent, which is always already one with the Force.

Notes

1 An extended Turkish version of this chapter, which includes much larger discussions, appeared with the title "'Güç Sizinle Olsun': *Yıldız Savaşları'*nda Posthuman Öznenin Yokluktan Çokluğa Serüveni" ("May the Force Be with You": The Journey of the Posthuman Subject in *Star Wars* from Absence to Plurality) in the author's monograph, *Posthümanizm: Kavram, Kuram, Bilim-Kurgu* (2020) (Posthumanism: Concept, Theory, Science-Fiction), published by Siyasal Kitabevi, Ankara.

2 This phrase is an allusion to Serpil Oppermann's (2010) article "Ecocriticism's Phobic Relations with Theory."

3 Black actors in the first trilogy were limited to Billy Dee Williams (as Lando Calrissian), Femi Taylor (as Jabba the Hutt's slave-dancer Twi'lek), and James Earl Jones, who gave Darth Vader his voice. The prequel involved only Samuel L. Jackson as Mace Windu. Episodes VII, VIII, and IX have more diversity with other nonwhite actors, such as John Boyega (as Finn), Lupita Nyong'o (as Maz Kanata), Kelly Marie Tran (as Rose Tico), and Oscar Isaac (as Poe Dameron), but *Star Wars* seems to have a long way to go to overcome its notoriety.

4 The character of Captain Phasma, the commander of the First Order stormtroopers, was first introduced in *The Force Awakens* (2015) and reappeared in *The Last Jedi* (2017), the animated series *Star Wars Resistance* (2018), as well as various comics and video games. "A progressive female character," in Christie's own words, to whom we feel connected not by the way she is "made flesh" but by her humanness (quoted in Young 2019), Captain Phasma is depicted as a mentally and physically robust character.

5 Timothy Zahn's *Star Wars: Thrawn Trilogy* (1991–1993) outlines this well.

6 This is a reference to Leia's famous bikini costume when she is held captive by Jabba the Hutt.

7 Although the binary opposition of rationality/emotionality is also problematic even in their reversed forms, I still wish to consider Shmi's portrayal as a strong figure with high reasoning skills an improvement in the positioning of the female characters in *Star Wars*.

8 I feel compelled to present a general criticism from fans and critics alike on Padmé's gradual reduction to "a weak damsel" who dies of "broken heart" in Episode III, and yet her influence as a warrior and a political figure is more visible in the animated series *Clone Wars*. This also raises the question of whether emotions make us really weak and is thus related to some of the key areas that Karen Jones defines (2003, 187) on "normative agency." Why does the one with emotions need to be the irrational or weak one? In search of an answer to this question, one can return, in the broadest sense, to the argument presented by Jones. She notes that emotions and rationality are not necessarily mutually exclusive, adding that the decision-making agent does not hold any agential privilege to decide whether an action is rational or irrational because the decision might depend on the circumstances.

9 I must note here that the new materialist view of matter is largely anti-representationalist due to the extreme power that discourse is granted (see Barad 2007). What we mean by representation only refers to the means that make it possible for the humans to claim access to knowledge and existence. However, in a literary or cultural reading, we, as humans, are limited to our own methods of understanding and interpreting any media product, and, as such, we cannot evade reading those codes via representations. This is why in this chapter, I follow Bruno Latour (1999, 214) and prefer to "have" my "cake" and "eat it too." If one can be a "monist" and "make distinctions," I see no harm in following a new materialist thread and using representations as my discussion point at the same time.

10 It is interesting how *oikos* came to be the root of the prefix *eco-*, as in ecology, hence the constant othering of nature along with all the others of Anthropos as the white, rational, able-bodied, male powerholder. What is paradoxical is that it is also the constant othering of something that originally means "home."

11 These pronouns are added to overcome the still-persisting gender-discrimination here.

References

Alaimo, Stacy. 2008. "Trans-Corporeal Feminisms and the Ethical Space of Nature." In *Material Feminisms*, edited by Stacy Alaimo and Susan J. Hekman, 237–264. Bloomington, IN: Indiana University Press.

———. 2014. "Oceanic Origins, Plastic Activism, and New Materialism at Sea." In *Material Ecocriticism*, edited by Serenella Iovino and Serpil Oppermann, 186–203. Bloomington, IN: Indiana University Press.

Alaimo, Stacy, and Susan J. Hekman. 2008. "Introduction: Emerging Models of Materiality in Feminist Theory." In *Material Feminisms*, edited by Stacy Alaimo and Susan J. Hekman, 1–19. Bloomington, IN: Indiana University Press.

Bai, Heesoon, and Avraham Cohen. 2008. "Breathing Qi (Ch'i), Following Dao (Tao): Transforming This Violence-Ridden World." In *Cross-cultural Studies in Curriculum: Eastern Thought, Educational Insights*, edited by Claudia Eppert and Hongyu Wang, 35–54. New York, NY: Routledge.

Barad, Karen. 2007. *Meeting the Universe Halfway: Quantum Physics and the Entanglement of Matter and Meaning*. Durham, NC: Duke University Press.

Bennett, Jane. 2010. *Vibrant Matter: A Political Ecology of Things*. Durham, NC: Duke University Press.

———. 2015. "Systems and Things: On Vital Materialism and Object-Oriented Philosophy." In *The Nonhuman Turn*, edited by Richard Grusin, 223–239. Minneapolis, MN: University of Minnesota Press.

Berger, Arthur. 2012. "Is *Star Wars* a Modernized Fairy Tale?" In *Myth, Media, and Culture in Star Wars: An Anthology*, edited by Douglas Brode and Leah Deyneka, 13–19. Lanham, MD: Scarecrow Press.

Braidotti, Rosi. 2006. *Transpositions: On Nomadic Ethics*. Cambridge, UK: Polity Press.

Brown, Jeffrey A. 2018. "#wheresRey: Feminism, Protest, and Merchandising Sexism in *Star Wars: The Force Awakens*." *Feminist Media Studies* 18, no. 3: 335–348. Accessed September 19, 2020. doi:10.1080/14680777.2017.1313291.

Chamary, J. V. 2018. "'*Star Wars: The Last Jedi*' Finally Explains the Force." *Forbes*, January 6. Accessed September 07, 2020. https://www.forbes.com/sites/jvchamary/2018/01/06/star-wars-last-jedi-force/#6ec955c17a32.

Christie, Gwendoline. 2016. "Interview." *PEOPLE*, January 4.

Coole, Diana, and Samantha Frost. 2010. "Introducing the New Materialisms." In *New Materialisms: Ontology, Agency, and Politics*, edited by Diana Coole and Samantha Frost, 1–43. Durham, NC: Duke University Press.

De Landa, Manuel. 2002. *Intensive Science and Virtual Philosophy*. London: Bloomsbury.

Dominguez, Diana. 2007. "Feminism and the Force: Empowerment and Disillusionment in a Galaxy Far, Far Away …." In *Culture, Identities and*

Technology in the Star Wars Films: Essays on the Two Trilogies, edited by Carl Silvio and Tony Vinci, 109–133. Jefferson, IA: McFarland.

Gibson, Caitlin. 2017. "How Princess Leia Became an Unofficial Symbol for the Women's March." *The Washington Post*, January 23. Accessed March 1, 2020. https://www.washingtonpost.com/news/arts-and-entertainment/wp/2017/01/23/how-princess-leia-became-an-unofficial-symbol-for-the-womens-march/.

Haraway, Donna. 2006. "When We Have Never Been Human, What Is to Be Done?: Interview with Donna Haraway." Interview by Nicholas Gane. *Theory, Culture & Society* 23, nos. 7–8: 135–158.

Jones, Karen. 2003. "Emotion, Weakness of Will, and Normative Conception of Agency." In *Philosophy and the Emotions*, edited by Anthony Hatzimoysis. Cambridge: Cambridge University Press.

Kac-Vergne, Marianne. 2016. "Sidelining Women in Contemporary Science-Fiction Film." *Miranda* 12. Accessed February 29, 2020. http://miranda.revues.org/8642.

Kirby, Vicki. 2011. *Quantum Anthropologies: Life at Large*. Durham, NC: Duke University Press.

Latour, Bruno. 1999. *Pandora's Hope: Essays on the Reality of Science Studies*. Cambridge, MA: Harvard University Press.

Lovell, Bronwyn. 2016. "Friday Essay: Science Fiction's Women Problem." *The Conversation*, September 15. Accessed May 21, 2020. https://theconversation.com/friday-essay-science-fictions-women-problem-58626.

McWhorter, Ladelle. 1999. *Bodies and Pleasures: Foucault and the Politics of Sexual Normalization*. Bloomington, IN: Indiana University Press.

Moravec, Hans. 1988. *Mind Children: The Future of the Robot and Human Intelligence*. Boston, MA: Harvard University Press.

Oppermann, Serpil. 2010. "Ecocriticism's Phobic Relations with Theory." *ISLE: Interdisciplinary Studies in Literature and Environment* 17, no. 4: 768–770. Accessed May 20, 2020. http://www.jstor.org/stable/44087671.

Sanz Alonso, Irene. 2021. "Alien Ecofeminist Societies: 'Sharers' in Joan Slonczewski's A Door into Ocean." In *Dystopias and Utopias on Earth and Beyond: Feminist Ecocriticism of Science Fiction*, edited by Douglas A. Vakoch, 114–125. Abingdon, Oxon, UK and New York, NY: Routledge.

Sheldon, Rebekah. 2015. "Form/Matter/Chora: Object-Oriented Ontology and Feminist New Materialism." In *The Nonhuman Turn*, edited by Richard Grusin, 193–222. Minneapolis, MN: University of Minnesota Press.

Simpson, Philip L. 2006. "Thawing the Ice Princess." In *Finding the Force of the Star Wars Franchise*, edited by Matthew Wilhelm Kapell and John Shelton Lawrence, 110–122. New York, NY: Peter Lang Publishing.

Star Wars. 1977. Film. Directed by George Lucas. USA: 20th Century Fox.

Star Wars: Phantom Menace. 1999. Film. Directed by George Lucas. USA: Lucasfilm.

Star Wars: Revenge of the Sith. 2005. Film. Directed by George Lucas. USA: Lucasfilm.

Star Wars: The Clone Wars. 2008–2020. Animated Series. Directed by Dave Filoni. USA: Lucasfilm Animation.

Star Wars: The Force Awakens. 2015. Film. Directed by J. J. Abrams. USA: Walt Disney Pictures.

Star Wars: The Last Jedi. 2017. Film. Directed by Rian Johnson. USA: Walt Disney Pictures.

Sullivan, Heather I. 2014. "The Ecology of Colors: Goethe's Materialist Optics and Ecological Posthumanism." In *Material Ecocriticism*, edited by Serenella Iovino and Serpil Oppermann, 80–94. Bloomington, IN: Indiana University Press.

van den Hengel, Louis. 2012. "Zoegraphy: Per/forming Posthuman Lives." *Biography* 35, no. 1: 1–20.

Wolfe, Cary. 1998. *Critical Environments: Postmodern Theory and the Pragmatics of the "Outside."* Minneapolis, MN: Minnesota University Press.

Wolmark, Jenny. 1988. "Alternative Futures?: Science Fiction and Feminism." *Cultural Studies* 2, no. 1: 48–56. Accessed February 29, 2020. doi:10.1080/09502388800490021.

Young, Bryan. 2019. "Age of Resistance: Captain Phasma and Her Origins – In-Universe and Out." In *Star Wars: Age of Resistance – Villains*, Written by Tom Taylor and Illustrated by Leonard Kirk. New York, NY: Marvel Comics.

10 Chinese Science Fiction and Representations of Ecofeminists

Mad Women or Women Warriors

Peter I-min Huang

Chen Qui-fan's *The Waste Tide* (2013) and Liu Cixin's *The Three-Body Problem* (2008) are two recent critically acclaimed works of science-fiction (sci-fi) that are examined here against ecofeminist theory in its latest, so-called fourth wave, manifestations. Those reflect more engagements with literature produced outside of the West and with work produced by scholars in the burgeoning areas of environmental theory and practice of queer ecology, environmental justice, (critical) animal studies, (critical) plant studies, postcolonial studies, and climate justice.[1] A comparison here of Liu's mainstream sci-fi novel and Chen's less well-known cyberpunk sci-fi novel, a comparison that is inspired by those latest directions in ecofeminism, sheds light on the ways in which *The Three Body-Problem*, which has been more successful from a financial and commercial point of view than has been the cyberpunk and sci-fi novel *The Waste Tide*, tacitly defers to and indulges in popular and dominant masculinist constructions of and fantasies about eco-terrorists and eco-fascists. Those constructions appear in and betray the novel's three apparently profoundly and disturbingly morally flawed main characters, individuals who become disillusioned with the direction in which small but powerful groups of humans who have no faith in Earth's oldest environments are steering the planet. Through two of those characters in particular, Ye Wenjie and Wenjie's daughter Yang Dong, the novel subtly and disingenuously depicts ecofeminists as violent women and madwomen. In contrast, *The Waste Tide* is more sympathetic to the kinds of environmental positions and goals upon which Liu's novel casts doubt. Chen's sci-fi novel expresses in effect that if one wishes to identify and challenge violent and militant eco-fascist agendas, rogue eco-cults, and eco-terrorists, then one must look to mainstream, dominant directions in society and industry. Those directions betray masculinist ideologies. The novel focuses on one of those directions in particular, that which identifies the electronics and electronic waste (e-waste) industries. Specifically, the novel questions the ongoing problem of illegal dumping of e-waste in China, a country that continues to be "the world's largest e-waste dumping ground" despite the government's ban on importing e-waste since 2000 (Healey 2017, 3). The novel's principal protagonist is an ecofeminist woman warrior, Xiaomi.

The Three-Body Problem

The emergence of sci-fi in China impressively owes to Liu Cixin (born in 1963), arguably the country's most prominent and popular contemporary sci-fi writer (Han Song 2013, 17; Mingwei Song 2013, 95) and certainly one of its most successful. Liu is one of the "Big Three" Chinese sci-fi authors, the other two of whom are Han Song (1969–) and Wang Jinkang (1948–) (Hua 2015, 519). Liu's *The Three-Body Problem*, the first in his sci-fi trilogy (*San Ti*), which includes *The Dark Forest* and *Death's End*, is Liu's most well-known and critically acclaimed work. The recipient of the prestigious Hugo Award in 2015 following the translation of the novel into English in 2014, *The Three-Body Problem* has earned high praise from the general public as well as literary critics. The former includes such notable figures as Mark Zuckerberg, founder of Facebook, and Barack Obama, former US president (Healey 2017, 1).

As Han and other literary critics recognize Liu's contribution to sci-fi, his work represents the most dominant strain of sci-fi, one that has inspired Chinese sci-fi since its inception in the first decade of the last century (Han Song 2013, 15). That is to say, Liu's science fictions reflect popular optimism and faith in science and technology and the ability of the human species to reach states of freedom and perfection through science and technology; they bestow relatively little interest on the moral and ethical questions that tug at the titanium sleeves of that faith, and are "the least influenced by Chinese politics" (Mingwei Song 2013, 95).[2] As sci-fi literature scholar Mingwei Song notes, the myriad actual and historical material struggles of humans on the planet Earth are "a minor" concern in Liu's fictions in contrast with the cosmic object of cynosure of the "extravagant and grandiose backdrop" of "the universe" (95). Liu thus also expresses little sympathy for, and even distaste and indifference toward, the natural world (the oldest extant environments of Earth (Ding 2019).[3]

Liu's utopian sci-fi *The Three-Body Problem,* is a salient example of the author's sci-fi output. The novel reflects mainstream popular beliefs that science and technology will bring great gains to the human species. It also reflects mainstream attitudes of skepticism and condescension toward the world's oldest environments and toward environmentalists' efforts to save those environments from being exploited and eradicated under projects that heavily rely on and enlist scientific and technological discovery. Those attitudes tie to Liu's portrayals of the novel's central female protagonist, the physicist Ye Wenjie, and two other main characters, Wenjie's daughter Yang Dong, also a physicist, and Mike Evans, a US animal rights and environmental activist. All three are more or less subtly portrayed as mad, deluded, and deranged thinkers and activists clinging to an obsolete vision of Earth; eco-terrorists and eco-fascists fighting an ethically moribund struggle against scientific and technological advances; and backward-looking "luddite" humans vainly holding onto the anachronistic belief that humans should share the planet with their "earthothers."[4] At the same time, these characters and their very centrality put into serious question what the novel seems to be lauding.

Described by critics as a novel that fits into the sci-fi subgenre of "technological utopias" (Hua 2017) and a novel that reads as a "complex apocalyptic space opera" (Yan 2013, 2), *The Three-Body Problem* follows the fates of Ye Wenjie (and her daughter Yang Dong and a fellow environmental thinker and activist, Mike Evans). It begins in the present when Wenjie, in her late sixties, is being interviewed by Wang Miao, a nanomaterials researcher who is taking part in the investigation of the suicide of Wenjie's daughter, Yang Dong. Subsequently, Wenjie herself is investigated and charged with conspiring with Mike Evans, the US environmentalist, entomologist, ornithologist, and animal rights advocate, to bring about the invasion and conquest of Earth by Trisolaris, an extraterrestrial civilization. During the interrogation and trial of Wenjie, she recollects her past, which includes two major events and turning points in her life that set her on the path to where she is now.

The first of the two events, both of which occur in the time of the Cultural Revolution (1966–1976), has haunted Wenjie for years. When she was a young student at the prestigious Tsinghua University, she witnessed the persecution of her mother and father, highly distinguished physics professors at Tsinghua. Her mother was forced to falsely testify against her father, and she lost her mind when she (and the young Wenjie) saw four Red Guard youths frenetically beat to death her husband (Wenjie's father). The second event refers to a slightly later time in Wenjie's life when she learned about and read *Silent Spring* (1962), an actual text by the scientist Rachel Carson. Wenjie reads Carson's book after she is assigned to work on a project in a remote area of Inner Mongolia and meets a journalist who recommends the book to her. What most catches Wenjie's attention in that world of old China are its giant ancient trees, and the massive felling of them that is taking place to make way for what people are being told will be a newer and braver world. The trees' deaths remind Wenjie of her father and mother, cut down in their prime, at the height of their intellectual capacities, because their knowledge threatens and impedes the Cultural Revolution projects. Wenjie thinks of *Silent Spring* and Carson's fight against the US government's widespread use of a pesticide ("DDT"), a fight that Carson helped to win with the publication of *Silent Spring*; and she compares that kind of totalitarianism to the Cultural Revolution, which is purging society of anyone or anything that stands in the way of the government's modern industrial blueprint for China.

Both of the aforesaid experiences, Wenjie's witnessing of the barbaric treatment of her family as a young girl and her reading of *Silent Spring* later in her life when she is assigned by the government to work in Inner Mongolia, shape Wenjie in different ways. She is distrustful of most humans, including her own husband. She has more faith in the nonhuman ecogenic world and its workings than in "the human" and its enterprises. Both experiences eventually lead her to committing extreme acts of violence (homicide) and attempting to carry out an ambitious but doomed eco-terrorist goal.

Following her work on the project in Inner Mongolia, Wenjie, an intrepid physicist, is assigned to work on a project at the Red Coast Base, a secret military base and high-level astrophysical and solar activity research center situated at the summit of Inner Mongolia's Radar Peak. She becomes familiar with the organization, Search for Extraterrestrial Intelligence (SETI), and is the first human to successfully send a message (to the sun) and receive an extraterrestrial reply.[5] However, because of her distrust of humans, Wenjie goes to great lengths to prevent her colleagues and supervisors from discovering her success of sending and receiving a message from extraterrestrials. She thus murders, without being found out for that, Commissar Lei, a senior project worker and official, and Chief Yang, who also is Wenjie's husband.

When the Cultural Revolution ends, Wenjie returns to Tsinghua University and takes up a teaching position there. In the meantime, she has given birth to a daughter, Yang Dong (whose father is Chief Yang, Wenjie's now-deceased husband). Wenjie raises Dong to spurn all scientific and technological research that is inimical to both women and the natural world. Thus, when Dong grows up, following in the steps of her mother to become a physicist, she joins a cult-like group called the Frontiers of Science. The goal of its members is to push science in directions that are opposite to the dominant and mainstream trajectories of scientific research of transforming, deliberately or by default, the planet into a predominantly anthropogenic (human-made) and human-controlled, planet. However, the Frontiers of Science disintegrate as its members become increasingly disillusioned with their species and even their own beloved profession. They reach the point when they reject altogether the merit of scientific inquiry and so spurn their lifelong engagement with physics. Out of despair, Dong commits suicide. In the note that she leaves behind, written down on a small piece of fragrant birch bark that is from one of the trees in the forest where she lives as a recluse, Dong states that the sum total of her scientific research amounted to nothing but a vainglorious and irresponsible, anthropocentric pursuit.

Sometime after Wenjie returned to Tsinghua University and took up a teaching position at the university while raising her daughter Dong, Wenjie met Mike Evans. Similar to Wenjie, Mike also has been profoundly influenced by an immensely popular and critically acclaimed work of anti-human-exceptionalism literature. In Mike's case, it is Peter Singer's *Animal Liberation* (1975), an actual animal rights text that brought widespread attention to the horrific exploitation of various animal species by humans. The son of a billionaire oilman, Mike first becomes involved in the animal rights movement after one of his father's giant oil tankers wrecks off the coast and spills crude oil into the Atlantic Ocean. When Mike sees the sea suffocating under a thick film of oil, the seabirds drowning in it, and countless carcasses of seabirds floating on the slick, he decides to devote his life to animal and plant life advocacy. At university, he studies biology and specializes in entomology and ornithology. In his estimation and according to his ecocentric value system, an insect or bird species is as unique and irreplaceable as the human species, and so he founds a "Pan-Species Communism" society, the main tenet of which is that all lives are equal. Subsequently, he travels to China because he believes that that tenet has long existed in that country and other regions in the East. When he and Wenjie meet, they find they have much in common.

Mike tells Wenjie about his "Pan-Species Communism" society and the close critical ties between it and both Buddhism and Arne Naess' movement of deep ecology. Although he believes that the Buddhist teachings of non-violence and reverence for life have more in common with the ecocentric principles of deep ecology than do Christian teachings, he is deeply disappointed when he arrives in China and finds much of what he sought to escape from in the West. He works in a remote and hilly region in northwest China, planting trees in an effort to slow the attrition of local swallow populations under markedly anthropocentric and dominant directions in industrialization and urbanization. Wenjie tells him about her work at the Red Coast Base and her communications with extraterrestrials. Together, Wenjie and Mike establish the radical environmental Earth-Trisolaris Organization (ETO), an ambitious plan to invite the extraterrestrial civilization Trisolaris to invade Earth and sabotage what Mike and Wenjie see to be their species' aggressive and appetitive colonization of Earth. Their plan is aborted when they are discovered by authorities. Mike is executed. Wenjie is put on trial. Liu's novel ends as the trial is taking place. The last sentence of the novel is spoken by Wenjie. "My sunset," she whispers, "And sunset for humanity" (Liu 2014, 390).

Through the three figures of failure of Ye, Yang, and Evans, Liu's *The Three-Body Problem* effectively launches a slippery slope and strawman argument: one cannot support environmental thinking and action that calls for sharing of the planet with other beings besides humans for the reason that that thinking and action are dangerous and doomed, akin to a juggernaut that rolls inexorably toward eco-terrorism and eco-fascism.

What Liu's novel disingenuously identifies as being eco-terrorist and eco-fascist in actuality are the opposite of that, as scholars in the areas of queer ecology, environmental justice, climate justice, indigenous studies, material ecocriticism, and postcolonial ecocriticism argue (Alaimo and Hekman 2015; Nixon 2015; Huggan and Tiffin 2010: Adamson, Evans, and Stein 2015). These scholars are united in their work of identifying and challenging the "logic of domination" that underwrites a wide range of humans' planetary pursuits (Gaard 2017, 35). That logic, which ecofeminists describe under the term "masculinist," functions according to five principles: homogenization, hyperseparation, background, instrumentalism, and denied dependency; and it stands opposite to and conflicts with ecofeminist principles and practices (35). They include compromise and sharing as opposed to competition and accretion; compassion for one's "earthothers"; and willingness to coexist with one's "earthothers" (22).[6] Those principles and practices are misrepresented in Liu's novel in the figures of Ye Wenjie, Yang Dong, and Mike Evans. Ye Wenjie in particular is castigated as a deranged and pathetic ecofeminist madwoman. The given principles and practices are more fairly and accurately represented in the figure of Xiaomi, a woman warrior in Chen's *The Waste Tide*.

The Waste Tide

Against *The Three-Body Problem's* subtle castigation and demonization of environmental activists, and in contrast with its "grand visions of the future" and adamantine optimism in the ability of science and technology to solve the planet's problems—hallmarks of Liu's work (Jia 2013, 104)—is Chen Quifan's sci-fi *The Waste Tide*. It does not scapegoat environmental thinkers and activists as being a threat to Earth. It targets other groups and entities, and it is part of a new wave of Chinese sci-fi by a younger generation of writers who are addressing environmental apocalypses that already are occurring (Shi 2020). They include the electronics industry and its offspring, the electronic waste (e-waste) industry. If Liu's *The Three-Body Problem* epitomizes the "technological sublime" (a term made famous by a study by David E. Nye entitled *American Technological Sublime,* which is about how faith in human-made technologies supersedes faith in natural phenomena in the modern period), then Chen's *The Waste Tide* foregrounds the dark sides of that sublime—namely, transhumanist posthumanist fantasies of biological transcendence and technological mastery as well an "affect of detachment" that enables technophiles to avoid questions of sentience and suffering (Han Song 2013, 19).[7] A cyberpunk fiction and technological dystopia, *The Waste Tide* confronts the heavy moral "masculinist" baggage of humans' uses of technology to control the planet and the many species that struggle against great odds to share their planet Earth with the human species.

The *Waste Tide* is set in a place based on the actual town of Guiyu ("Treasure Island") in Guandong Province (Chen 2019). The town is situated not far from Chen's hometown of Shantou (Chen 2019; Healey 2017, 2). The main industry in Guiyi is the e-waste industry. Since the 1980s, the industry has spawned multimillionaires in China, exploited and poisoned the bodies of millions of other people, and transformed the province of Guangdong into an e-waste industry capital (Healey 2017, 3). Guiyu is a microcosm of Guangdong Province, and, indeed, of China, "the world's largest e-waste dumping ground" despite the government's ban on importing e-waste since 2000 (Healey 2017, 3).

The central character of *The Waste Tide* is Xiaomi, a migrant worker who works as an e-waste recycler and becomes a cyborg after she is infected by a human-made virus created in the labs of a secret US military operation, the

Waste Tide Project. The virus enhances her preexisting physiological capacities and helps her to lead other migrant workers to revolt against the industry that poisons and oppresses them.[8] Xiaomi's name connotes several meanings: a small grain of millet, a little sweet thing, and a past China defined more by ecogenic than anthropogenic matter (if also overburdened by feudalism, emperors, and warlords). As Healey notes, Xiaomi's name also carries a reference to Xiao-mi Keji, a Chinese electronics company that was founded in 2010 and "rose to prominence" in the years before, during, and after the year of publication of *The Waste Tide* in 2013, the year in which the company also produced a popular smartphone product (2017, 22).

Another character, Scott Brandle, is a US business man who represents Wealth, a global corporate, rare earth extraction, and waste recycling company. He has come to Guiyu to negotiate a deal with the local families who control the e-waste business on the island. He hires Chen Kaizhong, a translator, to help him in the negotiations. Chen, who has studied in the USA and was born in Guiyi, is shocked to find on his return to his hometown that it has become a toxic dumping site. He meets the "waste-girl" Xiaomi and they fall in love. Their relationship is interrupted when Xiaomi is kidnapped by gangsters, who also gang-rape Xiaomi. They work for a rich boss of one of the local families who control the e-waste business, the Luo family. The family wants to use Xiaomi's body in a ritual to cure their son, who is gravely ill.

Brandle discovers that his company Wealth is being funded by the Waste Tide Project, which develops and researches chemical weapons. It was founded at the end of World War II. At that time, the US military recruited Suzuki Ninagawa, a brilliant young scientist who earned her PhD in biochemistry at New York's prestigious Columbia University. The name of the project, "Waste Tide," is the name that Suzuki gives to the project. She joins the project not long after her fiancé, a commander of a Japanese battleship during World War II, is killed when his battleship is attacked and destroyed by an American B-52 bomber.

Researching the activities between 1955 and 1972 of the Waste Tide Project, Brandle learns of project members' experiments on human subjects after an underground environmental group directs him to a website. There he finds a video that details the experiments. Those include scenes of human subjects hallucinating and tearing their eyes out of their heads under the influence of the drugs forced on them. The video also states that the US military secretly used some of the project's chemical weapons in such countries and regions as Ethiopia, Afghanistan, the former Yugoslavia, and the Persian Gulf. The video that Mike accesses also features an appearance by Suzuki (before she commits suicide on the anniversary of her fiancé's death 60 years earlier). In the tape, she is an elegant octogenarian. In calm and measured tones, she testifies before the camera. She states that she deeply regrets working on and inventing chemicals that caused unconscionable kinds of suffering to humans forced against their will to participate in the

Waste Tide Project. She incriminates herself for participating in a project that was branded as a project for world peace. She describes herself as both a criminal and a creator. In doing so, she implicitly critiques the generally positive terms in which acts of so-called creation and invention in science and technology are touted.

In contrast with such figures as Chen Kaizhong, Scott Brandle, and Suzuki Ninagawa, who are caught up in scientific and technological projects that purport to be for world peace and instead continue old conflicts, Xiaomi is a figure that speaks for some of the most underrepresented and demonized forms of struggling for world peace. Chen, despite his love of Xiaomi, is mostly a passive figure. Brandle, as Healey points out, "self-identifies" with Ninagawa and is, like Ninagawa, a "mere pawn in the larger games played by powerful shadowy organizations" (2017, 19). Xiaomi plays the most active role in struggling for peace. Her figure also speaks for impure so-called hybrid identities as opposed to pure identities. She is a combination of Xiaomi 0, a waste girl, and Xiaomi 1, a superman robot as a result of a virus from the Waste Tide Project that infected Xiaomi. Moreover, Xiaomi's character closely identifies with the work of ecofeminists.

As posthumanist scholar Elaine Graham defines the cyborg identity, it is a "hybrid of the cybernetic and the organic" that "straddles the boundary of the human and technological, "disrupts...distinctions between 'natural' and artificial" in its "hybridity and contingency," and challenges more than supports "transhumanist" fantasies of human immortality and transcendence (2002, 200). Such fantasies abound in mainstream, and well-funded, masculinist forms of "technoscientific innovation" (155). These forms reflect humans' longing for "invulnerability, incorporeality and omniscience" (155). Under them, the cyborg is seen mostly to herald "an emergent epoch of 'postbiological' humanity" and to promise the end of humans' "physical limitations (of strength and intelligence)" and conditions of "finitude (decay, disease and death)" (158). Such ideas trace to the "unalloyed faith in the primacy of the Enlightenment subject—rational, autonomous, self-determining"—and belief in an anthropogenic "[m]achinic evolution" that will "complete the task of natural [ecogenic] selection" (159).[9] As Graham observes, those ideas, and "technophilia" in general, are "polarizing the world into the connected and the isolated," stripping some humans of agencies, enhancing those of others, and making the divisions between sentient and non-sentient beings hard to distinguish (Jolly 1999, quoted in Graham 2002, 165). Those masculinist conditions and outcomes are amply illustrated in Chen's novel. For example, when Scott arrives at Guiyu, he notices the inscription on a stone at the entrance to the village. The inscription evokes Dante's Alighieri's description of the entrance to hell in the *Divine Comedy*: "I'll enter a city of misery; I'll enter an everlasting suffering; I'll enter men who are lost" (Chen 2013, 33).[10] He sees an artificial limb moving on the ground. The mutilated arm is "like an enlarged caterpillar" (33). Its fingers grab at the ground and drag the entire limb along it. A boy rushes to pick up the limb. He turns it in a different direction, playing with it as if it is a toy car. When Scott visits a local e-waste factory, in a scene in the novel that evokes the journey to the underworld in epic literature such as Dante's *Divine Comedy*, he sees a horrific accident in which the arm of a machine reaches out and grabs a migrant worker's head. A "low beastly whining sound" issues from the man's throat and his expression becomes "horribly distorted" (38). Such common, bizarre and miserable, scenes remind Scott again of Dante's description of hell in the *Divine Comedy*: "You who enter shall give up hope."

As Graham summarizes the work of Donna Haraway, the first to critically embrace cyborg identity in explicitly feminist terms, the cyborg, in inhabiting a world that is "simultaneously 'biological' and 'technological,'" is a welcome "blasphemy" against dominant, masculinist-biased ideas about technology and science (2002, 200). As an extension of humans' embodied agencies, it refutes masculinist-derived notions of ontology, essentialism, and naturalism. Xiaomi's extended physiological agencies, agencies created by scientists working for the Waste Tide Project for the purposes of destroying targeted groups of humans, help her to lead the migrant workers who work in Guiyu to revolt against their e-waste industry employers, many of whom are local townspeople. However, when a typhoon hits Guiyu and floods the town, Xiaomi persuades the migrant workers to give up their hate and resentment and help the local residents. She tells them,

> If we let ourselves be devoured by hate, then they will win. Instead, we will let them see clearly that we are not garbage that creates pollution... or parasites on their land. We are humans like they are. We have feelings and sympathies as they do, and so we will risk our lives to save them. Therefore, let's reach out our hands to help them.
>
> (Chen 2013, 228)

Through Xiaomi's efforts, the migrant community and local community come together. Chen describes the union thus, "Carols are loudly sung. At dawn, a tree full of pearls grows up to the sky" (2013, 230).

Two recent famous works of Chinese sci-fi reflect the two directions that sci-fi is taking in China today, one highly publicized and mainstream, the other less publicized and more politically and socially challenging. The first, represented by Liu Cixin's *The Three-Body Problem*, treats environmental concerns as being overrated and its activists as individuals who tread on the quicksand of eco-fascism and eco-terrorism. In the central figure of Ye Wenjie, ecofeminism in particular seems to be both demonized and condescendingly viewed according to popularized, reductive, and misunderstood notions about it as well as about areas of environmental engagement with which it closely intersects (environmental justice, climate justice, postcolonial ecocriticism, indigenous studies, critical animal studies, and critical plant studies). The second direction of sci-fi, represented by Chen Quifan's

The Waste Tide, provides a more challenging direction for Chinese sci-fi, one that popular, mainstream sci-fi has been in effect unwilling or reluctant to entertain because that direction broaches political and social realities and defends political and social work that seeks for greater awareness and respect for the nonhuman ecogenic world. *The Waste Tide* exemplifies the ability of art to critically address, more than to escape from, masculinist projects of eco-domination; and the ability of art to play a smaller or larger role as opposed to no role at all in the work of raising awareness about environmental problems that closely tie to privileged heteronormative identity and shadow scientific and technological discoveries that on their surface promise dazzling, utopic vistas into the future.

Notes

1 The stages in the evolution of scholarly disciplines are sometimes referred to as a three-step or three-wave process. The first is "the wide recognition of a few master thinkers" of a given discipline's "problematics and approaches" (Watts 2008, 251). The second is "the appearance of anthologies of current scholarship (typically written in an affirmative mode) and foundational texts that further circumscribe" the discipline (251). The third "late stage" is "the moment of interrogation—the simultaneously internal and external question of the assumptions of the field" (251). For more on those stages as they inform ecofeminism, and for more on the confluences between the areas of environmental theory and practice listed in the first paragraph, see Gaard (2017, xiii–xviii).

2 The Chinese Cultural Revolution, in fact, is central to the plot. Liu himself emphasizes that, as Alexandra Alter notes in a recently published article, "How Chinese Sci-fi Conquered America," in her interview of Liu. See also Liu's comments in "Coronavirus and Outer Space Aliens" (2020). As another article, a review of *The Three-Body Problem* by Chris Francis (2014), also makes clear, the novel is a "highly deserving blockbuster in China," not the least because it "serves as a crash course in both the historically important Cultural Revolution of the mid-twentieth century and the basics of astrophysics."

3 For more on those attitudes, positions, and stances, see Estok's "ecophobia hypothesis" (2018).

4 The term "earthothers" appears in Greta Gaard's study, *Critical Ecofeminism* (2017, 22). By that Gaard means plants and animals, the subjects of the second chapter of her study, where she introduces readers to the overlapping areas of ecofeminism of critical animal studies and critical plant studies.

5 SETI refers to an actual organization. For more on it, and on a closely related organization, Messaging Extraterrestrial Intelligence (METI), see Johnson (2017).

6 For more on the "logic of domination," see Plumwood (1993). See also Patrick Murphy's discussion of the feminist principle of invitational rhetoric in his chapter in this volume, "No Easy Answers: Karen Traviss's *Wess'har Wars Series*."

7 For a full account of the utopian, or "transhumanism," projects conducted under posthumanism scientific and technological research, see Graham (2002). For more on the "technological sublime" and the "affect of attachment," as those are stock ingredients of mainstream, popular sci-fi, see Estok (2017).

8 The significance of the cyborg in such cyberpunk sci-fi novels as *The Waste Tide* is the subject of Veronica Hollinger's essay, "Contemporary Trends in Science Fiction Criticism, 1980–1999." In it, Hollinger refers to Donna Haraway's seminal writing (first published in 1985) titled "A Cyborg Manifesto: Science,

Technology, and Socialist Feminism in the Late Twentieth Century." As Hollinger argues, it was the single most "influential document" in feminist studies of science fiction (1999, 256). Haraway is a staunch defender of science and technology and her work encourages more women to seek a profession in the sciences and in technological discovery. Differently from the dominant masculinist drivers of science and technology, however, Haraway advocates enlisting scientific and technological knowledge to encourage more openness toward, tolerance for, and understanding and embrace of female, queer, animal, plant, and other *cyborg* identities. Nothing or no being is inherently sinister or sublime; rather it is the way humans enlist and relate to a thing or being and how they themselves operate in the world that gives them that seemingly venal ontology.

9 Indeed, transhumanist ideas trace back further in history, to the ancient Greek distinction between *bios* and *zöe*, as Başak Ağın argues in "'The Force Is Strong with This One:' A Materialist Feminist Approach to *Star Wars*" (this volume).

10 The English translations of material cited from Chen Qiufan's novel, which is published in Mandarin, are mine.

References

Adamson, Joni, Mei-Mei Evans, and Rachael Stein. 2015. "Environmental Justice Politics, Poetics, and Pedagogy." In *Ecocriticism: The Essential Reader*, edited by Ken Hiltner, 135–142. London: Routledge.

Alaimo, Stacy, and Susan Hekman. 2015. "Emerging Models of Materiality in Feminist Theory." In *Ecocriticism: The Essential Reader*, edited by Ken Hiltner, 143–153. London: Routledge.

Alter, Alexandra. 2019. "How Chinese Sci-fi Conquered America." *The New York Times Magazine*, December 3. Accessed October 13, 2020. https://www.nytimes.com/2019/12/03/magazine/ken-liu-three-body-problem-chinese-science-fiction.html.

Carson, Rachael. 1962. *Silent Spring*. New York, NY: Houghton Mifflin.

Chen, Qiufan. 2013. *Huang chao* (*The Waste Tide*). Wuhan: Changjiang Literature and Art Publisher.

———. 2019. "Weisheme yao xie yi bu guanyu dianzi lese de kehuan xiaoshuo" ("Why Write a Science Fiction Novel about E-Waste?") *Science Fiction Studies in London*, August 22. Accessed October 6, 2020. https://mp.weixin.qq.com/s/8JsHwZPtkhZm4zaEZWnbkg.

Ding, Xiongfei. 2019. "Liu Cixin tan renwen zhuantong yu keji weilai" ("Liu Cixin Discusses the Humanities and the Technological Future") *Shanghai Dongfang Newspaper Co., Ltd.*, October 13. Accessed October 13, 2020. https://m.thepaper.cn/newsDetail_forward_4626136.

Estok, Simon C. 2018. *The Ecophobia Hypothesis*. London and New York, NY: Routledge.

———. 2017. "Pollution, Sci-fi, and the Sublime." *Tamkang Review* 47, no. 2: 3–16.

Francis, Chris. 2014. "Review of *The Three-Body Problem* by Liu Cixin." *Booklist*, October 15, 28.

Gaard, Greta. 2017. *Critical Ecofeminism*. Lexington, KY: Rowman & Littlefield.

Graham, Elaine L. 2002. *Representations of the Post/Human: Monsters, Aliens and Others in Popular Culture*. New Brunswick, NJ: Rutgers University Press.

Han, Song. 2013. "Chinese Science Fiction: A Response to Modernization." *Science Fiction Studies* 40: 15–21.

Haraway, Donna J. [1985] 2000. "A Cyborg Manifesto: Science, Technology, and Socialist-Feminism in the Late Twentieth Century." In *Posthumanism*, edited by Neil Badmington, 69–84. Basingstoke, Hampshire, UK: Palgrave.

Healey, Cara. 2017. "Estranging Realism in Chinese Science Fiction: Hybridity and Environmentalism in Chen Qiufan's *The Waste Tide.*" *Modern Chinese Literature and Culture* 29, no. 2: 1–33.

Hollinger, Veronica. 1999. "Contemporary Trends in Science Fiction Criticism, 1980–1999." *Science-Fiction Studies* 26: 232–262.

Huggan, Graham, and Helen Tiffin. [2010] 2015. "Introduction to *Postcolonial Ecocriticism, Literature, Animals, Environment.*" In *Ecocriticism: The Essential Reader*, edited by Ken Hiltner, 178–195. London: Routledge.

Jia, Liyuan. 2013. "Gloomy China: China's Image in Han Song's Fiction." Translated by Joel Martinsen. *Science-Fiction Studies* 40: 103–115.

Johnson, Steven. 2017. "Greetings, E.T." *The New York Times Magazine*, June 28. Accessed October 13, 2020. https://www.nytimes.com/2017/06/28/magazine/g reetings-et-please-dont-murder-us.amp.html.

Jolly, Richard, ed. 1999. *Human Development Report.* New York, NY: Oxford University Press.

Li, Hua. 2015. "The Political Imagination in Liu Cixin's Critical Utopia: China 2185." *Science-Fiction Studies* 42: 519–540.

Li, Hua. 2017. "Spaceship Earth and Technological Utopianism: Liu Cixin's Ecological Science Fiction." *Tamkang Review* 47, no. 2: 17–31.

Liu, Cixin. [2008] 2011. *San ti (The Three-Body Problem).* Taipei: Owl Publisher.

———. 2014. *The Three-Body Problem.* Translated by Ken Liu. New York, NY: Tor.

———. 2020. "Xin guan yiqing yu wai xing zen" ("Coronavirus and Outer Space Aliens"). *San ti shequ (Three Body Community)*, July 15. Accessed July 20, 2020. https://mp.weixin.qq.com/s/4uHEfj5_1Xz4xGfbKpZKqA.

Nixon, Rob. 2015. "Environmentalism and Postcolonialism." In *Ecocriticism: The Essential Reader*, edited by Ken Hiltner, 198–208. London: Routledge.

Plumwood, Val. 1993. *Feminism and the Mastery of Nature.* New York, NY: Routledge.

Shi, Jingyuan. 2020. "Weisheme kehuan keyi chengwei zhongguo ruan shili de mimi wuqi" ("Why Can Sci-Fi Become a Secret Weapon for Chinese Soft Power?"). *Chinese Sci-Fi Monthly*, June 9. Accessed October 6, 2020. https://mp.weixin.qq .com/s/nf34ev12DEQs7j8BVQiF7w.

Singer, Peter. 1975. *Animal Liberation.* New York, NY: Harper Collins.

Song, Mingwei. 2013. "Variations on Utopia in Contemporary Chinese Science Fiction." *Science Fiction Studies* 40: 86–102.

Watts, Richard. 2008. "Towards an Ecocritical Postcolonialism: Val Plumwood's *Environmental Culture* in Dialogue with Patrick Chamoiseau." *Journal of Postcolonial Writing* 44, no. 3: 251–261.

Yan, Wu. 2013. "'Great Wall Planet': Introducing Chinese Science Fiction." Translated by Wang Pengfei, with Ryan Nichols. *Science Fiction Studies* 40: 1–14.

Part 4
Capitalism and Colonization

11 Hegemonic Masculinity and Tropes of Domination

An Ecofeminist Analysis of James Cameron's 2009 Film *Avatar*

Lydia Rose and Teresa M. Bartoli

If ever there was a science fiction film that epitomizes modern ecofeminism, it is James Cameron's 2009 motion picture, *Avatar*. Cameron's groundbreaking use of 3D computer technology immersed moviegoers into a world based on idealized ecofeminism with vivid imagery never before seen. Through *Avatar*'s storyline, a worldwide audience was presented with a reflection of Western society's attitudes, values, and compulsion to dominate, while being provided a hypothetical case study of idealized ecofeminism, exposing the masses to an imagined world that viewed nature as essential and all life as valuable. The impact and cultural influence of Avatar is powerful and compelling. There is no denying the breadth of *Avatar*'s exposure: seen by millions worldwide, it endured as the highest grossing film in the USA for ten years (Glenday 2019). *Avatar* still remains as the second highest grossing film of all time and was the only film ever to earn $2 billion outside of the USA, making it the highest grossing film in the world (Childress 2019). Additionally, the powerful impact of *Avatar* is exemplified in the psycho-social-cultural responses to the movie; this includes "post-*Avatar* depression" (Alexander 2014), depression onset by recognizing the unattainable surreal world that seemed so real with 3D technology, and "the Pandora Effect" (Falquina 2014), also a condition of depression, but instigated by the historical, unresolved grief of colonized, traumatized peoples. Aside from *Avatar*'s cultural impact, this work of science fiction provides a powerful presentation of ecofeminism while serving as a prime example of how "hegemonic masculinity" and "tropes of domination" integrate, as well as reproduce, harmful psycho-social, behavioral, and political ideologies in interacting with nature and reproducing and/or manipulating cultures. In this ecofeminist analysis and critique of *Avatar*, a brief overview of the motion picture will be presented along with foundational elements of ecofeminism. Hegemonic masculinity will be described, followed by an examination of the construct depicted in this film. And lastly, an evaluation of the tropes of domination in patriarchal, capitalistic societies, and as portrayed in *Avatar*, will be presented, providing an explanation for the creation and continued development of harmful ideologies and cultural practices that create destructive divides between nature and culture.

Avatar and Ecofeminism

The science fiction film *Avatar* introduces the surreal moon, Pandora, inhabited by the Na'vi: human-like extraterrestrials with striped cyan (blue-green hue) skin and tails that have the ability to connect neurally with fellow species, other species, and nature. The Na'vi leadership includes a male clan leader and a female spiritual leader portrayed as being equal in power. The connection of women to nature is cemented in the Na'vi peoples' deity, the goddess Eywa, made up of all living things and personified by the Tree of Souls—a giant willow-like tree with roots throughout the moon. Na'vi religion focuses on interconnectedness and concern for the ecosystem as a whole. Life on Pandora embodies a society based on the ideals of ecofeminism where domination over women, other species, or nature is portrayed as nonexistent. The social ideologies and themes presented in the film include the following: power relations, speciesism, environmental ethics, ecological catastrophe, patriarchal domination, and resistance to colonialism/anti-colonialism. In addition, many of the major tenets of ecofeminism are presented in various ways throughout *Avatar*.

Consistent with a primary tenet of ecofeminism, life on Pandora is represented as interdependent with, and dependent upon, other beings, other species, and with nature, while recognizing the integrity and strength of all living things (Mies and Shiva 1993). James Cameron so clearly displays the cultural juxtaposition between the ideal ecofeminist society of the Na'vi people and modern Western ideology as Pandora is being colonized by human Earthlings who engage in a familiar/typical paternalistic, capitalistic, militaristic manner which exhibits power, aggression, and anti-speciesism.

Gaard and Gruen (1993) trace the development of ecofeminism to the goals of connecting feminism and ecology. Critical ecofeminist issues, such as sexism, patriarchy, violence against women, and violence against nature are addressed in *Avatar*. The audience is introduced to human colonizers who exhibit behavior based on patriarchy to justify their exploitation and oppression of Pandora. Murphy (1998) recognizes that from its conception, ecofeminism maintained that there is a correlation between the exploitation of nature and the oppression of women. Ecofeminists typically recognize that quality of life decreases, not only for men and women but children and people of color, due to the exploitation of the environment. Animals in the environment are typically constructed as part of nature and exploited as such. Kordecki (this volume) examines how the animalization of beings has a negative effect on human worth. Kordecki continues with the notion that women, children, people of color, "others" are typically feminized or constructed as (an)other gender if not straight out animalized in which to create normalized patterns of oppressive practices and behavior. Constructing an "other" is embedded in language, culture, and reproduced in cultural products (i.e., science fiction literature) utilizing embedded dominant ideologies or grand narratives such as patriarchy and capitalism. The issues and consequences of patriarchy and capitalism are displayed through the colonizing humans and their primary purpose on Pandora: capitalism.

Patriarchal cultures typically create a hierarchical structure based on male domination that not only gives power to men, but is the foundation for the exploitation of women and nature for capitalistic goals. Ecofeminism provides the framework that explains and exposes the complex connections between nature/culture and exploitation/oppression. Ruether (1995) recognizes that the foundation of ecofeminism is based on the "fundamental connection[s]" between Western, patriarchal cultures, and the domination of women and nature. According to Agarwal (1992), the exploitation of women and nature can be further explained by the idea that in patriarchal paradigms, men are connected to culture and women are viewed as being closely linked with nature whereby nature is regarded as inferior to culture. This view is grounded in the understanding that in patriarchal societies, masculine ideals are influential and feminine identification (based on a connection to nature) is seen as inconsequential in society. This ecofeminist idea is portrayed in *Avatar* through the patriarchal human colonists and their disregard of Pandora's environment and the indigenous Na'vi people.

Avatar's introduction of the human colonizers, who only seek to extract a rare mineral resource for financial gain, begin their exploitation of the natural environment which ultimately results in devastating consequences to all living beings on Pandora. The exploitation of the natural environment produces oppression and the widespread massacre of living beings on Pandora, particularly the indigenous Na'vi people. The exploitation of nature and the oppression of women, minoritized others, and other species, does not manifest at random as *Avatar* reflects another important tenet of ecofeminism: the interconnections between the domination of women, minoritized others, and nature (Warren 2000). *Avatar's* storyline provides the vehicle that brings forth an awareness for ecofeminism by revealing this interconnectedness through the movie's presentation of the exploitation of nature, the use of violence, and the oppression of minoritized others and people of color (in the case of *Avatar*, cyan blue). Ecofeminism reveals that the living environment and all living beings need to be recognized as important and valued entities in and of themselves. Domination and oppression are the natural consequence when nature is treated as a commodity for the generation of wealth. Gaard and Gruen (1993) contend that the problems addressed by ecofeminism are rooted in global oppression: unequal distribution of wealth, global water pollution, deforestation, and world hunger and food insecurity. These are issues produced by oppression and domination that did not exist on Pandora, until the human colonizers arrived.

Avatar addresses ecofeminist ideas about the connections between nature/ culture and exploitation/oppression, but also acknowledges the unjustified domination that results from racism and sexism. As ecofeminist theory and philosophy developed through the years, scholars began to recognize that patriarchy (culture) does not represent the primary domination for all oppressed people. Racism, classism, and sexism are the primary dominations for many individuals and these "-isms of domination" often intersect and produce multiple forms of discrimination (Warren 2000). *Avatar* addresses domination as a result of racism and sexism through the storyline and the major characters in the movie, revealing significant insights about the influence of race and gender.

James Cameron conceived of an indigenous Na'vi people that are very different from the human colonizers, not only in their body type, but in an important distinction that reflects the systemic racism inherent in Western society: color. The movie successfully exhibits an important tenet of ecofeminism: that the focus on difference is the basis of oppression. This idea is exhibited throughout the movie. The blue Na'vi people and their distinct qualities are unique as compared to typical alien beings found in many science fiction films. In addition, Cameron presents the Na'vi in a way that induces audiences to primarily identify with the culture of the Na'vi rather than with the culture of the earthlings. The Na'vi represent a vast contrast to the human colonizers from Earth, who are predominantly white males, including the protagonist who is positioned as the "superhero" in the movie.

Lastly, this science fiction storyline mirrors mainstream Western history where ecological values are subverted in the dominant culture of the USA. *Avatar* presents a reflection of Western society's compulsion to dominate, illustrated by the Earthling's attitudes and lack of value for women, nature, and the minoritized. Ecofeminist theory acknowledges the compulsion to dominate and seeks alternatives to domination through social transformation. The ecofeminist goal of social and ecological justice involves the examination of the compulsion to dominate and exposing the false logic of domination (Warren 2000).

These many social constructs of domination (i.e., racism, sexism, classism) lead to inequality on the basis of masculinity and patriarch. In this sense, "hegemonic masculinity" and "tropes of domination" provide insight into ideological practices that are both overt and covert. Understanding hegemonic masculinity and tropes of domination provides further insights into the analysis of *Avatar* by exposing complex interconnections between nature and culture while portraying and recognizing the significance of ecofeminist values.

Hegemonic Masculinity

The social construct of masculinity within a society founded on patriarchy is best understood in terms of "hegemonic masculinity." The concept of hegemonic masculinity evolved from the writings of Antonio Gramsci's "cultural hegemony" on the invisible or covert nature of power through "normalized" culture. The construct was then further developed and codified by scholars of masculinity (Connell and Messerschmidt 2005) and identified as the dominance of men over women and over other types of masculinities. In this way, hegemonic masculinity serves to "justify" domination. Embedded in the construct of hegemonic masculinity is the recognition of numerous forms of diverse masculinities. The existence of multiple masculinities within patriarchal societies generates a hierarchy producing a dominant group that establishes dominance over women and men of less powerful masculinities (Connell 1995).

In contrast to a "sex-role" perspective of masculinity based on fixed, individual personality traits, hegemonic masculinity addresses the influence of power on behavior. Connell (1995) contends that masculinities are not equivalent to men, but are defined by "patterns of practice" concerning power and position. Connell and Messerschmidt (2005) explain that hegemonic masculinity is founded on heterosexual power and that men engage in behaviors to position themselves into power over others. Hegemonic masculinity, therefore, is constructed upon the necessity to control and can be identified as a structure of domination. Additionally, although these behaviors are predominately employed by men, both men and women engage in the patterns of conduct that define hegemonic masculinity (Connell and Messerschmidt 2005).

Equally important to the construct of hegemonic masculinity is its connection to ecofeminism. Both ecofeminism and hegemonic masculinity examine the connection between Western, patriarchal cultures and domination. Patriarchy creates the setting for hegemonic masculinity and legitimizes men's dominant position in society. Ruether (1995) points out that patriarchy creates a hierarchical structure based on male domination. Patriarchal cultures, embedded with dominant ideologies of capitalism, give power to men and perpetuate oppressive practices and behaviors toward women, the feminized/minoritized, and nature that are justified and made to appear 'natural' and inevitable. The mutual conditioning of patriarchy and hegemonic masculinity creates patterns of behavior, based on power and domination, which serve to justify domination over others, and are reproduced and ingrained with intransigent opposition to ecofeminist values (Connell 1995).

Ecofeminist scholars examine patriarchy, capitalism, and colonialism as common themes within the science fiction genre. Deininger and Scammell (2021, 83) point out the supremacy of science fiction as a "form of environmental literature." *Avatar*'s narrative of colonialism on Pandora centers on the acquisition of a rare mineral resource by a corporation representing Western patriarchal culture. The conflict in the story is established by the location of the mineral: beneath the Na'vi's indigenous home and the Tree of Souls. The contrast between the Na'vi and the corporation reveals the subordination of ecofeminist values and explains the oppressive and destructive actions influenced by patriarchy, capitalism, and colonialism.

Gaard (1993, 2) explains that the framework that "authorizes these forms of oppression is patriarchy." Patriarchy is defined as an ideology where the self/other distinction is separate and atomistic (Gaard 1993). An example of the corporation's distinction between self/other is their designation of the Na'vi as "not human." Several times throughout the movie, the indigenous humanoids are referred to as "blue monkeys" and as "savages threatening the whole operation." Because they are separate from humans, and viewed as an obstacle, their environment and their existence is judged as unimportant and irrelevant.

Avatar's narrative explains further the link between the ideologies of capitalism and colonialism and the oppression/domination of nature and others. In a scene infused with power, gender discrimination, and overt misogyny, corporation leader Parker Selfridge is confronted by Dr. Grace Augustine. The doctor is angry and opposed to the inclusion of an ex-marine, rather than a researcher, on her science team. Dr. Augustine accuses Selfridge of "intentionally screwing me," although it is clear that she was inconsequential in the decision. Selfridge contemptuously expounds on his expectations. Dr. Augusine's is told that her job is to "win the hearts and minds of the natives" and gain their trust for the paramount objective of obtaining the rare mineral worth "twenty million a kilo." With abatement for the scientists, Selfridge declares that obtaining the mineral is "the only reason" for their presence on Pandora.

Themes of anti-colonialism are often explored in works of science fiction (Blend, this volume). *Avatar* is an anti-colonialism narrative providing its audience with insight from an indigenous viewpoint. As Jake is taught to value the ways of the Na'vi, the movie viewer is exposed to a different way of understanding nature and life. *Avatar* successfully engages the audience to identify with the Na'vi and to relate and value the culture of the Na'vi. The destructive and brutal attack on nature and the beautiful environment, the indigenous people, and the spirit of Pandora, creates intense emotional pain, not only for the Na'vi, but for the viewing audience. This emotional pain is most intense when the "Hometree" is destroyed. This harm is specifically exemplified in the film as necessary to the colonialism agenda of capitalism, exploitation, and oppression and serves to create an anti-colonialism sentiment.

Ruether (1995) points out that systems of domination are responsible for the structures that impact women, land, and animal inequality. Within the framework of patriarchy, hegemonic masculinity justifies the exploitation of nature for profit (Connell 1995). *Avatar* exposes the link between patriarchy and oppression of women and nature where ecofeminist values are subverted through hegemonic masculinity. The actions of the human characters on Pandora demonstrate the influence of power and provide an explanation for dominant behavior. The protagonist (Jake Sully), the antagonist (Colonel Quaritch), and the science team director (Dr. Grace Augustine) reveal patterns of behavior that are oppressive and incompatible with the principles of ecofeminism.

Avatar's Jake Sully engages in conduct based on constructing his masculinity through actions that propel him into positions of power. This behavior is exemplified by Jake's choosing of Neytiri as his mate. Heterosexual patterns of mate selection are an essential component of hegemonic masculinity. Heterosexuality is a "hegemonic ideal whereby men should be strong, tough, in control over women and their bodies, heterosexual and sexually dominant" (Jewkes et al. 2015, 11). Jake's action of mate selection establishes his power position over other males, specifically Tsu'tey, the leading warrior in the clan and the promised mate to Neytiri.

A nefarious attribute of hegemonic masculinity and the structure of domination is the power to control and dominate over others through voluntary compliance. This concept touches upon Antonio Gramsci's description of the covert nature of power. Anthony Lemelle (1995, 91) explains that "the powerful are able to win the voluntary consent of the ruled." Such voluntary consent is demonstrated by Neytiri, who allows Jake to choose her despite the fact that she was already betrothed to Tsu'tey. To further establish his complete dominance, Jake succeeds in bonding/dominating the great leonopteryx, Toruk, and becomes Toruk Maktos. These actions are consistent with Connell's (1995) identification of masculinities as defined by patterns of behavior that establish men in positions of power.

While Jake Sully's masculinity is constructed through heterosexual dominance, Colonel Quaritch displays masculinity through behaviors that exhibit his physical strength and aggression. Taylor (2020) examines hegemonic masculinity through an analysis of superheroes: "Superhero narratives typically celebrate physically strong, white, heterosexual masculinity, contributing to the inscription of this as the hegemonic model of masculinity in Western culture." This superhero narrative is exemplified in *Avatar* by Jake Sulley, a white man becoming the leader of the cyan-blue Na'vi. The military leader exhibits his superior physical strength by engaging in weight lifting when Jake arrives to meet him. While bench pressing an excessively large amount of weight in front of the paraplegic, Quaritch informs Jake that Pandora's gravity can "make you soft." This superhero narrative centering on workout scenes is typical of hegemonic masculinity whereby power dynamics are often negotiated in workout and training scenes (Taylor 2020). In *Avatar*, the workout scene establishes Colonel Quaritch's masculinity on two levels. The first level is demonstrating his physical strength, a trait of masculinity integrated into Western cultures (Beynon 2002). The second level is by confirming his dominance and power over Jake, a crucial part of hegemonic masculinity (Connell 1995). Colonel Quaritch further demonstrates his masculinity through aggressive behavior through the use of military "toys" (the weaponized robot suit, high-tech weapons, and various aircraft). Fiske (1987), identified the usage of "male toys" (such as motorcycles, cars, guns, and tanks) as a means to elevate males into positions of power over others.

While the characterizations of Jake Sully and Colonel Quaritch exemplify distinct demonstrations of masculinity, the female character, Dr. Grace Augustine, provides further insights into masculinity. Committed to displays of power and control over others, Augustine, as the leader of the science team, exhibits aggressive, traditionally male behaviors typical of patriarchal domination in capitalistic societies establishing the heteronormativity of the human culture on Pandora. Dr. Augustine demonstrates a demand for leadership recognition when she first meets Jake. Despite Jake's invitation by the corporation to participate in the science team's operations, Dr. Augustine rebukes and insults him. The leader of the science team then aggressively confronts corporation leader Parker Selfridge to establish her position in the operations. Although Dr. Augustine is unsuccessful in removing Jake from the team, she demonstrates her inclination to challenge the position of other leaders. Dr. Augustine continues to behave in ways that confirm her position of power, for example when she demands, from the entire science team, her cigarette the moment she "awakens" from her avatar. Dr. Augustine's behavior is designed to remind others of her position as a leader and of her power over them. Dr. Augustine exhibits power and leadership, traits of masculinity influenced by Western cultures (Aulette 2009).

The analysis of hegemonic masculinity in *Avatar*'s three main human characters provides an explanation for behavior that results in oppression and domination. The actions establishing the masculinity of Jake Sully, Colonel Quaritch, and Dr. Grace Augustine reveal the influence of power on patterns of behavior that are oppressive and incompatible with the principles of ecofeminism.

Tropes of Domination

With science being "the most celebrated tool for the domination of the world by Western man" (Lemelle 1995, 88), science fiction serves to further valorize science as a tool for domination, not only of Earth but of the fictitious worlds beyond. In *Avatar*, science is utilized in the unjustified domination of Pandora. The earthlings use biotechnology and genetic engineering to develop a hybrid body that can house the mind of the earthlings in a body that is similar to the native Na'vi. Although Pandora's atmosphere is a toxic environment for humans/earthlings, the control of nature through science and the manipulation of DNA allows the development and growth of hybrid bodies that are unaffected by Pandora's atmosphere. The creation of the hybrid bodies for the humans to use while interacting with the Na'vi was motivated by one primary objective: domination of their land and resources. The science utilized on Pandora is by no means the only tool of domination presented in the movie. In the case of *Avatar*, James Cameron flips the familiar science fiction trope of "invading evil aliens who seek domination" by introducing humans as the invading aliens and by exposing audiences to the actual Western colonial history of domination. The Western colonist mindset, based on domination, is easily crafted, reproduced, and recognized in *Avatar* and is positioned in contrast to ecofeminism as an alternative possibility. Modern domination of the world by "Western man" has been grounded in practices of colonization, internal colonialism, neocolonialism, and enslavement that exist as structures of domination. The utilization of tropes of domination are significant to the practice of colonization, internal colonialism, neocolonialism, and enslavement, and centered on the significance of racism (particularly the white/black color line) and sexism (hegemonic masculinity/heterosexualism) (Lemelle 1995); the same patterns of domination are evident in *Avatar*.

Upon close examination and critique of *Avatar*, the dominance of "hegemonic masculinity" and the absolute control of nature via science is reinforced through a number of common tropes of domination: race, gender, and sex. Race is signified through the white/blue distinction (humans/ the Na'vi people). The film makes visible the strong connections of racial tropes of domination to hegemonic masculinity. Similar to most science fiction superheroes, *Avatar*'s protagonist is a white male, despite his use of the blue avatar. This is consistent with Taylor's (2020) description of the superhero narrative as being "typically white" and explains why the number of Black superheroes in Western fiction is underrepresented. The primary exception is Marvel's Black superhero, the Black Panther. The 2018 *Black Panther* movie, with a predominantly black cast and black director, was embraced by audiences worldwide and resulted in overwhelming success, breaking numerous box office records to become one of the top ten highest grossing films of all time (Glenday 2019). The *Black Panther* movie is the only superhero movie ever to receive an Academy Award nomination for Best Picture and it destroyed the myth that films with predominantly black casts do not perform well (Robehmed 2018).

Not only is the color-line trope blatantly represented in *Avatar*, but so is the cultural distinction between the Eurocentric and the Afrocentric perspectives of culture. The Afrocentric perspective, represented by the Na'vi people, focuses on the connection among the mind, body, and spirit (Lemelle 1995), while the Western, Eurocentric perspective of culture focuses on the mind as completely separate from body and spirit. The Eurocentric perspective of separating the mind from the body is conducive to the ideology of accepting that what makes a person is the mind—one can transfer their mind to a different body and be the same person. This explains how Jake can easily transfer his mind into the blue avatar body and still be represented as "himself."

While racial-ethnic minorities are faced with the practice of "passing" or developing a "double consciousness," to participate in societies dominated by white men of power, on Pandora, earthlings utilize science and scientists to engage in passing as part of the Na'vi. The scientists that work to interact with the Na'vi, using the genetically engineered bodies, are faced with developing a double consciousness—one to interact with the Na'vi and one to interact with the men of power funding their research.

When Jake's mind is transferred to the hybrid Na'vi body, the body is initially constructed as merely a tool. However, through social interaction with Neytiri, Jake goes "native" by connecting his body, spirit, and mind together with animals, plants, and of course, Neytiri when mating with her as well as when he joins and bonds with Toruk to become Toruk Makto. In *Avatar*, the culture of the Na'vi people is understood as completely intertwined with mind, body, and spirit and goes even further to represent the Na'vi people as connected to Pandora's ecosystem as one with the Tree of Souls or Eywa. This is contrasted with the earthlings' traditional Western, Eurocentric representations of culture that emphasizes hierarchical power structures and science as superior in terms of technology and physical domination of Pandora.

Further, the domination and exploitation of the Na'vi people are represented through the eyes of the earthlings as a problem or issue separate and distinct from domination and exploitation of Pandora's animals and natural resources. The film pushes the boundaries of interconnectedness when Eywa is able to bring all of the moon's animals into the battle against the earthlings, blurring the lines that are typically drawn on the basis of race to include other species.

Many times throughout the movie, the racial tropes emphasize the dehumanizing element of the dominated. On Earth, the notion of domesticating, controlling, or destroying animals is justified as serving the betterment of the dominating group. In *Avatar*, the animals are respected as members of an ecosystem, valued as living beings, and eventually join the Na'vi as equals in the epic battle at the end of the film. Although the animals join the battle in concert with the Na'vi, the Na'vi are not ruling them. To some extent, the Na'vi are just another species in the battle; a playoff of the racial trope of dehumanizing the "other"—just another animal. From an ecofeminist perspective, this is a natural conclusion. Unfortunately from a hegemonic masculinity perspective, all animals are under the domain of men of power.

The use of tropes of domination to understand the covert cultural reproduction of domination of disempowered groups was best explained by Anthony Lemelle (1995) in theorizing on black masculinity. He writes that "racism is sexism" in that white males of power are constructed as superior to others. While Lemelle (1995) explains how black males are constructed as another sex/gender in scientific terms (98) in *Avatar*, a similar practice takes place in constructing the Na'vi as another sex/gender also in scientific terms. The neural connections of their tails to each other redefines sex and gender, redefining interconnectedness, redefining science as nature and nature as science.

The sexualized relationship of Neytiri and Jake Scully plays into the sexual trope of the "other" as the feminized exotic and the desexualized male. Neytiri's previously selected mate prior to the arrival of Jake, Tsu'tey, angry at learning that Neytiri has mated with Jake, ultimately represents the Western castrated non-male or a desexualized eunuch. The trope of "sex" and "love" is a tool to justify harm and overpowers the trope of "loyalty."

The fabricated trope of love versus loyalty becomes blurry for both the audience, as well as for Jake and Neytiri. The trope of choosing sides, love me or hate me, either-or thinking, or zero-sum game, makes one either friend or foe. Jake chooses to betray his loyalty to Colonel Quaritch; the Colonel betrays the initial mission; the fellow scientists betray the corporate backers and work to keep Jake in his avatar body; and the pilot betrays the security company by stealing a helicopter to take Jake and the team of scientists to an outpost.

The typical tropes of sex and sexual desire for Eurocentric men of power emphasizes phallic size. Possession of the penis—phallic masculinity—bigger is better—the "size matters" trope plays out figuratively throughout the film. When Jake first takes control of the hybrid Na'vi body, the oversized body, as compared to the earthlings, the audience experiences his long "tail" as out of control and destroying the lab. Later on in the film, to show his loyalty to Neytiri, Jake connects with, and takes control of Toruk, the largest dragon-like predator feared and honored by the Na'vi. While the other Na'vi warriors have been training for a lifetime, Jake, in a mere three months, is able to subdue and connect with Toruk to inspire and lead the Na'vi warriors in the epic battle. Jake riding Toruk is the phallic symbol of true masculinity—a man's man. By taking Toruk, he wins over Tsu'tey and is given a position of leadership and power over all the warriors in all the clans that have joined forces.

The epic battle scene is representative of the typical colonialists "machismo spectacle." Lemelle (1995) utilizes the understanding of the machismo spectacle to describe different brands of masculinity, whereby black men are subjected to a particular brand of masculinity through four cultural institutions: military, jails, organized athletics, and the entertainment industry. *Avatar* is part of the entertainment industry reproducing domination, power, and control for white men of power and feminizing all "others" but is situated as an ecofeminist product by playing into mild tropes of femininity and power struggles of "we can do it too," typical of liberal feminism. Female warriors and the female spiritual leader provide the pretense of feminine equality, but ultimately, *Avatar* is a machismo spectacle that utilizes masculine military tropes of domination well recognized and stimulating to the audience. The masculine, cyborg weapons of destruction that are utilized in the war against nature and the minoritized others, are tools to gain control and possession of the moon and its inhabitants. Even the death scenes of the female pilot and of the warrior Tsu'tey are a sad truth that the audience knows is expected. In this sense, the master/slave trope is reinforced and displayed as natural.

The master/slave trope of domination is evident when Jake Scully serves as the mastermind in the defense of Pandora and the Na'vi. Tsu'tey, who has been the finest warrior and leader of the hunters prior to the presence of Jake, works to get the other clan members behind Jake. Tsu'tey's valiant display during the battle ends with his death. Once the battle is over with the defeat of the earthlings, science and technology still prevail. The weapons of the colonizers are usurped and turned against them. The audience is left with the notion that Pandora is saved. However, the Western mindset is easily crafted, reproduced, and recognized in the process of sending the earthlings off the planet and in the complete transferring of the colonized mind permanently into the genetically created shell of the hybrid body. Again, on the surface, this colonialist mindset seems as if it was eliminated and the ecofeminist agenda is left successfully prevailing. This might be why there was such a depression among viewers who experienced some unresolved issues related to Western colonialism. Lemelle's (1995) utilization of various tropes of domination to understand the practice of colonization, internal colonialism, neocolonialism, and enslavement as structures of domination is well observed in *Avatar*. Race, gender, and sex are common tropes of domination founded on the dominance of "hegemonic masculinity" and the absolute control of nature via science.

Conclusion

James Cameron's *Avatar* may be one of the greatest science fiction films of all time that clearly promotes an ecofeminist agenda. Through the setting on Pandora, the film exposes viewers to a world that represents the highest ideals of ecofeminism: a healthy planet and environment with plentiful natural resources, populated with beings who exist peacefully with each other and in perfect harmony with nature and other species. In addition, audiences are introduced to many of the major tenets of ecofeminism through *Avatar*'s storyline. The primary aim of ecofeminism is to seek social and ecological justice; the ideal ecofeminist world is envisioned and presented through the Na'vi people in the way they interact with integrity and respect for each other, nature, and other species. The Na'vi culture embraces the ecofeminist tenet that there is interdependence with, and dependence upon, all living beings and with nature. The interconnections between the domination of women, of minoritized others, and of nature are displayed by the human colonizers on Pandora; their pursuit to exploit the planet's natural resources lead to the domination/obliteration of the Na'vi people, their home and sacred land, and other living species. The compulsion to dominate is demonstrated by the colonizers. Ecofeminists analyze the structures of domination exposing forms of linked oppressions and recognize that because they are linked, one type of oppression (e.g., over women or minoritized groups) cannot be overcome without addressing the other linked oppression (e.g., over nature). The human colonizers on Pandora focus on the difference between themselves and the Na'vi people, referring to the Na'vi as "blue monkeys."

Ecofeminist scholars recognize that focus on feminized difference is the basis of all oppressions. In contrast, the Na'vi people embrace an important tenet of ecofeminism: the value of cultural and biological diversity, which is necessary for social transformation to eliminate oppressive practices.

Like all great science fiction, *Avatar* challenges its audience, but instead of presenting the "what if" question, the movie reflects ecofeminist issues existing within current society, providing understanding about the consequences of domination over others and exploitation of the environment. While the futuristic setting on Pandora is a product of imagination, the exploitation of the environment for capitalistic goals is based on historical and current practices of Western societies. The disregard of the indigenous Na'vi people in the colonizer's quest for the rare mineral on Pandora parallels the Trump administration's authorization of the 1,100 mile Dakota Access Pipeline that runs through Sioux Tribe territory, violating an 1851 federal treaty and disproportionately exposing American Indians to serious health risks.

Oil pipelines are notorious for leaks, spilling toxic pollutants into the soil, waterways, and air, causing destruction to the environment, contaminating water sources, and resulting in serious health risks, injury, and death for people, animals, insects, and flora that live near pipelines. Since 2010, nearly nine million gallons of crude oil have spilled from pipelines across the USA, amounting to a pipeline leak every other day (Harrington 2016). US District Judge James Boasberg deemed Trump's executive order for the Dakota Pipeline as "highly controversial" since it provided permits for the construction of the pipeline without conducting the mandatory environmental impact analysis (Wamsley 2020). The federal judge further stated that the Energy Transfer Company should have never been allowed to build a portion of the pipeline under South Dakota's Lake Oahe, which serves as a drinking water source for the Standing Rock Sioux Tribe (Moore 2020). The federal court ordered the Dakota Access Pipeline to be shut down immediately until a full and complete environmental impact review is conducted, which takes approximately 13 months (Wamsley 2020).

Within days, a federal appeals court decided that the Energy Transfer Company would be allowed to continue operating the Dakota Access Pipeline and given time for any further legal proceedings (Moore 2020). In October 2019, the Keystone 1 Pipeline leaked about 380,000 gallons of oil into wetlands (Wolfe and Ries 2019). Even though the pipeline is opposed by environmental groups and American Native groups in which the pipeline would cross through their sovereign land, Trump signed an order approving construction of the Keystone XL pipeline (Wolfe and Ries 2019).

The link between reality and science fiction is palpable in *Avatar*. The exploitation of the environment and the oppression of indigenous people for capitalistic goals is an important ecofeminist issue that affects all living beings, as well as the health of the planet. Like all great science fiction, *Avatar* challenges the audience's thinking about these current issues in society and allows the viewer to observe many different sides of an issue from a distance.

The ecofeminist analysis of *Avatar* emphasized two core concepts: "hegemonic masculinity" and "tropes of domination." The application of these concepts in analyzing the film provided insight into ideological practices that are both overt and covert. Describing hegemonic masculinity and tropes of domination in this analysis of *Avatar* exposes the complex interconnections of capitalism, patriarchy, and colonialism as practices that oppress women, minoritized others, and nature, while still portraying and recognizing the significance of ecofeminist values.

Avatar, while progressive in terms of ecofeminism, also characterizes and reproduces harmful western cultural views. In many ways, the words of Neytiri seem to ring true: "Sky people cannot learn. They cannot see."

References

Agarwal, Bina. 1992. "The Gender and Environment Debate: Lessons from India." *Feminist Studies* 18, no. 1: 119–158. Accessed September 1, 2020. http://www.jstor.org/stable/3178217.

Alexander, Jonathan. 2014. "Aesthetics and Artificiality from *À Rebours* to *Avatar*: Some Varieties of the Virtual since 1884." *Science-Fiction Studies* 41: 502–523. Accessed September 1, 2020. https://www.jstor.org/stable/10.5621/sciefictstud.41.3.0502?seq=1.

Aulette, Judy Root, Judith Wittner, and Kristin Blakely. 2009. *Gendered Worlds*. Oxford: Oxford University Press.

Beynon, John. 2002. *Masculinities and Culture*. Philadelphia, PA: Open University Press.

Childress, Erik. 2019. "The 50 Highest-Grossing Movies of All Time: Your Top Box Office Earners Ever Worldwide." *Rotten Tomatoes*, March 2. Accessed September 14, 2020. https://editorial.rottentomatoes.com/article/highest-grossing-movies-all-time/.

Connell, R. W. 1995. *Masculinities*. Berkeley, CA: University of California Press.

Connell, R. W., and James W. Messerschmidt. 2005. "Hegemonic Masculinity: Rethinking the Concept." *Gender and Society* 19, no. 6: 829–859. Accessed September 1, 2020. http://www.jstor.org/stable/27640853.

Deininger, Michelle, and Gemma Scammell. 2021. "'Extinction is Forever': Ecofeminism and Apocalypse in Louise Lawrence's Young Adult Short Fiction." In *Dystopias and Utopias on Earth and Beyond: Feminist Ecocriticism of Science Fiction*, edited by Douglas A. Vakoch, 83–97. Abingdon, Oxon, UK and New York, NY: Routledge.

Falquina, Silvia Martinez. 2014. "'The Pandora Effect': James Cameron's 'Avatar' and a Trauma Studies Perspective/'Elefecto Pandora': 'Avatar,' de James Cameron, y una perspectiva de los estudios de trauma." *Atlantis* 36, no. 2: 115–131. Accessed September 1, 2020. https://www.researchgate.net/publication/289734576.

Fiske, John. 1987. *Television Culture: Popular Pleasures and Politics*. New York, NY: Methuen.

Gaard, Greta. 1993. "Living Interconnections with Animals and Nature." In *Ecofeminism: Women, Animals, Nature*, edited by Greta Gaard. Philadelphia,

PA: Temple University Press. Accessed September 1, 2020. https://www.research gate.net/publication/237404647.

Gaard, Greta, and Lori Gruen. 1993. "Ecofeminism: Toward Global Justice and Planetary Health." *Society and Nature* 2: 1–35. Accessed September 1, 2020. https://www.academia.edu/32438639/.

Glenday, Craig. 2019. "*Avengers: Endgame* Overtakes *Avatar* as the Most Successful Movie at the Global Box Office." *GuinnessWorldRecords.com*, July 23. Accessed September 2, 2020. https://www.guinnessworldrecords.com/news /2019/7/avengers-endgame-overtakes-avatar-as-the-most-successful-movie-at-the -global-box-584354.

Harrington, Rebecca. 2016. "Here's How Much Oil Has Spilled from US Pipelines Since 2010." *Business Insider*, December 15. Accessed September 14, 2020. https ://www.businessinsider.com/how-much-oil-spills-from-pipelines-us-america-na tural-gas-2016-12?r=MX&IR=T.

Jewkes, Rachel K., Michael G. Flood, and James Lang. 2015. "From Work with Men and Boys to Changes of Social Norms and Reduction of Inequities in Gender Relations: A Conceptual Shift in Prevention of Violence against Women and Girls." *The Lancet* 385, no. 9977: 1580–1589. Accessed September 1, 2020. https://www.sciencedirect.com/science/article/abs/pii/S0140673614616834.

Lemelle, Anthony. 1995. "The Political Sociology of Black Masculinity and Tropes of Domination." *Journal of African American Men* 1, no. 2: 87–101. Accessed September 1, 2020. http://www.jstor.org/stable/41819284.

Mies, Maria, and Vandana Shiva. 1993. *Ecofeminism*. London: Zed Books.

Moore, Mark. 2020. "Federal Appeals Court Allows Dakota Access Pipeline to Continue Amid Legal Battle." *New York Post*, July 15. Accessed September 15, 2020. https://nypost.com/2020/07/15/dakota-access-pipeline-allowed-to-contin ue-after-court-ruling/.

Murphy, Patrick D. 1998. "'The Women Are Speaking': Contemporary Literature as Theoretical Critique." In *Ecofeminist Literary Criticism: Theory, Interpretation, Pedagogy*, edited by Greta Gaard and Patrick D. Murphy. Chicago, IL: University of Illinois Press.

Robehmed, Natalie. 2018. "A $426.6 Million Opening Makes 'Black Panther' The Top-Grossing Film with A Black Cast." *Forbes*, February 20. Accessed October 13, 2020. https://www.forbes.com/sites/natalierobehmed/2018/02/20/a-426-6 -million-opening-makes-black-panther-the-top-grossing-film-with-a-black-cast/ #38c0a22712a6.

Ruether, Rosemary Radford. 1995. "Ecofeminism: Symbolic and Social Connections of the Oppression of Women and the Domination of Nature." *Feminist Theology* 3, no. 6: 35–50. Accessed September 1, 2020. http://journals.sagepub.com/doi/ abs/10.1177/096673509500000903.

Taylor, James C. 2020. "Renewing Hegemonic Masculinity Every Wednesday: Arrow and Television Form." In T*oxic Masculinity: Mapping the Monstrous in Our Heroes*, edited by Esther De Dauw and Daniel J. Connell, 34–51. Jackson, MS: University Press of Mississippi. Accessed September 2, 2020. doi:10.2307/j. ctv1595mq0.6.

Wamsley, Laurel. 2020. "Court Rules Dakota Access Pipeline Must Be Emptied for Now." *NPR*, July 6. Accessed September 14, 2020. https://www.npr.org/2020/ 07/06/887593775/court-rules-that-dakota-access-pipeline-must-be-emptied-for -now.

Warren, Karen. 2000. *Ecofeminist Philosophy: A Western Perspective on What It Is and Why It Matters*. Lanham, MD: Rowman and Littlefield Publishing Group Inc.

Wolfe, Elizabeth, and Brian Ries. 2019. "The Latest Keystone Pipeline Oil Leak Is Almost 10 Times Worse Than Initially Thought." *CNN*, November 20. Accessed September 14, 2020. https://edition.cnn.com/2019/11/20/us/keystone-pipeline-leak-10-times-worse-trnd/index.html.

12 Eco-Heroines and Saviors in Iraj Fazel Bakhsheshi's *Men and Supertowers* and *The Sun's Sons*

Zahra Jannessari Ladani

The roots of ecological crises have been found in a "failure of the imagination" and it has been claimed that literary imagination can create pathways for the realization of goals and, thus, can serve as a device for the purposes of ecocriticism. This failure can be interpreted in two ways: first, that there has been a "failure of the imagination" which has ended in ecological crises, and that if literary imagination becomes more active and concerned with ecological and environmental questions, it can serve as a remedy, at least by providing us with prospects of how we can avoid or survive such crises; second, that there has been literary imagination with regard to ecological crises, but there has not been sufficient recognition or appreciation of such imagination. My double interpretation of the phrase "failure of the imagination" (Bergthaller 2010, 730), at the beginning of this chapter, may lay the ground for the expression of the fact that ecological and environmental issues have been an essential concern to many science fiction writers whose fiction becomes home to diverse ecosystems and the way they are treated, that is, imbalanced, reconstructed, exploited, and destroyed. More specifically, the subgenre of ecofeminist science fiction devotes itself to the exploration of imagining and re-imagining neglected ecological and environmental issues to address serious philosophical and existential questions.

One such figure, with deep and serious ecological concerns, who needs to be recognized and appreciated on an international level is the Iranian science fiction writer Iraj Fazel Bakhsheshi with six novels and two collections of over 50 short stories, signifying a hallmark in the history of science fiction in Iran. He was born on April 19, 1965, in Mashhad. He studied at the University of Tehran and graduated as a mining engineer in 1989, and now he works in the mining industry. His novels and short story collections include *Men and Supertowers* (2006), *A Message Older than Time* (2007), *The Guardian Angel* (2008), *The Patient in Chamber 320* (2009), *The Sun's Sons* (2011), *Yellow River Mine* (2013), *Mr. Fourth Generation and Other Stories* (2014), *Travel to Planet Tera* (2016), and *52 Short Stories* (2017). In almost all of his novels, Fazel Bakhsheshi imagines an earth threatened by diverse types of imminent ecological and environmental disasters, from the extinction of particular species and inadequacy and lack of resources of energy to meteorite crash and the consequent forced immigration of elite groups to other planets to survive at the cost of the annihilation and perishing of other species and social classes. On the other hand, Fazel Bakhsheshi fantasizes planets that are to be future homes to the immigrant populations from the earth; these new ecohomes are to be terraformed and ecologically reconditioned, as a result of which their indigenous populations are going to suffer drastically. Besides these eco-concerns, Fazael Bakhsheshi also creates characters that become heroes and heroines in the course of their struggles against diverse forms of oppression, colonization, and corruption, either helping their fellow humans to regain what they lost by enlightening them, or improving the life conditions of other species by fighting colonial and oppressive forces. Women characters, particularly, in such struggles against the dominant power of the oppressive groups, emerge as eco-heroines and saviors in the works of Fazel Bakhsheshi.

Only a few of Fazel Bakhsheshi's stories, that is, "Murder," "Sorrow and Mirth," "World in World," and "Lilith," have been translated to Russian and Kazakh and published on some social networks such as Facebook. His science fiction has been appreciated for investigating and foregrounding human issues, culture, and the influence of techno-scientific progress on society. His characters usually have no names; this means that they can be understood universally, but simultaneously he shows his commitment to national and indigenous concerns by incorporating them in his fiction so skillfully that the Iranian reader will immediately recognize them. Fazel Bakhsheshi's amazing imaginative power encapsulates local/regional incidents and events, vocational matters, and social concerns in such unfamiliar fictional coordinates that the effect is almost always thought-provoking and even shocking. In this chapter, I will analyze two of his novels in terms of ecofeminism. Specifically, I will focus on the notion of eco-heroines and saviors in *Men and Supertowers* and *The Sun's Sons*.

Both novels mentioned above demonstrate fictional worlds fraught with the "ethics of rights"—"ethics of responsibilities" dichotomy, a distinction Gilligan and Attanucci make between two "moral orientations" of "justice" and "care" (1998, 74), which Gaard terms as men's seeking rights (ethics of rights), and women's taking care of responsibilities (ethics of responsibilities) (1993, 2). In *Men and Supertowers* and *The Sun's Sons*, rights are mostly what Fazel Bakhsheshi's male characters fight for, whereas responsibilities are what his female characters mostly undertake and accomplish. But this rights-for-males and responsibilities-for-females division does not always work as a fixed rule, particularly when his morally responsible male characters fulfill sacrificial and leading roles. At times, Fazel Bakhsheshi's male characters even turn into sublime souls with messianic commitments and a great sense of responsibility. As for his female characters, they are typically heroic souls who try to save their society; they help nature and the environment on the earth to thrive and even become leading figures whose contributions positively affect the life of alien beings and ecosystems on other planets. Here, ethics of responsibilities (care) highlighted as an ecofeminist code by the mentioned critics turns out to be an essential feature in the case of Fazel Bakhsheshi's female characters while ethics of rights (justice) is highly controversial regarding his male characters. This distinction between the two moral orientations will be discussed and exemplified in the following.

Men and Supertowers

As for Fazel Bakhsheshi's *Men and Supertowers*, the supertower as the locale of the narrative represents the dystopian world where capitalistic motives play a crucial role in the life of human beings. Here, the supertower is actually a gigantic space with millions of people living and working inside its autocratic system of control and surveillance. The concept of supertower is better understood when one imagines the contrast between the outside world as the natural ecosystem and the inside world of the gigantic structure of the supertower perceived as an artificial habitat. It is of equal importance to imagine the way the body and mind of the supertower's residents are affected by their mechanical lifestyle as opposed to the more natural lifestyle of people living outside the tower. Furthermore, regardless of the Freudian implications of a supertower, that is, being a vertical construct as well as a phallic symbol representing masculinity, the high tower can be viewed as a product of civilization and culture in opposition to nature, as male is opposed to female. From an ecofeminist perspective, the supertower may signify not just verticality, but also hierarchal mentality and the discourse of power and domination which leads the masculine figure to pursue ethics of rights through competitiveness and ambition:

> Man's conception of the world [...] consists in the dichotomous alternation of elements, useful to create a hierarchy in the world. Unlike this tendency, the feminist one seems to be more inclined to glimpse the commonalities rather than the differences; it is for this reason that Men would be more accustomed to competitiveness and contrast, while Women would be more conciliatory and able to mediate between opposite positions.
>
> (Valera 2017, 15)

Considering Valera's remarks, Fazel Bakhsheshi's supertower combines the hierarchal conception of the world and gender constructs and produces a unique horrible spatial entity that looms large in the eco-sphere of the earth, demonstrating a monstrous distortion in the natural course of life. In addition, Fazel Bakhsheshi's supertower can be taken as an allegory for the post-capitalist prison structure of man's existence in an era not far from our current time. In this structure, what we fear, based on Korody's remarks, is typically the capitalist *use* of technology, not technology itself. We recognise, often subconsciously, that we have very little power in this world, and that when a new technology is introduced, it will not be up to us how it is used. Big data could be a boon for the medical sector, for instance, but more likely it will be a way for companies to monitor our credit, our spending habits, our friends, our intimate relations, and our travel patterns. Technology is not to blame here; our economic system is.

(Korody 2016)

Men and Supertowres is the fictional rendering of the "architectonics" of post-capitalistic societies where urban architecture, in Korody's words, becomes the site of "ubiquitous surveillance and dataveillance guised as 'smart urbanism' and 'smart architecture'." This new architecture is so foreign to the natural living environment that it turns into a lethal site for the inhabitants. I would like to suggest that Fazel Bakhsheshi displaces the site of Darwin's theory of evolution by taking humans out of their original habitat—the natural environment where they are directly connected to the earth and breathe from the air—and positing them inside an artificial structure that gradually brings them to a decline and devolution.

A glimpse into the interior world of the supertower reveals that everything in the life of the inhabitants in *Men and Supertowers* is planned and arranged by the Department of Health and Regulation of Population and Mind (DHRPM), the central governmental agency that bears great resemblance to Foucault's "Panopticon." The strict hierarchical structure of DHRPM mandates that the inhabitants of the supertower be categorized as first-rate and second-rate humans, the latter naturally assigned menial and less complex jobs. Here, all human beings are named by codes, that is, letters plus numbers, rather than typical given names and surnames. This use of codes simplifies their identification and categorization, as well as their manipulation. In this world, men and women are an emaciated, disempowered, and mechanical race; they have lost whatever initially defined them as human through medicine and nutrition prescribed by DHRPM counselors. They listen to selected music, marry the partners chosen for them, and spend their time with humanoid holograms that spy on them. Isolation, lack of communication, and a palpable absence of humanitarian acts characterize life in the supertower. Human passions, emotions, and intuitions are diagnosed as abnormal and are constantly suppressed and controlled by diets enforced by DHRPM. The strict measures taken to control the lives of the supertower's inhabitants lead to their psychosomatic deterioration, which not only transforms them into unnatural beings and robotic mechanisms but also commodifies their labor in the post-capitalistic society of the tower. The commodification of the labor of the supertower's population here serves the ethics of rights, since reason dictates that progress and better life conditions are necessary assets to reach an advanced civilization and, to achieve this goal, the labor as well as the obedience of the majority of people are required.

The post-capitalistic economic system dominant in the supertower, according to the survey conveyed by one of the leaders (and narrators) in the story, emerges as a result of the economic conditions experienced in the past centuries. The survey reveals that since the mid-twenty-first century, the manufacturing of goods was affected significantly by "external factors, i.e., factors outside the workplace." At the beginning, these were limited to the "laborers' commute, their living place, and the costs of the towns where they worked." Considering these external variables, the economic scientists and sociologists of the society of *Men and Supertowers* decided to eliminate the bad effects of these factors on workers. To do so, the idea of building manufacturing towers was proposed quickly. The development of "vertical spaces" seemingly reduced environmental problems and expenses of purchasing land for manufacturing plants and workers' residences. In addition, it reduced the problems of workers' transportation. The building of these towers began in poor countries with large populations. They had millions of cheap workers who, unlike the workers in advanced countries, were after a comfortable and luxurious life, and worked merely to earn their meals. In this manner, the first tower was erected and the others followed quickly and employers gathered workers in the towers, lodging thousands of them there (Fazel Bakhsheshi 2006, 57–58).

In *Men and Supertowers*, therefore, the notion of the "tower" does not serve the function of a simple setting, but is a colossal spatial matrix, almost metamorphosed to become the central character, controlling the other elements of the story. As the "dominant" of this novel, the "supertower" is actually a highly advanced plantation where captive people work as producers/slaves. The tower determines the modes of living by turning the inhabitants into tools for the utilitarian project of the Market machine. Indeed, the tower is a post-capitalist gothic structure of 60 levels, each level like a little city, with all required services and facilities. The interesting point is, however, that the gigantic tower has no exit ways, or if it has, the inhabitants do not know about them. In fact, the inhabitants know nothing about the outside world and are not allowed to quit the place. The apartments are similar to very comfortable prison wards in which the single resident eats, sleeps, plays games, and does a limited range of activities under the incessantly observing eyes of a hologram that reports the slightest change or "abnormal" behavior to the counselors at DHRPM. Characters like A1475456 who are occasionally summoned to DHRPM for the slightest changes detected in their lifestyle, receive treatments for normalization. The treatment is a sort of desensitization that actually makes the patient indifferent to his/her instinctive urges.

Under such strict control, however, A1475456 succeeds in circumventing the treatment by little tricks he plays on his hologram, thus keeping his instincts awake though he is well aware of the risks of what he is doing.

Getting acquainted with a female hologram designer named B2357493, our eco-heroine who remains in the backstage till the end, he works against the rigid system and exits the tower to join the external world. But the consequences of his attempted escape are tragic for he is not biologically acclimatized to the outside world and will soon perish. Nonetheless, he is chosen as the first leader and savior of the tower's inhabitants and starts writing a manifesto to enlighten them about their life conditions and invite them to begin a normal life in the world outside the tower.

Here, I should add that before his acquaintance with B2357493, A1475456 was just trying to keep his instincts awake, having no serious thought of escaping the supertower. The discourse of resistance and emancipation comes into being only after their union, which inspires them to dream of a real world out of their habitat. Thus, the contribution of the female character as a figure whose natural instincts are incomparably stronger than the male protagonist's entails her close relation to nature and the external world as the real ecosystem, which affirms Françoise d'Eaubonne's essential delicate analogy between women and nature (Gates 1996, 9; Valera 2017, 10–11). This analogy emphasizes that women possess characteristics that resemble those of nature, like giving birth to offspring and being nurturers as well as being the domitable gender which makes them subject to domination and exploitation by the male gender. Françoise d'Eaubonne's analogy fits the condition of B2357493 very well, since she comes from an inferior category in the hierarchical system of the supertower precisely because she is very humanlike and her characteristic features often do not meet the leaders' mechanical expectations. B2357493's obviating the dietary plan arranged for her by DHRPM and her manipulation of her hologram are considered signs of abnormal behavior. When A1475456 asks about the nature of her abnormality, she responds: "I do not like the word 'abnormality.' I have a wish." Her wish (abnormality) is "to get out of here and see the outside world" (Fazel Bakhsheshi 2006, 33). This wish, based on an ecofeminist perspective, is just very natural and stresses her unique connection to nature. B2357493's position as a professional hologram designer never exonerates her from punishment for her attempted escape; she is retrenched and then given the hard job of a menial laborer, and eventually forced to resign and ostracized from the tower. Therefore, all her life in the supertower, she is dominated and exploited by the oppressive male system.

The story, however, is different in the case of A1475456. His abnormal behavior, ironically, promotes his status to that of a leader rather than putting him at risk of being recognized as a threat to the whole system. Actually, the leaders of the supertower decide to assign him a very confidential and important job, which takes him to the higher levels of the tower and allows him to have all the information he needs for a second escape. At this point, I should add that A1475456 is again under the influence of the dietary system specifically prescribed for him to control his instincts. Thus, he is back to his ethics of rights and considers his new position as a well-deserved achievement. Nonetheless, A1475456 gradually remembers B2357493 and their shared wishes, as a result of which he makes a prompt decision to flee and later comes out as a hero figure to enlighten people about their enslavement. The real savior at the back of the stage, however, is B2357493's heroine figure. Being an expert in the field of hologram technology, she risks her life against a technology-informed system that forbids maternal passion, family nucleus, love and human subjectivity, and natural life in general. Her ethics of responsibilities wins the male protagonist's awe and respect, thus modifying his ethics of rights and invigorating his moral responsibility.

In *The Techno-Human Condition*, Allenby and Sarewitz offer different levels of technology:

> If one thinks of a vaccine as a means of reducing levels of infection, it looks like a Level I technology; if one thinks of it as a means of improving economic growth, it looks like a Level II technology; if one thinks of it as a part of long-term demographic trends and subsequent political and social evolution in a developing country, it looks like a Level III technology.
>
> (Allenby and Sarewitz 2011, 40)

Timothy Clark believes that this excerpt asserts the degree by which "techne" can function as a determining factor in the transformation of biological-ecological as well as the sociopolitical condition of man (Clark 2015, 8). We should remark that the technoscientific autocracy that B2357493 revolts against goes beyond level II and reaches level III. It is only by reading this quote that the profundity of B2357493's agenda becomes apparent for her rebellion happens within a very complicated context, where the colossal supertower reaches beyond economic purposes to shape the sociopolitical evolution of the population born and living inside its complex structure. Despite her achievement, B2357493's heroic act remains in the background and is redirected in the manifesto written by A1475456 which divulges secrets related to the atrocity practiced in the supertower and calls for a public rise against and immigration from the tower's artificial ecosystem and return to their original ecohome, that is, the outside world. Here, the outside world is introduced as the original habitat still uncontaminated. However, one wonders how immigrants born in the supertower and raised in and adapted to such an artificial environment can survive in the adverse ecosphere of the outside world. As a consequence of this revolutionary manifesto, the false ecosystem in the supertower might be destroyed in the long run, but the emaciated human species accustomed to that false matrix may not obtain the necessary qualifications to acclimatize and adapt, and thus, to evolve into a strong species. The human body, here, like in Atwood's *Oryx and Crake*, is the "ecodystopic body," borrowing Brandao and Cavalcanti's

(2021) term, that is exploited and transforms into a new body that later becomes dysfunctional and alien when put into the natural environment. The whole prospect in *Men and Supertowers* seems tragic.

The Sun's Sons

Fazel Bakhsheshi's eco-heroines and saviors, nevertheless, are not always backgrounded and sacrificed as it happens in *Men and Supertowers*. In *The Sun's Sons*, the heroine emerges as a triumphant female figure who establishes herself as a source of power, justice, and wisdom among the humanoids living on Earth II. The story goes that the earth (Mother Earth as the sustainer of humankind) is to perish in near future as a result of the overexploitation of its resources by man. This is precisely the catastrophe which, in Žižek's (2020, 41) view, is needed to make men able to "rethink the very basic features of the society" in which they live, but in the case of Fazel Bahksheshi's characters and the society in which they live, this catastrophe leads to the recapitulation of the same tragic scenario of nature exploitation and perishing of species as well as ecological reconditioning on Earth II; in other words, little is added to the characters' wisdom.

The imminent catastrophe in *The Sun's Sons* turns out to be the reason behind a highly confidential project the United Nations has been working on for 300 years, which is now ready to be operationalized by an elect group including the topmost scientists of the world in diverse fields, among them M9 (the female space physician and project manager) and Z9 (the male linguist with expertise in ancient languages). The project has been planned to send part of the earth's population to Earth II and save the human race. Due to some unforeseen incidents in the course of operationalization, however, an emergency alert is given, the main project is canceled, and instead an ad hoc team, including M9, Z9, and T9 (the project's Chief Security Officer), is sent to Earth II for a period of five years. Earth II has been selected as the target planet because its ecological and climatic conditions as well as its life forms are similar to the earth. One evolved species, among other inhabitants on this planet, is the "humanoids" with analogous physical and skeletal features to man except for a big single eye in the middle of the forehead and a very primitive lifestyle. In other words, there is no civilization on Earth II and, thus, the ad hoc team has the duty to run civilization on the planet and make it ready, that is, homelike, for the acceptance of future travelers from Earth. But the project pursues its objectives by means of oppression, aggressiveness, and militarism dictated by Pharaoh (T9's adopted name on Earth II), the humanoids being sabotaged, subjugated, enslaved, and educated, whereby the resources on Earth II are heavily exploited for the purpose of building a great Empire. Finally, Pharaoh is overthrown by Z9's betrayal and later by M9's tactful and timely decision to poison and ostracize the whole team.

The violence practiced for man's empire-building in Fzael Bakhsheshi's *The Sun's Sons* is reminiscent of the discourse of "conquest and defeat" in

Le Guin's *Always Coming Home*, where the original inhabitants, that is, the Athsheans, are killed as a consequence of masculinist thinking, as Byrne interprets in this volume. This empire-building project which brings havoc to the whole ecosystem of Earth II and affects the life of the humanoids in unexpected ways is representative of the politics of the Anthropocene and its codes whereby, borrowing Zylinska's terms in *Minimal Ethics for the Anthropocene*, Pharaoh and his team's "idea of justice and 'good', their clamor for a 'better tomorrow'" becomes the humanoids' "horizon of horror" (2014, 124).

The Sun's Sons also represents Kate Soper's first category of the uses of "nature:" when

> employed in a metaphysical sense...nature is the concept referring to the difference and specificity of humanity. This concept of the natural as the non-human is presupposed in all debates about the interpretations of the distinction between the natural and the cultural (or between the human and the animal)
>
> (1995, 319)

which, as Merrick argues, signals either "human continuity with the non-human" or its "irreducible difference" (2008, 219). Taking the extraterrestrial humanoids as the natural, and consequently as the animal, the terrestrial biologists in *The Sun's Sons* hunt them for their laboratory experiments. The linguist (Z9) reads in the biologists' report on the humanoid's vocal tract that their vocal organ is less complicated than humans' and, therefore, their tongue moves less, which gives the humanoids a bizarre accent. Accordingly, humanoids have a very limited range of vocabularies for communication (Fazel Bakhsheshi 2011, 35). Thus, Z9 develops a special curriculum to teach speaking and writing man's language based on the zoologist studies conducted on humanoids. This means that in the first place, humanoids are considered as animals, a part of nature, and thus the subject of man's exploitation. Second, humanoids' inferior status paves the way for later stages of domination and oppression. Pharaoh's decision to take the Caliban-like humanoids out of their "Neolithic Era" or Dark Ages just serves to increase the chance of the humans' "survival" on Earth II (Fazel Bakhsheshi 2011, 84). One observes a similar condition in Le Guin's *The Word for World Is Forest*, where, according to Chan (2021), the new planet is going to be built after "Earth's image", and the ideology that supports this project is the primacy of humans over nonhumans.

Furthermore, for the consolidation of man's conquest of Earth II in *The Sun's Sons*, Pharaoh examines the possibility of producing a male heir out of female humanoids (queer sexuality) through a series of breeding experiments. The "Goddess of Healing" (M9's adopted name on Earth II) cautions Pharaoh that human's dominant genes avert the production of hybrid creatures as well as cross-species confusion and monstrous bodies. Nevertheless, Pharaoh's biotechnology leads to large-scale coercive copulation and oppression of the humanoid female sex, which bespeaks his dualistic attitude toward the Other (the alien, the animal, the natural, and the female in ecofeminist terms). This coercive interbreeding agenda is an example of "masculinism, solutionism and scientism" (Zylinska 2014, 125), or "the sort of bravado whereby men seek to exert control over everything around them by the force of instrumental rationality" (Barney 2011, n.p.). On the one hand, the Other is indispensable to guarantee Pharaoh's survival and strengthen his power relations, humanoids serving him as soldiers, builders, hunters, etc.; on the other hand, the Other is a non-entity (of no subjectivity) that can be altered, shaped, or even eradicated, for instance, the humanoid magician is killed and substituted with the High Priest (the position assigned to Z9 on Earth II) in the very first encounter between the humanoid public and Pharaoh.

The Sun's Sons also investigates the dichotomy articulated by Michel Serres in *The Natural Contract* about the role of the Anthropocene when he says,

> [t]he parasite takes all and gives nothing; the host gives all and takes nothing. Rights of mastery and property come down to parasitism. Conversely, rights of symbiosis are defined by reciprocity: however much nature gives man, man must give that much back to nature, now a legal subject.
>
> (1995, 38)

This is where Serres anticipates the danger of the Anthropocene at the same time that he looks at it with hope for a new form of humanism, that is, one "tied to a collective self-recognition of the human as 'steward' of the planet" (Clark 2015, 5) whereby, for example, the farmer "gave back, in the beauty that resulted from his stewardship, what he owed the earth" (Serres 1995, 38). Man's parasitic life on Earth II speeds up the prospect of an imminent apocalypse due to vast terraforming, uncontrolled exploitation of Earth II's natural resources, and the atrocious militarism practiced by various humanoid tribes. This time, the subject of domination is the ecohome Earth II, Mother Earth's substitute, where the same historical scenario of man's social evolution from the Stone Age to agrarian and capitalistic life is recapitulated. Pharaoh's political domination of this planet is simultaneously a bio(eco)terrorist agenda whereby the new ecosystem is quickly pushed to the edges, drastically altered, and even corrupted.

Thus, Pharaoh adopts a politics far from "rights of symbiosis" and "reciprocity;" his politics is rather just "parasitic." This politics, nonetheless, requires to be revolutionized if the humanoids and the rest of the species on Earth II are going to survive. Thus, Earth II is in urgent need of setting in motion, as Karen J. Warren states in *Ecofeminist Philosophy*, "an ethic *of* the environment," that is, an ethic that "asserts that the nonhuman natural environment...is deserving of moral consideration" as opposed to "an ethic *concerning* the environment," which "denies that the nonhuman environment...is morally considerable" (Warren 2000, 74). Here, I should stress that Earth II's nature is morally considerable, because it possesses properties "that are shared by all and only morally considerable entities," such as "rationality, sentiency, the ability to use a language, possession of a soul, possession of morally relevant interests, being 'the subject of a life,' and simply being alive" (Warren 2000, 74). It goes without saying that humanoids as a species belonging to Earth II's ecosystem possess almost all of these properties, and thus, are "morally considerable." Warren's concept of "an ethic *of* the environment" conforms to "ethics of responsibility" mentioned earlier in this chapter, as both express a concern for the Other, here Earth II and its nature, particularly the humanoids. Therefore, *The Sun's Sons* embodies the deft combination of the ecofeminist codes of "care" and "responsibility" and the environmental ethicists' code of "an ethic *of* the environment" in the figure of a heroine, that is, M9, who saves Earth II's ecosystem and population from the apocalyptic demise that made earth defunct.

The turning point of the novel comes with the subversive acts of Z9 and M9. The linguist takes over Pharaoh by poisoning and paralyzing him and thus rendering the monarch incapable of pursuing his interbreeding project. The poison is taken from a plant that grows on Earth II and is well known among the humanoids. The poison is shot by a simple missile, again made of natural material. Z9's *coup de ta* is not for the good of the humanoids, but serves as a step toward the selfish decision to establish himself as the heir to the monarchy, since he believes that he deserves most because he has been the most loyal and devoted subject during Pharaoh's reign. This indicates that the matter of successorship and competition for power is a central male characteristic in the human race.

Opposed to this competitive world is the conciliatory and responsible world of the female. This is best shown in *The Sun's Sons* (ironically not *The Sun's Daughters*) in the figure of M9 (or the Goddess of Healing) whose adopted name and vocation indicate that she has to tend to the psychosomatic problems of the humanoids, so unlike T9's and Z9's worldviews, hers is based on "ethics of responsibility" rather than "ethics of rights." Among the members of the ad hoc team, M9 is the most sympathetic and ethical toward the aliens and the ecology of Earth II. She realizes that the project of the colonization of Earth II and the education of the humanoids according to human codes has only corrupted the new ecohome and distorted life forms on this planet. In other words, she realizes that the "ultimate result of unchecked, terminal patriarchy will be ecological catastrophe" (Kelly 1997, 113), (eco)colonialism, and genocide. In order to stop this, she develops a gradual plot and orders her servants to reconstruct a battery by employing guidelines she remembers from her studies about the construction of electric batteries in ancient Iran. She plans to replace the discharged battery of her missile (a missile she brought from Earth at the beginning of the story and which has been out of use all these years) with this one. This is a form of military technology she develops in order to fight Pharaoh. It goes without saying that M9 has been raised and educated within the same patriarchal and hierarchal world in which T9 and Z9 have been raised. However, one essential difference between M9 and the other two is that she turns the patriarchal system on its head to emancipate the humanoids and save Earth II from disaster. And she is the only human that is truly guarded by the humanoids after the coup. She is not a suspect among the humanoids, because her life history on Earth II and her vocational contributions prove her to be incorruptible and trustworthy. So her queenship (which is humorously resembled to that of Cleopatra's by M9) is welcomed by the humanoids not as a political status but as a socio-ecological role (perhaps a "steward" in Serres's terms as quoted above) to support and improve life conditions on Earth II. In her overthrowing the monarchy of Pharaoh and thwarting the plot of Z9, M9 never kills, that is, she transforms "nonviolently the structures of male dominance" (Kelly 1997, 113). She makes intelligent and controlled use of poison and ostracizes the paralyzed bodies to a distant land where they can regain their health and return to normal life. Nonetheless, she writes a message on a parchment and puts it in their baggage to inform them that in case they return, the humanoids will certainly destroy them.

Conclusion

Unlike B2357493 who undergoes a traumatic experience and remains in the background in *Men and Supertowers*, M9 in *The Sun's Sons* is an eco-heroine who gets out of the backstage and comes to the fore to prove that if she is the victimized sex in the patriarchal system of the humankind, she can reverse this situation in the new ecohome. The new ecohome means to her a new existential status. M9 is not only the emancipator of an inferior race (humanoids) but also the savior and rectifier of an inferior sex (the female) as well as the brave soul that saves the ecosystem without claims of knighthood and heroism but with duties of a stewardess. Fazel Bakhsheshi's heroines are the initiators of a new version of heroism, one that collates social responsibilities with ethical mandates and an egalitarian outlook. The heroines in *Men and Supertowers* and *The Sun's Sons* can be taken as models that put into practice the critical codes and criteria of ecofeminism. In other words, the existence and contributions of such eco-heroines in these two novels make it possible for us to reevaluate "nature and environmental issues" and "uncover the perseverance of androcentric dualist thinking in society" (Yang 2017, 4).

References

Allenby, Braden, and Daniel Sarewitz. 2011. *The Techno-Human Condition.* Cambridge, MA: MIT Press.

Barney, Darin. 2011. "Eat Your Vegetables: Courage and the Possibility of Politics." *Theory & Event* 14, no. 2. Accessed October 13, 2020. doi:10.1353/tae.2011.0023.

Bergthaller, Hannes. 2010. "Housebreaking the Human Animal: Humanism and the Problem of Sustainability in Margaret Atwood's *Oryx and Crake* and *The Year of the Flood.*" *English Studies* 91: 728–742.

Brandão, Izabel F. O., and Ildney Cavalcanti. 2021. "Margaret Atwood's Ecodystopic SF: Approaching Ethics, Gender, and Ecology." In *Dystopias and Utopias on Earth and Beyond: Feminist Ecocriticism of Science Fiction,* edited by Douglas A. Vakoch, 114–125. Abingdon, Oxon, UK and New York, NY: Routledge.

Chan, Amy Kit-sze. 2021. "Re-reading Ursula K. Le Guin's SF: The Daoist Yin Principle in Ecofeminist Novels." In *Dystopias and Utopias on Earth and Beyond: Feminist Ecocriticism of Science Fiction,* edited by Douglas A. Vakoch, 126–137. Abingdon, Oxon, UK and New York, NY: Routledge.

Clark, Timothy. 2015. *Ecocriticism on the Edge: The Anthropocene as a Threshold Concept.* London: Bloomsbury.

Fazel Bakhsheshi, Iraj. 2006. *Men and Supertowers.* Tehran: Ghasidehsara & Mehran.

———. 2011. *The Sun's Sons.* Mashhad: Ahange Ghalam.

Gaard, Greta. 1993. "Living Interconnections with Animals and Nature." In *Ecofeminism: Women, Animals, Nature,* edited by Greta Gaard, 1–12. Philadelphia, PA: Temple University Press.

Gates, Barbara T. 1996. "A Root of Ecofeminism: *Ecoféminisme.*" *ISLE: Interdisciplinary Studies in Literature and Environment* 3, no. 1: 7–16.

Gilligan, Carol, and Jane Attanucci. 1998. "Two Moral Orientations." In *Mapping the Moral Domain: A Contribution of Women's Thinking to Psychological Theory and Education,* edited by Carol Gilligan, Janie Victoria Ward, Jill McLean Taylor, and Betty Bardige, 73–86. Cambridge, MA: Harvard University Press.

Kelly, Petra. 1997. "Women and Power." In *Ecofeminism: Women, Culture, Nature,* edited Karen J. Warren, 112–119. Bloomington, IN and Indianapolis, IN: Indiana University Press.

Korody, Nicholas. 2016. "Architecture after Capitalism, in a World without Work." *Archinect Features,* March 18. Accessed October 13, 2020. https://archinect.com/features/article/149935222/architecture-after-capitalism-in-a-world-without-work.

Merrick, Helen. 2008. "Queering Nature: Close Encounters with the Alien in Ecofeminist Science Fiction." In *Queer Universes: Sexualities in Science Fiction,* edited by Wendy Gay Pearson, Veronica Hollinger, and Joan Gordon, 216–232. Liverpool: Liverpool University Press.

Serres, Michel. 1995. *The Natural Contract.* Translated by Elizabeth MacArthur and William Paulson. Ann Arbor, MI: University of Michigan Press.

Soper, Kate. 1995. "Feminism and Ecology: Realism and Rhetoric in the Discourses of Nature." *Science, Technology and Human Values* 20, no. 3: 311–331.

Valera, Luca. 2017. "Françoise d'Eaubonne and Ecofeminism: Rediscovering the Link between Women and Nature." In *Women and Nature?: Beyond Dualism in*

Gender, Body, and Environment, edited by Douglas A. Vakoch and Sam Mickey, 10–23. London and New York, NY: Routledge.

Warren, Karen J. 2000. *Ecofeminist Philosophy: A Western Perspective on What It Is and Why It Matters*. Lanham, MD: Rowman and Littlefield.

Yang, Karen Ya-Chu. 2017. "Introduction." In *Women and Nature?: Beyond Dualism in Gender, Body, and Environment*, edited by Douglas A. Vakoch and Sam Mickey, 3–9. London and New York, NY: Routledge.

Žižek, Slavoj. 2020. *Pandemic!: Covid-19 Shakes the World*. London and New York, NY: OR Books.

Zylinska, Joanna. 2014. *Minimal Ethics for the Anthropocene*. Ann Arbor, MI: Open Humanities Press. Accessed October 13, 2020. https://quod.lib.umich.edu /o/ohp/12917741.0001.001.

13 Rethinking Resistance

An Ecofeminist Approach to
Anti-Colonialism in Louise Erdrich's
Future Home of the Living God, and
Oreet Ashery and Larissa Sansour's
The Novel of Nonel and Vovel

Benay Blend

This chapter addresses the intersection of ecofeminism, Indigenous Studies, and science fiction by focusing on Louise Erdrich (Ojibwe), *The Future Home of the Living God* (2017) and Oreet Ashery (Israeli) and Larissa Sansour (Palestinian), *The Novel of Nonel and Vovel* (2009), two works that model resistance to colonialism. As Nicole Anae (2021) observes in her study of four Australian writers, feminists are paying increasing attention to science fiction. For these authors, science fiction serves as a vehicle for exploring social issues like colonialism, racism, and climate justice, all from an Indigenous perspective. Both texts counter science fiction's colonial gaze by reshaping the boundaries of the genre. As Greta Gaard (1998, 3) discerns, though ecofeminism makes women central to its analysis in ways decolonial movements do not, it acknowledges that connections between patriarchal domination of women and nature are related to racism, colonialism, and class conflict. Through an ecofeminist lens, these texts raise important questions. Does science fiction have the capacity to correct the violence of the past by offering an alternative model of resistance? What is the relationship between art and political modes of struggle? How do these texts fit in the larger sweeps of ecofeminist studies? When Indigenous and Palestinian texts are read together, what sort of contextual conversations emerge across border lines? And, finally, why are creative forms of resistance so important to Native and Palestinian peoples? Linked by the overarching question of why ecofeminism is still needed to address the environmental emergencies and challenges of our time, such revisions of racialized spaces offer imaginative insights into the future. By expanding the genres to include women of color, a critical ecofeminist perspective offers, then, a more inclusive version of science fiction.

As Tania LaFontaine (2016, 6) explains, science fiction serves as a good vehicle for environmental themes. Moreover, the study of science fiction from an ecofeminist stance serves scholars of both fields as it provides a more expansive scope. At its core, ecofeminism grew out of activist social movements of the late 1970s to early 1980s. As such, it addresses gender relations between women and men and between humans and nature (Diamond and Feman 1990, ix). It shares with science fiction a checkered history in terms of failing to include the complexities of women's experiences as mediated by class, ethnicity, sexuality, and so on. As Justine Larbalestier (2006, xvi) notes, there are many feminisms, just as there are varieties of feminist science fiction. According to Grace Dillon (2012, 2), science fiction arose in the mid-nineteenth century as a genre that often conflated the abuses of colonialism with exploration stories. Ecofeminism, too, has been implicated in colluding with patriarchal modes; in particular, critics have leveled charges of essentialism at the idea that women's alleged biologically determined closeness to nature supports patriarchal claims of their inferiority. Moreover, argue Phillips and Rumens (2017, 3), highlighting the commonality of all women as victims of male oppression fails to address the diversity of women's lives across race, class, and national boundaries. In a colonial setting, adds Cathy Hawkins, any consideration of "Othering," with reference to gender, needs also to include an analysis of racial difference. "Despite its interest in war and the colonization of other worlds," Hawkins charges, science fiction has remained indifferent to issues surrounding race (2006, 208).

Nevertheless, Black women have fought against what Andrea Hairston terms a "narrowly defined feminism" that excludes the experiences of "other" women by labeling them "marginal or aberrant" (2006, 292). This chapter, then, contributes to the field by focusing on works that challenge the social construction of gender while taking into account other differences. It follows Vandana Singh's (2021) call for a multilayered approach to ecofeminism that goes beyond Western notions of individualism into a space that is more collective and profound. For women of color, including Erdrich and Sansour, opposing racism and genocide are struggles that they often share with men in a colonial society, even while they fight against sexism in their communities. According to Valerie Padilla Carroll, ecofeminism's more recent move towards intersectionality illustrates the fruitfulness of that discipline in dialogue with other studies. Moreover, writes Irene Sanz Alonso (2021), science fiction meshes particularly well with ecofeminism because it highlights that in many ways we are living in a dystopia, but it also provides alternative ecofeminist modes of living. What better terrain than the field of Indigenous science fiction to rethink resistance to colonial power? Both science fiction and ecofeminism can then benefit from an alliance with Indigenous Studies.

By embracing the conventions of science fiction in her novel, Louise Erdrich creates a space for self-determination as the Ojibwe use environmental chaos as an opportunity to reclaim their land. In most cases the colonizers have erased the colonized and define the future. So immersed in the past, still trying to reclaim history, how can the colonized imagine a future? This is the overarching question in Basma Ghalayin's *Palestine + 100: Stories from a Century after the Nakba*. How might science fiction writers imagine "fanciful ventures into fanciful futures" (2019, ix) when the past is still around? According to Ryan Poll, the decolonial project of Indigenous Futurism is to visualize a future that is "radically open," while taking into account the central role that epidemics and pandemics have always played (2020). It is the kind of challenge that Larissa Sansour and Oreet Ashery present in *The Novel of Novel and Vovel* (hereafter cited as *The Novel*). In their graphic novel, real-life artists Sansour and Ashery assume the persona of anti-heroes in order to grapple with such problems. According to ReemFadda (2009, 171), fundamental questions of "temporality, spatial rationale and existential continuum" are at the core of Palestine/Israel. How can a future be imagined that "reclaim[s] agency, through decolonization," Fadda (2009, 171) asks, in a not so far-off space where oppressed peoples reclaim sovereignty and self-determination? Indeed, as Deininger and Scammell (2021) argue, science fiction is capable of changing the world by reimagining it. Both texts employ science fiction as a venue for undermining patriarchal, capitalist, and colonial practices at the same time from within a genre that celebrates technoscience, a product of all of the above.

Despite thematic and narration differences, or perhaps because of them, there are advantages to reading these two texts together. Though they take different paths, each follows a multilayered approach to claim, interpret, and create viable understandings of sovereignty. Because the books never follow linearity from past to present, the action that occurs in the present also contextualizes the past and makes way for what Fadda terms the future "not" zone where anything is possible (2009, 171). If there is a trope connecting both novels it is this fluidity, what Dean Rader calls "floating tests" (2011, 81), a space that adheres to cultural and geographic boundaries yet defies the conventions of a traditional script. According to Sarah Bezan (this volume), feminist interpretations of embodiment also entail the interchange of past, present, and future states. In Erdrich's novel, for example, Cedar Hawk Songmaker, adopted Ojibwe child of Minneapolis liberals, finds herself at 26, pregnant, at a time when the world might be running backward, maybe sideways, in a decidedly mysterious way (2017, 3). As Russ (1995, 22) observes, science fiction revolves around what is not yet possible, a condition that draws the reply "nobody knows" (1995, 22), and an analysis that Cedar herself gives to her situation (2017, 3). The characters "Nonel" and "Vovel", typos of the word "novel," are by default uncontained. A pair of "borderline anti-heroes" (Ashery and Sansour 2009, 8), standing in for the two politically engaged artists who created them, their antics take them repeatedly in and out of the novel's storyboard. Both novels, then, reject what Miriam Spiers (2016, 4) calls a "linear, Euro-American" understanding of history by exploring the impact of colonial trauma both in the past but more importantly, in the present. In so doing the authors offer a means to reimagine the past while simultaneously proposing a model of resistance and sovereignty in the future.

Both novels also take up the theme of ethnic identity, but Erdrich carries it that much further by shouldering the additional burden of adoption. As Rader (2011, 85) notes, personal searches for identity are related to larger values held by the community. It is not so much how a person identifies, continues Rader (2011, 85), but who validates his or her personal self-perception. For Erdrich, it is tribal culture that embraces Cedar's presented self, the persona that she enacts after locating her biological family. In this way, Cedar participates in what Grace Dillon terms "returning to ourselves," a process of recovering traditional values in order to survive "our post-Native apocalypse world" (2011, 12). Indeed, as Erdrich claims in an interview with Erin Vanderhoof in *Vanity Fair*: "After the 2016 election, identity politics [were] questioned." But she continues: "I think finding out who we are—as a unified, diverse nation—is one of the most important things we can do to preserve our liberty, promote equality, and preserve democracy" (2017, 1). For Nonel, a pro-Palestinian Israeli, "being from here and anti-here" (Ashery and Sansour 2009, 147) is similarly complex. As a Palestinian living in the diaspora, Vovel, very much like Cedar who investigates for her roots, searches for a way to survive as an artist who wants to bring about change through her work. When she is offered a chance for super powers from the Virus Man, she decides that creativity means more to her than heroics (2007, 44). However, when she finds that the virus is not reversible, Vovel, along with her side-kick, Nonel, decides to use that power to free Palestine. Both novels, then confront structures of racism and colonialism in order partly to counter science fiction's complicity with them.

Both texts reflect upon how we deal with the transformation of nature taking place right now. Global environmental degradation appears in Erdrich's novel in the form of eco-dystopian descriptions of the landscape. Through an ecofeminist perspective, she focuses on the ways that genetic engineering and reproductive technologies are based on exploitation and subordination of nature, women, and Indigenous people. According to Maria Mies (1998, 175), the struggle for self-determination with regard to women's bodies serves as a foundation of the women's movement. This political aim of autonomy for women means liberation from occupation by patriarchal institutions. Like the Ojibwe, who seek tribal self-rule, women have sought emancipation but in this case on a personal level. In Erdrich's novel, backward evolution has created risks for pregnant women. Few healthy babies are being born. As a consequence, women like Cedar are rounded up to be placed in hospitals where their births can be controlled (2017, 72). Not only are babies the best "canaries," as Irene Diamond (1990, 210) states, in an economy based on toxic waste, Cedar's situation points to a dilemma inherent in women's demand for reproductive self-determination. As Mies

(1883, 221) explains, the movement for reproductive rights, while affording women writers like Erdrich the opportunity to write more books, has led to control by pharmaceutical companies, medical doctors, and increasingly the state, as exemplified ironically in this novel. Moreover, as Bezan (this volume) notes, the reproduction industry, through privileging the nuclear family, in turn promotes the tropes of whiteness and nationalism. While Nonel and Vovel are also victims of technoscience when accidentally infected by the Lab Man, they put their unwanted powers to good use by liberating Palestine. Perhaps because this is so clearly an imagined space the outcome was much brighter. Not so for Cedar, who represents the consequences of what happens when natural processes once mediated by women are now controlled by men. Both texts point an accusatory finger at profit and control in technologies' widespread domain. In her reading of the 1975 film *The Stepford Wives*, Katja Plemenitaš (this volume) addresses this ecofeminist concern that men develop technology for the express purpose of dominating women's bodies. For the Stepford wives, as well as women like Cedar, there seems to be no exit.

This conflation of science fiction elements with Indigenous Studies helps Erdrich cross over many themes, including contact, apocalyptic (post) colonial studies, and ecofeminist themes. Her writing also fits into the genre described by Iris Ralph (2021) as climate fiction (cli-fi), narratives that address the harmful impact of human beings on the earth. In her dystopian novel, women are enslaved for their capacity to produce healthy babies. In an interview with Margaret Atwood in *Elle*, Erdrich states that she began writing the narrative during the presidency of George Bush at a time when her own pregnancy coincided with a period that she saw as a disaster for women's issues (2017, 3). Erdrich thus wrote herself into the pregnant protagonist Cedar, an Ojibwe adoptee who spends most of the narrative evading the newly established evangelical government. Setting the plot aside to work on other novels, Erdrich picked it up again after the 2016 election because she sensed that life was once again literally moving backward. In her words: "Maybe I'm writing the biological equivalent of our present political mess" (2017, 4). Benign technology becoming dangerous repeats itself also in Sansour's text, but in Erdrich's work it is a more overarching theme: the ecofeminist notion that human reproduction remains a key to understanding how economic, cultural, and political forces have gone off track. Though the narrative has comedic relief, the overwhelming tone is one of cynicism and despair befitting a text that creates a dystopian future world that a reader might recognize as now.

Cedar's path in *Future Home* reflects Erdrich's belief in the importance of identity (Vanderhoof 2017, 1). Diverging from stereotypical scenes of Indigenous people, Erdrich writes a diverse and intermingling array of characters. Written as an extended letter to her unborn child, Cedar documents both her adoptive and biological families as well as musings on theology and life. The adopted daughter of "happily married vegans" (2017, 56) who are "green in their very souls" (2017, 4), Cedar, growing up, fulfilled her Waldorf classmates' romanticized notions of an Indian princess who enjoys a special "hotline to nature" (2017, 5) and its creatures. According to Andrea Hairston, "authenticity," such as the expectations that Cedar bore, is the "problem child of pseudo-science, commodity culture, and anxious nostalgia" (2006, 290) for a non-existent past. Indeed, she continues, such essentialist notions help maintain the status quo. After having internalized colonialist appropriations of her culture, Cedar's perspectives change. In talking circles with other Indigenous people, she absorbed a whole new stereotypical notion of contemporary Indigenous America. Playing with a trickster-esque portrayal of Cedar's friends who make fun by absorbing dominant stereotypes of Indians, Erdrich describes the former princess's anguish at finding that she fits in no better here than before. In her talking circles, she hears stories of drug use, suicides, folks with crises that she had not known in her sheltered life. Having been a "snowflake," now without her "specialness," Cedar says she "melted" (2017, 20).

Such efforts to conform, writes Andrea Hairston, contribute to making "self-determination/self-definition" (2006, 291) all that much more difficult for women of color, as Erdrich's novel shows. Indeed, Cedar's predicament reflects a hall of mirrors in which her classmates, in much the same way as some feminists, romanticize women and Earth-based cultures as essentially closer to nature than men. As Phillips and Rumens (2017, 5) note, naming the cultures of others in a way that they have not, white feminists at times appropriate Indigenous beliefs for the use of others. Earth-centered spiritual traditions can plant seeds in the imaginations of ecofeminists, but as Ynestra King (1990, 113) explains, white Westerners must first take responsibility for their own history. Though Cedar's parents supported her quest for identity, they also participate unwittingly in appropriation of what is in fact their own version of Native culture. According to Cedar, her adoptive parents give her unqualified support, but they have always wanted a "piece of Native pie" (2017, 56), she explains, when she has no pie of her own at all.

Cedar's first encounters with her birth family's tribal life destroy any essentialist notions that she has left. Much in the same way that women of color charged ecofeminists with operating in an ahistorical vacuum, thus disregarding the complexity of Native life, Cedar herself finds illusions broken when her invented Native parents are not equipped with "both-sided braids," engaged in perhaps "fasting themselves to death" (2017, 6) or sundancing to exhaustion. Instead, they are "bourgeois" owners of a Superpumper franchise "first stop before the casino" (2017, 5). As Ynestra King observes, humanity cannot "jump off, or jump out" (1990, 111) of historical phases, meaning that cultures remain embedded in complex, evolving traditions that are not accessible to others looking for belief systems perceived as better than their own. When Mary Potts Almost Senior, better known as Sweetie, describes her daughter's biological father, Cedar is relieved; an "Indian Darth Vader" (2017, 14) who appears far closer to her dream. Nevertheless, Cedar's real motives for connecting with her family involve providing her unborn baby with a tribal "web of connection" (2017, 6) that she was lacking as a child. "Returning to ourselves," claims Grace Dillon, serves as a healing balm necessary to slough off "dirty baggage" (2016, 9) inflicted by colonial oppression. Cedar's journey in *Future Home* consists of moving from socially imposed persona to contemporary native woman with all of the expected complexities.

Shape-shifters mark the characters in *Future Home* (Atwood 2017, 12). No one is really what they seem. As in her other novels Erdrich views the circularity of past and present as crucial for a more inclusive notion of Indigenous identity. According to Dean Rader (2011, 76), tribalography, a term conceived by Lee Ann Howe, more accurately describes the links between past and present, the ability of regional narrations to contextualize the ways that past events shape what is happening today. Moreover, notes Miriam Spiers (2016, 1), what better mode than Indigenous Futurisms to decolonize the future than reinterpreting the past in a new framework. In Erdrich's work storytelling becomes the means for transmitting and preserving traditional knowledge. Cedar's identity becomes enmeshed with that of her biological grandmother as Mary Potts Senior transcends her own memories to include those of her relatives and tribal community. In Grandma's mind, as perceived by Cedar, time becomes a rubber band, a "pinball machine" (2017, 34), claims Cedar, one of the old not electric kinds, stretchable, or as tiny loops, retrieving her community's voice. "The narrative is all that matters" (2017, 34), explains Cedar, her Grandma's history that is a multiplicity, an unrolling of many scrolls. Erdrich honors not only this tribal past but also its impact on a common future.

Not only do characters shift shapes in *Future Home*, but evolution is also reversing itself. Animals and plants are shifting through random mutations, Cedar learns from the rare news she hears on television (2017, 44). According to Tania LaFontaine (2016, 20), all science fiction contains at least one novum, a fictional invention that the reader still perceives as plausible. On the one hand, Cedar's world appears destroyed, dead, extinct, or sick and dying, particularly pregnant women who can no longer give birth safely to healthy children. "Ducks are not ducks and chickens are not chickens," and insects are now a food source, especially "ladybugs the size of cats" (2017, 90). If nature is already under siege in the world today, though, then these are simply already known mutations exaggerated by novums in the novel. Standards of plausibility are derived not only by Cedar's observations but also from science. As Iris Ralph (2021) explains, science fiction has increasingly turned to biology and the life sciences to clarify changes to the climate. What Erdrich makes up in her dystopia follows this path, but with a distinctive Native twist; Cedar falls back on scientific musings to explain what she believes to be metaphorically or simply literally true. Sure that someone might come up with an explanation for what is happening, Cedar focuses on "the invisible, the quanta" (2017, 8) of life forms. Here Erdrich takes advantage of the ambiguous evolutionary glitch to introduce a particularly Indigenous perspective, one that challenges Euro-American world views. Moreover, she weds science fiction theory with Indigenous science literacy and Western science. According to Grace Dillon (2012, 5), Western science provides Native authors with an opportunity to enlist Indigenous literacies as an integral part of their writing (2012, 3). The field of quantum physics, which Erdrich employs, recalls the Indigenous concept of what Dillon terms "multiverses" (2012, 5), a space, she claims, consists of several alternate worlds. Musing on the state of the world Cedar often juxtaposes Western science with what Dillon terms "Indigenous scientific literacies" (2012, 7), to illustrate that traditional knowledge holds as much credence as Western thought. Indeed, Cedar comes to believe that "the end of science "(2017, 61) has arrived, signaling a phenomenon that Joanna Ross considers integral to science fiction when explanations are "neither impossible nor possible" (1975, 22), when nobody really knows. By restoring the mystery to her knowledge base Cedar turns to Catholic and Ojibwe teachings that place value on what is not necessarily known.

Narratives about climate change, global transformation, and/or destruction of the environment on earth, like the one discussed in *Future Home*, take place in the future but imply a landscape that has already been transformed. In their discussion of Margaret Atwood's Maddaddam trilogy, Izabel Brandão and Ildney Cavalcanti (2021) claim that most feminist dystopias are really part of our contemporary time. Ironically, Cedar finds that corn, a crop sacred to the Ojibwe but now technologically produced, might backslide not as much because it has been genetically enhanced (2017, 98). Through her focus on corn, Erdrich draws attention to a particular technical violence of neo-colonial systems that have replaced Indigenous literacies. Most traces of the natural world are presented as absences. The contrast between nature that still exists and the increasing desolation caused by climate change leave Cedar with nostalgia and grief. If she could no longer look at trees, thinks Cedar, she would surely collapse under the fear invading her world (2017, 80).

At the core of *Future Home* are the destruction of the environment, death of nature, and exploitation of women, too. As the novel closes, Cedar's wonder at where her son will be the last time it snows on earth highlight humans' responsibility for failure to solve environmental concerns before this catastrophic stage. As Joanna Russ (1995, 16) observes, dystopian fiction describes events that have not happened yet, a cautionary tale that the author hopes to prevent. In the Welsh writer Louise Lawrence's young adult novels, discussed by Deininger and Scammel (2021), there remains the possibility of surviving the Anthropocene, a term used to describe a period in which climate change has reached the tipping point. Cedar's world is a post-apocalyptic view, but there is beauty, too, personified by the floral details of a window tile decorating one of the many places where Cedar can take refuge. Holed up in a post office turned underground safe house, Cedar speculates that humanity's survival depends on everyday grace such as this (2017, 194). Erdrich's cautionary tale juxtaposes the technologically compromised environment with ecofeminist world views. In particular, she suggests that subordination, appropriation, and exploitation of women and the natural world are interconnected and such connections extend to the treatment of Indigenous people. According to Phillips and Rumens (2017, 3), contemporary ecofeminists highlight not only environmental concerns but also contextualize these issues within a broader social, political, and historical framework.

Specifically, Erdrich addresses new developments in biotechnology, genetic engineering, and reproductive technology that propose to colonize women's bodies. Just as Palestinians and the Ojibwe are displaced by colonial and neo-colonial regimes, so Vandana Shiva claims that the medicalization of childbirth views women as a source of "raw Material" from which the "product" (1993, 26) is produced. Indeed, in the dystopic world of *Future Home*, women are reduced to "womb volunteers," inert vessels from which babies are extracted in a world in which healthy births are rare (2017, 90). Very similar to the way that Brandão and Cavalcanti (2021) describe Margaret Atwood's dystopic science fiction, themes of confinement, power, and surveillance appear here. In this scenario, Cedar's womb becomes literally a container to be captured to ensure the reproduction of the race. In Fairview Riverside Hospital, Room 624 (2017, 20), Cedar finds herself alongside a young Asian pregnant woman, nicknamed Spider Nun for her severity but also incessant tearing apart and reweaving of her blankets. In an environment where women are objectified as mothers of the race and made passive by drugs to keep them calm, Spider Nun, alias Tia Jackson, "weaves and unravels" (2017, 142), an activity providing not only an escape rope but also a web of care, responsibility, and justice that are at the core of Indigenous literacies and ecofeminism.

Eventually with the help of Sera the two escape. Picked up by a recycling truck they travel to an underground facility that provides shelter for hunted women. In a small room, really a cave, Sera, in her professional capacity as midwife, delivers Tia's baby, but the child is born dead (2017, 181, 182). According to Arisika Razak, midwifery represents core values of ecofeminism—a profession that employs "intuition, empathy and touch" (1990, 170) in a process that is attuned with nature. In *The Blue Jay's Dance*, Erdrich recounts how she herself had much the same agenda (1996, 3). "It was no accident," she recounts, that she employed for all four births a midwife "unafraid to make emotional connections" (1996, 36) with her family. Sera's expertise cannot save Tia's baby, born at a time when babies are the "canaries" in a thoroughly poisoned world.

Here is the conundrum. In *The Blue Jay's Dance*, Erdrich writes of wanting always to be with her children, especially newly born, but also wanting to be, through her writing, her own self (1996, 215). "Reliable birth control is one of the best things that's happened in contemporary literature" (1996, 145), Erdrich claims, a sentiment echoed by the women's movement's quest for self-determination. As Irene Diamond (1990, 204) notes, contemporary feminists look to reproductive technology as a means to women's freedom. But this places women's reproductive capacities under the control of corporations and perhaps eventually the State, as has happened to Cedar in *Future Home*. When Cedar asks her adoptive mother how she will know when labor starts, Sera tells her that she will know by "knowing" (2017, 231) things, an ecofeminist ethic that privileges women's instinctive knowledge over science. In the end, Cedar is recaptured by another mother who needs the bounty money to feed her children (2017, 247). Although the novel ends with Cedar musing about Hildegard of Bingen—"Everything is penetrated with connectedness, penetrated with relatedness" (2017, 247)—it seems clear that she will live out her days in the hospital producing babies for the state.

Erdrich presents a conflict not between peoples, as in much science fiction, but between ecofeminist and Indigenous values in conflict with individualist standards of settler capitalist colonialism. Moreover, it is not a case of dominant masculinity vs. women's values in the manner that Lydia Rose and Teresa Bartoli (this volume) describe in their analysis of James Cameron's 2009 film *Avatar*. In *Future Home*, the struggle is between communalism (tribal) and individualism (Western), so that in this mix women can be villains, too, depending on their social construct. Because the struggle for post-apocalyptic survival is not personal, but community-based, Cedar falls victim to corporate scientific institutions, but she leaves behind her tribe which is better equipped as a community to endure. Practically speaking Erdrich's work itself challenges received knowledge about the "Vanishing Indian." Indeed, in a recent blog, Erdrich (2020) declares: "When treaties were made it was thought that Native people were going to vanish, but no. We are still here," despite the European-born epidemics that she claims have always plagued her people. In her novel, then, she implies that the Ojibwe will thrive on their homeland, both in the readers' present and in the near future in which the story lives. According to Cedar's step-dad Eddy, the Native apocalypse has already taken place. "Indians have been adapting since before 1492," he tells Cedar, so he figures they will continue to endure. The world, he concludes, is always "going to pieces" (2017, 28), so this feels no different than before. From an Indigenous perspective, pandemics—whether in Erdrich's dystopia or in our world today—are not breaks from a normal pattern. For the colonized, claims Ryan Poll, whose populations have long been under siege, the apocalypse is ongoing (2020).

According to Grace Dillon (2012, 8), many writers of Indigenous futurisms, though, imagine an optimistic future in which Natives come out on top or at least become the subjects of their own work. Erdrich's *Future Home* encompasses a cycle from the trauma of the Dawes Act of 1862, which divided the land into individual parcels, to the future in which the tribe takes advantage of the crisis to regain land (2017, 213). As the novel closes, Cedar's future does not look good, perhaps because in the end she is left to carry her burdens all alone. But for the Ojibwe, who recoup traditional ways, there is a communal path to sovereignty based on self-determination, a vision that echoes Singh's (2021) description of Chipko villagers who also embraced ecofeminist ethics of care and connectedness to nature.

Rather than focusing on various members of the community, as does *Future Home, The Novel* values the spectacle of hero and villain. Based on the plot alone, it seems to fit easily into the genre of mainstream science fiction. After deciding to write a graphic novel, Sansour and Ashery created their respective alter egos, "Vovel" and "Nonel" (Ashery and Sansour 2009, 8), names based on repeated typos of the term "Novel" in their initial Skyping. According to Reem Fadda (2009, 174), their comic book style reflects their other work, art that is in full flight from an almost unbearable reality, Palestine/Israel. Transformed into superheroes after having been infected by a virus, Nonel and Vovel are faced with the choice of remaining crusaders or returning to their status as artists. Upon learning that their heightened powers might be permanent, the pair transgress what Fadda terms "times of potentialities" (2009, 174) by springing into action. Much like *Future Home, The Novel* concerns itself with what has not yet happened. Reclaiming agency by imagining a liberated Palestine of the future, perhaps the only place self-determination can exist, the pair go on to fantasize about destroying the separation wall as well as the Israeli Occupation Forces. Their dreams become even more grandiose when they learn that the real puppet master is Dharq Djumper, ruler of the Fifth Planet, and a villain who plans to turn earth into an intergalactic vegetable garden divested of human beings. Along with a hive of feminist purple ninjas, the duo destroys the gaseous planet by flinging a bomb from their giant slingshot transported on their backs (Ashery and Sansour 2009, 175).

Like *Future Home, The Novel* "returns us to ourselves" (Dillon 2012, 10) by highlighting an Indigenous writer who writes about an Indigenous-centered world liberated by the imagination. Despite its muscle-flexing duo, *The Novel* is collective in outlook and also quite didactic, focusing as it does on collaboration between the writers who strive to educate readers about the occupation. Indeed, as the authors claim, one important goal of the book is to address the problematic collaboration of Palestinian and Israeli artists. In so doing, they strive to make the region's issues more accessible while trying to avoid what is often termed "normalization," meaning dialogue between two unequal parties, in this case Palestinian and Israeli, in which the participants gloss over the reality of occupation.

The focus of *The Novel* is not so much on the individuals'/personas' identities as it is on how best to organize collaboration. As Joanna Russ (1995, 5) observes, science fiction almost always highlights communal, never individual, concerns, though she admits that protagonists often serve as extraordinary figures. Ecofeminists hold cooperation, too, as a core value. For Nonel and Vovel, the work is more complex, specifically how to best collaborate when neither believes that dialogue groups do much good. In their words, not only are such efforts "all talk and no state" (Ashery and Sansour 2009, 7), but they also gloss over the brutality of facts on the ground. Moreover, while "mutually extended olive branches" (Ashery and Sansour 2009, 7) might sound appealing, most Palestinians, according to this duo, feel that this "creates a dangerous aura of moral equivalence" (Ashery and Sansour 2009, 7) between two unequal parties.

In this case, consensus regarding the occupation had been reached before starting this project (Ashery and Sansour 2009, 7). Still, they devote a chapter to "normalization" by presenting various means to explore this subject. Ever witty, the writers tried posing questionnaires but felt uncomfortable with this process. They toyed with blank pages to convey the frustration of their efforts. Finally, they decided to carry on with this "discursive ride" (Ashery and Sansour 2009, 9) by simply moving on with the writing of this novel. Very much like *Future Home*, their trajectory is non-linear. Erdrich's meanderings spring from an Indigenous perspective, one that emphasizes space over time. According to Spiers (2016, 9), Native world views defy a linear conception of time by existing in both the past and present, a time frame that exposes how attempted genocides of the past continue to impact the present. According to Fadda (2009, 171), Ashery and Sansour, too, imagine alternative pasts, presents, and futures, but their web of words and of geographies are different. For Palestinian writers, as Reem Fadda (2009, 171) claims, there has been an actual break from history since the time of the 1948 war (*Al-Nakba*, or the catastrophe), and even since then recurring events have severed people from the land in such a way that there is no continuous understanding of time. Because of this ruptured sense of chronology, continues Fadda (2009, 172), Palestinians hold obsessively to the past while also longing for a "not yet," an imagined future, which inspires agency and free will to make it happen. Rather than trying to resist past events, Sansour and Ashery suggest new avenues by which contemporary Palestinians can confront historical trauma by using it as a springboard toward a liberated future. By creating frames within frames, stories upon stories, the authors deploy narrative style but also photographs, screenshots of email shots, and other non-traditional, multimedia forms. Interrupting the tale Nonel and Vovel sometimes leave behind their personas and the storyboard to discuss things in the present tense. At one point, Vovel Says no, "I'm sorry, Nonel, but that frame refers to my ex-persona only. Stop clinging to the past, woman" (Ashery and Sansour 2009, 135). Their goal now, says Fadda (2009, 173), is to enter into a "revolutionary moment" when the present remains anchored in a past that is nevertheless left behind.

Attuned with much of women's writing, the section titled Virus Story focuses on the everyday lives of the authors. Written mostly in the conversation mode, Nonel and Vovel share their dismay over discovering that they have been accidentally infected with a virus. Though assured by the Lab Man that it is a good bug, not bad, they are not happy to learn that in return for superpowers their creative cell will decline (Ashery and Sansour 2009, 8). According to Joanna Russ (1995, 4), such tropes in science fiction hinge first on the bizarre that has buried in it the familiar but with an unusual angle that makes it, in turn, bizarre. Shape shifters, much like Erdrich's characters who are never what they seem, Nonel and Vovel turn into the role of anti-heroes, in Nonel's words: "big fat stupid superman, spiderman and batman, all rolled into one" (Ashery and Sansour 2009, 77). Like all good trickster tales, including those Indigenous tropes analyzed by Dean Rader (2011, 87), Nonel and Vovel both "mirror and mock" (2011, 87) those involved in the Palestinian struggle.

In the authors' world view, politics and poetics are inextricably mixed. According to Reem Fadda (2009, 172), art is an area capable of not only producing change but also interpreting the world in such a way that it opens up for reflection. In *The Novel*, both artists tackle the question of making real change as practitioners who barely make a living. This question relates to ecofeminism in two ways. An allegiance between anti-capitalist and ecofeminist discourses provide strategies for toppling the market system, an economic arrangement that in this case reduces the duo to "well-intentioned over-producers" with very little funding. In an economy based on mutuality and care, which also honors women's work, the pair might not have this problem. Ecofeminism, moreover, seeks to overcome dualities such as alleged male/female characteristics, a binary that Nancy Chodorow sees as socially imposed (1974, 66). In this case, Nonel and Vovel struggle between their roles as underpaid artists with communal values and the opportunity for enacting real change as super individuals.

According to Manal Deeb (2013, 1), a Palestinian-American artist born in Ramallah but based now in D.C., art forms serve as "better tools than political and military solutions for they are "emotional forces, powerful" (2013, 1) means for communication. Moreover, Deep does not see exilic angst as "essentially material," nor even political, but rather a "deep spiritual aspiration in the soul" (2013, 3) of all Palestinians in exile, an emotion surely shared by Vovel. "Me with Powers?" she asks, a question made more poignant by her knowledge that she lacks the power to return even to her own home (2013, 88). At this point, though, she learns that the virus is not reversible.

In order to reconcile the power/creativity dyad, the authors turn to collaborative practices that also model ecofeminist modes of connection. In order to highlight processes behind the book, explain the authors, as well as highlight the fact that all artists often build on the work of others, they decide to turn over portions of the work to artists and writers whose portfolio best suits their own. For example, in the Virus Story, various artists render their interpretations of events. In the section titled Intergalactic Palestine, they turn over not only illustrations but writing, too. This shift mirrors the duo's metamorphosis into superheroes (2019, 7). For two control freaks, this process of muddling the distinction between puppet and puppet master proved consuming (2019, 152). Coming out of the storyboard to voice an answer, Larissa decides that it's "really quite liberating" not to be in charge, especially if they get to "flaunt [their] powers" at the "all out good vs. evil showdown coming up" (2019, 153) in the next section.

In conclusion, "Galactic Palestine," Nonel and Vovel most fully explore the decolonizing potential afforded by the appropriation of popular genres. In this section, they put their new identities to use in Occupied Palestine. Though the Lab Man brushes them off as "impotent idealists in capes" (Ashery and Sansour 2009, 130), the duo quickly meet the Ninja Aida, who takes them to Resistance Headquarters, where they encounter thousands of feminist Ninjas prepared to seek their aid. Inhabited only by women, the Ninjas' space reflects the kind of separatism that Christy Tidwell (2021) critiques in her review of two opposing tendencies within ecofeminism. Rejecting the notion that women's difference is a source of strength, Tidwell finds this version of ecofeminism quite risky because it often rebuffs science and technology, too. In particular, she is concerned that this path involves the rejection of birth control, a branch of medical science that she believes beneficial to women's rights. While Erdrich might agree, her novel highlights the core conundrum in this line of thought. Returning to the superpower duo, both welcome the Ninja's help, but that assistance involves technology in the form of space travel that allows them to annihilate the forces controlling Earth. As notes Reem Fadda (2009, 172), "to do," "to make," "to create" and other action verbs are inextricably joined to the Palestinian sense of statelessness. Phillips and Rumens (2017, 13), too, explain that ecofeminism is more than a useful theory. It is also linked to action, suggesting that theorists should always push for social justice. At the Ninja's beehive, Aida explains that Dharq Djumper, the evil ruler of the Fifth Planet, plans to use the already existing separation wall as a seal around what he hopes to use as a storage plant for a fertilizer that will nourish Planet Earth after it is turned into a giant veggie garden for his peoples' use (Ashery and Sansour 2009, 146). Clearly opposed to ecofeminism's focus on sustainability, the Fifth Planet's scheme also counters the Ojibwe's desire to go back to traditional modes of farming.

Although Vovel has a hard time believing that America's support for the "neo-colonial legoland" (Ashery and Sansour 2009, 149) that has become Israel is not the real cause for the Palestinians "being royally screwed" (Ashery and Sansour 2009, 149), she agrees to fly to the Fifth Planet along with Nonel where the pair employ a giant slingshot to launch a bomb that blows the planet to smithereens (Ashery and Sansour 2009, 163). Back on Earth, they gather for a picture with their Ninja allies in which everyone is in the frame (Ashery and Sansour 2009, 166). Implying that the consequences of Occupation will continue long after liberation, Vovel notes that "it was more like a saturated pre-credit to a 007 flick than a full-blown epic" (Ashery and Sansour 2009, 168). Nonel replies that "every ending is a new beginning and besides, it would seem wrong to believe that they had managed to solve an old dilemma by dressing up in capes and tight suits" (Ashery and Sansour 2009, 168). Though simplified by taking the conflict out of its present arena where it seems impossible to solve, the authors understand that peace will only bring about a complex reconstructive process that could last for years.

As Salma Monani (2017, 46) explains, science fiction space travel is a story of frontiers. As such, it highlights this genre's uneasy relationship with the Western. Yet *The Novel* undermines colonial underpinnings inherent in these genres by emphasizing a Palestinian theme. In another part of the Middle East, Zahra Jannessari Lanani (this volume) addresses the Iranian writer Fazel Bakhsheshi's *The Sun's Sons*, a tale in which a woman's superpowers save the ecosystem. Not only does the heroine overcome a totalitarian regime, claims Jannessari Lanani (this volume), she does so by using ecofeminist values of responsibility and collaboration. In that text and *The Novel*, the women undermine the plans of male scientists who think mostly of their own agendas and respective needs. As the pair reach the outer edges of space, they enter a place akin to the "statelessness" that Fadda claims allies with the "diasporic … state of becoming for the artist" (Fadda 2009, 175). A place that makes possible a "bigger picture" (Fadda 2009, 175) in which new perspectives are possible, it is similar to what SalmaMonani (2017, 52) describes as cosmo-ethics, that is, diasporic space in which art and politics are entwined. Perhaps, Reem Fadda muses, "something intergalactic" (2009, 175).

In the era of coronavirus and general uncertainty about the future, the present feels increasingly dystopic. How then do practitioners of science fiction continue to view this genre as a vehicle for creating an alternative future? How can society be restructured in the future when the present seems so bleak? Flash forward to Sansour's installation *Heirloom* for the Danish Pavilion at the 2019 Venice Biennial. At its center is the short film *In Vitro* set in a post-apocalyptic bunker in Bethlehem. In this film two survivors of an ecological disaster—Dunia (Hiam Abbass), a dying fighter, and Alia (Maisa Abd Elhadi), her progeny and clone, discuss the past and future. Sansour's current work has none of the whimsicality of her graphic novel. As Nat Muller, the film's curator explains, her work has shifted from "absurdist," an effort to resist portraying Palestinians as either victim or terrorist, to "dystopian" (D'Arcy 2019), much more like Erdrich's book and perhaps more in tune with the times.

References

Anae, Nicole. 2021. "Ecofeminist Utopian Speculations in Henrietta Augusta Dugdale's *A Few Hours in a Far-off Age* (1883), Catherine Helen Spence's *A Week in the Future* (1888), Mary Anne Moore-Bentley's *A Woman of Mars; Or, Australia's Enfranchised Woman* (1901), and Joyce Vincent's *The Celestial Hand: A Sensational Story*." In *Dystopias and Utopias on Earth and Beyond: Feminist Ecocriticism of Science Fiction*, edited by Douglas A. Vakoch, 98–113. Abingdon, Oxon, UK and New York, NY: Routledge.

Ashery, Oreet, and Larissa Sansour. 2009. *The Novel of Nonel and Vovel*. New York, NY: Charta.

Atwood, Margaret, and Louise Erdrich. 2017. "Inside the Dystopian Visions of Margaret Atwood and Louise Erdrich." *Elle*, 1–18. Accessed September 16, 2020. http://www.elle.com/culture/books/a13530871/future-home-of-the-living-god.

Brandão, Izabel F. O., and Ildney Cavalcanti. 2021. "Margaret Atwood's Ecodystopic SF: Approaching Ethics, Gender, and Ecology." In *Dystopias and Utopias on Earth and Beyond: Feminist Ecocriticism of Science Fiction*, edited by Douglas A. Vakoch, 37–49. Abingdon, Oxon, UK and New York, NY: Routledge.

Carroll, Valerie Padilla. 2018. "Introduction: Ecofeminist Dialogues." In *Ecofeminism in Dialogue*, edited by Douglas A. Vakoch and Sam Mickey, 1–13. Lanham, MD: Lexington Books.

Chodorow, Nancy. 1974. "Family Structure and Feminine Personality." In *Woman, Culture, and Society*, edited by Michelle Zimbalist Rosaldo and Louise Lamphere, 43–66. Stanford, CA: Stanford University Press.

D'Arcy, David. 2019. "Artist Larissa Sansour on Representing Palestine in the Danish Pavilion at the Venice Biennale." *The National*, June 3. Accessed August 30, 2020. https://www.thenational.ae/arts-culture/art/artist-larissa-sansour-on-representing-palestine-in-the-danish-pavilion-at-the-venice-biennale-1.869497.

Deeb, Manal. 2013. "Visualizing a National Narrative: Art, Resistance and the Consciousness." *The Palestine Center*, July 31. Accessed September 16, 2020. http://www.thejerusalemfund.org/4255/visualizing-a-national-narrative.

Deininger, Michelle, and Gemma Scammell. 2021. "'Extinction is Forever': Ecofeminism and Apocalypse in Louise Lawrence's Young Adult Short Fiction." In *Dystopias and Utopias on Earth and Beyond: Feminist Ecocriticism of Science Fiction*, edited by Douglas A. Vakoch, 83–97. Abingdon, Oxon, UK and New York, NY: Routledge.

Diamond, Irene. 1990. "Babies, Heroic Experts, and a Poisoned Earth." In *Reweaving the World: The Emergence of Ecofeminism*, edited by Irene Diamond and Gloria Feman Orenstein, 201–210. San Francisco, CA: Sierra Club Books.

Diamond, Irene, and Gloria Feman Orenstein. 1990. "Introduction." In *Reweaving the World: The Emergence of Ecofeminism*, edited by Irene Diamond and Gloria Feman Orenstein, ix–xv. San Francisco, CA: Sierra Club Books.

Dillon, Grace. 2012. "Imagining Indigenous Futurism." In *Walking the Clouds: An Anthology of Indigenous Science Fiction*, edited by Grace L. Dillon, 1–15. Tucson, AZ: University of Arizona Press.

Erdrich, Louise. 1995. *The Blue Jay's Dance: A Memoir of Early Motherhood*. New York, NY: Harper Collins.

———. 2017. *The Future Home of the Living God*. New York, NY: Harper Collins.

_____. 2020. "Postcolonial Love Poem." *Louise Erdrich's Blog*, April 1. Accessed October 13, 2020. https://birchbarkbooks.com/blog.

Fadda, Reem. 2009. "Not-Yet-Ness: Towards the Intergalactic." In *The Novel of Vovel and Novel*, Written by Oreet Ashery and Larissa Sansour, 171–176. New York, NY: Charta.

Gaard, Greta, and Patrick D. Murphy. 1998. "Introduction." In *Ecofeminist Literary Criticism: Theory, Interpretation, Pedagogy*, edited by Greta Gaard and Patrick D. Murphy, 1–15. Urbana, IL: University of Illinois Press.

Ghalayin, Basma. 2019. "Introduction." In *Palestine + 100: Stories from a Century after the Nakba*, edited by Basma Ghalayin, vii–xiii. Manchester, UK: Comma Press.

Hairston, Andrea. 2006. "Octavia Butler—Praise Song to a Prophetic Artist." In *Daughters of Earth: Feminist Science Fiction in the Twentieth Century*, edited by Justine Larbalestier, 265–305. Middletown, CT: Wesleyan University Press.

Hawkins, Cathy. 2006. "The Universal Wife: Exploring 1970s Feminism with Lisa Tuttle's 'Wives'." In *Daughters of Earth: Feminist Science Fiction in the Twentieth Century*, edited by Justine Larbalestier, 190–217. Middletown, CT: Wesleyan University Press.

King, Ynestra. 1990. "Healing the Wounds: Feminism, Ecology, and the Nature/Culture Dualism." In *Reweaving the World: The Emergence of Ecofeminism*, edited by Irene Diamond and Gloria Feman Orenstein, 106–121. San Francisco, CA: Sierra Club Books.

La Fontaine, Tania. 2016. *Science Fiction Theory and Ecocriticism: Environment and Nature in Eco-Dystopian and Post-Apocalyptic Novels*. Saarbrücken, Germany: LAP Lambert Academic Publishing.

Larbalestier, Justine. 2006. "Introduction." In *Daughters of Earth: Feminist Science Fiction in the Twentieth Century*, edited by Justine Larbalestier, xv–xix. Middletown, CT: Wesleyan University Press.

Mies, Maria. 1993. "New Reproductive Technologies: Sexist and Racist Implications." In *Ecofeminism*, edited by Maria Mies and Vandana Shiva, 174–197. North Melbourne, Australia: Spinifex Press.

_____. 1993. "Self Determination: The End of a Utopia?" In *Ecofeminism*, edited by Maria Mies and Vandana Shiva, 218–230. North Melbourne, Australia: Spinifex, Press.

Monani, Salma. 2017. "Science Fiction, Westerns, and the Vital Cosmo-ethics of the 6th World." In *Ecocriticism and Indigenous Studies: Conversations from Earth to Cosmos*, edited by Salma Monani and Joni Adamson, 44–62. New York, NY: Routledge.

Nazif, Perwana. 2018. "Arabfuturism: Science-Fiction and Alternate Realities in the Arab World." *The Quietus*. Accessed August 30, 2020. https://thequietus.com/articles/24088-arabfuturism.

Poll, Ryan. 2020. "Colonial Pandemics and Indigenous Futurism in Louise Erdrich and Gerald Vizenor." *Pop Matters*, August 3. Accessed August 30, 2020. https://www.popmatters.com/louise-erdrich-gerald-vizenor-2646854556.html.

Phillips, Mary, and Nick Rumens. 2017. "Introducing Contemporary Ecofeminism." In *Contemporary Perspectives on* Ecofeminism, edited by Mary Phillips and Nick Rumens, 1–17. New York, NY: Routledge.

Rader, Dean. 2011. *Engaged Resistance: American Indian Art, Literature and Film from Alcatraz to the NMAL*. Austin, TX: University of Texas Press.

Ralph, Iris. 2021. "Ecofeminist Climate Fiction: Merlinda Bobis's *Locust Girl*." In *Dystopias and Utopias on Earth and Beyond: Feminist Ecocriticism of Science Fiction*, edited by Douglas A. Vakoch, 67–79. Abingdon, Oxon, UK and New York, NY: Routledge.

Razak, Arisika. 1990. "Toward a Womanist Analysis of Birth." In *Reweaving the World: The Emergence of Ecofeminism*, edited by Irene Diamond and Gloria Feman Orenstein, 165–172. San Francisco, CA: Sierra Club Books.

Russ, Joanna. 1995. "Speculations: Subjunctivity of Science Fiction." In *To Write Like a Woman: Essays in Feminism and Science Fiction*, edited by Joanna Russ, 15–26. Bloomington, IN: Indiana University Press.

———. 1995. "Towards an Aesthetic of Science Fiction." In *To Write Like a Woman: Essays in Feminism and Science Fiction*, edited by Joanna Russ, 3–14. Bloomington, IN: Indiana University Press.

Sanz Alonso, Irene. 2021. "Alien Ecofeminist Societies: Sharers in Joan Slonczewski's *A Door into Ocean*." In *Dystopias and Utopias on Earth and Beyond: Feminist Ecocriticism of Science Fiction*, edited by Douglas A. Vakoch, 114–125. Abingdon, Oxon, UK; New York: Routledge.

Shiva, Vandana. 1993. "Reductionism and Regeneration: A Crisis in Science." In *Ecofeminism*, edited by Maria Mies and Vandana Shiva, 22–35. North Melbourne, Australia: Spinifex, Press.

Singh, Vandana. 2021. "Foreword. Ecofeminism and Speculative Fiction: A Writer's Reflection." In *Dystopias and Utopeias on Earth and Beyond: Feminist Ecocriticism of Science Fiction*, edited by Douglas A. Vakoch, xviii–xxvii. Abingdon, Oxon, UK and New York, NY: Routledge.

Spiers, Miriam. 2016. "Reimagining Resistance: Achieving Sovereignty in Indigenous Science Fiction." *Transmotion* 2, nos. 1–2: 1–32. Accessed September 16, 2020. doi:10.22024/UniKent/03/tm.224.

Tidwell, Christy. 2021. "'The Revolt of the Mother': Romanticizing Nature and Rejecting Science in Sally Miller Gearhart's *The Wanderground* and Other Feminist Utopias." In *Dystopias and Utopias on Earth and Beyond: Feminist Ecocriticism of Science Fiction*, edited by Douglas A. Vakoch, 150–162. Abington, Oxon, UK and New York, NY: Routledge.

14 The Road to Sinshan

Ecophilia in Ursula K. Le Guin's Early Hainish Novels

Deirdre Byrne

In this chapter, I identify and explore some of the precursors to Ursula K. Le Guin's postmodern, multimedia masterpiece of ecofeminist literature, *Always Coming Home* (*ACH*). I find these forerunners in her less renowned early Hainish novels, *Rocannon's World* (*RW*), *Planet of Exile* (*PE*), and *The Word for World Is Forest* (*WWF*). In my discussion, I draw on Gilles Deleuze and Félix Guattari's theory of assemblages in order to explain the novels as heterogeneous, shifting, and fluid artistic constellations. I also refer to Karen Barad's theory of new materialism in order to delve into the role/s of nonhuman nature in Le Guin's earlier fiction. I conclude by suggesting that *Rocannon's World* and *Planet of Exile* can be considered "ecophilic" and as demonstrating a fledgling ecofeminist sensibility, while *The Word for World Is Forest* may be called a work of "angry ecofeminism". These three works articulate ecofeminist leanings in Le Guin's early writing.

ACH has long been hailed as an outstanding work of ecofeminist fiction (cf. Murphy 1991; Hanafy 2014; Abdullah and Sharif 2019). I read the text as an assemblage in the sense that Gilles Deleuze and Félix Guattari use the term in *A Thousand Plateaus* (1987, 588 and elsewhere) of heterogeneous parts and genres, each shifting, changing and diverse, with motile relations between them. This holds true of the components of the text's presented world as well as of its formal elements. The Kesh people, who live in the village of Sinshan on the Na River in Northern California, practice active respect and celebration of human and nonhuman beings, as well as a profound aversion to injuring any being. Le Guin consciously masculinizes the violence inherent in natural despoilation, as well as the habit of warmongering. These behaviors are found among the Condor people, while the Kesh have crafted a gender-egalitarian community in dynamic harmony with nonhuman nature. I find *ACH* more ecofeminist than "pastoral" (Sawyer 2006) or utopian (Wytenbroek 1987), although it includes elements of both genres.

The textual components that make up the work, including narratives, poetry, drama, fictional anthropology, and metafictional commentary are connected insofar as they represent the same imaginary future community, but they are not otherwise linked. The heterogeneity of the textual components, together with the populist structure of Kesh society, lead me to refer to classify *ACH* further, via Deleuze and Guattari, as a nomadic assemblage, where "people demand to formulate their problems themselves and to determine at least the particular conditions under which they can receive a more general solution" (1987, 588). Nomadic assemblages are "absolutely incompatible with territorial hierarchies based on essentialist meanings, state hierarchies based on centralized command, and capitalist hierarchies based on globally exchanged generic quantities" (Nail 2017, 33). This is not to say that the text has no "consistency" or organizing structure: the concepts of equilibrium of energies and of wholeness-in-diversity pervade the work.

One of the shorter narratives in *ACH*, "The Life Story of Flicker of the Serpentine of Telina-na", has a visionary recount a vision that changed her life direction:

> It was the universe of power. It was the network, field, and lines of the energies of all the beings, stars and galaxies of stars, worlds, animals, minds, nerves, dust, the lace and foam of vibration that is being itself, all interconnected, every part part of another part and the whole part of each part, and so comprehensible to itself only as a whole, boundless and unclosed.
>
> (1986, 290–291)

Flicker's visionary epiphany may have been modeled on General Systems Thinking, with its insight that wholes are interconnected to form bigger wholes. But it also has much in common with Deleuzian assemblages. It reveals the "abstract machine" (Deleuze, Guattari, and Stivale 1984, 14–16) that structures the cosmos as a "universe of power." This ordering principle, operating on heterogeneous entities, is invisible to Flicker (as to most people) in their usual state of mind, but is visible when she is in a trance state that exposes the intricate lines connecting such phenomena. The vision also resonates with Barad's understanding of diffraction and intra-action as conceptual tools for reconfiguring our perception of matter as agentive and active. Barad uses diffraction, a concept derived from "the way waves combine when they overlap and the apparent bending and spreading of waves when they encounter an obstruction" (2007, 74) as a method of analyzing the effects and patterns of difference. Diffraction is a way of making sense of assemblages and entanglements, and highlights the ordering principles in epistemology. "Intra-action," a term Barad prefers to "interaction" (cf. 2007, 128), highlights the processual becoming of the world and the co-emergence of agents within relational processes of change. If the cosmos is seen as made up of entangled lines of energy, then Flicker's vision, and by extension, Le Guin's is markedly compatible with Barad's new materialism.

Flicker's vision also has affinities with feminist politics' realization that women's struggles for equality are indissoluble from the struggles for justice by racial and sexual minorities. This realization underpins Greta Gaard's description of ecofeminism:

> [T]he way in which women and nature have been conceptualized historically in the Western intellectual tradition has resulted in devaluing whatever is associated with women, emotion, animals, nature, and the body, while simultaneously elevating in value those things associated with men, reason, humans, culture and the mind. One task of ecofeminism has been to expose these dualisms and the ways in which feminizing nature and naturalizing or animalizing women has served as a justification for the domination of women, animals, and the earth.
>
> (1993, 5)

Sam Mickey identifies different approaches within ecofeminism: "Although the word 'ecofeminism' is a singular noun, it refers not to a monolithic or homogeneous ecofeminism but to a plurality of ecofeminisms" (Vakoch and Mickey 2018, ix). In this chapter, I approach Le Guin's writing from the starting point that all forms of oppression are entangled and form a territorial assemblage in which "concrete elements are coded according to a natural or proper usage" (Nail 2017, 28). "Natural or proper usage", as Deleuze and Guattari recognize, does not designate inherently natural or proper functions, but those that have been ascribed to phenomena in order to serve political interests. Deleuze and Guattari do not analyze patriarchy in-depth, although, as Pelagia Goulimari argues, their ideas of becoming-woman and minoritarian politics are strikingly compatible with feminism (1999). Gaard aptly notes that patriarchy underpins all forms of oppression, despite variation in specific instances (1993, 1). Maria Mies and Vandana Shiva note that "everywhere, women were the first to protest against environmental destruction" (1993). This implies that women are more keenly aware of environmental injustice than men are (whether because of their psychology or socialisation, the authors do not explain). They go on to assert that:

> As activists in the ecology movements, it became clear to us that science and technology were not gender neutral; and in common with many other women, we began to see that the relationship of exploitative dominance between man and nature, (shaped by reductionist modern science since the 16th century) and the exploitative and oppressive relationship between men and women and prevails in most patriarchal societies, even modern industrial ones, were closely connected.
>
> (1993)

Here, as elsewhere, Mies and Shiva connect hegemonic masculinity, violence toward women and exploitation of the environment. These connections enable the authors to identify "capitalist patriarchy" as "the paradigm

that destroyed women and nature" (Mies and Shiva 1993). (The term "capitalist patriarchy" is drawn from Claudia von Werlhof (2007, 4).) The logic
of exchange for profit, for Von Werlhof, Mies and Shiva, as for Deleuze
and Guattari, is one of the mechanisms by which elites (read: patriarchal
elites) subordinate all Others: women, nonhuman nature, the poor, gender-
nonconforming people, and people of color. The motive, simply, is to make
money and derive profit by using Others to benefit the male, white (heterosexual) western Self. Mies and Shiva continue:

> Th(e) capitalist-patriarchal perspective interprets difference as hierar-
> chical and uniformity as a prerequisite for equality. Our aim is to go
> beyond this narrow perspective and to express our diversity and, in dif-
> ferent ways, address the inherent inequalities in world structures which
> permit the North to dominate the South, men to dominate women, and
> the frenetic plunder of ever more resources for ever more unequally
> distributed economic gain to dominate nature.
>
> (1997)

Early Hainish Novels

Many critical responses to *RW* and *PE* see these works as simply early
installments in Le Guin's Hainish cycle (a loosely connected series of texts
including *City of Illusions* (*CI*), *WWF*, *The Left Hand of Darkness*, *The
Dispossessed*, and *The Telling*). The texts in the Hainish cycle are connected
by being set in the interplanetary League of All Worlds, a cooperative fed-
eration of all eight planets that were colonized (the euphemism "seeded"
is used) by the Hainish. Unfortunately, critics, including Le Guin herself
(cf. 1993, 129, 136, and 140), tend to view *RW*, *PE*, and *CI* as juvenile
interim stations on the way to the mature achievement of *The Left Hand of
Darkness* and *The Dispossessed*. They view these texts as significant mainly
because of their contribution to the reader's understanding of the Hainish
universe (cf. Brigg 1997). All three of the novels include a recurrent science
fiction trope, presenting the League as under threat from the Faradayan
rebels in *Rocannon's World*, from the Gaal in *Planet of Exile*, and from the
Shing in *City of Illusions*. The threats provide the catalyst for what Rafail
Nudelman sees as the shared plot development of all of the Hainish novels
toward a Campbellian hero-journey:

> Le Guin's heroes have the mission of attaching a lower-level culture to
> a higher-level (finally—to a universal) one. Culture is here interpreted
> as a unity retaining variety (i.e. the resistance to absorption shown by
> all unique life-forms), as a structural unity—in contrast to *Nature as an
> unstructured monotony.*
>
> (1975, 218, emphasis added)

In contrast to Nudelman, I argue that nonhuman nature in the Hainish novels is not "an unstructured monotony", an unfeeling backdrop, but is agentive and active in intra-actions with human beings, sparking the protagonists' realizations of its inalienable ontology. Accordingly, I will conduct a contrapuntal ecofeminist reading of three of Le Guin's early Hainish texts: her first published work, *RW* (1966b), her second, *PE* (1966a), and *WWF* (1972), as well as referring finally to the ecofeminism explicit in *ACH*. My aim is to ascertain whether there are ecofeminist impulses in the early texts. I also hope, as a side effect, to rescue these early texts from the comparative obscurity to which they have been relegated by critics who are (in my view) unresponsive to their complexity and creative vision.

Rocannon's World (RW)

By Le Guin's own admission, *RW* is not an entirely successful mixture of "fantasy and science fiction" (1993, 129). Elements of fantasy are evident in the work's allusions to Norse mythology, feudal economy, and the patriarchal hero-story. The hero-story (cf. Campbell 1949) centers a male hero tasked with saving or rescuing a person, species, or community. The formula privileges the human and the masculine above the nonhuman and the feminine in ways that are not always compatible with feminism: "Joanna Russ describes this Real He-Man as 'invulnerable...super-potent...absolutely self-sufficient...never frightened [or] indecisive' and 'he always wins.' In short, she conclude[s], 'an alien monster'" (Kelso 2006, 247).

The ethnologist Gaverel Rocannon, the main protagonist of *RW*, is certainly not "an alien monster". He is more a questioner than a quester, being, by trade, an ethnologist whose job is to establish communication, rather than to conquer either the enemy or their territories. The text, however, sides with patriarchy in the use of violence to neutralize enemies: there is at least one airborne battle between Rocannon's party and those who oppose their quest, in which swords strike off heads in the best tradition of macho heroism.

In appearance and social structure, Fomalhaut II is very similar to consensus reality but exhibits what Fredric Jameson, writing about *The Left Hand of Darkness*, calls "world-reduction" (1975): a technique of isolating particular aspects of the twentieth-century experience in order to examine them. Jameson explains: "The existence of modern technology in the midst of an essentially feudal order is the sign of this imaginative operation" (1975, 228). In *RW*, the rampant consumption and commodity fetishism of twenty-first-century capitalism are absent, both because there is a smaller population and because there is no system of monetary exchange. A lack of money, however, does not mean that there is no drive to acquire or competition relating to possessions. "The Necklace," which forms the prologue to the main narrative, is centered on Semley of the Angyar, who travels through space and (though she does not know it) time, motivated by jealousy of a fellow gentlewoman's jewels, to retrieve a gold chain with a blue jewel as a pendant, with which she hopes to outshine her competitor. While "The Necklace" serves the plot function of introducing the hero of the main narrative to the heroine, it also demonstrates the value of acquisition and ownership to the planet's inhabitants.[1]

Rocannon narrates the motive behind his survey of Fomalhaut II to Semley's grandson Mogien:

> [A]fter I met Lady Semley, I went to my people, and said, what are we doing on this world we don't know anything about? Why are we taking their money[2] and pushing them about? What right have we?
>
> (Le Guin 1966b, 453)

His meeting with Semley leads him to question the entire settler-colonial project, which he frames aptly as "taking their money and pushing them about" (a succinct description reminiscent of Joseph Conrad's (1984, 31–33) more cynical "the conquest of the earth, which mostly means the taking it away from those who have a different complexion or slightly flatter noses than ourselves"). Rocannon is a fairly typical humanist scientist, for whom the category of the human is much more important than the nonhuman. Consequently, he does not take note of imperialism as also destructive of nonhuman nature: a realization that is implicit in the text. I will refer to two central episodes that demonstrate an emerging ecophilia.

The first episode occurs when the unnamed "enemy" destroys Rocannon's ship during his ethnographic survey of highly intelligent life-forms (hilfs) on Fomalhaut II. The scene is described first, and most importantly, as one of natural devastation:

> Suddenly beneath them a hole dropped away in the side of the hills, a black pit filled with smoking black dust. At the edge of the wide circle of annihilation lay trees burnt to long smears of charcoal, all pointing their fallen tops away from the pit of blackness.
>
> (Le Guin 1966b, 455)

In this passage, the destruction of Rocannon's spaceship, which, almost coincidentally, traps him on the planet, is secondary to the burning of the trees. The black burnt trunks contrast strikingly with the previous paragraph, which describes green, "damp, cool thickets" still alive. The trees play an agentive role in dramatically highlighting the enemy's threat as foremost environmental, and only secondarily socio political.

After this event, Rocannon, Mogien, and a few servants or "midmen" (Fomalhaut's feudal system does not permit any enquiry into servitude as a destiny) set off for the uncharted South of the planet to neutralize the threat to the environment and its cultures of human and nonhuman beings. As Rocannon's party flies over the landscape, he expresses delight in and cares for the rolling green landscape. Rocannon is not only being courted by the landscape, the undulating curves of which recall a sensuous lover, but he is also, to paraphrase Deleuze and Guattari, *becoming-ecology*, which is also to say, becoming-woman and becoming-minoritarian. The (patriarchal) driving force of the quest leads Rocannon to overcome numerous environmental challenges and military obstacles, while on the other hand, the ethnologist's desire to establish relations through intra-action goes beyond categorizing nonhuman nature as non-Self: he is drawn to it by experiences of wonder and care that, in my reading, mobilize ecophilia. These are also the hallmarks of the "enchantivism" that Craig Chalquist describes as crucial to deep, transformational change in the way humans relate to each other and to the planet (2007, 4).

Rocannon receives the gift of mind speech that enables him to defeat the enemy with the assistance of an agential landscape. Looking for succor for a wounded midman, Rocannon finds "A tiny stream, smoking as it ran, wound along the base of a drift of hard, shadowed snow. He looked for the stream's source and saw a dark gap under the overhanging cliff: a cave" (Le Guin 1966b, 1616). Surrounded by rock and cloud, Rocannon enters the cave and speaks with its guardian, a humanoid avatar of the cave's mysterious ontology, who gives him the gift he needs. The cave is the opposite of a hospitable refuge: it feels like an ontological wound in the landscape, recalling Barad's statement that "[m]atter feels, converses, suffers, desires, yearns and remembers" (in Dolphijn and Van der Tuin 2012, n.p.). Rocannon's panic, which seems at first reading to be an emotional response to the supernatural force in the cave, is actually an extension of the terror felt by the whole environment (wind, rocks, snow, and sun) in the face of the destruction that is to happen. The gift of partial telepathy is only one part of the gift Rocannon receives on the hillside: he also receives the gift of onto-ethical entanglement with the very matter of the world that comes to bear his name.

Planet of Exile (PE)

The eponymous "planet" of *PE* this novel is Werel, a planet with a single orbit of 60 Earth years, which makes its 15-year winters, with blizzards and persistent below-freezing temperatures, life-threatening. Le Guin uses Werel's orbit as a chronotope, a creative device that brings together place and time. Bakhtin describes the chronotope's functioning as follows:

> In the literary artistic chronotope, spatial and temporal indicators are fused into one carefully thought-out, concrete whole. Time, as it were, thickens, takes on flesh, becomes artistically visible; likewise, space becomes charged and responsive to the movements of time, plot and history. The intersection of axes and fusion of indicators characterizes the artistic chronotope.
>
> (1981, 84)

Likewise, on Werel, time becomes a determiner of human spatiality: as the marauding Gaal and damaging winter both threaten the Tevaran and human settlements, these chrono-ecological events force an alliance between previously mutual aliens. In the midst of a defense of the human settlement of Landin, Jakob Agat Alterra muses on the way time and space are fused in indigenous Tevaran worldviews:

> They did not look down over time but were in it as the lamp in the night, as the heart in the body. And so also with space: space to them was not a surface on which to draw boundaries but a heartland, cen-tered on the self and clan and tribe.
>
> (1966a, 74)

Agat's condescending reflections are colored by his settler mentality, which perceives the Terrans' linear mode of thinking as superior to that the Tevarans'. To the Tevarans, time and space are assemblages where phenom-ena such as consciousness, community, environment, and enemy are laid out in constantly shifting and porous webs of intra-action. The approaching winter causes axes to intersect and indicators to fuse to create an agen-tial landscape of snow which is anything but "unstructured monotony" (Nudelman 1975, 218). Humans and Tevarans alike are at the mercy of the winter. Economies of scale come into play here too: underpinning the cli-matic change is a subtle change in the biology of the humans, making them able to conceive children with the Tevarans.

Le Guin uses Rolery, "the girl born out of season," to undermines Agat's colonial and patriarchal racism. Amongst the Tevarans, Rolery is destined for "some Spring-born fellow [to] take her for third or fourth wife" (1966a, 17). Yet Rolery is *the one who chooses* (Le Guin 1993, 136, original emphasis) in the text. Her courageous venture outside Tevar and to the alien settlement leads her to an entangled encounter with ocean waves, which inaugurates both her union with Agat and the realization of the biological shift that will bring the two cultures together. Her joy in the sand on the beach gives way to embodied expression: "Firm and level and endless, the sand lay under her feet. She ran for the joy of running" (1966a, 10). Soon, though, she is nearly drowned as the tide comes in:

> Water crashed and boiled below them with a roar that shook the solid rock. The waters parted by the island joined white and roaring, swept on, hissed and foamed and crashed on the long slope to the dunes, stilled to a rocking of bright waves.
>
> (Le Guin 1966a, 11)

Rolery and Agat's personal entanglement is as powerful and potentially damaging to both of them and their societies as the crashing waves that nearly sweep her away to her death. From this diffractive event, the ripple effects of their telepathic meeting will spread throughout Werel, changing it, in the same way as Barad observes waves "bending and spreading when they encounter an obstruction" (2007, 74). This incident enables both Rolery and Agat to perceive the intra-action of weather, hostility and culture in weaving their peoples' destinies together. The culture of the Terrans and Tevarans is entangled with their planet's extreme meteorology. Werel's 15-year winter means that both Rolery and Agat will become part of their ecology—but Rolery will also change it when she bears his child. She becomes a harbinger of ecofeminist activism, bringing about an alliance between the Terrans and Tevarans which will enable them to resist the Gaal and survive the winter by working together with the weather, not against it as is the anthropocentric norm.

The Word for World Is Forest (WWF)

WWF takes place on a planet whose indigenous name is "Athshe" or "forest", but the settlers call it "New Tahiti" in a brutal act of imposing identity on indigenous places and people. The settler in charge, Davidson, exemplifies an anthropocentric and androcentric approach to it when he arrives and sees "nothing. Trees. A dark huddle and jumble and tangle of trees, endless, meaningless" (Le Guin 1972, 15). These trees constitute an assemblage of plant life, but this is only visible through indigenous eyes, much like Flicker's vision in *Always Coming Home*. Davidson approaches life as a series of conflicts. His first conflict is with Kees, a conservationist, who is concerned that the humans (whom the Athsheans call "yumens") are poaching the Athshean wildlife. Davidson fails to see the entanglements of human and nonhuman nature. His ontology is hierarchical and stratified:

> When I say Earth, Kees, I mean people. Men. You worry about deer and trees and fiberweed, fine, that's your thing. But I like to see things in perspective, from the top down, and the top, so far, is humans.
>
> (Le Guin 1972, 14)

After this discussion, Davidson smugly reflects "you've got to play on the winning side or else you lose. And it's Man that wins, every time. The old Conquistador" (Le Guin 1972, 15).

Davidson is portrayed as purely patriarchal and purely destructive of the nonhuman natural world: his character springs from Le Guin's anger at the Vietnam War, which, in 1968 when she wrote the novel, was in full swing (1993, 146–147). Le Guin recognizes that she "succumbed, in part, to the lure of the pulpit" (1993, 146) and that Davidson's portrayal as "purely evil" is not realistic (1993, 147). In her Introduction to *WWF*, she accurately identifies patriarchy and colonialist greed as the culprits for the destruction of indigenous human and nonhuman beings in Vietnam:

[I]t was becoming clear that the ethic which approved the defoliation of forests and grainlands and the murder of non-combatants in the name of "peace" was only a corollary of the ethic which permits the despoliation of natural resources for private profit or the GNP, and the murder of the creatures of the Earth in the name of "man."

(Le Guin 1993, 146)

Although Le Guin's analysis does not use the term "capitalist patriarchy," her discussion of the destruction to the environment being carried out by men has much in common with Mies and Shiva's ecofeminist understanding of patriarchy as the source of exploitation of women and nature. She also recognizes that patriarchy is the ideology that creates and pursues war.

By contrast to this relationship of exploitative dominance, the assemblage of trees that cover the surface of the planet Athshe shape the social, cognitive, and emotional practices of the forest's inhabitants:

No way was clear, no light unbroken, in the forest. Into wind, water, sunlight, starlight, there always entered leaf and branch, bole and root, the shadowy, the complex....Nothing was pure, dry, arid, plain. Revelation was lacking. There was no seeing everything at once: no certainty. The colors of rust and sunset kept changing in the hanging leaves of the copper willows.

(Le Guin 1972, 36)

To surrender to a "forested" way of thinking and feeling is an example of *becoming-forest*. This forested way of thinking prefers forking and indirect paths to (phal)logocentric, linear, and teleological forms of thinking. A canopy of leaves, constantly changing colors as the light filters down, makes the senses less reliable than under an unchanging blue sky, and unsettles empiricism and certainty. This is more than an arboreal literary imagination: Le Guin's vision of how Athsheans think, led by indirection and mutability, is both decolonial and rhizomatic. It is decolonial in the sense of insisting that context matters: the material components of geospatial location make an enormous difference to the structures of thought, emotion, and sociality. Despite taking its starting point from the interbranching forest branches and roots, it is not an arborescent approach that structures hierarchy, but a flattened vision which is "open and connectable in all of its dimensions" (Deleuze and Guattari 1987, 13). The Athshean practice of "dreaming" is one rhizomatic practice, allowing them to reshape personal and collective memory through non-linear connections between them. Le Guin uses this idea as an alternative to what she calls the predominance of "yang" civilisation:

In one way or another, from Plato on, utopia has been the big yang motorcycle trip. Bright, dry, clear, strong, firm, active, aggressive, lineal, progressive, creative, expanding, advancing, and hot.

(1989, 90)

The humans who have settled Athshe are definitely on a "big yang motorcycle trip," where the logic that subtends colonialism is premised upon the assumption that there is a direct line of progress for one species only. Davidson and his ilk pervert the green world of Athshe by bringing violence and death to a pacifist society. When the central character, Selver, finally understands that the humans are not going to listen to reason or learn to appreciate the Athshean way of dreaming through difficulty and challenge, he teaches his people how to kill. The Night of Eshsen, when Selver leads the Athsheans in revolt, killing many humans, becomes an angry plea to against capitalist patriarchy not to pursue the exploitation of nonhuman and non-western Others for profit. The "arborescent" (Deleuze and Guattari 1987, 13) hierarchical thinking of the settlers does not admit compromise or connection. Even though Lyubov is not a typical settler, he is part of the settler-colonial assemblage, and this is why he, too, loses his life. Le Guin's rhizomatic vision of the entanglement of action, psyche, and matter leads her to portray violence as damaging the Athsheans and their environment as much as it does their human victims.

Always Coming Home (ACH): A Parable

ACH contains a parable, "Big Man and Little Man" (Le Guin 1986, 157–159), where Little Man poisons every living thing in the world and then dies "of fear" (159). Big Man and Little Man are analogous to a patriarchal God and a first man. Little Man is one of the bringers of the Law of the Father into human society; both of them have their heads on backward. This condition of thinking wrongly, which, for the Kesh, seems to have been "the literalisation of a metaphor" (159). She explains:

So these things human beings had done to the world must have been deliberate and conscious acts of evil, serving the purposes of wrong understanding, fear, and greed. The people who had done these things had done wrong mindfully. They had had their heads on wrong.

(Le Guin 1986, 159)

The patriarchal God (Big Man) and first human (Little Man) are both male and Little Man's deliberate destruction of nonhuman life is attributed to his masculinity. Believing in human exceptionalism, as Rosi Braidotti notes, is no longer tenable, especially from a feminist perspective:

the alleged universalism of the Eurocentric paradigm of 'Man' rests on
entrenched dualisms....This reduces the notion of 'difference' to pejo-
ration: it spells inferiority and social and symbolic disqualification for
those who get branded as 'Others.'

(2015, 677)

Little Man dies of fear because he is terrified of losing his position at the
top of the hierarchy of power. His fatal terror contrasts strikingly with the
female character of Coyote who restores fertility and life: "Where she walked
she made the wilderness. She dug canyons, she shat mountains. Under the
buzzard's wings the forest grew" (Le Guin 1986, 159). Coyote exemplifies what Braidotti calls a "relational ontology [which] is *zoe*-centered and
hence nonanthropocentric" (2015, 690). Le Guin's Coyote is a female version of the legendary trickster of Oregon Indian legend, who is described by
Jarold Ramsey as a nonbinary being:

[T]hrough the mediation of Coyote the Trickster, the people could
have their morality both ways: they knew that his relentless pursuit of
women, wealth and pleasure would come to no good end, according
to tribal values – but before that end arrived, they could richly enjoy
themselves, as though on holiday!

(1977, xxxi)

All the coyotes in *ACH* (as in Le Guin's (1987) "Buffalo Gals, Won't You
Come Out Tonight") are female, and this is a significant diversion away
from Coyote as male, which is the default position in American Indian
folklore. Non-patriarchal and nonanthropocentric thinking is necessary to
counteract the damaging masculinity of Big Man and Little Man. Coyote
becomes a symbol for the ability to open oneself to the experience of the
other, whether human, nonhuman or non-sentient. Her nurturing of life on
earth in the wake of environmental destruction is of a piece with her mothering of the abandoned blind girl Myra in "Buffalo Gals, Won't You Come
Out Tonight," and she becomes a symbol for the ecofeminist vision of the
entire text of *ACH*.

Conclusion

My chapter has traced Le Guin's concern for the nonhuman nature in her
earlier works of science fiction, where alien is used as a metaphor for oth-
erness, as Julia Kuznetski (2021) suggests. *RW*, like *PE* (and many other
works of science fiction), uses an external threat as the catalytic event that
drives the narrative. When antagonists attack one another with explosives,
as has frequently happened in human history, and occurs at the beginning and end of *RW*, a landscape which has evoked sensitivity and care
is destroyed, or at best, damaged beyond repair. The "gorge where they

camp near a waterfall," which Le Guin cites as one of the work's best features (1993, 133), along with the peaceful grassy plains that Rocannon and his companions navigate on their journey south, form an assemblage with the human and humanoid occupants of the planet. The whole assemblage, including and importantly its nonhuman components, will be annihilated if the war to come is not stopped. Although Rocannon is no ecofeminist, Le Guin's concern for the nonhuman natural features of Fomalhaut II can only be called ecophilic. Similarly, in *PE,* the world of Werel seems alien to the Terrans because of the long seasons that stretch for nearly 15 years each. The settlers are, nevertheless, faced with difficulties arising both from the planet's extreme meteorology and from invading others, which force them to realize that Werel has become their home. They are, in fact, emerging and entangled elements of the planetary life-assemblage. No such resolution is available in *WWF,* where the Athsheans are confronted with a different kind of settler, who proves impossible to change. In this scenario, the only way to deal with the settlers is to kill them or imprison them. Unfortunately, the violence that concludes the action of *RW, PE,* and *WWF* means that the texts succumb to masculinist responses to conflict. As Murphy observes in this volume, though:

> Such questions as when is intervention necessary for ecological rebalancing and how extreme should be the measures taken, when is nonintervention an appropriate form of action even when a species is being self-destructive, and what is the difference between violence that reduces one population for the benefit of another and unintentional environmental degradation that leads to extinction, all require ethical approaches and moral behaviors.
>
> (102)

The question of the Other, becoming more and more urgent in the Anthropocene as we realize that agency is shared with nonhuman and material elements, requires avoidance of violence. In *ACH* Le Guin writes "The image of the other's pain is the center of being human" (1986, 478). The impulse of an ethical compassion that is encapsulated in these words includes marginalized others (nonhuman nature and women) is profoundly feminist, albeit not restricted to biological women, and gives expression to a *zoe*-centered care, that is more important attention than ever in the Anthropocene.

Notes

1 The catastrophic consequences of Semley's desire for a beautiful necklace serve as a warning against commodity fetishism.
2 Despite Rocannon's guilt over "taking their money," *RW* does not document the use of money on the planet at all.

References

Abdullah, Danaz Abubaker, and Azad Hamad Sharif. 2019. "The Contrasting Worlds of Ursula K. Le Guin's *Always Coming Home*: An Ecofeminist Study." *Journal of University of Garmian* 6, no. 3: 232–244.

Bakhtin, Mikhail. 1981. "Forms of Time and of the Chronotope in the Novel: Notes toward a Historical Poetics." In *The Dialogic Imagination: Four Essays*, edited by Michael Holquist and Translated by Caryl Emerson and Michael Holquist, 84–258. Austin, TX: University of Texas Press.

Barad, Karen. 2007. *Meeting the Universe Halfway: Quantum Physics and the Entanglement of Matter and Meaning*. Columbia, NC: Duke University Press.

Braidotti, Rosi. 2015. "Posthuman Feminist Theory." In *The Oxford Handbook of Feminist Theory*, edited by Lisa Disch and Mary Hawkesworth, 673–698. Oxford: Oxford University Press.

Brigg, Peter. 1997. "A 'Literary Anthropology' of the Hainish, Derived from the Tracings of the Species Guin." *Extrapolation* 38, no. 1: 15–24.

Campbell, Joseph. [1949] 2008. *The Hero with a Thousand Faces*. London: New World Library.

Chalquist, Craig. 2007. *The Enchantivist Alternative: Transmutation through Inspiration*. Accessed October 12, 2020. https://chalquist.com/writings/ench antivism-transmutation-inspiration/.

Conrad, Joseph. [1902] 1984. *Heart of Darkness*. Harmondsworth, UK: Penguin.

Deleuze, Gilles, and Félix Guattari. 1987. *A Thousand Plateaus*, 2nd Edition. Translated by Brian Massumi. Minneapolis, MN: University of Minnesota Press.

Deleuze, Gilles, Félix Guattari, and Charles J. Stivale. 1984. "Concrete Rules and Abstract Machines." *SubStance* 13, nos. 3–4: 7–19.

Dolphijn, Rick, and Iris van der Tuin, eds. 2012. *New Materialism: Interviews & Cartographies*. Ann Arbor, MI: Open Humanities Press. Accessed October 12, 2020. https://quod.lib.umich.edu/o/ohp/11515701.0001.001/1:4.3/--new-mate rialism-interviews-cartographies?rgn=div2;view=fulltext.

Gaard, Greta, ed. 1993. *Ecofeminism: Women, Animals, Nature*. Philadelphia, PA: Temple University Press.

Goulimari, Pelagia. 1999. "A Minoritarian Feminism?: Things to Do with Deleuze and Guattari." *Hypatia* 14, no. 2: 97–120.

Hanafy, Iman A. 2014. "Ecofeminism across Cultures in Le Guin's *Always Coming Home*." *Review of Always Coming Home*. Accessed October 13, 2020. https ://fart.stafpu.bu.edu.eg/English%20Language%20and%20Literature/2008/pu blications/Iman%20Adawy%20Ahmed%20Hanafy_Final%20Le%20Guin%2 0-%20Cairo%20conference.pdf.

Jameson, Fredric. 1975. "World-reduction in Le Guin: The Emergence of Utopian Narrative." *Science-Fiction Studies* 2, no. 3: 221–230.

Kelso, Sylvia. 2006. "Evolutions of the Fantasy Hero in Peter Jackson's *The Lord of the Rings* and Lois McMaster Bujold's *The Curse of Chalion*." *Paradoxa: Studies in World Literary Genres* 20: 247–262.

Kuznetski, Julia. 2021. "Ecofeminist (Post) Ice-Age Ecotopia: Doris Lessing's 'Mara and Dann' Books." In *Dystopias and Utopias on Earth and Beyond: Feminist Ecocriticism of Science Fiction*, edited by Douglas A. Vakoch, 50–66. Abingdon, Oxon, UK; New York: Routledge.

Le Guin, Ursula K. 1966a. *Planet of Exile*. New York, NY: Ace Books.

———. [1966b] 1994. *Rocannon's World*, Kindle version. London: Gollancz.

———. 1972. *The Word for World Is Forest*. New York, NY: Tor.

———. 1986. *Always Coming Home*. London: Victor Gollancz.

———. 1987. "Buffalo Gals, Won't You Come Out Tonight," *The Magazine of Fantasy & Science Fiction*, November, 131–158.

———. 1989. *Dancing at the Edge of the World: Thoughts on Words, Women, Places*. London: Victor Gollancz.

———. 1993. *The Language of the Night: Essays on Fantasy and Science Fiction*. Edited and with Introduction by Susan Wood; Revised edition edited by Ursula K. Le Guin. New York, NY: G. P. Putnam's Sons.

Mies, María, and Vandana Shiva. 1993. *Ecofeminism*. Ann Arbor, MI: Fernwood Publications.

Murphy, Patrick D. 1991. "Ground, Pivot, Motion: Ecofeminist Theory, Dialogics, and Literary Practice." *Hypatia* 6, no. 1: 146–161.

Nail, Thomas. 2017. "What is an Assemblage?" *SubStance* 46, no. 1: 21–37.

Nudelman, Rafail. 1975. "An Approach to the Structure of Le Guin's SF." *Science-Fiction Studies* 2, no. 3: 210–220.

Sawyer, Andy. 2006. "Ursula K. Le Guin and the Pastoral Mode." *Extrapolation* 47, no. 3: 396–348.

Vakoch, Douglas A., and Sam Mickey, eds. 2018. *Literature and Ecofeminism: Intersectional Voices*. London and New York, NY: Routledge.

Von Werlhof, Claudia. 2007. "Capitalist Patriarchy and the Negation of Matriarchy: The Struggle for a Deep Alternative." In *Women and the Gift Economy: A Radically Different World View Is Possible*, edited by Genevieve Vaughan, pp. 139–153. Toronto: Inanna Publications. Accessed October 13, 2020. http://emanzipationhumanum.de/downloads/capitalistpatriarchy.pdf.

Wytenbroek, J. R. 1987. "*Always Coming Home*: Pacifism and Anarchy in Le Guin's Latest Utopia." *Extrapolation* 28, no. 4: 330–339.

Index

For Product Safety Concerns and Information please contact our EU
representative GPSR@taylorandfrancis.com
Taylor & Francis Verlag GmbH, Kaufingerstraße 24, 80331 München, Germany

www.ingramcontent.com/pod-product-compliance
Lightning Source LLC
Chambersburg PA
CBHW071604110726
47908CB00007B/2244

* 9 7 8 0 3 6 7 7 2 0 2 2 3 *